- WA

THE DEVIL
TO PAY

Marshall Cavendish
Editions

Other Marshall Cavendish Offices:
Marshall Cavendish International. PO Box 65829 London EC1P 1NY, UK • Marshall Cavendish
Corporation. 99 White Plains Road, Tarrytown NY 10591-9001, USA • Marshall Cavendish
International (Thailand) Co Ltd. 253 Asoke, 12th Flr, Sukhumvit 21 Road, Klongtoey Nua, Wattana,
Bangkok 10110, Thailand • Marshall Cavendish (Malaysia) Sdn Bhd, Times Subang, Lot 46, Subang
Hi-Tech Industrial Park, Batu Tiga, 40000 Shah Alam, Selangor Darul Ehsan, Malaysia.

Marshall Cavendish is a trademark of Times Publishing Limited

National Library Board Singapore Cataloguing in Publication Data
Woon, Walter, C.M.
The devil to pay / C.M. Woon. – Singapore: Marshall Cavendish Editions, c2005.
p. cm.

ISBN: 978-981-4302-66-1
1. World War, 1939–1945 – Secret Service – Malaysia – Malaya – Fiction. I. Title.

PR9570.S53
S823 — dc21   SLS2005045681

Printed in Singapore by Times Printers Pte Ltd

I dedicate this book to my dear wife Janis

1

I TOOK to crime at a relatively early stage in my career. It wasn't my idea. My employer forced me into it.

If I had had my way, I would have done conveyancing or solicitor's work. A spot of chancery work or commercial litigation now and again wouldn't have been bad either. But Clarence d'Almeida, my boss and senior partner of the firm of d'Almeida & d'Almeida, had taken me on as his personal devil, assistant and general do-it-all. For some reason, he had formed the impression that I was cut out for criminal litigation. He himself thrived on it. Not that it paid well – crime almost never pays. The only rich clients one gets are the successful criminals; and d'Almeida didn't represent those as a matter of principle. He had an uncanny nose for smelling out innocence and guilt. Being a gentleman of independent means, he could indulge his altruism by helping the indigent innocent.

Anyway, for good or ill, crime became my metier. The work was interesting. On that score, I had no complaint. It must also have been tiresome, routine and often sordid. But my memories of that time are sepia-tinted by nostalgia, and the bad parts have somehow faded beyond recollection. We didn't know it then of course, but we were living in the last halcyon days of an era. I remember 1939 as a year of kingfisher-blue skies, with not a cloud on the horizon. It was the year of Gone with the Wind and Snow White. Neville Chamberlain had proclaimed peace in our time, and in Singapore, we were little concerned with the quarrels far away amongst people of whom we knew nothing. The sun shone, people made money and pursued their lives and loves in blissful ignorance of what went on in the wider world. The distant rattle of sabres being drawn did not disturb our idyll.

For me, the end began with the return of a ghost from the past.

SUNDAY AFTERNOON tea with d'Almeida was a little tradition that he had instituted for the junior members of his chambers. There were three of us at that time – George Singham, Ralph Smallwood and myself – so we took it in turns, appearing dutifully at four o'clock precisely on our allotted Sundays. D'Almeida used the occasion to grill us on various aspects of the law to ensure that we were keeping up with latest developments. It was not unlike a viva voce examination. Personally, I didn't mind too much, as d'Almeida was an excellent teacher despite his rather intimidating manner and reputation. The other two had a different view. As far as Ralph and George were concerned, Sunday tea with d'Almeida was a fête worse than death.

This particular Sunday was different, though. I was shown to d'Almeida's study in the usual way by his manservant, a large and laconic Sikh by the name of Palvit Singh. To my surprise, there was someone with him. The visitor turned round when d'Almeida rose to greet me. With an unpleasant shock, I recognised him.

"Ah, Chiang, good of you to join us," said d'Almeida. "May I introduce Flight Lieutenant James Thornton? My assistant, Mr Dennis Chiang." Thornton rose and held out his hand uncertainly, which I shook rather limply.

It was obvious that he didn't remember me. I, on the other

hand, had a very vivid recollection of James Thornton. My uncle, who had taken me in when my parents died, determined that I should be raised as a proper English gentleman. To that end, he had packed me off at an early age to Fenton Abbey, a Gothic pile stranded in the middle of the Fens not far from Ely. My time at Fenton Abbey was not a happy one. The weather was cold, the masters and students colder. When I finally escaped the clutches of that dismal institution, I swore that I would never again have anything to do with anyone whom I had had the misfortune to meet there. And so it had been – until now. James Thornton had been a Sixth Former and prefect when I arrived. He and his friends made life purgatory for me during that first year. There was nothing personal in it, of course. To them, First Formers were a lower form of life, to be tortured at whim.

I took my seat next to d'Almeida, eyeing Thornton warily. He still showed no sign of recognition.

"Mr Thornton wanted to consult me discreetly on a sensitive matter," continued d'Almeida, passing around the tea and biscuits. "I invited him to tea. I hope you have no objection to his presence at our usual tête-à-tête?"

"Not in the least," I responded, suppressing the urge to walk out there and then. Snap out of it, I told myself. It's been more than a decade. He doesn't even remember.

"Now that Mr Chiang is here, perhaps you would be so kind as to begin at the beginning," invited d'Almeida.

"Well, umm, yes," began Thornton, fidgeting a little in his chair. He began stroking his moustache. "It's a delicate matter. A woman, you see. A bit of trouble at the Club." His voice trailed off.

"Come, Mr Thornton, if I am to help you, it will not do if you cannot bring yourself to tell me the problem."

Thornton took a deep breath as if to steel himself and took the plunge. "Mr d'Almeida, I must tell you right out that it wasn't my idea to consult you." D'Almeida raised his eyebrows, but said nothing. "That was Mr Newman's idea. He said that you were the man to talk to."

"Mr Newman?" responded d'Almeida almost absently, "I am not sure I know a Mr Newman."

Thornton was taken aback. "Mr Fredrick Newman, our President. He seems to know you."

D'Almeida nodded non-committally. Thornton continued. "As I was saying, I'm the Honorary Secretary of the Icarus Club. It's not a big club, just a few dozen of us out at RAF Seletar. We've got our own clubhouse on the base for the chaps to drop by and have a stengah and a chat."

"Only military men?" asked d'Almeida.

"Mostly," responded Thornton. "A couple of civvies retired from the Forces. Like your friend Mr Newman; or Major Newman as I should properly call him, though he's not bothered about the rank. We've got army types, a couple of naval chappies but mostly RAF. No ORs of course."

"ORs?"

"Sorry, Other Ranks – non-commissioned officers and below. Only officers as members. That's the normal rule. The ORs have their own club somewhere."

And no natives either, I thought to myself. That's the normal rule too. Officers and gentlemen, Other Ranks, natives; the colonial caste system. It was just like that in Fenton Abbey. The prefects and the Sixth Formers lorded it over the lesser mortals. It was part of the system. But my antipathy to Thornton stemmed from more than mere distaste for the public school ethos.

Seeing him in the flesh brought the whole horrid episode back from the deepest dungeon of my mind, to which I had consigned it long ago. Wilberforce was a boy in my Form. I scarcely knew him. I never had the chance. My last memory of Wilberforce was of his body sprawled on the cobbles of the Outer Court. The snow was red around him. It was my first experience of death. I had never seen a dead body before. He looked like a broken toy. Violent death was still a horror to me then, not the banal thing that it became in later years. I ran away shuddering and cried myself to sleep that night. The nightmares continued for years. The coroner's conclusion was that Wilberforce had slipped while climbing through one of the third floor windows, presumably on his way to another dormitory after lights-out. A childish prank gone tragically awry. Our Form knew differently. Wilberforce had been dangled out of the window by some Sixth Formers for some petty infraction of the rules. Someone's slippery hands hadn't been strong enough to hold him … Of course, none of that group ever owned up. They all left Fenton Abbey with their testimonials and honours intact. Thornton was one of them. He may have forgotten, but I hadn't.

Thornton continued, oblivious to my glare.

"We have a Ladies' Night once a month. You know the sort of thing, a couple of drinks, dancing, dinner. We had one on Friday night. There was an unfortunate incident." He stopped.

"Do go on," urged d'Almeida.

"There was … an alleged indecent assault."

"Alleged?"

"Well, no, 'alleged' isn't the word I want. One of the lady guests complained of an indecent assault. By one of the members."

"The way you phrase it, I surmise that you do not entirely believe her," commented d'Almeida.

"Mr d'Almeida, I'll be frank with you. It's not that I disbelieve her. But the woman in question is a Eurasian. One of the chaps chatted her up at Great World and brought her along for a drink. She was out for a good time. People had a few drinks. She seemed the sort not to mind a little slap and tickle."

"Just a slap and tickle?"

"Well, no … There was an attempt at intercourse. Against her will."

"In a word, rape?"

"In a word, yes. She ran right into me after the assault. She was in a dickens of a state, crying, hysterical. I called Mr Newman after I twigged what she was going on about. But by the time we got back to the place where it happened, the blighter had done a bunk."

"You have a suspect?"

"We have. The woman gave a full description."

D'Almeida held up his hand. "Mr Thornton, I do not know why your Mr Newman recommended me. This would more appropriately be a case for the police. If you are asking me to defend your members against the accusations of the young lady, I must tell you that I do not as a matter of principle act for those who are guilty of a crime. Whatever the popular view of lawyers may be, we do not exist to manipulate the system in the interest of malefactors."

Thornton shifted uneasily. "Please hear me out, Mr d'Almeida. Then if you decide that you won't help, I'll take my leave."

D'Almeida nodded. Thornton went on. "It's more or less certain that the woman was attacked. We even know who the assailant is. Or more exactly, we know it's one of two people: either William Fitzhugh or his brother David. The trouble is, we don't know which one. They're identical twins."

"So," said d'Almeida softly, "the lady can identify her assailant, but she does not know exactly which twin it was."

"That's exactly the problem, Mr d'Almeida. As I said, by the time Mr Newman and I got to the scene of the crime, he was gone. I just managed to catch a glimpse of him as he scooted off down the driveway. I think it might have been William, but then again, I can't tell them apart either – certainly not from the back and at night. When Mr Newman confronted them yesterday, William claimed to have been at some restaurant in town. So did David. We can't do anything."

D'Almeida leant back in his armchair and placed his fingers together. The sunlight streaming through the study window glinted off his steel-rimmed spectacles. "An interesting conundrum," he mused, almost speaking to himself. "The law does not allow a joint prosecution on the basis that one of the two must have done it. The case must be proven beyond a reasonable doubt against an identified assailant. As long as both gentlemen maintain their story, a reasonable doubt will always be present. Interesting." He lapsed into silence. Thornton looked over to me. I tried to avoid his glance by pretending to study the books on the shelves.

D'Almeida spoke suddenly. "What is it exactly that you wish me to do?"

Thornton jumped a little at the sound. "Ah ... I ... we hoped that you might be able to suggest some way to resolve the problem." D'Almeida raised his eyebrows. Thornton continued. "Mr Newman said that you have a knack for solving knotty issues effectively, though unconventionally."

"Why not take it straight to the police? It is their job to deal with cases of this sort."

"Normally, yes. But the Fitzhughs are very well connected. Their father Lord Rushton was Undersecretary for Far Eastern affairs in the last Cabinet. We can't just turn up at the Central Police Station and say that one of the two did it. Knowing who's involved, the police won't touch the case. Not unless we've got something much more solid."

"Why even bother?" asked d'Almeida provocatively. "It was only a native girl out for a good time."

"That's what some of the chaps are saying. She asked for it and she got what she asked for. I must admit that that was my first reaction. But she didn't ask to be raped. We can't just turn a blind eye to that sort of thing. It won't do to have it spread about that women aren't safe at our Club. And it's a matter of justice for the woman, even if she isn't entirely pure as the driven snow."

I was surprised. This wasn't quite what I had expected of him. A sense of justice didn't fit in my picture of James Thornton.

D'Almeida nodded approvingly. "Very well, Mr Thornton, I shall take the case. The first thing of course is to establish the facts. The Fitzhughs and other witnesses have been interviewed by you?"

"The Members' Committee meets tomorrow to discuss the matter. We've called them down to explain themselves."

"May I suggest that your hearing should be at someone's house and not at the Club?"

Thornton's brow creased in puzzlement. D'Almeida explained himself, "I would like to be present, discreetly. Your Club presumably does not allow non-Europeans. It would be a matter of comment if I should turn up there."

Thornton looked embarrassed. "Of course. It hadn't occurred to me. But you're right, it would cause comment. We'll fix it so you can be there when we talk to the Fitzhughs."

Evidently relieved that he had secured d'Almeida's aid, Thornton took his leave. Palvit showed him out, leaving me alone with d'Almeida. I braced myself for the examination to come. It wasn't long in coming.

"Well, young man, define 'rape'," he shot at me.

I rummaged in the recesses of my mind. "Er ... sexual intercourse without the consent of the victim?"

"To be precise, against her will or without her consent. So what is the first thing we must establish?"

"Her consent?" I ventured weakly.

He made an impatient sound. "Of course she did not consent.

What we need to know is whether she did anything to lead him to believe she was inviting intercourse."

I nodded dumbly. Having been brought up in a rather sheltered and conservative environment, I felt vaguely uneasy discussing such matters. When I was about eleven, I had, in a moment of innocent boldness, asked my uncle (who was my guardian) how he had managed to produce five daughters from his two wives. My uncle, who was by nature rather distant and Victorian, had coughed and hrumphed and squirmed and turned a delicate shade of pink behind the ears. He told me somewhat shortly that one day I would get married to a nice girl and everything would become clear. I recall wondering how a nice girl would know about such things when my worldly-wise uncle could hardly bring himself to discuss the issue. The experience did not make me more comfortable talking about sex. I didn't relish the prospect of asking a woman what she had done to encourage rape.

D'Almeida had an uncanny knack for sensing people's thoughts. "It will not be pleasant, but the task must be done. You can see the lady tomorrow. Take Singham with you. You might need a man of the world."

I bristled a little at his assumption that I was not a man of the world, but was glad all the same that George would be in on it too. Fortunately, d'Almeida felt that I had had enough for one day and released me early. I fled as fast as my old jalopy could manage down his long driveway.

I DIDN'T go straight home that Sunday. Normally, Sunday dinner was a family affair, with Mak supervising Gek Neo and June doing the cooking while our black-and-white amah Ah Sum hovered around making clucking noises. The two younger girls Julie and Augusta would get under everyone's feet until they were chased physically from the kitchen. My role was to lounge around like the lord and master of the house (which I was in theory, in the absence of any other male relatives), a task which suited my talents admirably. This particular Sunday, however, I had been invited to dinner with my cousin May and her husband Ralph.

May and Ralph were newly wed and had set up home in his bachelor apartment. The usual Baba custom was for the man to join the woman's household. But given the fact that there were already eight people in our house and a fluctuating population of dogs, cats, chickens, ducks and goldfish, it had seemed a good idea for May to move out. They came back regularly for meals, though. Since May had to give up her job as a nurse when she married, she also turned up most days to exchange gossip with her sisters and half-sisters. It was like she never left.

Nevertheless, the time had to come when May would have to put into practice all the things Mak had taught her about being a good wife and housekeeper. This was the pinnacle of a good Nonya's ambitions, to have her own household to run. May was ahead of her time in holding a job, and as a result, her domestic education had suffered somewhat. Mak thought that it would be good for her to get some live practice. So the amah was given the afternoon off and I was deputed to be the guinea-pig.

I arrived to the smell of unidentified frying objects emanating from the kitchen. "Good to see you, old man," said Ralph when he met me at the door, looking somewhat harassed. Evidently, he had been roped in to help, a most un-Baba-like proceeding. As a bachelor, Ralph had taken all his meals at restaurants and coffeeshops. I knew that he was just about capable of making toast without triggering an alarm at the Fire Brigade, but that was the extent of his culinary expertise.

He flopped down into an armchair and thrust a bottle of beer into my hand.

"Everything in order?" I enquired politely. Mentally, I was calculating whether it would be possible for me to get back home in time to be fed.

Ralph nodded glumly and took a swig from his bottle. "May's been at it all afternoon. The chopping, pounding, slicing... You can't imagine."

I could, actually. Preparing a proper Nonya meal was not a matter of popping a couple of eggs in a pot to be boiled. Everything had to be done by hand – the slicing, cutting, pounding, blending, frying. There were no recipe books, only the distilled experience of generations, passed down from mother to daughter. When done right, the result was exquisite. When done wrong ... my stomach churned at the thought.

"Er ... I think your wife's trying to communicate with you," I said to Ralph. "There are smoke signals coming from the kitchen."

"Oh, Lord!" he exclaimed, and hopped off to help.

Left to myself, I looked around the place. I had been there during Ralph's bachelor days. The flat was a big one which he had inherited from his parents, with high ceilings and a pleasing geometrical Art Deco look. The furnishing had been somewhat spartan then. All this had changed, for the better I thought. May had brought some of her favourite pieces of furniture from the house, a large glass-fronted almeirah for china, an easy-chair, a couple of side tables. She had a flair for decoration. The flat felt like a real home.

I made myself useful setting the table. May soon appeared, laden with dishes. I gave her a cousinly peck on the cheek and relieved her of her load. She had really prepared a feast – nasi kunyit, achar, sayur lodeh, bakwan kepiting, babi pong teh. I marvelled at the amount of food. She had, of course, done it single-handedly, as Ralph's only talents (apart from eating) were carrying things and keeping flies away. Despite my initial gloomy prognostications, the meal actually tasted quite good – not as good as Mak's, but a worthy first effort. I said so and she beamed.

After we had cleared the dinner things away, I discussed the afternoon's events with Ralph.

"The key issue is consent. D'Almeida says that it isn't enough for her to say she didn't consent. If he thought she was leading him on, the jury could very well let him off."

"Hmm, ticklish one," commented Ralph. "She sounds like a good-time girl, at least from the description. It's always easy to cry rape after giving a fellow the come-on. You know what they say about the difference between a diplomat and a lady ..."

"No," I replied, "I don't know what they say about the difference between a diplomat and a lady."

"Well," continued Ralph, "it goes like this. If a diplomat says 'yes', he means 'maybe'; if he says 'maybe', he means 'no'; and if he says 'no', he's no diplomat. Whereas when a lady says 'no' she means 'maybe', if she says 'maybe' she means 'yes'."

"And if she says 'yes'?" I inquired.

"And if she says 'yes', she's no lady," concluded Ralph with a smirk.

"That is the most terrible thing to say about a woman," interjected May, who had returned without us noticing. "You are a bad influence on my husband, Dennis Chiang."

I was about to protest the injustice of this, but she continued, "Why should men think because a woman is friendly that she wants to be taken advantage of? I did not hear the first part, but I do not think this woman you talked about wanted to be molested."

"No, I'm sure she didn't," I said, "but apparently he picked her up in a bar and she followed him to his club."

May's expression hardened. "A bar? Why was she in a bar?" Well brought-up girls did not frequent bars, and disapproval was etched all over May's face. I knew immediately that we would have a problem if the case went to a jury of her peers.

WALTER WOON | 17

"I don't know why she was in a bar. But she was and that's the problem. There's no doubt that the blighter took advantage of her, but if it goes to a jury, they will have to decide whether he thought she wanted … er … it."

"It?" asked May innocently, "what is 'it'? I do not understand what 'it' is that she wanted." May had been a nurse. She knew very well what I meant. She looked at me challengingly, her eyes twinkling with mischief.

"Intercourse," I said, my ears reddening, "whether she wanted to have intercourse."

May giggled. "You are so funny, Denny. You cannot even say the word without blushing. How are you going to do the case?"

HOW INDEED, I thought to myself glumly. It wasn't my day. Singapore was just about as far as one could get from Fenton Abbey without falling off the globe, and there he was – Thornton, of all people, when I had thought that I was rid of the whole lot of them forever. Then, on top of that, to be lumbered with a rape case personally assigned to me by the sharpest criminal lawyer in the Straits Settlements. Asking a strange woman about her sexual activities would be bad enough. To have to report it all in lurid detail back to d'Almeida … it just wasn't my day.

2

FORTUNATELY, George wasn't squeamish about birds, bees, love, lust, sex or anything else of that sort. He took over as soon as the problem was explained to him. I must admit that George was a lot brighter than most – certainly brighter than me and Ralph at any rate. Being related to d'Almeida on his mother's side, he had genetics to thank for this; though he was most uncommonly touchy about being reminded of the familial connection.

We got the woman's name from Thornton and duly turned up at her flat. It was in a nice part of town, right next to Amber Mansions and across from the Presbyterian Church. Rather a fancy sort of place, well-kept and redolent of middle-class affluence. The flat was on the fourth storey. I had a look at the names on the doors as we went past each landing – all very European, with only one distinctly Chinese name.

"This is it," said George, reading the plate on the door when we got to the top, "Gilbert. Such a very white name."

The door was opened by a striking blonde. "Miss Elaine Gilbert?" asked George suavely, "We're from d'Almeida & d'Almeida. Our office called earlier. May we come in?"

"No, I'm not Elaine," she replied, "but come in anyway. My name's Daphne Ford. I live in the apartment across the hall. Elaine will be out in a minute. Why don't you gentlemen have a seat? Over there, on the couch."

George needed no second invitation. I followed in his wake. He performed the introductions and manouevred himself onto the end of the settee next to Daphne Ford. I looked around while he made conversation with her. Elaine Gilbert had taste, that much was evident. Framed prints by Mucha, Klimmt and Hokusai adorned the walls. The furniture was modern, copies of pieces by Le Corbusier and Mies van der Rohe. At least I assumed that they were copies, since I didn't know enough to tell an original from a reproduction. Whatever they were, the flat looked expensive.

I turned my attention to Daphne Ford. She clearly wasn't English. No Englishwoman would have been so informal with two total strangers – certainly not with two Asiatics. I guessed from her accent and bearing that she was American; probably from somewhere south of New England, with perhaps a touch of finishing school about her. She was attractive in an unsophisticated way – nouveau riche rather than old money, I would have said. I guessed her to be in her early twenties. I left George to do the chatting while I sized her up. My examination was interrupted by the entrance of Elaine Gilbert.

Despite her European name, Elaine Gilbert was quite obviously of mixed parentage. Her complexion and hair were dark. She was thirtyish, well-dressed, with perhaps a little too much powder on the cheeks. She greeted us a little hesitantly. George got straight to work. "Miss Gilbert, thank you for seeing us. I know that this must be painful for you, but we're here to help. We'd like to ask you a few questions if we may."

She helped herself to a cigarette from a round tin on the side table. George produced a lighter like a conjurer. She inhaled deeply and let the smoke drift out. I thought her manner wary, but then again, who could blame her? "What do you want to know?" she asked cautiously.

"To begin with, what do you do? Have you a job?"

"Yes, at the League of Nations Health Bureau here in Singapore. I'm personal assistant to the Deputy Director." The answer was crisp and controlled. George nodded and indicated that I should take notes.

"Are you married?" She shook her head.

"Tell us how you met the man. Was he the one who took you to the Club?"

"Yes," she said in an emotionless tone, "he was the one. I was having a drink at the Blue Lagoon in Great World. He seemed friendly enough. We had a couple of drinks and he invited me to go to his Club." She fidgeted a little with her skirt.

"You'd never met him before?"

"No, never."

"Do you know his name?"

"He told me he was Hugh. That was it."

"So you went with him to the Icarus Club. What happened there?"

"What happened? The bastard took advantage of me. I told him no, but he wouldn't listen. He forced himself on me." She stopped abruptly. Her hand was shaking. The ash from her cigarette dropped onto the carpet.

"I know this is hard," said George soothingly, "but we must ask. Did you do anything to encourage him?"

"Encourage him? You think I led him on?" Her eyes flashed. "No, I didn't encourage him. Not with a word, not with a look. He attacked me. I fought him but he was too strong. He's a bloody bastard!" she said with vitriol and stubbed out her cigarette in the ashtray forcefully. Then she began to weep, with little suppressed sobs. Daphne came over and put an arm around her comfortingly.

I was disconcerted, but George forged onwards. "I'm sorry to have to press you, but have you ever done this before – gone off with a strange man to a club or restaurant or bar?"

Daphne interjected, "How could you! To suggest such a thing! Elaine's not the one on trial."

"Miss Ford," replied George evenly, "in a rape case, unfortunately the victim often ends up on trial. You can be sure that the defence lawyer will take every opportunity to cast Miss Gilbert as a loose woman. He will rake up the past mercilessly – every lover, indiscretion, whiff of scandal that he can find. Anything to cast doubt on her virtue. We have to know if we are to help."

Daphne fell silent. Elaine made an effort to compose herself. The sobs stopped. She buried her face in her hands. "Let it drop," she said woodenly.

This took us both by surprise. "Miss Gilbert, both the President and the Secretary of the Icarus Club are keen to see justice done. They want your assailant to answer for his crime. But we do need your help," cajoled George.

"Please go," she said in a low voice.

Daphne reacted with astonishment. "Elaine! These gentlemen are here to help you. You've got to talk to them."

"Please GO!" she repeated more forcefully.

George motioned to me to leave. "We're sorry to have troubled you," he said. "Perhaps we might come back later. When you feel ready to talk." Elaine said nothing, but waved us away without looking up.

"Yes, come back later," said Daphne quietly at the door, "she's still in a state."

"Maybe we could talk to you, if you don't mind," said George.

"Sure, if you think it'd help." She showed us into her flat, which was directly across from Elaine's. It was smaller and much less expensively furnished – just a bedsitter with a tiny kitchenette attached.

George settled himself on the only settee in sight, right next to Daphne. I took one of the hard dining chairs. "Could you tell us anything, Daphne? May I call you Daphne, by the way?" he asked.

"Yes, sure, do call me Daphne. I don't really know much really. I heard Elaine get in late Friday night – the walls are so thin, you can hear everything. She was crying. So I went out to see what was up."

"You're close friends then?"

"Well, not exactly close. But we got to know each other when I moved in here a half year ago. Anyway, she was in a real state – clothes rumpled and all that. I took her into her apartment and made her some Ovaltine. She told me she'd been attacked by a man. I put her to bed."

"Did she give you any details? A name perhaps?"

"No, not much. She told me he was a British officer. But she didn't know his name. He'd picked her up at a bar."

"Did she do this a lot? Go to bars, I mean."

Daphne hesitated. "Well," she said, pursing her lips, "I can't rightly say. She's out most nights, 'specially weekends. I guess she gets around a bit."

"Did she have any men friends? Anyone who called regularly?"

"No, not that I know. But she never told me anything about her love life, if she has one. She's very English about things like that – reserved, I mean. We talk about art and books mostly, and music. I adore music. She has great taste. I guess she's pretty loaded, to be able to afford her place. Anyway, she was quite happy to find someone to talk to. I guess it's not easy out here in the East to find anyone interested in those things."

Having let George dominate thus far, I felt it time to venture a question myself. "Miss Ford, it's been suggested that Miss Gilbert was something of a good-time girl. From what you've just told us, she sounds like an intellectual. What would your assessment of her character be?"

Daphne furrowed her brow a little and paused before answering, "If you mean by good-time girl whether she has a lot of admirers and goes to parties and that sort of thing, I don't really know. She doesn't have any men callers at her apartment – not that I've seen anyway while I've been here. As for being an intellectual, she knows a lot about art and books and music. If that's what makes an intellectual, then I guess she's one."

George smoothly took control of the conversation again. "Do you know why she didn't call the police?"

"No, I guess she was too shook up. She went out all day Saturday and again Sunday. I offered to go with her but she didn't want company. It's been a shock to her, this whole business. Her nerves are pretty shot, as you saw. I didn't want to push her to go to the police. At least, not till she's recovered a bit."

George got up. "Well, thanks, Daphne, you've been a great help. We'll see you again later." She watched us descend and then went back to Elaine's flat.

Outside, George commented, "We'll have to come back again."

"Yes," I replied, "I suppose we'll have to speak to Elaine Gilbert when she's in a calmer frame of mind."

"Correction, my young friend," responded George. "*You* can speak to Elaine Gilbert. I shall take care of Miss Daphne Ford." He sauntered off whistling down the road.

D'ALMEIDA was already back when we returned to the office. George filled him in on our interview with Elaine Gilbert as well as the little information we had gleaned from Daphne. He listened impassively, glancing at me occasionally for confirmation.

When we had finished, he recounted to us what had happened

at the Members' Committee's hearing for the Fitzhughs.

There wasn't actually much to tell. The Committee consisted of Mr Newman as President, Thornton and another member whose name escaped me. D'Almeida had sat quietly in the corner, pretending at his own suggestion to be a clerk taking notes. He blended perfectly into the background. William and David Fitzhugh had duly appeared, somewhat cocky in their confidence. It transpired that the Fitzhughs were well known to be men-about-town. Money, rank and looks conspired to convince them of their divine right to have their way with women. They were examined separately. Both denied having been at the Icarus Club on Friday night. They each maintained their well-rehearsed story of having had dinner at Foster's Restaurant that night – alone, so there were no independent witnesses. As there was no shaking them, the Committee had to let them go with a stern warning that further shenanigans would not be tolerated in future. And there the matter stood.

D'Almeida, as was his wont, had already verified the alibi. He sent Ralph to the restaurant. Ralph was to pretend to be an acquaintance of the Fitzhughs in order to find out discreetly whether either of them had been seen there on Friday night. The answer from the waiters was expected – yes, one of the Fitzhughs had been there, but no one knew which. All white men look alike and in this case, we were dealing with identical twins.

"Devilish clever, those two," grumbled George when we got back to the Assistants' Lounge. "As long as they stick to their story, no one can get the real rapist."

"Maybe we should just get the police to haul both of them in," commented Ralph. "Rape is rape, after all."

"And do what? Rub chilli powder into their eyes until one confesses? And since when has it been a police matter for a white man to force a native girl? If it had been a white girl and a native man, maybe. But you know jolly well that the police aren't going to touch the noble Earl of Rushton's precious heir and spare unless they are given an absolute, watertight, incontrovertible case on a platter. Not for the sake of a half-breed woman of dubious repute who gets picked up in a bar and follows a strange man back to a quiet room at the back of his club."

"Steady on, aren't you being a bit harsh on her?" asked Ralph.

"Only saying what the police will say if we bring this case to them half-baked." George started to pace. "We've got to find some way to break one of them."

I was feeling uncomfortable. I had been trained to believe that justice was blind – colour-blind at any rate. George's cynicism unsettled me, but deep down, I couldn't help feeling that he might be right. Without a clear case against one of the brothers, it would take a daring prosecutor to charge them. This was the kind of gaffe that was liable to get a promising young man posted to Mashonaland to register livestock. "Well, unless Elaine Gilbert decides to cooperate, this case is down the drain," I commented.

"I think she'll cooperate if we can get the goods on the Fitzhughs," said George. "To use the phrase of the delectable Daphne, she's still 'pretty shook up'. Let it wait a while. When she realises that we can put the bastard away, she'll come around to helping us."

"Easy to say," I responded, "not so easy to pull off. Just how do you suggest we go about getting the goods on them?"

George frowned. "I don't know yet. But I'll think of something."

We were interrupted by the entrance of Moraiss, the Chief Clerk, trailing an air of mildew behind him. Moraiss spent all his time in a dusty nook surrounded by decaying copies of ancient law reports and the smell had become part of him. "Telephone," he said shortly, addressing George, "A woman called Gilbert." With that, he shuffled out again.

"Ha!" said George triumphantly, "I knew she would change her mind."

He was back in a couple of minutes. "Progress?" I inquired.

"Might very well be," answered George. "She called to say that she's got something important to tell us. We're to meet her at her flat at seven o'clock. She wouldn't discuss it over the 'phone."

"So I suppose there's no chance of my getting home for dinner?" I ventured hopefully.

"You suppose correctly," he responded. "I think there will be significant developments."

3

WE GOT to Elaine Gilbert's place just before seven o'clock, in style this time. D'Almeida had decided that it was time for him to meet Elaine, so he had dismissed his syce and got me to drive his Rolls down to the flat. George installed himself in the back seat with Uncle Clarence. I parked the car right in front of her entrance, under a street-light which had just begun to glow in the gathering dusk. The street was almost deserted although the hour was early. That was normal. All the nightlife of the city went on in Chinatown, not in the genteel quarter of town or the affluent residential suburbs. As a rule, we dined early and went to bed, a fact of which my rumbling stomach forcefully reminded me as we climbed the four flights of stairs to Elaine Gilbert's flat.

The door was ajar when we got there. The radio was on. I distinctly heard the chimes of Big Ben signal the news on Radio Malaya as we reached the top of the landing. "Odd," said George and pushed open the door.

The living room was a shambles. The side-table was overturned and the settee cushions thrown on the floor. The shards of a glass tumbler lay scattered around. D'Almeida pushed his way past us. "Do not touch anything," he commanded.

We made a quick tour of the flat. There were three bedrooms, a kitchen and a dining room. We went through all the rooms.

The master bedroom was large, with two gigantic wardrobes and an en suite bathroom. I peeked in the wardrobes. Full of clothes and shoes, as one might have expected. No sign of anyone anywhere.

"Here, look at this," called George from the kitchen. There was a small servant's room attached, with a lavatory outside in a small balcony. The metal grille gate was open. From the look of the lock, someone had forced it with a screwdriver. A spiral stone staircase led down from the top balcony where we were, past the flats on the floors below, all the way to the ground level. An alley ran there between the blocks of flats, with dustbins arrayed along the side. In the twilight, it was impossible to see whether anyone was hidden there. D'Almeida instructed us to investigate.

George and I split up at the bottom of the stairs and took one end of the alley each. We met in front of the block. There was no sign of anyone. When we got back up to Elaine's flat, d'Almeida had a magnifying glass out and was minutely examining the floor around the settee.

"No one," puffed George. "It looks like whoever it was who jimmied the back gate, he or she got away."

"He," said d'Almeida shortly.

"How can you be so sure?" asked George with surprise.

"I note that the toilet seat in the master lavatory is up. Ladies habitually do not leave the toilet seat up. I surmise that there has been a man in the flat – unless of course it was one of you two during your earlier visit?"

We shook our heads. "It looks like she's been kidnapped," I said, somewhat superfluously.

"It would appear so," replied d'Almeida evenly. "I think we should send for the police, if you would be so kind, Chiang."

I went across the landing and rapped on Daphne's door. She opened it in a moment. She had on a kimono-like garment but was still dressed. "Sorry to bother you, Miss Ford. Something's happened. Can I use your 'phone?"

"Surely," she said, puzzled. "What's up?"

I got the police straightaway and gave them the address, explaining briefly what we had found. "Kidnapped!" exclaimed Daphne, horrified. "It can't be! And I didn't hear a thing."

D'Almeida had joined us. He introduced himself and shook Daphne's hand with a small bow. "You saw and heard nothing then, Miss?" he inquired.

"No, nothing, not at all." She sat down heavily on the settee.

"You were in all day?"

"Well, yes," she said. "After your two gentlemen left, I stayed with Elaine a while. We had lunch. Then I came back to my apartment. I've been writing letters all day here." She indicated her writing bureau, which was open and strewn with envelopes and notepaper.

"You can hear everything that goes on in the landing?"

"Yes, normally, 'specially when I'm at my desk. I'd have heard if there'd been anyone in the hallway. I'm pretty sure no one went in or out the front door all afternoon."

"It appears that the intruder gained access through the back gate. The lock seems to have been forced."

"How terrible!" exclaimed Daphne with a shudder. She glanced nervously at her back door. "Should I check my gate?"

"I shouldn't think it necessary," said d'Almeida comfortingly. "The intruder had a specific purpose in mind."

To their credit, the police were there within half an hour. The inspector in charge was a thick-set man, who greeted d'Almeida warmly. "Ah, Mr d'Almeida, a pleasure to see you again, sir. All in order, I trust?"

"The pleasure is mine, my dear Inspector Fergusson," responded d'Almeida with equal warmth, "we have touched nothing."

"Good, good. All by the book, then. What can you tell me?"

D'Almeida gave the inspector a quick summary of the whole case, stating just the facts with no embellishment. The inspector took it all down competently in his little book. The men with him searched the flat in the meantime.

"There is just one thing," said d'Almeida as we got ready to leave. He pointed to a little white square of paper just under the settee. "There appears to be something there. It might be worth examining."

"So there is," said the inspector, picking it up with a pair of tweezers. He held it up to the light for us to see. It was a book of matches. From the Icarus Club.

DAPHNE WAS in such a state of excitement that we thought it best not to leave her alone. George suggested that we should all go to dinner, a suggestion that she accepted with alacrity. D'Almeida kindly put his car at our disposal provided we dropped him off at the office first. This we did gladly.

George, of course, managed to arrange it so that he and Daphne rode in the back seat while I did the driving. "Where to?" I asked.

"The Raffles," commanded George. "I'm sure we can get something palatable at the Raffles Café."

I was sure we could, but the prices scared me. I hoped that George had brought enough cash, because all I had on me was a couple of creased dollar notes and a handful of shillings, mostly one-cent.

We left the Rolls parked in the forecourt of the Raffles and walked over to the Café, which was in the arcade of shops fronting Bras Basah Road. A waiter approached us immediately as we entered the premises.

"Ah, Ngiam," said George jovially, as if he owned the place, "a table for three. We'll take the one over there in the corner by the plant."

The waiter beamed and conducted us to the table, bowing politely.

"I didn't know you knew the waiters personally," I whispered to George.

"I don't," he whispered back. "The waiters here are Hainanese. They're practically all called Ngiam. By the way, I hope you've got money with you. I'm skint."

I would have made a cutting reply, but we were already sitting down at the table. I glanced at the menu despondently. The only thing I could afford was a cup of coffee.

"You're not eating?" remarked Daphne with surprise.

"No," I lied. "Had a heavy tiffin. No appetite left." The last was true. The prospect of being arrested for cheating at the Raffles completely took my appetite away.

George obviously had no such qualms. He ordered a copious meal, complete with dessert.

"Nice joint," said Daphne, looking around approvingly. "I guess you must come here all the time, seeing as how you know all the waiters."

"On and off," said George nonchalantly, "It's quite a pleasant place for a quiet chat. The food's quite good too." He produced a pack of cigarettes, which he offered around. "Have a smoke?"

"No, thanks, not for me," said Daphne. George put the cigarettes away. I was quite glad, having just managed to give up the habit. Mak hadn't said anything about it, but my five girl cousins were vociferous in their opposition to tobacco in the house. There is nothing like being nagged from five directions simultaneously to help one quit.

"You know we found a book of matches in Elaine's flat," said George. "From the Icarus Club."

"The Icarus Club," responded Daphne. "Wasn't that where Elaine got attacked?"

"Yes, precisely. It's very suggestive. There are two possibilities – one, that her kidnapper is a member of the Club and dropped them during the abduction. Two, that the matches were planted to make it look like a member of the Club did the kidnapping."

I didn't want to be left out. "We should look at the motive for the kidnapping."

"Yes, indeed, we should. She seems quite well-off. The most obvious motive would be that someone has kidnapped her for money. Would you know if she has relatives – a rich papa or uncle or something like that?"

"No, I don't think she has anyone here," she replied. "She told me once that she's alone in the world. She said I was her only friend here."

"So we tentatively rule out kidnapping for ransom. Extortioners seldom resort to abduction. Which leaves us …"

"You think that the guy who attacked her at the Club grabbed her to silence her?" asked Daphne.

"It's an obvious possibility. Either the attacker or someone who wanted to protect him. She called me earlier to say that she had something important to tell me. You wouldn't happen to know what it was, would you?"

"No idea. She didn't tell me anything during lunch. I asked her to call the police, but she only said she'd think it over."

"Anyway," continued George, "it seems that we can start with the working hypothesis that her abductor is the same person as the one who attacked her on Friday night, or someone trying to protect him."

"If there's something I can do to help nail the scumbag, count me in," said Daphne with feeling. "What should we do first?"

Our food arrived – or more precisely, their food and my coffee.

"The first thing we should do," said George, "is to devote ourselves to this splendid meal. You're sure you won't join us, Dennis?" I shook my head glumly, wondering whether we could get away with just washing up the dishes.

We had a convivial time, chatting about this and that. Daphne proved a lively companion. She had just attained her majority and had persuaded her parents to let her spend some time in the Straits Settlements, her father being a businessman in Jesselton. He had reluctantly agreed, knowing that the wilds of Borneo were no place for a young girl. He arranged for her to stay with friends, but she had given them the slip and rented a place of her own, out of money that her grandfather had left her. Singapore might not exactly have been the centre of the civilised world, but she found the independence itself to be exciting. Her only regret was that there was not more culture. She was fascinated with literature, art and music. George carried his end of the conversation, though I knew that his taste in books and music tended towards Erle Stanley Gardner and Cole Porter more than the classics. Still, he spread what knowledge he had admirably, managing to sound informed without being pinned down on details.

At the end of the meal, Daphne left to go to the powder room. George got up to leave. "We can't just walk out like that, you know," I hissed to him urgently. "They'll bung us into the chokey for not paying."

He clicked his tongue at me. "No need to get excited. I'll just put it on the tab."

"Tab? What tab?"

"D'Almeida's tab, of course. He won't mind us entertaining a witness, I'm sure. I'll just sign the chit as we leave."

I would have growled at him, but my stomach did a much better job.

4

IT WAS two days later that Ralph burst into the Assistants' Lounge with news. "Have you heard? They've found Elaine Gilbert."

"Found her? Where?" asked George, folding up his newspaper.

"In a car wreck in a rubber estate. Burnt to a crisp. I just heard Inspector Fergusson telling d'Almeida."

The three of us bundled out of the Lounge and headed to d'Almeida's room. We bumped into Inspector Fergusson as he was leaving. D'Almeida saw us and beckoned us in.

"So you have heard the news?"

"Yes," said George breathlessly. "Tell us about it."

"The police found a wrecked car in a rubber estate at Jalan Kayu late last night. There was a body in it, burnt beyond recognition."

"Isn't Jalan Kayu near RAF Seletar?" asked George.

D'Almeida nodded.

"How can they be sure it's Elaine Gilbert if the body's burnt beyond recognition?" I asked.

"They found a handbag with identity papers near the wreck. Inspector Fergusson is convinced that the victim is indeed Elaine Gilbert."

"Well," said George, "it looks like we've got a murder on our hands."

"The police think so," said d'Almeida. He took off his spectacles and began polishing them.

"Have they completed the forensic tests yet? Do they know the time and mode of death?"

D'Almeida looked at him. "This is not Scotland Yard, you know," he said witheringly, "The tests will take some time yet due to the state of the body."

"Has anyone checked up on the Fitzhughs?" persisted George.

"They have an alibi for the time of the abduction," said d'Almeida somewhat absently, staring out of the window. "Both are staff officers attached to General Dobbie's headquarters at Fort Canning. There was a staff meeting that day. Inspector Fergusson informs me that they both signed in that afternoon and signed out after midnight."

We looked at one another. From George's expression, I could tell that he was far from satisfied.

D'Almeida continued, "I asked Mr Thornton to come by this morning to discuss the case. It appears that events have overtaken us. Would you be so kind as to deal with him, Chiang? He should be here in a quarter of an hour. There are several things that I must attend to." With that, he got up and left.

My mind was still reeling from the news. The last thing I wanted was a tête à tête with James Thornton. I turned to George. "Well, it looks like the Fitzhughs are off the hook on this one. You can't get a better alibi than the GOC himself."

"I wouldn't cross off the Fitzhughs just yet," said George firmly. "It's quite possible they pulled another fast one and managed to get out to grab Elaine Gilbert – or at least, one of them did. The question is how. Maybe you can ask Thornton if he's got any ideas."

"Aren't you staying?" I asked, somewhat plaintively.

"No, old son, someone has to tell Daphne. I'll do it. Meet you there when you're done with Thornton." With that, he too left before I could protest further.

THORNTON was late, which did not improve my mood. I decided to meet him in d'Almeida's spacious office rather than in my broom-closet. I toyed with the idea of sitting behind d'Almeida's massive teak desk during the interview, but my courage failed me at the last moment.

He finally arrived about ten minutes after the appointed time. We sat across from one another in d'Almeida's leather armchairs. Although he was in mufti, he still had a military look about him. The moustache was neatly clipped, his leather shoes shone and his carefully-brushed hair was slick with Vaseline. He listened without comment as I told him what had happened.

"Well," he said at the end of my résumé, "I suppose that's the end of that. The rape case is closed and Fitzhugh will get away with it." His tone suggested disappointment.

"Not quite yet. We think that whoever abducted her must have done it to protect Fitzhugh," I said. "In some way or another, the Fitzhughs are in it up to their necks. The problem is getting the proof."

"Really?" he said, raising his eyebrows. "Is there a chance of getting the proof?"

"Yes," I said cautiously, "we're working on it. But why are you so keen on pinning the deed on Fitzhugh? I didn't think you were the sort who'd be interested in abstract justice."

This took him by surprise. "What do you mean by that?" he shot at me.

"You really don't remember me, do you?" I asked, staring him directly in the face.

He returned my stare and shook his head.

"Chiang. Fenton Abbey, 1927. You were a prefect when I was a First Former."

I was unprepared for his reaction. For a moment he sat completely still. Then he let out a groan and sank back in his chair.

"Oh God!" he moaned. "Fenton Abbey! How I've tried to forget that damned place! You weren't really there, were you?"

I nodded, somewhat dumbfounded. "Yes, I went up in '27."

"1927! You say you were in the First Form then. You don't remember a boy called Wilberforce?"

"I remember Wilberforce. I saw his body. It gave me nightmares for years."

"Damn you! Wilberforce has haunted me ever since. I left England to forget. I thought out here in the East there wouldn't be anything to remind me. Damn you for raising old ghosts!"

His outburst took me completely aback. Thornton slumped in his chair. He seemed to be wrestling with some powerful emotion. I sat stupefied. At length, he mustered himself and spoke. His voice was strained.

"Sorry, sorry ... it was the shock of being reminded. I didn't think it would still be so hard after so many years."

"Would you like a glass of water? Or something stronger ..."

He waved aside my offer. "I suppose I owe you an explanation ..."

"You were the one who let Wilberforce fall," I began.

"No, no, you've got it all wrong. It wasn't me. It was that bounder Vandeleur. Wilberforce was late with his tea. We thought it would be a good idea to teach him a lesson. So Vandeleur dangled the boy out the window while we egged him on. I was there when ... when ..."

"When he let go of Wilberforce," I completed the sentence for him.

He nodded. "Yes. Vandeleur was in a blue funk. We all agreed not to say anything – not to the masters, not to anyone."

"Everyone in my Form knew."

"Yes, I daresay everyone knew – or suspected. Even Dr Chalmers, the Headmaster, had his suspicions about us. But there was no proof as long as no one spoke. I was there at the inquest. Misadventure. I saw Wilberforce's mother leave in tears. She almost had to be carried away. It was as much as I could do to keep silent."

"You could have said something," I said accusingly.

"Yes, I could. I should have. But there was that damned code. A Fentonian doesn't snitch. It's a rule of honour. Of honour!" He laughed a short bitter laugh.

"So you let Vandeleur get away with it …"

"Yes, I let him get away with it. But Wilberforce tormented me. I never realised before how real Banquo's ghost must have been to Macbeth. After a while, I couldn't bear it any more. I chucked it all in … University, the City, everything. I signed up with the RAF and came out here – to get away from everything that might remind me. Hong Kong first, then Malaya. I'd done a pretty damned good job of forgetting – until you come along, out of a clear blue sky …" His voice trailed off.

I felt rather awkward. The event had been traumatic for all of us First Formers. I had spent the next decade hating Thornton and Vandeleur, Tomlinson and De Vere … I forget the other names now, but at the time the memory was still vivid. It hadn't crossed my mind that Thornton might have been equally affected by the incident.

"I'm sorry I sprang it on you," I said, feeling quite embarrassed. "I hadn't realised …"

"Not your fault," he replied, somewhat stiltedly. The stiff upper lip was beginning to reassert itself.

An idea struck me suddenly. "You don't have to let the bounders get away again, you know. You could help us nail Fitzhugh."

"Yes, I suppose I should," he said hesitantly. "But I'm not sure what exactly I can do …"

"Neither am I," I confessed, "but come along and meet the others. We'll think of something."

IF GEORGE was surprised to see Thornton in my company, he didn't show it. He made the introductions.

"We were just about to have another look around Elaine Gilbert's flat. Will you join us?"

"Are you quite sure this is legal?" asked Thornton doubtfully.

"Trust me," said George smoothly, "I'm a lawyer. Besides, our good friend Inspector Fergusson and his men have already done the place once over, so there's no problem there."

Thornton still hesitated. "Shouldn't we just leave it to the police?"

"We could do that," replied George, "just as you could have done with the rape. But you came to d'Almeida because he gets results that the police can't get. Are you in or out?"

"Anyway," chipped in Daphne, "Elaine left me her key so that I could let people in to tidy things. We're going to tidy things – sort of. It's okay."

"All right," said Thornton resignedly, "count me in."

Daphne let us in with her spare key. The flat was a bit dustier, but as far as I could see, nothing had been moved. The cushions and shards of glass still lay on the floor.

"What're we looking for?" asked Daphne with a little note of excitement in her voice. She seemed to be enjoying the adventure.

"I don't know," responded George. "Anything unusual. Out of the ordinary. Something that might give us a clue who the kidnapper was." He went out onto the rear balcony with Daphne. Thornton wandered aimlessly into the master bedroom. I started examining the lounge. A pile of papers on the writing desk caught my attention. I began leafing through them.

"I've found something interesting here," I called out. George and the others joined me. "Look at these – rent receipts for this flat, but all made out to a Dr Tate. Any idea who Dr Tate might be?"

"No idea," said Daphne. "I always thought it was her apartment. 'Least that was the impression she gave me. But look here, there's a card." She picked up a calling card from a nook and read it out: "Dr S Tate, Deputy Director, League of Nations Health Bureau. I guess that's her boss. She was personal assistant to the Deputy Director."

"Interesting," said George. "So, our Miss Gilbert did have a love life after all. Her assistance must have been very personal if Dr Tate was paying for all this."

"I don't see how this takes us any further, though," I commented.

"Well, it more or less rules out kidnapping for money as the motive, if this lot wasn't hers," rejoined George, "Let's take stock. Fact: Elaine Gilbert was raped by one of the Fitzhugh brothers. Fact: she calls on Monday afternoon to say that she has something important to tell me. Fact: she's kidnapped immediately after. Fact: her body is found in a burnt-out car a day later. What's the conclusion?"

"It looks pretty clear that someone grabbed and killed her to shut her up," I said. "No one has a motive except Fitzhugh and his brother. But they've got an alibi. Or maybe an accomplice?"

George turned to Thornton. "Anyone that they're particularly close to? Close enough to be an accessory to murder?"

Thornton shook his head. "Not that I know of. The Fitzhughs aren't the most popular of blokes. They're pretty conscious that their blood is bluer than the Danube and they don't let others forget it. I'd say they're tolerated rather than liked, and then mainly because they're so free with their money. Except with women. They seem to get on pretty well with the ladies. Friday wasn't the first time that one of them had brought a woman to the Club Social."

"Anyone in particular?"

"No, they're not the type to get tied to one woman. They're the love 'em, lay 'em, leave 'em sort. There've been stories. Money can buy anything here, though. That and a pedigree."

"So, we continue with the working hypothesis that the Fitzhughs did it by themselves."

"You're forgetting that they were at Fort Canning all afternoon and night Monday," I reminded him. "They both signed in and were seen. I think we can take the word of Malaya Command that they were there."

George pursed his lips. "Yes, I grant that. But the Fitzhughs are still the key. We need to get them to talk. If only there was some way to get one of them to open up, to confide in someone ... "

"We could set a honey trap," said Daphne slowly.

"Pardon?" I queried.

"A honey trap. You must've read about things like that in the last war. The Mata Hari kind of caper. You said that both of them have an eye for the girls, right?" she asked Thornton, who nodded. "So if some lady were to get real close, they might spill the beans."

"In theory, yes," I began doubtfully, "but you're not seriously suggesting that we get some poor woman to ... "

"Not some poor woman. Me." declared Daphne.

I shook my head emphatically. "It's too dangerous. There's no knowing what they might do."

"Doesn't have to be. I'd be careful to keep to public places. Look, it's the only way. Have you any other suggestions?"

I shook my head again.

"And if the Lieutenant would introduce us, I could simply take it from there."

Thornton looked uncomfortably at me. I still had serious

doubts. Daphne looked directly at me. "Look, I know what you're thinking. But Elaine was my friend – my only friend here. I want to help nail her killer."

George chimed in, "Daphne's right, there doesn't seem to be any other way to make them talk. I think it's worth giving it a shot. It's either that or let them get away with murder. What d'you say?"

Reluctantly, we both agreed. Deep in my heart, I had a niggling sense that we were courting disaster. But there wasn't any other way I could see. And I didn't want the ghost of Elaine Gilbert haunting me with the accusation that I'd let her killer get away.

5

AFTER further discussion we agreed that getting Thornton to introduce Daphne to the Fitzhughs would likely have put the wind up immediately. The best thing was for her to "accidentally" meet one of them at the Blue Lagoon Bar, where Elaine Gilbert had been picked up. To avoid other predators moving in on her first, George, Thornton and I would take turns to haunt the place. Our brief was to sit around every evening until one of the Fitzhughs put in an appearance. Daphne would only be called in when the target showed up. The rest would be left to her looks and their lechery. So followed one of the most mind-numbingly boring fortnights that I have ever spent.

As far as dens of iniquity go, the Blue Lagoon was pretty mild. There were much worse places in Singapore for someone in search of serious booze, sex or drugs. The proprietor of the Blue Lagoon was evidently a fan of American gangster movies. The whole place was set up like a speakeasy that wouldn't have been out of place in 'twenties Chicago. The smoke at any rate was authentic, even if the clientele was exotic. The crowd was a comparatively genteel one, unlike in some other places in town. Most were men, usually European, with a sprinkling of Asiatics. There were normally about half-a-dozen women. It wasn't really socially acceptable for young ladies to wander around town at night unescorted. Only the more Westernised and emancipated ones dared. There were always a few in the Blue Lagoon, mostly Eurasian. They came in twos and threes, occasionally alone. It was a statement of independence more than anything else, to shock their staid elders. The whiff of wickedness was evidently the draw.

We almost had immediate success. A couple of days after our council of war, George gave the order to scramble, having sighted a Fitzhugh at the Blue Lagoon. Unfortunately, by the time Daphne got there he had moved in on other prey. I was just escorting her to the door of the bar when George emerged to warn us off. It was just as well. We had barely time to turn around when Fitzhugh came out with a Eurasian tart on his arm. He headed off into the night while I took Daphne home.

That early near-miss encouraged us. The fact that Fitzhugh had zeroed in on one of the women gave us hope that the honey trap might actually work. Unfortunately, we then hit a dry patch. There was no sign of either of them for a fortnight. We stuck it out doggedly, but our enthusiasm began to flag. Sitting in smoky bars has never been one of my favourite pastimes. The combination of smoke, warm beer and noise made my head ache. After two weeks, I was all ready to give it up when, lo and behold, in strolled a Fitzhugh swaggering like God's gift to womankind. He cast a practised eye around, dismissed the local talent with a glance and sat down at the counter. I rushed off to the public 'phone to alert Daphne. Thornton had her there in a quarter of an hour.

Her entrance caused quite a stir. Unattached white females did not habitually frequent places like the Blue Lagoon. She sat herself down at a table and ordered a drink. For a moment, I had a horrible feeling that someone else would move in on her. However, my fears were groundless. True to form, Fitzhugh detached himself from the bar, oiled smoothly over and seated himself at her table. I was too far away to hear their conversation, but evidently, he was an entertaining companion, judging from the laughter that emanated from their corner. After half an hour, she got up to leave. He would have followed her, but she made it quite clear that she was going alone. I half expected that he would insist, but he didn't. I gave her a good headstart before I too left.

WE were all elated with our successful contact. Daphne was flushed with excitement. To her, the whole thing was a game of cloak and dagger, a Mata Hari caper as she put it.

"I knew you could do it," said George effusively. "You were superb!"

"Piece of cake," she responded, evidently pleased with the compliment. "I understand how Elaine might've been taken with him. He's pretty good company. And handsome."

George's brow clouded for a moment, a strange look which I couldn't quite interpret. It was gone in a flash. "Yes, he's a handsome dog," he agreed nonchalantly. "Evidently quite a ladies' man. You'll have to watch your step."

"Which one was it?" asked Thornton. "William or David?"

"Well," said Daphne, "he introduced himself as Hugh. But I pressed for a name. He called himself Hugh Rushton."

"So it could be either one," said Thornton.

"William, David, Hugh, it doesn't matter," exclaimed George. "The important thing is that we've made contact. Which is more than the police have done in the last fortnight."

"Yes, there doesn't seem to be much movement on that front," I commented. "Nor from d'Almeida." A sudden thought struck me. I turned to George. "You did mention this business to d'Almeida, didn't you, George?"

He avoided my gaze.

"Didn't you?" I pressed.

"Well, as a matter of fact, no, I didn't. He's been busy lately, as you know, and the opportunity never presented itself."

I let out a sigh of exasperation. It was just like George to drag us off on a frolic of his own.

"In any case," he continued jovially, "we'll let him know the results when we have some. What's next, Daphne?"

"Well, he asked if he could see me again."

"And …?"

"And I said maybe. I didn't want to be too eager. I gave him my number. Did I do right?"

"Absolutely right, darling," he said, patting her hand. "So Daphne plays hard to get and gives him a challenge. If he's the man we think he is, he won't give up so easily."

"What if he doesn't call?" asked Thornton.

"Oh, he'll call," said Daphne with certainty. "You can bet your life on that."

HER confidence wasn't misplaced. "Hugh Rushton" called the very next day to make a date for dinner. Daphne agreed but only on condition that she got to choose the place. She chose Emerson's, a fancy and slightly pretentious establishment near the Jinrickshaw Station.

On the appointed day, George got to Emerson's early to keep a discreet eye on Daphne. Oiling his way into the confidence of the maître d'hôtel in his inimitable way, he contrived to place himself just a couple of tables away. There he waited with anticipation for the man to make a wrong move. I think he rather fancied the thought of rescuing Daphne from the clutches of the villain. Unfortunately, Fitzhugh acted the perfect gentleman throughout. The evening passed without anything untoward happening. Nor did he make a false move on their next date, or the next … I began to wonder whether we'd got the wrong twin. It would have been just our luck to have picked up the good one.

Then came news. "He's invited me to the Club Social this Friday," announced Daphne after about a fortnight.

I was surprised. "The Club? After what happened the last time? You'd think he'd have better sense."

"Not really surprising," commented Thornton. "His sort doesn't think he can be called to account. Both of them were like that in front of the Members' Committee. They practically dared us to call in the police."

"Excellent," declared George, "the man seems incapable of learning from previous experience. Let's hope he makes his move."

I was still worried that George and Daphne hadn't thought through the consequences. "It's all very well hoping that he makes his move, but have you considered the danger to Daphne if he does? Remember, we're dealing with someone who won't stop at rape – or even murder."

Daphne patted me on the hand. "It's sweet of you to worry, but I don't think he's like that. He's a ladykiller, sure, but not a killer-killer. And I won't let it get too far. All we want is for him to give some hint that him or his brother attacked Elaine, right? I'll find some way to bring the talk round to that."

Thornton chimed in. "No, I think Chiang's right. We can't take a chance. Someone's got to keep an eye on Daphne. I can't do it. I'm too obvious."

"Well, then," contributed George, "I vote for Dennis. He's always been the knight errant for damsels in distress. He could go as a waiter. You can always use another good waiter, can't you Thornton?"

"But he's seen me before, at the Blue Lagoon," I remonstrated.

George clicked his tongue. "Nonsense, dear boy, he probably

didn't even notice you skulking in the corner. Anyway, waiters are invisible. No one pays any attention to them. And orang puteh can't tell one Chinaman from another."

"Yes, that's a jolly good idea," Thornton said, "a waiter could move around without attracting attention. And I've got the perfect spot for Daphne to have a quiet chit-chat with him – the Library."

"What's so special about it?" asked Daphne.

"Well, for one thing, no one ever uses it. Our chaps aren't the bookish sort. But more importantly, it has these speaking tubes that one of our naval members rigged up back in the 'twenties. For people to call the waiters. They're not used any more. They lead to a little pantry that's usually kept locked. But as Secretary, I can get the key. We could sit there and listen in on the conversation."

"Great!" exclaimed Daphne. "So I get him to the Library and get him talking, right?"

"Right," proclaimed George. "And with a little bit of luck, he'll spill all to our lovely Daphne. Give the man enough rope and he'll hang himself."

I DULY arrived at RAF Seletar that Friday afternoon and presented myself at the guardhouse. The sentry waved me through with hardly a glance at my pass. Walking through the gate, I noted that the streets were all named after roads in London. It was an odd sensation to be walking down Picadilly in the heat, surrounded by coconut palms and hibiscus bushes. The Icarus Club was located in a large detached bungalow behind Hyde Park Gate, set somewhat apart from its neighbours.

Thornton had me kitted out and introduced as a probationary waiter. He took the opportunity to show me the Library, a small corner room with a couple of bookcases filled with mouldering volumes. I picked one up. Silverfish scuttled from the spine in a cascade of paper dust. "Here are the speaking tubes," he said, indicating two trumpet-like objects attached to the wall by rubber tubes. "You put one to your ear and speak into the other."

"And how do we get Fitzhugh to do that?" I asked.

"We don't. Just leave the covers off. It should be able to pick up a conversation if we just move the settee over here. I'll pop into the pantry and you can say something. Whatever comes into your head." He left me. I sat on the settee and racked my head for something to say. In the end, I recited a couple of nursery rhymes, feeling totally foolish.

Thornton was back in a moment. "Loud and clear," he proclaimed. "It's jolly lucky it's only me, though. I can't imagine what another member would have said if he'd caught a waiter declaiming 'Mary Had a Little Lamb' to himself in here." He gave me a thin smile. It was the first time since I met him that he'd unwound enough to attempt jocularity. "Well, good luck," he said. "I'll pop in here when I see Fitzhugh and Daphne arrive. Come and join me when they go into the Library."

He assigned me to serve drinks in the ballroom together with the usual waiter, an old Hainanese who pointedly ignored me. Members began drifting in around half past six o'clock, most with a female companion. No one paid me the least attention, taking the drinks from the proffered tray without so much as a glance.

Fitzhugh turned up with Daphne on his arm just before seven. She certainly was a head-turner. Most of the other women there were Asiatics, no doubt picked up for the occasion like Elaine Gilbert. The few white women were frumpy and wilted, their limp frocks hanging forlornly from their frames. Daphne contrived to look radiant. To the chagrin of their dates, many of the men made a beeline for her. They swarmed around her but Fitzhugh made it clear that he wasn't letting anyone move in on his turf. I managed to get through the scrum to serve her a drink, which she accepted coolly without betraying a hint of recognition.

It was only after I got back to the bar counter that I noticed someone sitting quietly in a corner nursing a drink. I glanced quickly at Daphne's escort and back to the newcomer. They were completely identical, down to the immaculate parting of their hair. This one seemed to be more reserved, scanning the room with a wary eye. His gaze fell on me and lingered for a moment. I felt my neck hairs prickle as he stared directly at me. I averted my eyes and bent quickly, pretending to fumble for a glass. His glance glided on.

The ballroom was fairly small. Actually, it was an annex to the main building which must have housed the servants' quarters in the past. I hovered as near as I could to Daphne. The gramophone was on full blast and couples were on the floor. Despite the open windows and ceiling fans whirling like dervishes, it soon became uncomfortably warm. I heard Daphne say to Fitzhugh, "Say, let's get out of here. I'm cooking."

His eyebrows arched in surprise. "Aren't you enjoying yourself, darling?" His deep baritone was as smooth as satin.

"No, if I don't get out, I'm going to faint. I heard that you've got a library of sorts. Can I get a book?"

He seemed surprised by the suggestion, but went with her anyway as she slipped out the door. I followed discreetly in their wake. They went back into the main building where the Library was. I was afraid that he would try to get her into one of the other rooms, but to my relief, he took her straight to the Library. As they disappeared inside, I headed directly to the pantry where Thornton was waiting.

I was just about to step inside when a voice halted me. "I say, you! Yes, you there, boy! What the devil are you doing here? What've you got in there?"

I was stupefied to see Fitzhugh descend on me. For one brief moment, I thought he had spotted me shadowing him. Then I realised that it must have been his brother. Before I could stop him, he wrenched open the door of the pantry and stepped in.

The sudden irruption startled Thornton, who jumped up guiltily. "What the devil!" exclaimed Fitzhugh, "Thornton?" The voices of Daphne and his brother emanated distinctly from the speaking-tubes. The acoustics in that small pantry were marvelous. Every word was crystal clear. No wonder they had stopped using the place. There would have been no secrets left if the servants had been allowed to listen in from there.

Fitzhugh's expression changed from bewilderment to anger when he realised what Thornton was up to. "Of all the damned cheek!" he ejaculated. "You bloody spying bounder ... " Totally without warning, Thornton strode up and gave him a hefty punch on the jaw. He reeled back right into my arms.

"Sorry, sorry," I mumbled, struggling to place the dead weight in an armchair. "He must have seen me leave after his brother and decided to follow."

Thornton was nursing his fist. "I think I've broken my bally hand."

"He's out cold," I said after examining Fitzhugh.

"I don't know what came over me," said Thornton. "He was going to ruin everything. I had to stop him."

I nodded. "Can't be helped now. We'd better pay attention to what's going on. If Daphne gets something out of the other one, we want to have witnesses."

Leaving Fitzhugh in a somewhat untidy pile in a chair that was close by, we turned our attention to the speaking tubes to catch the conversation.

"…I hear you've got quite a way with the ladies, Mr Fitzhugh," said Daphne. Every word came clearly over the tubes.

There was a pause before Fitzhugh answered. "So you know my name. How did you find out?"

"I've got ears," she answered, "I heard some of the guys call you that. So what's your real name then?"

"David," he replied, "David Fitzhugh."

"Well, David Fitzhugh," said Daphne coquettishly, "you've got me here alone. Are you going to have your wicked way with me too?"

I drew my breath in sharply. Thornton glanced at me. "My God, she plays a dangerous game!" he remarked.

Fitzhugh's satin voice floated through the tube. "My wicked way..." he said suavely. "Whatever can people have been telling you?"

"Oh, nothing much. Just that Mr Fitzhugh has a different lady friend every time. And sometimes he plays rough, like last month."

He laughed shortly. "Yes, the chaps will talk. There was that unfortunate incident last month. But that wasn't me. It was William."

"William?"

"Yes, William, my twin brother. We're alike as two peas in a pod. William's always getting into scrapes. I'm covering up for him constantly. For the sake of the pater. William's the heir. It would kill the pater if there was trouble with the police."

We had been so engrossed in this revelation that we hadn't paid attention to the other Fitzhugh. Before either of us could react, he bolted out the door. We spun round and gave chase immediately.

William made straight for the Library with us at his heels. He burst in with the fury of a tornado, wrenched the surprised David out of his chair and began pummelling him.

"You scum!" he roared, "You lying worm!"

Thornton and I plunged in and managed with great effort to separate them. David's nose and lip were bleeding copiously.

"You lying bounder!" repeated William. "After all the times I've covered up for you, cleaned up your mess, squared the pater for you … You have the gall to accuse me …" He became incoherent. I could barely restrain him.

David wiped the blood from his mouth and said, "Steady on, old boy, don't forget yourself …"

"Don't you 'old boy' me," he spat out. Addressing Thornton, he said with venom, "You want the truth about last month? The truth is that dear brother David was here that night, doing his lady friend. I was at Foster's. And I'm not going to lie to save his skin any more."

David went livid in turn. "You bastard!" he yelled and struggled to get out of Thornton's grip.

"That," said William coldly, "is something you can't accuse me of being."

6

I LEFT Thornton to sort out the mess and took Daphne home. She was shaken and uncharacteristically quiet during the trip. George came round immediately to her flat when I called him. He was jubilant.

"Darling, you're a marvel," he gushed. She nodded wordlessly, sipping a glass of brandy.

"I suppose you'd better tell d'Almeida," I said.

George was on the 'phone immediately. I sat quietly next to Daphne. To my astonishment, she put out her hand and squeezed mine, giving me a wan smile.

The receiver clicked. "He wants to see us now," said George.

"What, at this time of the night? At the office? Wasn't he pleased?"

"Don't know," responded George shortly, "he didn't say. He's sending the car."

Daphne was still in a mild state of shock and wanted nothing more than to go to bed. We made sure that she was comfortable and left to wait downstairs.

The car finally arrived after an interminable time, driven by d'Almeida's syce Ahmad. After about ten minutes, George suddenly commented, "This isn't the way to the office. Where are we going?"

"Tuan say take you to Robinson Road," answered Ahmad.

"Robinson Road?" George glanced at me. "What's at Robinson Road?" I shrugged my shoulders. Personally, I didn't much care. The night's events had left me drained.

We drew up at a grey building at the end of Robinson Road, not far from the Old Market. D'Almeida was waiting for us, together with a large European. He made the introductions. "Gentlemen, may I present Mr Fredrick Newman." He indicated us. "This is my senior associate, George Singham. Mr Chiang, you already know."

Newman shook hands and said to me, "Well, young man, I hear you've been up to mischief again. Your little escapade has brought things to a head."

I realised with a shock that we had met before, under somewhat unhappy circumstances. I had had a little trouble with the police the previous year over certain Communists with whom I had unwittingly become involved. D'Almeida got me out of that tight spot. Newman had been the man in charge. Evidently, he hadn't forgotten me.

We followed them past the police guard and through a series of locked doors. "How do you know that Newman?" hissed George at me. "And where the devil are we?"

"Unless I miss my guess," I replied quietly, "we're in the bowels of Special Branch."

D'Almeida darted a quick backward glance at us and nodded.

We came at length to a small door with a peephole in it. A policeman stood outside. He unlocked the door and let us in. The room was small, with a naked bulb and a plain wooden table with two chairs. A blond woman was sitting at the table. She looked up when we entered.

"Elaine!" exclaimed George. "But you're dead!"

WE STOOD transfixed for a moment. Elaine seemed not to recognise us at first. Then she said, "Oh, it's you two again." Her tone was flat. Despite her new blond look, it was unmistakably her. She seemed older in that harsh light.

"Thank you, gentlemen, for the positive identification," said Newman.

Elaine's eyes flashed at him. "What are you holding me for? I've done nothing wrong. I want my lawyer." The irony of that seemed not to have struck her.

"You don't consider betraying your country as something wrong?" rejoined Newman.

"Betraying my country?" responded Elaine with some heat. "All of a sudden, I am accepted as a Briton. When it comes to this, I am British. But not at the Tanglin Club or the golf links; not in society. Don't talk to me about betraying my country. Asia is for the Asiatics. You have no right, no right at all to accuse me. And besides, I haven't done anything to betray anybody."

"What about murder then? An accomplice to murder," said Newman quietly.

"Murder!" Elaine blanched visibly.

"A young woman was found in a car, with your identity papers. She didn't die naturally. You must have known."

"No!" exclaimed Elaine, looking alarmed. "I never … I haven't … I knew nothing. He said he would fix things. He said he'd get a cadaver or something. I left it all to him …"

"We shall see about that," said Newman shortly and ushered us out of the room.

WE WERE taken to Newman's office and given a cup of coffee. "Well, gentlemen, your antics have forced us to act sooner than we would have liked. I should have kept a closer eye on young

Thornton. It was my mistake to have put him in touch with your people, Mr d'Almeida."

D'Almeida nodded and half-smiled. "The fault is also mine, Mr Newman. I had not realised what these young gentlemen were up to."

George could contain himself no longer. "For God's sake, will someone tell us what's going on? What's Elaine doing here? And where do the Fitzhughs fit in?"

"They don't," responded Newman. "But perhaps Mr d'Almeida will oblige. The credit belongs to him."

D'Almeida inclined his head to acknowledge the compliment. He took a sip from his cup and began, "Elaine Gilbert's kidnapping troubled me from the start. It seemed that she had been taken to stop her identifying her assailant. Her flat was in disarray. The broken glass on the floor, the forced back gate. All calculated to point to an abduction against her will." He took off his spectacles and polished them.

"But, I asked myself," he continued, "why would her abductor leave the front door open, as we found it? And, as I pointed out, someone had used her lavatory and left the toilet seat up. Only a man would do that. What sort of kidnapper would use his victim's lavatory calmly before or after the act? It had to be someone she knew, someone she was comfortable enough with to allow entry into her bedroom. This immediately ruled out either of the Fitzhughs. I looked around the flat for something unusual. I found some interesting rent receipts …"

"In the name of Dr Tate!" exclaimed George.

D'Almeida looked blank. "I beg your pardon?"

"Dr S Tate, the Deputy Director of the League of Nations Health Bureau. Her boss. We found the same rent receipts."

"Ah," said d'Almeida, light dawning, "you mean Dr Tah-tay. Dr Shigeru Tate. He is a Japanese gentleman. I met him once at the Governor's New Year Reception. A charming man. And you are correct in surmising that he is her boss."

"A very charming man," added Newman. "Dr Shigeru Tate is well known to Special Branch. He's the head of the Japanese intelligence network in Singapore."

"Indeed," continued d'Almeida. "Mr Newman recognised the name immediately when I confided my doubts to him. It seemed to us that the kidnapping had been staged. Our suspicions were confirmed when Miss Gilbert's body was apparently discovered. The body was burnt beyond recognition, but her handbag with identification papers was found not far away. What sort of kidnapper takes the victim's handbag with him and then leaves it where it can be found? A very slipshod way of carrying out a kidnapping. It seemed a calculated move to make the police believe that the body in the car was Elaine Gilbert's."

"But if it wasn't Elaine, then who … ?" I interjected.

"We don't know for certain," responded Newman. "Possibly some poor indigent plucked from the streets who happened to be the right build. Or a rubber tapper who happened to be in the wrong place at the wrong time. We're still checking for missing women. But Mr d'Almeida was telling you about Dr Tate. He managed to confirm that Elaine Gilbert was Tate's mistress."

"How on earth did you do that?" asked George.

"I introduced myself as her grieving uncle at her office," replied d'Almeida, with a wicked twinkle in his eye. "Her colleagues were most comforting. And very free with office gossip. It appears that their liaison is something of an open secret."

"I'm thoroughly confused," said George, shaking his head. "We'd figured that Tate must have been Elaine's lover or something, from the fact that he was paying for her fancy flat. But what has any of that got to do with the case – or cases, since we seem to have two separate ones now?"

"That, my dear Singham, was the final piece of the puzzle," continued d'Almeida. "Shigeru Tate is the head of a Japanese intelligence network here. Both David and William Fitzhugh are aides to General Dobbie. We surmised that Elaine Gilbert, besides being his mistress, was also one of his operatives. She was evidently assigned to seduce and compromise a young officer on the GOC's staff. How did our young Miss Ford put it – a honey trap?"

We stood aghast. "Damn! So Fitzhugh was innocent after all," exclaimed George.

"On the contrary," responded Newman, "as you and Thornton so clearly proved, David Fitzhugh was guilty of rape. You see, Jap intelligence slipped up badly. They thought there was only one Lieutenant Fitzhugh on General Dobbie's staff, the heir of the Earl of Rushton. Their calculation was that he would do anything to avoid a scandal that would stain the family name. No doubt Elaine was supposed to have an affair with him and, at the right moment, threaten to make public their relationship unless he cooperated. An affair with a half-breed Eurasian would hardly have been welcome to the noble Earl and his heir. Or so they thought."

"But they got the evil twin!" exclaimed George.

"Precisely. They got the wrong twin. David Fitzhugh is, as we all know, an out-and-out cad. William has evidently been trying to cover up for him all this time. Elaine, thinking that she is dealing with a proper English gentleman, gets David. Instead of her seducing him, he rapes her. And of course William is forced again to help his brother out of the scrape. Apparently, from what you told Mr d'Almeida of her condition when you saw her, it was a complete shock for her."

"Yes," I confirmed. "She was in quite a state. She seemed very keen to make him pay. Until she heard that her past would be raked up if there was a trial."

"But why the need for the elaborate rigmarole, the kidnapping?" interjected George.

"I believe that when you and Chiang visited her, she realised that Mr Thornton was determined to push the issue," answered d'Almeida. "She also realised that if it came to a rape trial, her liaison with Tate would be exposed and awkward questions asked. They may have panicked a little. Something had to be done quickly. So they hatched the idea of a kidnapping and apparent murder. With Elaine Gilbert dead, the rape case dies. The police are distracted looking for her murderer. Or better still, trying to prove that David Fitzhugh did it – which I believe was the point of leaving the Icarus Club matches to be found; a piece of pure, calculated malice on her part. Meanwhile, she changes her hair colour and goes underground. Perhaps they hope to use her again somewhere else."

"How did you find her?" asked George.

"It was simple, once Mr d'Almeida set us on the right track," replied Newman. "We had Tate followed. He led us to her. We've been watching her. And we would have kept on watching her if you hadn't intervened."

George and I looked at one another uncomfortably. "So what's next?" I ventured. "What happens to her and Tate?"

"Nothing," said Newman. "I think she can be persuaded to work for us. It's not comfortable being an accomplice to murder. She's obviously not a professional operative. I doubt she'd be willing to swing for her convictions, if she really has any. We'll work on her. If all goes well, she'll go on with Tate as if nothing had happened. But she'll be telling us what he's up to in future."

"What he's up to in future … ," said George with an edge in his voice. "So he gets away with murder."

"Yes, that's what it amounts to," replied Newman solemnly. "We can't touch him. He has diplomatic immunity. We could write to the League of Nations in Geneva to lift his immunity, but that would mean giving away everything we know. Otherwise, the most we can do is expel him. With this trouble brewing in Europe, His

Majesty's government would find an incident with Japan at this time somewhat inopportune."

"And I suppose David gets away with rape," said George with unconcealed bitterness.

"Not entirely. Special Branch will make a report to General Dobbie. To be caught once in a honey trap is unfortunate. To be caught twice smacks of gross negligence. Not something that one takes lightly for a staff officer in a sensitive position at Malaya Command. I'll see to it that the Earl of Rushton gets a copy of the report. And William isn't going to be kept on either, you can mark my words on that. Covering up for his brother instead of reporting the incident – a security lapse of the worst sort."

"What about Daphne and Thornton?" I asked. "Can we tell them?"

"No," said Newman decidedly. "Elaine Gilbert is dead. Let her stay buried."

SO THAT was that. We told Daphne and Thornton that despite what we had discovered, our evidence wouldn't be enough for a conviction in a rape trial – which was true. They were understandably outraged. To assuage their sense of injustice, we let on that Mr Newman would use his influence to ensure that David and William were disgraced – which was also true. They were sent packing with an enormous black blot on their escutcheon. They never served in a position of trust again. I was told that old man Rushton had a fit when he heard and nearly disowned the pair of them.

It was only many years later that I discovered what finally became of them. William was awarded the Distinguished Service Order for gallantry at Tobruk. David won the Military Cross at Arnhem. Both awards were posthumous. It seems that their code of honour had demanded a human sacrifice to wipe out the shame.

7

THE ELAINE GILBERT affair disquieted me. All my life I had had it repeatedly drummed into me that the enemy was Germany. I grew up devouring the Hannay and Biggles books. The Hun was always the villain. We were given a big dose of Empire history at Fenton Abbey. The Great War pervaded the atmosphere. In the Great Hall where we congregated for formal dinners, right above the High Table was an enormous plaque with the names of all the old boys of the school who had fallen in battle during those terrible years – at Mons, Ypres, the Somme, Gallipoli, Cambrai, Passchendaele and a score of other familiar and unfamiliar places. Right at the top, in gold letters, was the legend "Our Glorious Dead". There was not a village in East Anglia that did not have a memorial of some sort in the church or on the village green. The prospect of another general European war hung like an incubus over my undergraduate years. Beneath the veneer of gaiety that we affected, I sensed in my college-mates a growing unease.

All that had evaporated when I returned to Singapore. The atmosphere in the Straits Settlements was insouciant. As long as there was money to be made, hardly a soul cared about world politics. September 3rd, 1939 was an anticlimax. I heard Neville Chamberlain proclaim on the radio that a state of war existed between the British Empire and Germany. It didn't come as a surprise. Nor did it make a great difference to our lives. To us in the Straits Settlements, Europe was far away and the rumble of war indistinct. We had hardly been touched by the Great War. We didn't expect that things would be any different this time.

So it was a shock to discover that the enemy was someone else besides the Germans and in fact much closer than I had ever suspected. In my naïve way, I had always thought of the Japanese as our friends. The year I was born, the 5th Light Infantry mutinied in Singapore. For several days, the mutinous sepoys rampaged through the island killing Europeans. Among the forces who put down the uprising were sailors from Japanese warships in the harbour. My uncle had told me when I was quite young about the trials – he and my father had assisted d'Almeida in defending some of the mutineers. They got them off with a jail sentence. The ringleaders were shot outside the walls of Outram Road Gaol. The bullet holes were still there for all to see. The Japanese had been on the right side that time. They were allies during the Great War, having fought and beaten the Germans in Shantung. My uncle had spoken of them in complimentary terms.

There was in fact a big Japanese community in British Malaya, with their own shops and restaurants all over the place. We patronised Baba & Co, the large department store in Middle Road. It was as large as Robinson's. We bought fish brought in by Japanese trawlers. The Japanese ran rubber estates and mines up-country. There were Japanese photographers, shopkeepers and prostitutes; even a geisha house in Katong. My own barber was Japanese. I found it hard to think of them as enemies.

It was different for some of the other Chinese. We Babas were British subjects and had little interest in what went on in distant China. For the non-Babas, or Sinkhek as we called them, China was home. To say that they were agitated by the Japanese invasion of China would be an understatement. They went off the deep end in a big way. The Marco Polo Bridge incident in 1937 touched off a wave of protests and a boycott of Japanese goods. There was even street violence in Penang. To me and my intimate circle, however, Japanese aggression in China was no different from Italian aggression in Abyssinia; regrettable, to be sure, but nothing to get overly excited about. When it came to that, the Japanese were acting no differently from the French in Indochina or the Dutch in the East Indies.

But the discovery that a Japanese agent had tried to suborn a member of the GHQ staff, and had even committed murder to do it, shook me. It made me look askance at my Japanese acquaintances. It was therefore in a different frame of mind than usual that I made my regular visit to Mr Takeda, my barber.

Takeda was a pleasant, rotund fellow with a wide smile and round glasses. When he smiled, his eyes disappeared. He ran a bright, clean establishment just off South Bridge Road not far from the Subordinate Courts. It was well patronised by both Europeans and non-Europeans. I had been going to him ever since I came back to Singapore from England. He had always given satisfaction. Better still, he didn't feel the need to jabber constantly while cutting my hair, unlike some of the Indian barbers I had tried previously. He just smiled and snipped away. I don't recall that we actually spoke. I would come in, he would bow, smiling, and conduct me to the chair. When the process was over, he would bow again, still smiling, and I would pay. So I was surprised when, this time, he actually addressed me. Maybe it was the fact that I had been watching him surreptitiously in the mirror while he cut my hair, trying to divine the thoughts behind the façade that encouraged him. Whenever he noticed, he flashed me his searchlight grin and I would avert my gaze in embarrassment. But after the third time, he evidently decided that the ice had been broken.

"Sir," he said in a curious sing-song tone, "they say you lawyer, yes?"

"I am a lawyer, yes," I confirmed cautiously.

"I hope you will help me, sir, please."

"Of course, if I can." He was quite the most polite person I had ever met and I felt compelled to be equally courteous. That, plus the fact that he had in his hand a cut-throat razor, which he was energetically stropping on a leather strap prior to shaving me. I had no desire for a closer shave than usual.

"I live here in Singapore many years," he continued, "nearly 10 years now. I come from Nagasaki by boat, become barber in shop near Toyo Hotel. Then when I have enough money, I buy this shop." As he had begun to lather me copiously, I could only incline my head slightly in acknowledgment.

"It is lonely to be here alone," he continued wistfully, expertly scraping away the lather with deft strokes of the wrist, "I have no family." He was silent for a while, evidently concentrating on giving me a good shave. At the end of the process, he wiped my face with a hot towel. He held up a hand mirror behind my head so that I could examine the result of his ministrations. I nodded in approval. "I want to get married," he said. "For this, I need your help."

"You don't need a lawyer to get married," I told him, fishing out the change to pay for the haircut.

He looked crestfallen. "But it is ... there is problem," he stammered, fumbling for the words. The customary smile had disappeared. He looked so woebegone that I sighed and replied, "If it will make you happy, I'll see what I can do."

He brightened up immediately. His smile increased several degrees in magnitude. "Thank you, thank you, sir," he went on, shaking my hand as if he were pumping water out of a well. "You come to my house tonight? I make you dinner." He pressed a scrap of paper with his address into my hand. Having retrieved my limb from his grasp, I made my exit rather more hurriedly than was polite. He didn't seem to notice the rudeness. He was standing at the doorway, still smiling and bowing away like a clockwork toy.

THE OFFICE was almost empty when I got back from my haircut although there was still half an hour to go before quitting time. Things were much more easy-going then. A three-hour tiffin followed by early tea at four o'clock wasn't uncommon. D'Almeida himself was immured in the Library behind a great wall of books, as was his habit when business was slow. He was at heart a pedagogue, and nothing pleased him more than to run to earth some obscure point of legal philosophy in one of the ancient tomes. As for the others, there was no sign of either hide or hair. I had expected to have the Assistants' Lounge all to myself. It was with some surprise then that I discovered George preening himself there, freshly scrubbed and pressed, and wearing a flower in his lapel.

"All tarted up, I see," I commented. "Going out on the town?"

"Yes," he replied, admiring himself in our full-length mirror. "I have an assignation. With Daphne. Or, to be precise, I shall when I have asked her."

I reacted with mild astonishment. "With Daphne? You're going to make an overture?"

"My dear boy," he responded confidently, "not just an overture. I am going to give her the whole operetta – flowers, chocolates, dinner, the works." My doubts must have shown on my face. "Don't think I can get a date with her, O ye of little faith? Just watch me."

"It's not that," I replied hastily, "it's just that … that…"

"That she's white and I'm not?"

"I wouldn't have put it quite so bluntly myself, but now that you mention it, yes."

George stopped fiddling with his tie and looked me straight in the eye. "Dennis, I know there's a colour bar and all that, but Daphne's different. She's not prejudiced – not in the least like those sniffy memsahibs and their snooty daughters. She's American. Where is it written that her knight in shining armour can't be a black knight?"

"Well, good hunting," I wished him, somewhat doubtfully. We lived in a society of cascading snobbery. The Babas, coming from old established families, looked down on the Sinkhek, who were considered to be country bumpkins from the back of the beyond. The Sinkhek in turn looked down on the Tamil coolies, whom they derided as working class and black to boot. Within the Indian community itself, there were castes within castes. Right on top of the social pile were the white Britons, who despised everyone else. The womenfolk were the worst. Daughters of clerks and minor functionaries who would have been shown the tradesmen's entrance in London society put on the airs of duchesses when transported to the non-white colonies.

Strangely enough, racial prejudice was much less evident in England. I had found the English in general to be polite, helpful and even friendly on occasion, if a trifle reserved. But out in the East, where a few thousand Britons held sway over millions of non-European subjects, the rules changed. The whole edifice of Empire was built on the bedrock of racial superiority. Each and every newcomer was told in no uncertain terms that maintenance of the Raj depended on the prestige of the White Man. Going native was frowned upon. Of course the menfolk did it, especially up-country. A lonely planter or miner had to have his distractions. But in Singapore, the capital of the Crown Colony, mores and morals were stricter. A white man who took a native wife or mistress was just about tolerated, though excluded from polite society. But if an Asiatic man, especially a dark-skinned one, so much as looked at a white woman … There would be poisonous glares and dark rumblings about miscegenation. Daphne might have been American, but I wasn't sure that she hadn't been infected by the climate of the place. George, though, was supremely confident. He had enjoyed great success with ladies of every colour and creed. Daphne was of course the ultimate challenge. If anyone could pull it off, he could.

"The reason I have been hanging around here," he continued, "is that I need your help."

"My help?" I responded with surprise. "Since when did you need anyone's help with the ladies, let alone mine?"

"Well, dear boy, as you know, Daphne's pretty much into this art and music business, and I thought that you could give me a quick introduction to it."

"So I'll be Cyrano while you woo Roxane?" I said doubtfully.

"Exactly, except for the nose. I just need a couple of lines on some of the things we were talking about that night in the Raffles Café."

I knew there was no use protesting that one couldn't cram a liberal education into half an hour. I let him have as much as I could, which wasn't a lot. He seemed quite happy though. George had a talent for making a little knowledge go a long way. We always felt that he had a brilliant career ahead of him as a lawyer or politician with his special gift.

GEORGE AND I parted company, he to woo his latest lady-love and I to keep my appointment with Mr Takeda. I can't say that I was looking forward to it. I had heard somewhere that the Japanese ate seaweed and raw fish. The prospect of dining like a pelican did not appeal much to me.

Takeda's place was not far from his barber shop, deep in the warren of small lanes that made up Chinatown. I wasn't at home in this part of town. The sights and smells and sounds were alien to me. Two hundred yards from the main road, I was lost. Takeda had given me a rough sketch plan with his address. I wandered around a bit in the gathering gloom, looking for some landmark to orient myself. There were signs all over the place, but in Chinese. For all the use that was to me, they might have been in Etruscan. I was on the verge of giving up when I spotted Takeda peering anxiously out from a dark staircase at the side of a shop. He saw me at the same time. His grin flashed in my direction like a lighthouse. He beamed at me, waving to attract my attention. I made my way over to him, carefully avoiding the potholes full of dark water.

The row of terrace houses was seedy. The walls were black with moss and mildew. The open drains stank. I heard little furtive scurrying sounds and glimpsed dark shadows the size of small cats scampering into the cracks. The ground floor of each terrace unit was occupied by a shop, with signs painted in red and gold on black backgrounds. Their shuttered fronts betrayed no clue of what lay within. A pair of dimly-lit windows above the darkened shopfronts gave each house a face, as blank and inscrutable as an Asiatic's to a European.

I followed Takeda up the dark narrow stairs to his flat. The gloom of the staircase was intense. An anaemic bulb lit the landing at the top, barely sufficient to allow one to negotiate the uneven steps. The place smelt vaguely of partly-dry laundry. Takeda fumbled momentarily with the lock, then stepped aside and ushered me in with a bow.

The first thing that struck me was the absolute simplicity of the interior. He had no furniture. The room extended the whole width of the flat, as was normal with these terrace houses. At one end of the room, two large windows looked onto the street, practically peering into the flat opposite. At the other end, was a delicate partition made of paper and bamboo, lighted from behind by a subdued glow. The floor was spread with straw matting. In the middle of the room was a single low square table. On the table were two place settings, each comprising a lacquer box containing several covered dishes, a bowl and chopsticks. The centrepiece was a delicate porcelain vase with two chrysanthemums and two reeds, arranged with elegant simplicity. The whole place was spotlessly clean and very well-kept.

"Welcome to my humble house," said Takeda, bowing deeply.

THE FOOD was exotic to my taste. The sight of mottled purple tentacles complete with suckers peeping out from a bed of what looked like grass unnerved me. I had thought that I would retch, but I found the dishes surprisingly palatable. Besides the octopus, there were slices of a white fish alternating with a dark reddish fish and delicate small prawns, firm and sweet despite the absence of condiments. The fish was completely fresh and tasted cleanly of the ocean. I thought back to the wood-hued kippers and battered cod of my youth. In some European countries, one ate fish on Fridays as a penance; the way fish was prepared in Europe, it was a real penance to eat the stuff. I hadn't thought that I would develop a taste for raw seafood, but Takeda made me an instant convert.

When dinner was over, Takeda cleared the table efficiently. "Now we have coffee," he announced. "Coffee after dinner, in European manner."

He clapped his hands. A young girl entered, bearing a tray with a porcelain coffee pot and two cups. She was dressed in a samfoo, which struck me as incongruous in such Japanese surroundings.

"This is Yeng Nam," said Takeda, "she will be my wife." The girl blushed and bowed. She poured the coffee wordlessly and offered me a cup with eyes modestly downcast and a shy smile.

I examined Yeng Nam as I accepted the cup. She didn't seem to be very old. I guessed that she was still in her late teens. Her complexion was tanned, pointing to a life in the sun. She had a blank, round, inscrutable face, like a stereotypical china doll. It was a pleasant peasant face, homely rather than beautiful, almost child-like in its innocence. She did not move with the accustomed fluidity of an accomplished hostess. She handled the coffee things hesitantly, almost clumsily. When she had finished serving us, she retreated to a corner where she sat quietly on her haunches.

"So, Miss Yeng Nam is to be your wife," I ventured conversationally. "I congratulate you both. When is the wedding to be?"

Takeda's face clouded. "We have no wedding date. There is problem." He stopped. I waited. At length, he sighed and continued, "Big problem." I fidgeted. Sitting on the floor was an unaccustomed strain on my bottom. Besides, my legs didn't bend that way. I was impatient to get to the point, and I said somewhat abruptly, "So you keep saying. But what's the problem? And what do you need me for?"

Takeda did not register any irritation at my lack of grace. He just sighed again and said shortly, "She is already married."

I was taken aback at this. She hardly looked old enough. "Suppose you begin at the beginning," I suggested.

Takeda began, "Two years ago, I save enough money to buy another barber shop. A small one, in Nee Soon Village. Business is good there. I meet Yeng Nam. She live with her aunt. She is – how you say – orphan. Parents both die when she is young. Her aunt has vegetable farm."

I glanced at Yeng Nam. She was smiling uncertainly and

uncomprehendingly in my direction. Takeda went on, "I buy vegetables in market, I see her. She is beautiful to me. I am lonely, I have no family. I want to ask her aunt to marry her, but she is only fifteen. So I wait. But I wait too long." He stopped and sighed.

"Last year, rich towkay see her. He ask aunt and she agree. He give money to her and take Yeng Nam as wife. They come to town to live. I am sad because I think I will not see her again. But by good luck, they live near my shop in town. So I see her every day as she pass my shop. I see that she is not happy. Then one day she run away from husband and come to my shop. I say she must go back. She does not want, but I say must. So she go back to him. But he is bad man. He beat her hard."

At this point, he paused and said something I did not understand to Yeng Nam, in Japanese or dialect possibly. She turned round and lifted her blouse. There were weals on her back, half a dozen of them, like zebra stripes against the pale skin. I flinched at the sight. There and then I resolved to do all I could to help her.

Takeda spoke again. "She run away again last week and stay with me. I ask her to marry me. She has agree." He beamed at her, and she smiled shyly back.

"Right," I said, "I understand your problem. She needs a divorce first. I can help you there. There should be more than adequate grounds for divorce if he's been beating her like that. You both come down to the office first thing tomorrow and we'll fix you up. We'll have him in court and she can tell the judge all about it."

Takeda looked alarmed. "No, no, you do not understand. Her husband do not know she is here with me. She cannot go out. He will kill her if he find her." He paused and took a deep breath. "Her husband is big gangster boss."

8

"EVEN BIG gangster bosses get divorced," said Ralph, who had some practical experience in matrimonial law.

"I'm sure they do," I replied, "but the point is that they divorce people, not the other way around. There is a difference. That sort of fellow tends to have a nasty temper and I don't fancy ending up in the Kallang River in a concrete waistcoat."

"Do they do that here too?" asked Ralph disingenuously. "I thought it was a New York speciality."

I had been mulling over Takeda's problem. Despite his comical outward appearance, I found that he had a streak of steely determination. He wanted to rescue Yeng Nam from the clutches of her husband, Lim Beow Sin, better known locally as the Black Cat. Some quixotic impulse drove him to take care of her. He was preparing to go back to Japan (a fact that filled me with dismay, since good barbers are hard to find). But she would not go except as his wife, so he had to do things the legal way. Unfortunately, law is a game that takes two players and it was by no means certain that Black Cat would abide by the rules.

A thought struck me. "Damn!" I exclaimed. "It's just occurred to me that Yeng Nam and this Black Cat fellow won't have undergone a registry wedding. Can a Chinese customary marriage be dissolved by the High Court? And how do you do it?"

"Search me, on both counts, old boy," answered Ralph, shrugging his shoulders.

Suddenly, I made up my mind. "I'm going to ask d'Almeida. He'll know what to do. You coming?"

Ralph shook his head. "Not on your life. You know what he's like. He'll give us a viva voce. If I don't say anything, he'll conclude that I'm completely clueless and if I open my mouth, he'll have that diagnosis confirmed right away. You go ahead and tell me what the solution is."

I found d'Almeida in the library surrounded by ramparts of old law reports. He looked up when I coughed to get his attention.

"May I ask your opinion on a point of matrimonial law?"

"Certainly," he answered, indicating that I should sit down. "But be brief. I have much to do."

I summarised the problem briefly. He remained silent for a moment, polishing his glasses. Replacing them on his nose, he spoke in a dry expository tone, as if addressing an invisible class of undergraduates.

"A Chinese customary marriage as recognised in the Colony requires no formalities. All that is necessary is that the parties intend to enter into matrimony and not a merely meretricious relationship. This can be proven by cohabitation and repute, a purely evidentiary issue. The dissolution of the conjugal bond under Chinese customary law takes two forms.

"Firstly, by mutual consent and secondly, by unilateral repudiation on the part of the husband. There are no prescribed formalities for the former. It is sufficient that the divorce is announced publicly and that the relatives are informed. In the case of the latter, there is some doubt as to whether it is permissible in the case of a tsai, that is to say a principal wife, as opposed to a tsip, a secondary wife. One would be best advised to procure expert testimony as regards the law obtaining in China appertaining to this issue. Again, as in the case of divorce by mutual consent, there are no formalities. All that is required is a definite intention to dissolve the association and notoriety given to the decision. You may wish to refer to the case of Sim Siew Guan, which you will find reported in the Malayan Law Journal some seven or eight years ago. A case decided by the Chief Justice himself, I believe."

I sat open-mouthed for a moment, overwhelmed by this deluge of erudition. I wasn't even sure of the meaning of most of the big words he used. D'Almeida, who had a form of X-ray vision, saw the gears working overtime in my head. "In plain English," he continued severely, but with a twinkle in his eyes, "you should first establish that the parties intended to marry and not merely live together as man and mistress. The marriage can be dissolved by mutual consent, or, in the case of a secondary wife, by the husband unilaterally. No grounds for divorce need be specified. Is that sufficient?"

Recovering myself, I remarked, "This doesn't help us at all. I don't know if the girl is a principal or secondary wife, but that would seem irrelevant in any case. She can't divorce him and he won't divorce her."

"Have you asked?"

"Pardon?"

"Have you asked the man whether he is willing to divorce his wife?" repeated d'Almeida evenly. "You will not know unless you do." With that, he returned to his books.

I BUMPED into George back in the Assistants' Lounge. "Had a good time last night?"

He made a strange face. "We didn't go out."

"She didn't accept your invitation?" I asked incredulously.

"Oh, she did. We're meeting for tea at the Adelphi on Sunday afternoon. But she wants you to come along."

I was thunderstruck. "Me? Why me?"

"She seemed to think you'd be good company."

I didn't know quite how to react. Normally, I have no hesitation accepting invitations to tea with attractive young women. But in the last year, my heart had been if not actually broken, at least severely dented. The last thing I wanted was to start something with Daphne; certainly not when George was interested in her.

"No, I can't come," I said.

"Why ever not?" persisted George.

"Well, for one thing, I know you've got a crush on her and I don't want to get in the way."

"A crush on Daphne!" responded George with a short laugh. "My dear boy, do you think I'm some amorous adolescent anaconda? No, I absolutely insist that you come. I need the company. I need the support. I need you."

I began to waver. George pressed home his advantage.

"Look, Dennis, she's not entirely comfortable being alone with me. Not yet. You're comforting. You're brotherly. She won't feel threatened if you're around. The first rule of the hunt is not to spook the prey by moving too fast too soon. That's why hunters use camouflage and blinds. You're mine."

Oh, all right then," I conceded. "I'll be there."

"Good man!" said George, patting me on the shoulder. "And I hear that you've got yourself a case. Ralph's been filling me in."

"Well, out with it. What's d'Almeida's solution?" chimed in Ralph.

"Rather less complicated than I'd expected," I replied. "D'Almeida thinks we should ask the husband whether he'll give her a divorce."

Ralph whistled. "Not an appealing prospect at all. You won't look good in concrete."

"No, no, I don't think it's a bad idea," commented George.

"The direct method is often the best." He put his arm around my shoulder. "I'll come with you. I've never met a gangster boss before. This could be quite interesting."

WE GOT the Black Cat's address from Takeda, who had little confidence that a frontal attack would work. Neither did I for that matter, but we had a duty to try at least. The Black Cat's lair was among the godowns along the Singapore River, across from the police barracks in Hill Street. I brought along our interpreter, Tan Peng Ann, to translate. He was less than overjoyed. George provided a steadying influence. Left alone with me, it was more than likely that Tan would have done a bunk at the first sign of trouble.

The area was far from salubrious. The river lapped dispiritedly at the steps that lined its banks, invisible under a layer of flotsam that seemed to connect the moored tongkangs. There was a distinct smell, a compound of soggy doggy and unwashed humanity, with a hint of decayed rat thrown in.

We found the address quite easily, a nondescript building jammed between two undistinguished neighbours. There were several men at the entrance, lean, wiry and mean of mien. They sat playing cards or just watching the river. Tan spoke to one of them who looked a little older than the rest, handing him my business card. He glanced at it contemptuously and probably without comprehension, detached himself from the group wordlessly and went into the godown, casting a black look at us. The others stopped their activities to stare. One spat loudly and ostentatiously into the drain, never taking his eyes off us. I felt an odd tickling sensation between my shoulder blades, half-expecting a knife in the back.

After an eternity (in actuality, only a couple of minutes), a minion emerged from the dark depths of the godown and indicated that we should follow him. We passed between tall rows of stacked bales and gunny sacks. The smell of pepper and spices pervaded the air. "Nice setup," said George quietly in my ear, "it hides the scent of the opium neatly."

"Opium?" I whispered back, out of the corner of my mouth. "You think that's what they're up to here?"

"I wouldn't be surprised," replied George. "That, or maybe something even stronger."

We were ushered into a room at the far end of the godown. Through the open window, I saw a grimy alley and the back wall of the building behind. The room was dingy and poorly lit. Apart from a calendar featuring a Chinese beauty with improbably pink cheeks and red lips, the walls were bare. A passageway ran off to the side, presumably leading to more rooms. There was practically no furniture, except for a large teak desk in the centre.

A middle-aged man sat ensconced behind the desk, squinting at us with his little piggy eyes. We were not introduced, but I assumed that I was in the presence of Lim Beow Sin, alias the Black Cat. In contrast with the lean and mean minions surrounding him, he was round and soft. His face was impassive. We were not invited to sit down. A thin young man about my age stood next to him, whom I assumed was a major-domo or something of the sort. He fixed us with a dark malevolent gaze that bored right through us. Then he bent over and whispered something in Lim's ear, pointing at me. Lim looked at me and raised his eyebrows interrogatively. I indicated to Tan that he should speak. A momentary look of surprise flitted across Lim's face at this, but he remained otherwise mute and inscrutable while Tan recited what we had come for.

There was an extended silence when Tan stopped. The minions behind Lim's large form seemed frozen. Then, all of a sudden, Lim laughed, not out of mirth, but a joyless mocking laugh. There was no humour in it. His eyes remained steely cold. This was the signal for his men to laugh too, raucously, derisively. Just as suddenly,

Lim's laugh was cut off as though by a steel blade and he resumed his stern demeanour. The others stopped abruptly too, as if turned off by a switch. There was silence.

I took it that our request had been rejected. "Thank you for your time," I said to him, turning to leave.

I was stopped by a peremptory exclamation from Lim. I turned to Tan for an explanation. "He asks why you do not address him in Chinese," said Tan. "He thinks you do not give him face by speaking in the language of the orang puteh." He added sotto voce with a hint of panic, "Say something quick-quick or it will be bad for us all."

I turned slowly and faced Lim, trying hard to appear respectful. "Tell Mr Lim," I said in my most humble tone, "that I'm sorry that I can't speak any Chinese. I meant no disrespect." Then, for some odd reason, I bowed to him as Takeda might have done. It was a spontaneous gesture and completely unpremeditated. Lim laughed again, but this time with a little more genuineness. He addressed a couple of gruff phrases to Tan, who replied in a polite tone, bowing a little too. "We should go now," said Tan to me, with a little quaver in his voice.

The three of us turned slowly and retraced our steps through the godown at a measured pace, not looking back. I felt a dozen pairs of eyes boring into my back. It took all my willpower not to hurry. It was only when we were some way down the quayside, beyond view of Lim's godown that I relaxed.

"Damn," I ejaculated, "I've never been so tense in my life. My palms are all wet."

"Yes," said George, who had kept silent throughout, "quite an awkward moment."

"It was good that you made a kow-tow to him," said Tan, wiping his brow with a handkerchief. "Otherwise, I do not think we would be out here now."

"Well," I declared grimly, "so much for that. We aren't going to get his cooperation to let Yeng Nam go. I suppose I'll have to break the bad news to Takeda."

"No need to give up just yet," said George. "This is just the opening skirmish. The battle's far from over yet."

He set off in a decided fashion along the quayside towards the office. I followed despondently, without the faintest idea of what the next move in the campaign would be.

9

SUNDAY CAME with unexpected suddenness. I had broken the bad news to Takeda, who took it stoically. Yeng Nam, on the other hand, broke down in tears. It pained me enormously that I could do nothing more for them. She deserved better. They both did. Normally, I didn't take my failures so personally, but I brooded on this one constantly in the days that followed. For that reason, I didn't notice that my tea-time date with George and Daphne was imminent until reminded by the chimes of Big Ben introducing the Sunday afternoon news on Radio Malaya. All was quiet on the Western Front. After the rapid fall of Poland, the Blitzkrieg had degenerated into a Sitzkrieg. It didn't look like the war would be over any time soon, certainly not before the leaves fell. I thought of my friends, on the Continent as well as in England. I didn't even know if they were alive or dead. That made me even more depressed. I switched the radio off and went out.

I wasn't really in the mood to be sociable, but since I had promised George, I determined to make the best of it. There was no traffic on the streets, which was a blessing since my jalopy would have been hard-put to keep up with even a superannuated carthorse. I had stopped driving during normal working days to spare myself the poisonous glares of other drivers whom I held up because of the old banger's inability to proceed at more than 15mph without giving out in a wheeze of steam. I parked at Connaught Drive and went for a walk along the Esplanade, breathing in the cool sea air. There had been a little rain just before and the breeze was fresh. The slight overcast made walking pleasant. I took the long way past the Obelisk and the Memorial Hall, rather than cutting directly across the Padang. My mind was still occupied by the problem of Yeng Nam's divorce.

George was already in the lobby of The Adelphi when I got there. He looked very dapper in his pale linen suit and straw boater. It made quite a contrast with his dark complexion. For one brief fleeting moment, I was reminded of a minstrel in a minstrel show, but I didn't think it wise to mention it.

"Good of you to turn up, dear boy," he greeted me jovially.

"You're welcome," I replied, without much enthusiasm.

"Come now," he said, "you look like an undertaker who's mislaid his hearse. A little more jollity, if you please."

Daphne wafted in at that moment, fresh as a morning glory. Even old men turned their heads. We were conducted to our table among the potted plants. George was ebullient and Daphne effervescent. I sat there like a damp rag, feeling glumly that I was depriving them of privacy without providing company. Daphne tried to get me involved in the conversation. She turned to me and said, "You know, I did what George suggested and went for a walk along the River. It's really grand, seeing all the bustle. You really get the feel of being in a port. It took my breath away. Especially the smell. That really took my breath away."

"It's the local fragrance," commented George. "Canal No 5."

She laughed her little tinkling laugh.

"It smells like Venice on a bad day," I said, trying hard to sound like I was enjoying myself.

"Have you really been to Venice?" asked Daphne brightly. "It's on my must-do list. Ever since I saw that movie with Fred Astaire and Ginger Rogers, you know, the one where he follows her to Venice and she thinks he's married to her friend? You know it, Dennis, the one with the Irving Berlin tunes."

"Top Hat?" I ventured.

"Yes, that's the one, Top Hat. Venice is one place I must see."

"You'll be disappointed," I warned. "The reality isn't anything like Hollywood."

"But I've seen pictures, in Life magazine and National Geographic.And the paintings by all those artists. It's glorious. What do they call it – the Pearl of the Adriatic?"

"Don't pay any attention to Dennis. He's had too much sour grape juice to drink. You'll really like Venice," said George, smoothly insinuating himself into the conversation. As far as I knew, he'd never been on the Continent beyond Calais, but that didn't stop him. "Speaking of art, you should see the views of Venice by Vaporetto."

"Caneletto," I hissed to him when Daphne was distracted by a dropped serviette, "Caneletto was the artist who painted the views of Venice. A vaporetto is a water-taxi."

If he was discomfited, he didn't show it. With breathtaking sangfroid, he continued, "Yes, there's nothing like the view of Venice from the water in a vaporetto. And of course, you really mustn't miss the Caneletto paintings of Venice either."

Having retrieved her serviette, Daphne continued, "Yes, I'll go someday. When this nasty business is all over and people get back to their senses. Maybe next year."

The allusion to the war punctured what little enthusiasm I had managed to summon up. It must have shown, since she continued immediately, "I'm sorry, Dennis. I didn't mean to upset you. I know you've got friends in Europe."

I managed a slight smile. "No, it isn't that," I assured her. "Well, not mainly that. It's this case I took on. Trying to get a divorce for some poor girl married to a brute of a gangster who beats her. I can't do anything. It's getting me down. But please, don't mind me. I don't want to spoil your afternoon."

As I got up to go, Daphne said, "No, don't go yet. I mean, not unless you really want to. Stay and talk. Maybe you'll feel better. George told me all about the kid. It's not your fault you can't do anything for her."

I relented and sat down again.

"It's a lousy break. What a shame life's not like the movies. Otherwise you could do what Fred did in Top Hat. Discover that the priest who did the marrying isn't on the level and that Ginger's not married after all."

"Say that again," said George.

"What – that it's a lousy break?" asked Daphne with surprise.

"No, the bit about the priest. What was that about?"

"Well," explained Daphne, "in the movie, Fred's in love with Ginger but she thinks he's married to her friend. So she goes out and gets married to some fashion designer who's got designs on her. Then she and Fred find out that he really isn't married to her friend, but they can't get married because of the designer. To cut to the chase, in the end, it turns out that the priest who did the ceremony wasn't a priest so they're all right and live happily ever after."

"Daphne, darling, you're a wonder!" exclaimed George. "You've done it again."

"Done it again? Done what again?"

"Nothing, just gone and solved Dennis' problem, that's all. You see it, don't you?" he said, turning to me. I looked blankly at him. He gave an impatient tut. "What was it that d'Almeida said about Chinese marriages?"

"That they can be unilaterally dissolved by the husband?" I responded tentatively.

"No," he replied, a mite impatiently. "Didn't he say that you first have to establish that there was a marriage? By cohabitation and repute? From what you told me, it didn't seem that they made a big deal of the wedding. Was there a banquet? A big do? Anything to mark the happy event?"

"No, now that you mention it, I don't think there was. At least Takeda didn't mention any such thing. He just said that Black Cat paid the aunt and took the girl."

"There!" exclaimed George triumphantly. "No ceremony, no long cohabitation, no reputed marriage. No need for long and messy divorce proceedings. Just get a declaration that there was no marriage at all."

I was infected by his animation. It could work ... I was miles away for the rest of that afternoon, considering how to make it work. For once, I could hardly wait to get into the office on Monday morning.

IN FACT, it proved a lot easier than I had anticipated. Takeda confirmed from Yeng Nam that there had been no ceremony or contract. Money had changed hands and she had been taken away. It was almost like buying a pig or buffalo. They certainly had not had time to establish any reputation as man and wife, though he did introduce her as his wife when she met his cronies, which wasn't that often. There were the makings of a good case. I decided that the best thing would be for Yeng Nam to apply for a court declaration that there had been no proper customary marriage. The papers were duly drawn up, filed in court and served on Lim Beow Sin. Lim's lawyer filed an appearance on his behalf to acknowledge that he would be contesting the suit. Then we waited for his response to our allegations... and waited ... and waited.

As is so often the case, the proceedings went into suspended animation. The judicial process had its own pace and rhythm, something like a sea turtle hauling itself up a beach to lay eggs, but without the same sense of urgency. The press of other work and world events drove Yeng Nam's case from my mind. I had set up a large map in my room, the better to follow the drama unfolding on the other side of the world. Every day I conscientiously marked the progress of the war, insofar as it was possible to do so from the news bulletins. There was plenty of action at sea, with the sinking of the Graf Spee and the dramatic boarding of the Altmark. On land, though, nothing moved. The same held true for Yeng Nam's case. Christmas came and went, Chinese New Year loomed. I went for my haircuts at regular intervals and each time, Takeda asked me hopefully whether the matter had been settled. Each time, I had to tell him ruefully that there was no progress. Meanwhile, Yeng Nam continued to sequester herself from the world in Takeda's flat. She never left its sanctuary, not for a moment. Takeda insisted on this to prevent her being seen by anyone who might tip the Black Cat off, but I wasn't sure that the precautions were necessary. Her putative husband seemed to have lost interest in her totally.

Except for one thing. Practically every day, I would see Lim's sinister dark-eyed major domo lurking outside my office. Sometimes, he tailed me when I went to court. He even followed me to Takeda's shop once, making little effort to hide himself. Ralph suggested that he might be trying to find out where Yeng Nam was hiding. I didn't think so. He took no pains to avoid being seen. George said he was trying to intimidate me. If that was his aim, he succeeded. I stopped going out alone and developed the habit of checking that all the windows and doors of our house were locked before retiring to bed. In a perverse way, this psychological game strengthened my resolve to win Yeng Nam's freedom. What would come after that was something I tried not to think too much about.

The Registrar called at long last the week before Chinese New Year to offer a hearing date. It was a slack period as the whole town generally shuts down for the festivities. This was the only time in the year when the Chinese community put up the shutters and took a breather from the serious business of getting rich. We could have an early date if we didn't mind working during the festive period. I jumped at the chance to settle the matter quickly. I called the other side's lawyer to find out what he proposed to do. He told me that he had received no instructions from his client and had accordingly discharged himself. I relayed this information to Takeda.

"I ask about Lim Beow Sin," Takeda informed me. "He go away up-country. No one know where. Not come back."

"What do you mean?" I asked. "Isn't he ever coming back?"

"I do not know. All they tell me is that he go up-country. This is good, yes?"

I pondered a moment. My shadow had disappeared during the past week. It did seem as if the Black Cat had just forgotten the whole matter. "Well," I replied, "if he doesn't bother to contest the application, the court should grant it."

"Please?" asked Takeda plaintively.

"It means," I explained patiently, "that if Lim does not come back, Yeng Nam wins and you can marry her."

Takeda's smile was so wide it seemed to slice his face in half.

WANDERING BACK from Takeda's shop, I was surprised to bump into Daphne along High Street. I hadn't seen her since she turned up at the office Christmas dinner ostensibly as d'Almeida's guest. The hand of George was behind this I was sure. However, as he no longer bothered me with requests for tutoring on European culture, I had assumed that all was well on that front.

"Hi there, stranger," she greeted me brightly.

"Hello," I returned. "Haven't seen you in some time."

"Yes, must be a couple of months I guess. Say, it's a bit of luck running into you like this. I need to talk to you. Got a minute to spare? Maybe we could have a bite together."

I was in a good mood and the company of a young lady was always welcome. "Let me buy you lunch," I offered in a spontaneous burst of generosity which I regretted almost instantly.

"Sure," she responded. "How about the Cricket Club? I've always wanted to eat there."

My heart sank. Even if they condescended to waive the colour bar and let me in, the Chinese New Year bonus had disappeared with distressing rapidity and payday had yet to come round again.

"Er, I was thinking more on the lines of the Polar Café. I hope you don't mind."

"Okay, no problem," she replied understandingly, "I'm a bit tight myself till my trustee wires the next instalment of my allowance."

Relieved, I guided her to the Café, which was crowded with young members of the Bar. They did a good lunch there for a reasonable sum. We found a small table at the back, where there was a modicum of privacy away from the stares that a mixed-race couple inevitably attracted.

Daphne was her usual self, bright, lively and interested in anything and everything. I found myself enjoying her company immensely, despite the knowledge of George's declared interest lurking at the back of my mind. At the end of the meal, she dabbed her lips daintily, fixed me with her clear blue-eyed gaze and asked, "Well, Dennis, what do you think of me?"

I nearly choked on my coffee. Recovering myself, I replied, "Well, … er … to tell the truth … ah … I think that you're a … a really nice girl." It wasn't the most elegant compliment I had ever paid to a lady. She didn't appear to be pleased. She pursed her lips and frowned a little. "There you go. Always so polite and reserved."

I didn't know how to react. Daphne carried on, saving me the embarrassment of saying something meaningless to fill the gap. "I'm not fishing for compliments or asking you to declare your undying love for me, if that's what you thought. Look, we're friends, right? And I need it straight from a friend. What do you think of me? Am I prejudiced?"

I was totally taken aback. "Prejudiced? Absolutely not. You're the most unprejudiced person I know. None of the memsahibs would be caught dead having lunch with one of the natives like this."

She giggled. "A native! It's hard to think of you as a native. You're so ... so ... English. If I close my eyes and listen, you could be white."

So English ... I grimaced inwardly. There was a time when I would have been flattered to have been called English. After two years back in the Straits Settlements in close contact with the master race, I wasn't quite so sure. I felt vaguely uncomfortable. Whatever I might have been, in British Malaya I was not English.

"Well, I think you are the most unprejudiced person in the world," I repeated earnestly.

"Thanks," she said, giving my hand a little squeeze. "Then why do I feel the way I do about George?"

"How do you feel about George?"

"Listen," she said conspiratorially, drawing close to me, "this is between the two of us, okay?" I nodded.

"I've known quite a number of guys. They've been interested in me but none of them really clicked, if you know what I mean. Now, George, he's fun and cultured and great company and I like him ... but there's something inside of me that says 'hold on' and 'back off' when he gets too close. I know he'd like to be more than friends with me."

"And you? What do you want?"

"I don't know. I'm not sure."

"Listen to your heart."

"That's the problem." She sighed. "I can't hear clearly what my heart's saying. On one hand, I think he's a real swell guy. But on the other hand... back where I come from, if a black man pays court to a white girl, folks tend to get really upset. My Daddy would have a fit if he knew I'd been going out with George."

"Not just where you come from," I commented. "You must have caused quite a commotion in the white community here."

She frowned a little at that. "I don't care what folks 'round here think. It's my life. And my crowd don't mind one bit. They're okay with George. But it's me. What do I do?"

I wasn't accustomed to the role of counsellor and confessor. Knowing George as I did, I wasn't entirely sure that he really felt something for Daphne. Was it serious, or was she just another trophy to be added to his wall? I fumbled for something to say. Again, she saved me the trouble.

"I know I've got to make up my mind on my own. I guess I talk too much. But thanks for listening. It's easy to talk to you. I hope you don't mind. You're the only one I can really open up to … you're like a brother to me." She leaned over and gave me a quick peck on the cheek, then left.

Like a brother … somehow that made me feel discontented. I had no designs on Daphne myself; not consciously anyway. My head told me that I should keep out of the fray. My heart told me … what? Cyrano had fallen for Roxane. I didn't quite know what I felt.

10

THE HEARING was very much an anticlimax. It was Chap Goh Mei, the fifteenth and last day of the Chinese New Year period. There was no one else around. I was in and out of the judge's chambers in five minutes in the absence of any opponent. The judge gave no trouble at all, just read the affidavit and granted the declaration. I had the impression that he was keen to be off somewhere else, probably golfing with his peers. With that stroke of the pen, Yeng Nam's marriage to the Black Cat was pronounced non-existent from the start. Winning such easy cases normally doesn't give one much of a boost, but this was different. I was elated. Pausing only long enough to doff my robes, I set off for Takeda's shop as quickly as I could.

The streets of Chinatown were ankle deep in red paper, the remains of the barrage of fire-crackers that had been set off practically continuously since the previous night. The air was still acrid from the smoke. Takeda and Yeng Nam were waiting for me at his barber shop. His customary smile was twice as broad. She stood demurely a little behind him, smiling shyly. It was probably the first time in months that she had left his flat. Takeda closed up the shop and led me to the celebratory feast that he had prepared in the back room. I toasted the happy couple in sake. Their obvious delight mitigated my unhappiness at the imminent prospect of having to find a new barber.

We were just sitting down to eat when there came the sound of shouting from outside. At first, I thought it was just more revellers having a good time. But the voices sounded angry and the noise grew in intensity. Takeda rushed to the front room to see what was up. I followed. Yeng Nam was just behind, but he called out peremptorily to her and she stopped. A crowd had gathered outside the barber shop, yelling and shouting. I was bewildered. Then the first stone came, hitting the wooden door with a sickening thud. More followed. The windows shattered.

"What the devil's going on? What do they want?"

Takeda looked at me. "They say I am Japanese pig. They call for my business to close down. They say all Japanese must leave. Because of war in China."

I stared again at the crowd, which seemed to have grown by another couple of dozen in the meantime. There must have been fifty people out there. Some were carrying sticks. At the fringe, I caught sight of the Black Cat's sinister major-domo. He was half-hidden in the shadow of a pillar but there was no mistaking him. "The war in China be damned," I exclaimed. "That mob's been got up by Lim Beow Sin. His man is out there."

Takeda blanched. "Lim Beow Sin! He come for Yeng Nam."

Another volley of stones came through the broken windows and clattered on the floor. We retreated to the back room. I looked around. The door didn't seem as if it could resist a determined assault for any length of time. "Have you something we can use to fight back?" I asked urgently. "Anything, a broom even. We've got to hold them off until the police get here. It's our only chance."

Takeda shook his head. "We no fight. They too many. You take Yeng Nam. Out back door. Take her to safe place. Go!"

I was transfixed. He spoke to her quickly. She opened her mouth to protest, but he cut her short. Turning to me, he repeated, "Go! Go now. I beg you." With that, he went to the front door, unlocked it and stepped out.

For a moment, my mind stopped working completely. The crowd had fallen silent when faced by the sight of the pudgy bespectacled barber standing fearlessly in front of them. Then there was a yell and the mob surged forward. Yeng Nam screamed. Takeda was engulfed. I saw his arms flail; two opponents dropped. The rest recoiled, shocked by this unexpected display of martial prowess. He stood there, hands held before him in a guard position. Then they came forward again. I knew we had to leave. He had sacrificed himself to buy us time. Grabbing Yeng Nam by the wrist, I bolted through the back door.

The back street was empty. Those who weren't part of the mob were keeping their heads low. I ran as fast as I could, dragging the sobbing Yeng Nam behind me, cursing myself for my cowardice. I should have gone to help him … but my head told me that the only thing that that would have achieved would have been to increase the body count. Flight was the only reasonable course, I told myself. I felt totally rotten.

WE STOOD near the bed silently while they ministered to him. He seemed very small, bandaged and tucked up between the sheets. The sister and her entourage finished at last and let us through, with a stern admonition not to trouble the patient too much.

"How do you feel?" I asked.

Takeda managed a weak smile and tried to say something.

"No, don't talk," I urged, "you've got concussion, a couple of broken ribs and a fractured arm. Lie still."

"Yeng Nam?" he whispered feebly, his eyes closed.

"She's fine. I took her to my cousin's place. She'll be safe there."

I had deposited Yeng Nam with May and Ralph. It was the only safe place I could think of, since I had been tailed to the office and home by the Black Cat's goons. May was wonderful, taking charge of the girl immediately. Ralph was inclined to be apprehensive, but May asserted herself and he didn't persist in his objections.

"My cousin's a nurse. Yeng Nam will be safe, I promise you."

I don't know if Takeda heard me, but he stopped trying to speak. The ward sister reappeared and shooed us out.

In the corridor, I said again to Ralph and George, "It was the bravest thing I ever saw. He just stepped out and faced them. If he hadn't, I wouldn't be here."

"The man's got spunk," agreed George.

"Any luck catching the ringleader?" asked Ralph.

I shook my head glumly. Fortunately for Takeda, the police had arrived within minutes. Otherwise, we would have been at the morgue rather than the hospital. The mob vanished miraculously, leaving him senseless on the road. I gave what information I could to the police but there was precious little they could do. No one else would say anything. Even if people weren't scared witless by the Black Cat's gang, there wasn't a lot of sympathy for a Japanese in Chinatown. The police didn't expect to make any arrests.

We hadn't had time to plan what to do next. I had some vague idea that Yeng Nam might hide out at d'Almeida's place, which was big enough and out of town. We were still discussing how best to proceed when we got back to Ralph's flat. The door swung open even before he turned the key in the keyhole. I had a prickling sensation on the back of my neck.

"May?" called Ralph worriedly as we entered. There was no sign of anyone.

"Maybe they've gone out," I said, trying more to reassure myself than Ralph. He nodded, but didn't seem convinced. He went from room to room, looking for some indication where they had gone.

The flat was perfectly in order. There was no sign of anything untoward. I began to relax.

George, who had gone out to look around the building, called to us. "Here, I've found something."

We ran out into the alley behind the block. George was squatting next to the drain, trying to fish something out with a stick. He lifted it up. It was a pocket watch, just like a nurse would have. Around it was wrapped a scrap of paper. George unfolded it for us to see. There was a picture, a few circles and lines as a child might draw – a drawing of a black cat.

Ralph grabbed the paper and stared at it. He let out a groan. "Oh God, he's got them." My mind was numb. I could only think how stupid I had been. "I'm sorry, I'm sorry, I shouldn't have brought Yeng Nam here. They must have followed me."

George was galvanised. "There's no use moaning about what you should or shouldn't have done. The most important thing is to get them back before Lim gets them out of town." He grabbed Ralph by the shoulders. "Get a grip, man. Tell d'Almeida what's happened." Ralph nodded dumbly. George turned to me. "Let's get going."

"Get going? You know where they are?" I asked incredulously.

"As Quasimodo said to Esmeralda, I've got a hunch," he replied grimly and strode off.

WE CREPT along the alley behind the Black Cat's godown. No one was about. It was getting dark and families were settling down to the last feast of the New Year festivities.

"How can you be sure they're here?" I whispered to George.

"I can't be," he replied shortly, "but if they're not here, we're out for a duck. This is the only lead we've got. We'll have to trust to the gods of fortune."

But the gods of fortune beamed on us that night. We peeked

into one of the windows in the back wall of the godown. May was there, together with Yeng Nam, in what appeared to be a large store cupboard. I tapped on the sill to get her attention.

"Dennis! George! I am so happy to see you," exclaimed May, coming over to the window. Yeng Nam looked up and tried to smile, but remained crouched in the corner.

"Are you all right? Did they hurt you?" I asked.

"We are fine," May whispered.

"I am not so stupid to fight with men with knives. When they said come, we came without trouble. But you found my watch and message, right?"

"Right," I replied. "Now the problem is getting both of you out of here." I tried the bars of the window. Although they were wood, they didn't budge no matter how hard I shook them.

George nudged me out of the way. "You won't get out that way," he said. "There's a back door. I had a peek. No lock, only a bolt. How many goons are there?"

"There were two who took us," said May. "I did not see any more when we came. They are all home eating their Chap Goh Mei dinner, I guess."

"Only two goons and wooden bars," I commented. "They're pretty lax about their prisoners."

"Simply the psychology of the criminal mind, my son," replied George. "This is the lair of the Black Cat. People don't break into such places and live. Only idiots would try."

"Meaning us, I presume?"

George nodded. "Meaning us. Or one of us, at any rate."

I didn't like the sound of that, but before I could probe further, May continued urgently, "We must get out quick. They said they will move us by tongkang when it is dark"

"Right," said George. "Hang on, we'll have you out of there."

AT GEORGE'S insistence, we made a reconnaissance first rather than charge in blindly as my instincts urged me. Strings of crackers were going off all over the place as we slunk around the building. The air was full of smoke. It was like being in a war zone. We noticed two of the Black Cat's minions lounging in front. They appeared to be no more than teenagers. The buildings on either side seemed to be deserted.

We came back to the alley behind. A peek through the window into the room where we had been received by Lim Beow Sin revealed a third goon, built like gorilla, apparently engrossed in picking things out of his hair.

I examined the back door. It wasn't particularly sturdy. In fact it would have been child's play to break the bottom louvre of the window next to it, reach in and unbolt the door. "Not much of a problem there. But we've got to get through the guards first. Three to two. Not good odds, even if the ones out front are shrimps. But we've no choice. As you said, only idiots would try, so maybe they won't be expecting us."

"Correction," replied George, "only one idiot necessary to do the breaking in. And we can shorten the odds. Wait here. Keep out of sight and keep your eyes open." Before I could remonstrate, he had disappeared into the twilight without further explanation.

I scrunched up in the shelter of some crates, barely able to contain my annoyance at George's penchant for popping off suddenly and leaving me in suspense. However, since there was nothing else to be done, I kept on watching. From the back window, one could in fact see through the length of the building, out to where the tongkangs were moored at the quayside. A small boy came to the loungers at the front and handed them a couple of tiffin carriers. One of them came back bearing food to his colleague in the rear room. I ducked hurriedly, praying fervently that he hadn't noticed me peering in through the window. At length, I ventured to have a peek again. The nit-picker was having his dinner, as were the other two in the front.

George returned after about half an hour, carrying an assortment of things. It looked like he had raided a jumble sale. "Where the devil have you been?" I stormed at him. "Did you get the police?"

"Surely you jest," he replied shortly. "On Chap Goh Mei, when every able-bodied flat-foot is out keeping the drunks and pyromaniacs in line? By the time it filters through official channels, the girls will be half-way to Batavia. No, old son, we're on our own if we want to get them out now."

I was crestfallen. "Where'd you get all this junk and what's it in aid of?" I said, somewhat truculently.

"Let's just say I've been calling in IOUs from people who owe me favours. This junk, as you so graphically call it, will make the difference between getting out with or without your skin in one piece. Here." He thrust a large towel and a tin of something or other into my hand. I looked the label. It was Lyle's Golden Syrup.

"What do I do with this?" I asked plaintively.

He explained slowly, as to a small child. "You smear it liberally on the lowest pane, put the towel on it and bang with something solid. The pane will break, the sticky mess will make sure it doesn't crash to the ground so you can remove it quietly. Then you reach in with your paw, unbolt the door, get in, get the girls and get the dickens out. Okay? Clear? Good!"

He produced a bottle from his sack and splashed half the contents on his suit. It was brandy. "Don't move until you see the gorilla in the back leave. Then move like lightning. I'm going out front." Then he was off again.

I didn't have long to wait. George reappeared in front, shirt hanging out, swaying drunkenly and singing loudly. He held a bottle in each hand. Doubtless, he reeked like a distillery. The two minions in front looked up from their meal. George approached them, gesticulating wildly. He had a wide knowledge of swear words in a dozen languages. I couldn't hear him, but presumably he was treating them to some of the choicest ones. The two guards got up to confront him. George started screaming at the top of his voice, brandishing his bottle. This was too much for the gorilla in the back room, who went out to see what the commotion was and give aid to his fellows. That was my cue.

The pane gave way after a couple of hefty whacks with a handy plank. As George had predicted, the syrupy goo held the broken glass in place. I got the door open without trouble and headed down the passageway straight for the girls' cell, praying that it wasn't locked. Again, the gods of fortune smiled. The door was simply bolted from the outside. I yanked it open.

"Quick, out!" I called to the surprised pair. "We haven't any time to waste."

Yeng Nam seemed stupefied, but May grabbed her by the wrist and dragged her towards the door. Out front, I could still hear George making a racket. It could only be a matter of minutes though until the three goons collared him and threw him in the river or he was forced to make a bolt for safety. May and I half-carried Yeng Nam out of the cell. She seemed to have lost the power of independent movement.

We stumbled towards the alley door. At that moment, a large form waddled into the room. I was shocked into immobility by the apparition. It was Lim Beow Sin himself, his little piggy eyes distended with astonishment. Without a thought, I launched myself at him, hitting him right in the belly. It was soft as a feather pillow. He went down with a strangled gurgle.

"Get out! Don't wait for me! Go! Go!" I yelled to the girls. May, with commendable presence of mind, didn't stop to argue. She pulled Yeng Nam after her and disappeared into the smoky alley-way.

For a gangster boss, Lim seemed to have curiously little fight in him. He wallowed around on the floor, screaming in a shrill voice while I grappled with his bulk. The gorilla from outside was upon me in a couple of seconds. I felt his big, hairy arm around my neck. I elbowed him in the groin, but it made no impression. The brute was impervious to my feeble blows. He hit me several times with a rock-like fist. After about the third punch, I ceased to be able to think properly. I had the impression of many hands seizing me. I felt myself being manhandled across the room and thrown on a hard floor. I vaguely heard the sound of a bolt being shot. Everything was hazy. I was just glad that they had stopped hitting me.

HOW LONG I lay there, God only knows. I lost all sensation of time. The blood dripped from my lip and my vision was blurred. My head felt like some infernal dwarf was in it, banging on an anvil. Through the haze I discerned that I was in the same closet-cell that the girls had been in.

The bolt was drawn. Two men entered and dragged me out of the cell. The light was harsh in the back room and hurt my eyes. Lim's major-domo was there, sitting behind the teak desk. A cigarette drooped from the corner of his mouth. The guards let go and stood behind me as I faced him.

"Why you attack my uncle?" he asked suddenly.

I was taken completely aback. "You speak English?"

"You think I stupid or what?" he said scornfully. "Yes, I speak English. I go to school six years. I can read and write." He glared at me malevolently. "Why you attack my uncle?" he repeated.

My brain still felt dislocated. "Your uncle?" I responded stupidly. "Lim Beow Sin is your uncle?"

He made a derisive noise. "My uncle is Lim Chin Huat." He

stood up and fixed me with his dark threatening eyes. "I am Lim Beow Sin."

It took a while to sink in. "You're the Black Cat?"

He smiled evilly. "Yes, I am the Black Cat."

I gathered myself. "Look, I'm sorry I hit your uncle. But I had to. You kidnapped May and Yeng Nam."

His eyes blazed. "Yeng Nam! She is mine. I pay her family. I make her my wife. Why you take her from me?"

"She doesn't love you," I shot back, surprised at my daring. "You treated her like a dog. I know you beat her. The law is on her side. She's a free woman now."

He came over and slapped me on the face, twice, hard. "She is mine. She must learn to work properly, to be proper wife. Yes, I beat her. I am husband. I teach her to do right. It is not for you to tell me what I cannot do." He cursed me in Chinese and spat in my face. "I will teach you not to take my things." He gave a curt command to his men.

The two toughs grabbed me and pinioned my arms. I was marched out of the room, through the godown and out onto the quayside. The moon was full and the night air cool. I felt my head clear somewhat. They frog-marched me towards the moored tongkangs.

"Where are you taking me?" I demanded, teeth clenched in pain.

"Some place where no person will find you," replied Lim with an evil grin. "The fish will eat your bones."

I tried to lunge to the side, but the goon holding me tightened his grip and folded my arm even more deeply into my back. The pain was excruciating. He forced me up the gangplank. Lim and his other minion followed.

I'm not quite sure exactly what happened next. All of a sudden, there was the sound of police whistles and voices yelling, "Mata lai liao! Mata lai liao! The police are coming!" I saw a group of men running along the quay. The air was suddenly full of small explosions. I thought at first that someone was shooting and ducked instinctively, then I realised that it was strings of crackers exploding all over the place. Lim spun around uncertainly, taken entirely by surprise. I felt my captor loosen his grip. At that precise moment, George ran up the gangplank, screaming like a dervish and flinging lighted strings of crackers at them – not the small petas padi that the kampong kids played with, but the large ones, the thickness of a finger, that hung in strings like red lianas from the shophouses. Lim caught one string directly, juggled it for a moment as the crackers went off deafeningly in his hands, lost his balance and fell off the gangplank onto the quayside. George punched the other gangster, who promptly fell over too.

I gave my captor a thump in the belly with all the force I could muster and watched with satisfaction when he doubled up in pain. George tipped him aside and grabbed me. "Jump!" he yelled. I needed no second bidding.

The river water tasted as bad as it smelled, but I didn't care. We struck out for the opposite shore, pushing our way through the foul flotsam. I was barely able to make it. George hauled me out. "Thanks," I gasped. "I owe you my life."

He waved my thanks away. "Didn't I say," he panted, "that that junk would get your hide out in one piece?" He produced a police whistle from his pocket and blew. It gave a feeble watery tweet. For some reason, both of us couldn't stop laughing.

WE GOT back to the office sopping wet. To my surprise, d'Almeida was there, dressed in a police uniform. Ralph was with him. He jumped to his feet when he saw us. "Thank heavens, you're okay."

"The girls?" asked George.

"The two young ladies are now with Inspector Fergusson," replied d'Almeida. "I trust that you both are well?"

I was totally confused. George saw my face and gave a short laugh. "I guess I'd better explain," he said. "It's thanks to Mr d'Almeida that you're here in one piece. He and the office staff provided the distraction that let me get to you. They were the crowd on the quay making all that din."

"It wasn't the police?" I said weakly, sinking down into a chair.

"No," said d'Almeida, with the ghost of a smile, "we could not count on them arriving in time. When Singham telephoned and told me of your predicament, I knew we had to act instantly. Fortunately, we had these two costumes at hand from our Christmas gaieties."

"You took an awful risk," I said. "Lim and his gang might have been armed."

"It was a calculated risk," replied d'Almeida. "A lot of noise in the dark, police whistles, explosions – I had counted on the confusion to shield us from retribution. I was not disappointed."

"So the police have got the Black Cat and his gang."

D'Almeida looked serious. "Unfortunately not. As we feared, by the time they arrived, the birds had flown. Lim is still at large."

"Which means that Yeng Nam isn't safe. She'll have to go into hiding again."

"It is not the young lady who gives us concern," said d'Almeida gravely. "It is you."

"Me?" I replied in astonishment.

"You're the only one who actually saw him do anything," explained Ralph. "May didn't see him at all. Yeng Nam can only testify that he beat her while she was under his roof. He wasn't there when his goons grabbed her and May. Your barber friend Takeda didn't see him at the riot, and in any case can't identify him since they've never met."

"What about George?" I asked.

George shook his head. "Sorry, old son, I couldn't positively swear to anything. I don't even know which of the ugly mugs I hit was the Black Cat."

"It seems," continued d'Almeida, "that you are the only one who can give direct testimony that links Lim Beow Sin to these crimes. It is only you who can connect him in any way to rioting, kidnapping and even attempted murder."

It took me a while to comprehend what he had just said. "So I'm the only witness."

D'Almeida nodded. "The only witness who can threaten him. Your testimony could send him to prison for a very long time."

The implications were beginning to dawn on me. "I suppose," I said slowly, "that this means that he'll be after my hide."

D'Almeida nodded gravely. "I am afraid so. He will not hesitate to kill you if he can."

I felt a knot in the pit of my stomach. "I guess I'll have to lie low until they catch him."

"I fear that is the only way," said d'Almeida. "But not in the Colony. We will find you a safe place up-country somewhere."

There it was then. I knew I had no choice, but it didn't seem just. Lim Beow Sin had committed the crimes, and I was the one being punished.

11

STANDING ON the beach at Kuantan, one can see across the ocean all the way to America. Maybe not literally, but that's the way it seems. The sea stretches out to infinity, where it blends into the sky. For someone brought up in the crowded waters of Singapore, it's like being on the edge of the world.

I had a lot of time to stand on that beach and contemplate the ocean. The police had agreed with d'Almeida that as star witness against Lim Beow Sin, alias the Black Cat, I had to be protected at all costs. Their idea of protection was to offer me accommodation in the Police Barracks at Hill Street, where I would be surrounded by burly Sikh policemen 24 hours a day. The prospect did not appeal to me. D'Almeida's suggestion was that I should go off to join a friend's firm in Kuantan. Faced with a choice between indefinite police hospitality and exile in the wilds of Malaya, I chose exile.

Kuantan was almost literally at the end of civilisation in British Malaya. Most of the development was on the west coast. The tin mines and rubber plantations that formed the basis of the prosperity of the Straits Settlements and the Malay States were all in the west. On the eastern side of the Main Range, lashed by the monsoon for three months a year, only one tenuous main road linked Kuantan with the rest of the Peninsula. It snaked across the spine of Malaya, switchbacking over the mountains, with jungle bordering it for most of its course. Along the coast from Johore were a series of small roads crossing a succession of small rivers by an assortment of ramshackle ferries and rickety bridges. I went by steamer, a journey that took two days on account of the heavy seas, arriving during a tropical downpour that whipped the waves into white horses all along the shore. I could hardly keep my lunch down. It was not a happy introduction.

As the metropolis of Pahang, the largest and least developed of the Federated Malay States, Kuantan had all the amenities one would expect, including a law court and a whites-only Club. Since the local folks were by-and-large a law-abiding lot, there was little to occupy the former. The latter was the haunt of the planters from around the place – a sorry, sodden crowd of misfits who had been sent to rot in the ulu by their companies. Of course, I wasn't invited to join the Club; not that I cared. I was at least saved the awkwardness of declining membership at the premier social institution of the town. For recreation, there were a couple of cinemas. It was deader than Highgate Cemetery and far less interesting.

I found myself in limbo. People of my own race and age found me incomprehensible. I had nothing in common with them, and they left me to myself. My own circle of family and friends was far away. They might have been on the moon for all the contact I had with them. I missed Mak and the girls. It had only been three years since I got back from England and it was a wrench to have to go away once more. I was especially reluctant to leave Mak again, but she pointed out that my presence in fact put everyone in danger. She wasn't any keener than me about it, but we both saw clearly that I had to keep my head down until they caught the Black Cat. We left unsaid the thought that it might take weeks or even months, perhaps even years.

Of my circle of friends, to my surprise I found myself thinking most about Daphne and wondering what developments there might have been with George. I hadn't realised until then how much I had enjoyed talking to her. It was as if I had discovered a spring after wandering years in the desert, and now that spring had dried up. Even though we had only spoken together half-a-dozen times at most, I missed our conversations more than I cared to admit.

As far as work was concerned, there wasn't much. My employer, Mr Chidambaram, was a pleasant enough sort of fellow, but his passion in life was his garden. He popped by the office for a couple of hours a day just to see if by some chance a client had been washed up on his doorstep by the tide of fortune; otherwise, he was off tending his orchids in the compound of his large house, set on a small hill overlooking the sea. I had a lot of time to myself. The days and nights were long and stretched out before me interminably.

I DID eventually make a friend. He was a Frenchman called Michel Courtois, who managed a plantation owned by Courtois Frères et Cie, which as the name suggests was a family concern. He was in his fifties as far as I could tell and had been at it for ten years, banished on account of a disagreement with his elder brother over a woman. I actually made his acquaintance professionally. He had gotten drunk as usual one Friday night and knocked over a telephone pole with his car. It was, I gathered, rather a regular occurrence, though usually it was coconut palms or banana trees that were the victims. Since municipal property was involved, it was felt necessary to prosecute. I was counsel for the defence when he was hauled up before the magistrate.

The magistrate listened with unconcealed boredom to my mitigation plea. At the end of it, he eyed Courtois severely and pronounced sentence: "Fifty dollars. And don't let me catch you driving under the influence again, or I shall have no hesitation in sending you directly to jail."

I thought it was a reasonable sentence. Besides being blind drunk, Courtois had also been belligerent. It had taken four Malay constables to subdue him. He was lucky not to have been jailed. The magistrate banged his gavel and I was just packing up when my client pulled urgently at my sleeve. "Tell him I should get to keep the telephone pole," he hissed to me.

"What?" I responded stupidly, taken completely aback.

"Tell him that since I pay fifty dollars fine, I should get to keep the telephone pole."

The magistrate stared with irritation at us. "Was there something else, Mr Chiang?"

"Ah, your Honour," I replied, somewhat embarrassed, "my client desires to keep the telephone pole."

The magistrate was silent for a moment. "Your client desires what?"

I coughed awkwardly. "Er … my client feels that as he has to pay fifty dollars, he should be entitled to keep the telephone pole."

The magistrate drew himself up to full height and eyed us frigidly. "Kindly inform your client, Mr Chiang," he said in a voice that would have frozen a penguin, "that one cannot acquire telephone poles by the simple expedient of knocking them down."

COURTOIS didn't hold the loss of the case against me. In fact, as I said, we became friends. He was very much a loner and hardly ever went to the Club or mixed with his own kind. He had the reputation of being bellicose when drunk, which happened on a fairly regular basis. In short, he was a thorough misanthrope. Being cut off from Gallic civilisation did not improve his temperament.

He disliked the English and despised the Dutch. That was the reason he had chosen us to represent him rather than some white lawyer. Given his disposition, it was a surprise to me that he hadn't long ago been beaten to a pulp by an irate horde of tipsy planters whom he had insulted.

Our acquaintanceship started in the run-up to his hearing. As he declined to come to town, Chidambaram sent me up to his rubber estate to discuss the case. He spent most of the time talking about other things. It was as if he had been waiting all this time to release everything that was pent up in him. When he discovered that I had done some French at school, he became even more voluble, talking with wild gesticulations while I struggled to keep up with what was left of my schoolboy French. In the end, we worked out a modus vivendi. He would start off speaking English, but then lapse into French when the going got tough. I replied in fractured Franglais with a large component of pantomime. It took several visits to piece together his version of the affair and to cobble together a mitigation plea.

After the case was over, he invited me to continue visiting. I was glad for the diversion and accepted. Courtois' estate was about an hour's drive north of the town, set amid unkempt lawns right on the edge of the jungle. The sea could be glimpsed a mile away through the ranks of rubber trees. The bungalow was a plain single-storey whitewashed wooden structure, with wide verandas all around, festooned with bougainvillea. I motored up around four o'clock every weekday and we spent the evenings playing cards, talking and reading. We found that we had something in common besides loneliness and a sense of being outcasts. He was also a fan of crime fiction. I introduced him to Lord Peter and Monsieur Poirot; he in turn introduced me to Commissaire Maigret. He had a well-stocked library in his bungalow, mostly in French. It would be an exaggeration to say that we spent many happy hours there debating the relative merits of Christie, Sayers and Simenon, but it took the edge off the tedium of life. After tea, I would motor back along the deserted road to reach home just as the street lights were coming on.

We also had a common interest in what was going on in Europe. Courtois had fought in the Great War and been severely wounded. If he was acerbic about the English and the Dutch, when it came to the Germans, he was positively vitriolic. There was also a personal reason. The only being he cared for in the world was his son François, who was a matelot on the battleship Bretagne. I think it might have been the fact that I was about the same age as François, and was one of the few persons within a hundred miles who could speak anything that resembled his native language, that allowed me to get closer to him than the others of his race. He followed the progress of the war on a massive shortwave radio that allowed him to pick up news from French Indochina. He took a great interest in my map, which I had brought with me and conscientiously updated. On it, we followed the invasion of the Low Countries and waited anxiously for news of the battle for France.

I spent practically every night at Courtois' place that May and June. We listened attentively to the news from whatever station his shortwave radio managed to pick up. Despite the unrelenting optimism of the bulletins, the news was all bad. The Germans were through the Ardennes, they had crossed the Meuse, the BEF had been evacuated from Dunkirk… it went on and on without respite. In his heart, Courtois was convinced that there would be another miracle of the Marne, but we waited in vain that summer for such happy news. His only consolation was that there was no action at sea, and François remained safe aboard the Bretagne. When news came of the armistice, a black mood of the deepest hue descended on him. I found it prudent to stay away.

IT WAS more than a fortnight later that I bumped into him again – almost literally. Walking back to the office after a particularly pointless day in court arguing over some dreary couple's petty squabbles over matrimonial property, I came across the remnants of a crowd outside one of the town's watering holes. There had clearly been a fight shortlybefore. The crowd was just breaking up. A couple of the participants were stumbling away, dripping blood on the five-foot way from broken noses and cut lips. The loser was lying crumpled up on the road. I was about to sidestep him when I realized that it was Courtois.

He was barely conscious. I leaned over him gingerly to check how badly he was injured and was rewarded with a gust of breath compounded of alcohol fumes and halitosis in equal proportions. Reeling from the assault on my olfactory senses, I turned to the small group of spectators.

"*Siapa sini chakap Inggeris?* Anyone here speak English? What happened here?"

A young Malay spoke up. "Ya, I speak a little. Tuan-tuan fight together after drink. Si-Peranchis there," he said pointing to Courtois, "call the Inggeris bad names. The Inggeris get angry. So they fight."

I had expected something of the sort eventually, given Courtois' sunny nature. I checked to see if he had been badly hurt. His comatose condition seemed to owe more to alcohol than to the battering he had received. "Come," I called to the young man, "help me get the tuan to his car. I suppose that it's parked around here somewhere."

It wasn't too hard to find Courtois' car. He drove the only French car in town, a small black Citroën that looked somewhat like an upturned pram. The two of us half-dragged, half-carried Courtois' inert form over to it. We bundled him in and I drove back to his house in the gathering dusk.

The fireflies were out by the time we got there. The door wasn't locked, which was usual in those more-trusting times. I fumbled for the light switch and flicked it on. The front room was in a total state of disorder. My first impression was that someone had ransacked the place. On second look, however, it became clear that the mess was entirely of Courtois' own doing. From the evidence, it appeared that this drunken binge had started some time before. I cleared away the bottles from the settee and set him down.

I wandered into the bedroom to find a place to leave him for the night. On the side table next to the bed was a framed photo of François. The frame was draped in black. There was a telegram next to it. I couldn't restrain my curiosity. It was from Courtois' eldest brother. After the first line, I realised what had set him off. The Bretagne had gone down. François was not among the survivors.

With a heavy heart, I draped him over my shoulders as gently as I could. I laid him on the bed and debated whether I should just leave him there. In the end, I decided that common decency at least demanded that someone should stay the night with him. Since I was the only sentient being within ten miles, the job fell to me. I dined simply on some bread and cold meat I found in his 'fridge and settled myself down for the night on one of the less grubby settees. The gentle lullaby of the jungle soon put me to sleep.

COURTOIS was up before me. I awoke to find him pottering away in the kitchen, apparently none the worse for wear. He heard me stirring and came out. "Come, we eat," he said laconically.

We breakfasted on the veranda, looking out into the deep green of the estate. The sun had just risen above the treetops and the air was still cool. The shadows were dark between the rows of rubber trees, standing ramrod-straight like files of guardsmen. I watched a couple of hornbills flit from one tree to another. Courtois had of necessity learned to bake and we had a couple of very passable croissants with coffee. At the end of the meal, we cleared away the things in silence. He was like that sometimes. We could go for long stretches without conversation, when the mood was on him. It was on him now.

After we had washed up, he said simply, "Thank you that you pick me up last night."

"No need for thanks," I replied.

"If not for you, I would still be in the gutter, no? You have save my life." He gave me a Gallic bear hug and placed his grizzled cheeks against both of mine in turn. I was deeply uncomfortable and tried to suppress the urge to push him away. I had been taught at a tender age that one does not show emotion. And grown men don't kiss.

"You save my life last night, and now maybe I save yours," he continued. He beckoned me to follow him into his study. He went over to his large desk, unlocked one of the drawers and drew out an object wrapped in cloth. "I want to give you this."

I took the thing and unwrapped it. It was a pistol. "Boche," he said shortly. "A souvenir from Verdun."

"I can't accept this," I said, somewhat at a loss for the proper response. "I don't even know how to use it."

"I teach you," he responded. "I think maybe you may need it."

"Why ever would you think that?" I asked.

"I think," he said slowly, "that a clever young lawyer does not come to Kuantan of his own free will. I think that such a man only comes if he has trouble in the big city. Do I speak true? A woman, maybe?"

I smiled sourly. "No, not a woman."

"No matter," he said. "It is of no importance to me. But it may be useful for you to learn to shoot, no?"

I thought it over for a moment. It was a skill that might come in handy some time. I thanked him for the offer.

"Good," he responded. "We start now."

He took me out to the back of the bungalow and showed me how to dismantle and reassemble the pistol, a Parabellum 08 of the sort that a German officer might have used. I didn't press him how he had obtained it as a souvenir. He had plenty of ammunition. We spent the morning taking pot shots at empty bottles, of which he seemed to have a copious supply.

FROM THAT time, he took a sort of proprietary interest in me. He never asked again why I was stuck in that forsaken corner of the world, but he must have been able to get a pretty shrewd idea from the information I let slip during the course of our conversations. I discovered that he was an amateur naturalist of sorts. He was completely at home in the jungle and would often camp out. I sometimes accompanied him, out of boredom more than interest. He had an affinity with the natives, born perhaps out of antipathy towards the members of his own race. His Malay was passable, although he spoke it with a quaint French accent.

We often went hunting among the rubber trees and in the jungle around. I had little taste for killing wild things, but went along anyway for the experience. Courtois was a good shot and we often had game for dinner, exotic fare that I never dreamed I would ever taste. He was only a fair cook but I was glad not to have to eat the somewhat insipid slop that was served up at my boarding house. I was supplied with a shotgun on these expeditions. The first time I fired it, the recoil practically took my shoulder off. The second time happened when we were walking through a field of lallang on the way back from a succesful expedition. Courtois was ahead of me, carrying a couple of flying foxes tied to a stick on his shoulder. I was hot, tired, itchy and unattentive in my eagerness to get back to the house. Suddenly, a cobra appeared on the path, right next to Courtois. He didn't notice it. I have an abhorrence of snakes of all sorts, so what happened next was instinctive. To my shocked senses, it appeared to be the size of a giant man-strangling python. Before I knew what happened, the shotgun had snapped shut as if of its own volition and both barrels went off. I was knocked backwards. When I recovered, Courtois was on the ground, his left leg covered with blood. Fearing the worst, I approached him. It turned out that I had hit the cobra smack in the hood, spattering it all over Courtois. He came and gave me another series of Gallic hugs.

"Again you save my life," he said, between prickly kisses on my cheeks. "I will not forget. Never."

I thought it wise not to confess that I could just as easily have blown his foot off in my panic. I gave up carrying the shotgun after that.

Gradually, I found myself spending practically all my free time at Courtois' estate. I began to think of his bungalow as home. Even when he was out on some errand in some other town or inspecting the acres of trees, I would let myself in and listen to his gramophone records or browse through his books. One thing we no longer did together was to tune in to news of the war. He made no mention of it and I didn't care to broach the subject. I consigned my map to the rubbish heap. Europe and the war were far away.

I later discovered that he was still tuning in to the foreign news. "The Japanese have occupy Tonkin," he said to me one morning in late September, out of the blue.

"Does that mean that you're at war with them?" I asked.

He shook his head. "There was no fight. The Japanese just walk in," he said, in a bitter tone. "They retain the French administration, but Tonkin is – how you say – under new management."

"Does that bother you?" I asked cautiously.

He shrugged his shoulders. "*Ça m'est égal*. It is all the same to me – the Vichy regime, the British, the Japanese. Let them come, it is of no consequence to me. Maybe the little yellow men take Malaya next. They are already here."

I was taken aback. "Here? Where?"

"Everywhere. Japanese own the estates to the west of here. Also many fishing boats in the harbour. You did not know this?"

I shook my head. "No, not at all. I had no idea."

"This disturbs you?"

I had to admit it did. I told him all about Elaine Gilbert and her lover Shigeru Tate. He listened intently with narrowed eyes. At the end, he said, "They show much interest in my estate. They are forever mapping and drawing and walking down the estate roads to the beach like ants. I will watch closer from now on."

Walking all over the estate like ants … for some reason I could not pin down, I felt a vague sense of unease at the thought.

12

AFTER about nine months' exile, I felt I could stand it no longer. The constant hiss of the monsoon was wearing out my nerves. The drip, drip, drip of the raindrops falling from the eaves of the house between showers was like a Chinese water torture. I missed my family. I missed my friends. I even missed my work. I was determined to go back to Singapore even if a legion of Black Cats of Hell were lying in wait for me. I shot off a telegram to d'Almeida informing him that I had given my notice to Chidambaram and would be back on the first available train.

To my surprise, the following morning I found someone waiting for me at the office. He got up and offered his hand when I came in. "Well, my boy, I trust you are well?"

At first, I couldn't place him. Then it clicked. "Major Newman?"

"Yes," he replied. "I'm glad you remembered. I've something to ask of you. In private. Not here though. Is there somewhere we might meet later, discreetly?"

I could only think of Courtois' place. He was outstation for the day, visiting someone or other deep in the ulu. "Perfect," said Newman. "I'll meet you there. Let's say in two hours' time."

AT THE appointed time, I showed up at Courtois' bungalow. A

nondescript dark blue Austin was parked in front of it. There was no sign of Newman. I assumed that he had already gone in. To my surprise, there was no one in the bungalow. I wandered out the back door. A familiar voice wafted from the veranda.

"As you see, Mr Newman, the Malay Peninsula is a paradise for the lepidopterist. Just in this small cleared area at the edge of the jungle, we can already discern two species of Precis among the mimosas. There at the stringbush shrubs, you might notice a few specimens of Danaus chrysippus ..."

"Mr d'Almeida, whatever are you doing here?"

"Ah, my dear Chiang," said d'Almeida, turning to me, "I trust that you are well and in good spirits?"

"As well as might be expected," I replied, a trifle sourly. "I suppose you got my telegram. How did you get here so fast?"

"Indeed," he replied evenly. "I received it yesterday. It brought certain matters that I had been discussing with Mr Newman to a head. He was kind enough to arrange transport in an RAF aircraft."

"I don't suppose they've caught Lim Beow Sin?"

"I am afraid not."

I heaved a great sigh. If he had come to dissuade me, he had another think coming. I was already climbing the walls with boredom. Another week and I would be ready for the loony bin. I set my jaw and prepared to lock horns.

"I understand your frustration," continued d'Almeida soothingly. "But Mr Newman here has a proposition that you may find interesting. Perhaps we might go in?"

I led the way. We settled ourselves in Courtois' settees and helped ourselves to his beer. When we were comfortable, Newman looked me in the eye and began.

"I take it you'd like to get out of here?"

I nodded emphatically.

"But until they catch Lim Beow Sin, you can't return to Singapore. I would go so far as to say that none of the big towns in the Colony is safe for you, or even KL for that matter."

I grimaced.

"I'll come straight to the point," he said briskly. "How'd you like to work for me?"

"Work for you?" I responded, surprised. "In what way?"

"As you already know," he continued, "I'm with Special Branch. I've been concerned these three years now about Japanese espionage in the Straits Settlements and Malaya. They've been active here for some time, very active. You've had a taste of it yourself with the Elaine Gilbert affair. I'm convinced that there will be war."

The news came as a shock to me. At the back of my mind, I knew that war was possible, but to have it confirmed so bluntly by a man of Newman's standing ... My mind reeled. "War," I murmured. "When?"

"Soon. It could be a matter of months or even weeks. There's been an increase in activity. Japanese agents have been coming across the Siamese border. Army and naval officers. They come disguised as businessmen or planters. 'Disguised' is too strong a word. They hardly bother to hide their identities except in the most cursory way."

I thought about what Courtois had told me about the Japanese owning the estates adjoining his. "And the authorities know all about this?"

"The authorities are blind, deaf and dumb," said Newman bitterly. "We're being disgracefully complacent. There'll be the devil to pay, you mark my words."

"Why don't you at Special Branch just pick them up?"

"Our hands are tied. We have our plates full with Germany. Even as we speak, the Wehrmacht is massing on the Channel Coast, ready to launch a full-scale invasion of Britain. The last thing we need now is an incident with Japan. The official policy is non-provocation. So all we can do is watch. And pray that the Japanese do not move now, when we're so desperately weak."

"And where would I fit in?" I asked cautiously.

Newman got up and went to the topographical map of Malaya tacked to the wall. "I need a man up north," he said, his finger stabbing at the map. "There's an Indian Army garrison around there. Japanese agents have been undermining morale. Some subversives have been stirring up the troops with talk of Indian independence. If this goes on, they won't fight when the balloon goes up. We need to find out who's responsible and stop the rot now. A white man can't do it. Will you work with us?"

I fell silent. The thought of war didn't really bother me. It was a concept of which I had no experience. Of course, I would fight if my home and family were threatened. But my blind faith in the Empire had taken a beating over the last three years since I got back to the Straits Settlements. In my heart, I wasn't sure I wanted to help the British quash aspirations for independence amongst Indian troops. George had told me all about Congress and the struggle for swaraj, home rule for India. When I was in school or university, I would have branded them as traitors to the Empire; now, having had a taste of the practice of Empire, I wasn't sure at all. I thought of the specimens of the ruling race I had come across since my return from England. A wave of revulsion swept over me.

D'Almeida spoke up. "Perhaps you would be so kind as to give us a moment alone," he said to Newman. Newman nodded, lit his pipe and went out onto the veranda.

"I have accepted Mr Newman's request to work with him," said d'Almeida mildly.

I was thunderstruck. "You, Mr d'Almeida? But what of the firm? What about your practice? You can't be serious!"

"I am perfectly serious," he said solemnly. "There comes a time when a man must make hard decisions. I shall withdraw from the firm. Cuthbert and Aziz will take over. As far as the world is concerned, I shall have retired to the Cameron Highlands to live the life of a country gentleman. I think I have earned a peaceful retirement." His eyes twinkled for a moment, then became serious again. "I believe that Mr Newman is right. It will come to war with Japan, if not tomorrow, then in a few months. We must do what we can to prepare for it."

I could hardly contain myself. "But to help perpetuate British rule? This ... this ... regime that demeans us all everyday?" I burst out.

D'Almeida sighed. "I am older than you and have seen more of the world. War is not a matter to be taken lightly. I saw service in the South African War. It was one war too many for me."

I hadn't known that. The more I learnt about d'Almeida, the more he surprised me.

"The only hope we have is to be ready for the storm when it comes. This is why I will help Newman," he continued. "He too knows what war is. He served on the Italian Front in the Great War. Those who have lived through the experience know that we must do our utmost to spare others such a hell."

"But the British have no right to be in India – or here in Malaya for that matter. If someone's been getting the Indian troops to think for themselves, then jolly good for them I say." I felt myself get hot. "I'm not going to betray the Indians. They have a right to be free."

D'Almeida put his hand on my arm and looked me straight in the eye. "Do you seriously believe that if the Japanese conquer Malaya or India, they will let us go? All that will happen is that we will trade a white master for a yellow one. The British at least have a conscience. Not every Briton is an imperialist or bigot. The sacrifices of India and Malaya will make it impossible for them to deny us our freedom, in due time."

I fell silent, abashed. D'Almeida went on. "The garrison of Malaya consists substantially of Indian troops. They are being subverted and their will to fight for the Raj undermined. If the agitators succeed in breaking morale, we will be defenceless. Whether India has a right to be free is beside the point at this juncture. We face a common enemy, we and the British both. Newman needs us to find the agitators. I cannot do this task alone. That is why I suggested you."

This revelation put a new complexion on things. I was flattered that d'Almeida should have such faith in me. I suppressed my doubts.

"All right, Mr d'Almeida," I said, hoping to heaven that I was doing the right thing, "I'll do it. But only if you're there too."

"Good man," he said with a smile. I think it was the first real smile he had ever given me in all the time I had known him.

RELEASE FROM exile didn't come as quickly as I had hoped. After my talk with d'Almeida, I withdrew my notice and went back to work for Chidambaram. I thought that it would be a matter of days before I could leave. Instead, the weeks dragged on and the year changed. It was still depressing, but the prospect of getting out of Kuantan kept me going. It was hard being a stranger in a strange land at Christmas. Courtois went off to spend the festive season with friends at Fraser's Hill, where they maintained a bungalow. He let me have the run of the estate. The rain kept me indoors most of the time. It was the most miserable Christmas of my life, bar none.

With the new year came new hope. I got a cryptic telegram after Chinese New Year, purportedly from Mak, telling me that

Aunt Clara in Gemas was poorly and that I should stay with her for some time. Since I had no Aunt Clara, in Gemas or any other part of the world, I deduced that the summons had come. I took my leave of Courtois, who received the news with apparent regret. He gave me another series of hugs and kissed me on both cheeks, wishing me well. I had gotten used to this by now and managed to sufficiently overcome the English reserve which I had imbibed to hug back without feeling utterly foolish. I packed and gave notice with a light heart. Chidambaram must have thought me particularly callous to be so evidently delighted at Aunt Clara's precarious state of health.

LEAVING KUANTAN was a major undertaking. It involved a day's journey by bus and launch to Jerantut, a hundred miles inland from Kuantan, and thence to Gemas, a major railway junction at the Johore border. Of course, it was Uncle Clarence instead of Aunt Clara who met me there. I hadn't known what to expect, so it was a complete surprise when d'Almeida met me as I stepped off the train, dressed like a Malay driver. I knew enough to play along, though. He took my bags and led me to a car parked outside the station.

To my surprise, Thornton was there. After the business with Elaine Gilbert, I had visited him a couple of times. He knew I was interested in aeroplanes and had invited me over to watch the first Sunderland flying-boat land at RAF Seletar. Despite its ungainly shape in the air, the Sunderland was a magnificent beast in the water, like a great white whale as it ploughed through the waves to the landing dock. We managed to have a quick peek aboard after the crew went ashore. I was delighted at the opportunity. As far as I was concerned, all was forgiven regarding Wilberforce. Thornton was quite a decent sort, I found – not at all the beast that I had thought him in school. I was quite pleased in fact to see him again, and it appeared that the feeling was mutual.

D'Almeida was posing as Thornton's servant, since it would have attracted unwelcome attention if he were seen in the company of a native on apparently equal terms. After the initial round of greetings, I was about to climb into the back seat with Thornton when d'Almeida stopped me. "Not there," he whispered, "up in front with me. Let the tuan sit in the back by himself." I complied, though I couldn't help feeling just the tiniest bit put out by this treatment.

We drove for about three-quarters of an hour to an isolated bungalow on a rubber estate. Newman was there waiting for us. He greeted me formally, like a senior officer welcoming a subaltern on board.

"Well, gentlemen," he said in his brisk way when we were settled, "to business." He uncovered a map on a stand. "This is the border between British Malaya and Siam," he said, pointing with a stick. "The main road goes along here, from the border and the coast to Batu Sembilan. It's right in the ulu, miles from anywhere. The nearest big town is Kota Bahru, here. But Batu Sembilan is strategic. If the Japanese land on the east coast of Siam or Malaya, they'll be coming down this road. In its infinite wisdom, the RAF has built an airfield right here." He tapped a spot on the map. "Damned stupid," he continued in an acerbic tone, "because it's indefensible with all these hills around. The bloody fools never thought to talk to the army before putting the thing up." Thornton shifted uncomfortably in his seat. "But defend it we must, if the Japanese land in southern Siam. Or perhaps I should say, when the Japanese land."

I was shocked at the idea. For years we had been told that the jungle was impenetrable and that any attack on Singapore would have to come from the sea. The great 15-inch guns of the Buona Vista Battery in the west and the Johore Battery in the east of the island made such an assault impossible. Singapore was the Gibraltar of the Far East. Or so we were assured.

Evidently I wasn't the only one who was taken aback by the prospect. Thornton raised his hand, like a schoolboy. "Pardon me, sir. My impression was that it's considered strategically unlikely that an enemy would land there. It does appear to be a trifle far from Singapore and there is all that jungle to get through."

Newman tapped the map again. "You're right. It is considered strategically unlikely. But only by our brass-hats in Whitehall. The former GOC General Dobbie thought it possible and so does the new GOC General Bond. I've had a dekko myself. It's not impossible. We did a tactical appreciation. An enemy force, landing here, could fight its way down the Peninsula in a matter of weeks unless we get substantial reinforcements. The jungle isn't a brick wall. A lot of it is like that." He gestured to the estate beyond. The trees were widely spaced, in straight rows with no undergrowth. "Umpires in wargames can mark this as impassable on a map. But real troops can get through. The Argylls have done it on exercises. If Scotsmen can pass through, so can the Japanese. Anyone with eyes can see it all for himself. And the Japanese have their spies all over the Peninsula. You can be sure they know that the jungle's not the green barricade it's made out to be."

Thornton subsided. Newman continued. "More to the point, the airfield at Batu Sembilan is the key to our air defence in that sector. Its defence has been entrusted to the 1st Battalion of the Bhurtpore Regiment, an Indian State Forces unit. This means, for those who aren't familiar with such things," he said, turning to me, "that it's not a part of the regular Indian Army but rather a unit raised and maintained by His Highness, the Rajah of Bhurtpores for field service. The 1st Bhurtpores are not a happy outfit. We've had reports that there are agitators among their ranks, spreading sedition about Indian independence. Someone has been stirring them up – possibly

Japanese agents, possibly members of the Indian Independence League, maybe both. As I said before, if they're not stopped, the Bhurtpores won't fight when the time comes. So we've got to root out the bad apples before the rot sets in too far. And unravel their network, if we can. This is where you gentlemen come in."

He picked up an envelope and handed it to Thornton. "Flight-Lieutenant Thornton, here is your posting order as Ground Liaison Officer at RAF Batu Sembilan. Officially, you are the man who will coordinate relations between the Army and the RAF. Unofficially, you will function as the central clearing house for information obtained by the other two operatives, reporting directly to me. I have met the Station Commander, Wing-Commander Jackson, and the CO of the Bhurtpores, Lieutenant-Colonel Holmes. Neither of them knows what you will really be there for. They have no idea that you have any connection with me, except in a social context. I have convinced them that it would be a good idea to set up a branch of the Icarus Club in Batu Sembilan. I have suggested that as you have fortuitously been posted to Batu Sembilan, you would be the ideal man to establish the Club and function as Club Secretary. They have agreed. The Club will provide you with ample cover for your activities. You will leave in two days' time. Understood?"

"Perfectly, sir," answered Thornton.

He turned to d'Almeida. "Mr d'Almeida, as we have discussed, you will be placed as an accounts clerk with the Bhurtpores. Everything has been arranged. The necessary background information is in this file. At the proper time, Thornton will request Lieutenant-Colonel Holmes for your assistance with the Club accounts. Of course, no one has any idea that you and Thornton are already acquainted. I have full confidence in you." D'Almeida inclined his head in acknowledgement.

It was my turn next. "Mr Chiang," he said with the ghost of a smile, "after your sterling performance as a waiter at the Club, I am going to ask you for an encore." Before I could protest, he put up his hand. "Hear me out, please. As you so effectively discovered when you and Thornton cleared up that Fitzhugh case, a waiter is invisible. As Club waiter, you will be in a position to find out many things that will elude Thornton. We have persuaded Wing-Commander Jackson and Lieutenant-Colonel Holmes that the Club should also be open to the Indian officers – that was a tough fight, I assure you. Not everyone was or will be happy to have a mixed club. Thornton will have you placed at the Club after he is securely established. You will be able to circulate freely amongst the Indian officers and report on what you hear. No European would be able to do that. Your task is crucial."

The taboo against being a sneak was deeply ingrained as a result of my public-school upbringing. I found the thought of having to eavesdrop on others distasteful. For a moment, I toyed with the notion of backing out. Then I caught d'Almeida's eye and I knew that I couldn't let him down. I took the file that Newman proffered without a word.

"Very good, gentlemen," concluded Newman. "None of these files is to leave this building. Please study them carefully. Tiffin will be served at 1300 hours in the dining hall. We will have a discussion at …," he looked at his watch, "1600 hours to go over operational details. I shall see you then."

That was it. I was disappointed. I had half-expected that induction into the spy game would be more mysterious, with secret ceremonies and rituals. The reality was more businesslike than joining a golf club. I went away feeling a little like I had missed out on something.

D'ALMEIDA disappeared to do his swotting alone, as was his custom. He had tiffin sent to his room. Newman too had vanished on some mysterious business, so it was only Thornton and me at the table. My mind was uneasy about the role I was to play. I confided my doubts to Thornton.

"I was thinking," I said, "that it's going to be jolly difficult for me to play the part of a waiter for any length of time."

"You did a spiffing job when you worked at the Icarus Club," he replied.

"But that was only for a couple of hours. And I didn't have to say anything to anyone. The moment I open my mouth, people will know immediately that I'm a fraud."

Thornton's brow furrowed. "You've got a point there. That accent of yours is a dead giveaway." His face brightened. "But then, again, you don't have to speak English, do you? What do the natives speak? Malay? Chinese?"

I shook my head glumly. "That doesn't help. I don't speak a word of Chinese and my Malay's pretty basic. I give them two days to rumble me, if that."

We carried on in silence for a while. The houseboy came and cleared our things away. I watched him as he moved around in his practised fashion, removing the crockery and cutlery unobtrusively. It really was an ideal position for a spy. No one ever notices the domestic help.

"It's just struck me," said Thornton suddenly, "that you don't have to talk at all."

"Pardon?"

"Seriously," he continued. "I used to spend the hols at my uncle's house in Devonshire. He had a footman who used to serve at the table. It was years before I discovered that the man was dumb."

"So," I said, turning the idea over in my mind, "I play the part of the mute. My accent won't give me away if I don't open my mouth. It could work."

"Yes, I'm sure it'll work. Can you pull it off?"

"Believe me, James," I replied with feeling, "I've spent the better part of the last year without human company for most of the time. I shan't have a problem playing a mute."

13

RAF BATU SEMBILAN proved to be one of the more isolated outposts of the Empire. It had been carved out of the jungle a couple of years previously, in the bowl formed by two ridges of low hills. The jungle pressed in on three sides, the fourth being formed by the main road. The station was laid out neatly, with one metalled runway and two grass ones forming a triangle in front of the administration buildings and hangers. The cantonment of the Bhurtpores was at the far end, a collection of Nissen huts and ruler-straight rows of tents. A mile away was the village of Kampong Batu Sembilan itself, straggling along the main road to Kota Bahru, the capital of Kelantan. Technically, Kelantan was a sovereign state, albeit one under the protection of the British Crown. This made our mission that much more ticklish, since the Sultan might very well take umbrage at the Straits Settlements Special Branch operating on his territory without his permission.

As I rolled through the gates in the back of an RAF Bedford three-tonner, I had a good look around. A perimeter fence enclosed both the aerodrome and the army cantonment. A few white groundcrewmen were playing soccer on the field, stripped to the waist. A row of barrel-bodied Brewster Buffaloes lined the grass dispersal area. Beyond them, I recognised the sleeker shapes of Blenheim reconnaissance light bombers. From the cantonment of the Bhurtpores came the sound of a hundred pairs of feet square-bashing. I watched them as they marched back and forth, up and down, like clockwork soldiers.

The three-tonner deposited me unceremoniously in front of the officers' mess. An orderly came out and growled at me, "What d'yer want 'ere?"

I adopted a slight cringe and proffered to him my letter of introduction. He snatched it from me and read it, eyeing me suspiciously all the time.

"So yer want Flight-Lieutenant Thornton, eh? Well, c'mon then, I ain't got all bloody day." He gestured impatiently towards the mess. I gave him a bland smile.

"Whassa' matter, cat got yer tongue?" he growled. I smiled blankly at him again. "Bloody brainless Chink," he muttered. I trotted dutifully behind him, shoulders bent and head held low.

Thornton was in the mess, along with another officer. The orderly saluted smartly and presented me, "This 'ere Chinaman 'as a letter for you, sir."

It had been over three months since I had last seen Thornton. He left the Gemas house after our operational briefing by Newman. D'Almeida and I stayed on. For a month, we were briefed, instructed, trained and rehearsed in our roles until we could play them unconsciously. Then d'Almeida too left. After that, I was alone with the house-boys, waiting for instructions. I spent the time practising on the firing-range with a Webley service revolver that Newman had supplied, waiting to be released.

The orderly pushed me in the small of the back, "Go on, give the gentleman yer letter." I shuffled forward and presented it to Thornton.

"Yes, Davenport," he said, addressing the other Flight-Lieutenant, "this is the man I told you about. He used to work for me at the Icarus Club in Seletar. Had to leave Singapore in a hurry on account of some gambling debt, or so I'm told. Major Newman took pity and had him shipped out here to us."

Davenport looked me over like a buyer examining a buffalo. "He doesn't look too bright."

"Not overburdened with brains," responded Thornton, "but a good worker. You know how hard it is to get good help among the natives."

"A good worker, eh? Speaks English?" commented Davenport, still looking me up and down. "Well," he said, addressing me directly, "do you?"

I hesitated. We hadn't really discussed how much English I was supposed to understand. Clearly, if I were too fluent, the officers would curb their tongues. As I struggled to react, Thornton leapt into the breach. "As a matter of fact, he's mute. Has a basic understanding of English anyway, from my experience. He's from the Dutch East Indies. Better speak Malay to him, if you can." We'd agreed on this cover story to account for my inability to understand Chinese.

"From the East Indies? I suppose he understands Dutch then," continued Davenport. "Geeft u mij een whisky," he said to me.

I struggled to comprehend the guttural syllables. Thornton looked alarmed at the prospect of my cover being blown immediately. Latching onto the only familiar word, I headed for the bar and looked for the whisky bottles. I poured one with shaking hands and brought it over to Davenport.

"I didn't know you spoke Dutch," said Thornton with a slight quaver in his voice.

Davenport laughed. "Hardly. I spent two months in Batavia on an exchange with the KNIL – you know, the Dutch East Indies Army. Picked up a couple of phrases, mostly to do with drinks. Damned ugly-sounding language." He took a sip of his whisky.

THORNTON hurried me out of the mess with a little more alacrity than I would have thought advisable, purportedly to brief me on my duties. We left the building and crossed the green sward towards a small stream which separated the aerodrome from the Bhurtpores' cantonment. This bisected the area within the perimeter fence and marked the boundary between the army and the RAF. With the originality characteristic of the military, it had been christened the Boundary Brook. I trotted dutifully a couple of paces behind Thornton, keeping a properly servile attitude. Situated on a small rise by the Boundary Brook, close to the perimeter fence, was a bungalow that had seen better days. On the door was nailed a white board proclaiming it to be the Icarus Club. In smaller letters below were the words "Officers Only". When we were inside the bungalow, Thornton checked around to make sure we were alone.

"That was a damned close shave," he said, wiping his brow.

I nodded. "I'd better keep clear of that Davenport. Does anyone else speak Dutch?"

"Not that I know. It's just jolly bad luck that Davenport does. But you can manage, I'm sure. The drinks are the same, and I've already established that you're not playing with a full deck," said Thornton, tapping his temple.

"Thanks for that," I said sarcastically. "Not only mute, but dumb as well."

"Anyway," he continued, "I hope you like it here, because this is where you'll live. It used to belong to some chap from the Forestry Service. The station commander was supposed to have it, but it was in such a bad shape he decided to take one of the new bungalows instead. The natives say it's haunted. I hope you're not scared of ghosts."

I felt a frisson down my spine. I don't believe in spooks. I just don't want to meet one.

He led me through the building, which was a simple rectangular structure with a red-tiled roof and wide verandas all around. There was a large sitting room, a dining-room and two bedrooms. The kitchen and servants' quarters were at the back. They were in a ruined condition, with mildew on the walls and plants growing in the cracks. Evidently, no one had been there for years.

"Your quarters," said Thornton, showing me into one of the bedrooms. It was sparely furnished, but actually luxurious compared to what the other ranks had in their barracks. I had my own bathroom, and didn't have to share with anyone. I stowed my gear in the almeirah and followed him out to the bar, which had been set up in the sitting room.

"Fill me in," I asked.

"Well," said Thornton, "the Club isn't officially open yet, but the CO of the Bhurtpores and the Station Commander will do the honours on the 26th; that's next Friday, in case you've forgotten." I nodded in acknowledgement. I had in fact almost lost track of the days, since there was no one in Gemas to tear off the pages of the calendar in my room for me.

"You'll be in charge of the Club, serving the officers, simple cooking, washing up, that sort of thing. No one will bother you here. As I said, the natives and camp-followers think the building's haunted and it's off-limits to ORs; the sergeants have their own mess over there, next to the RAF officers' mess. There isn't a separate army mess – they've been using a tent – so the clubhouse will fill that role for the Bhurtpores. The Indian officers will be full members of the Icarus Club."

I was a little puzzled by this. "Aren't all officers automatically members of the officers' mess and Club?" I asked naively.

Thornton rubbed the back of his neck. "It's a bit complicated with the Indian Army," he explained. "It took me a while to figure everything out. Viceroy's Commissioned Officers, to use their proper term, aren't treated on par with British officers. So the subedar-major, subedars and jemadars have always had their own mess, separate from the British officers. But the 1st Bhurtpores are an Indianised unit. That means they've got Indian Commissioned Officers, graduates of the Indian Military Academy at Dehra Dun – second-lieutenants, lieutenants, captains – as well as the normal complement of VCOs. Follow?" To tell the truth I didn't, but nodded my head anyway.

Thornton sensed that I was lying and patiently explained. "Indianisation is a new thing. The idea is that a unit should be commanded by Indian and not British officers. So some battalions have ICOs instead of British subalterns and captains. That notion isn't wholly accepted in the Indian Army, I'm told. People say that an Indian-officered regiment can never be as good as one officered by British officers. The Rajah of Bhurtpore, who's a progressive sort of chap, decided that the 1st battalion of his regiment should also be Indianised; and the powers-that-be reluctantly agreed. So the Bhurtpores are a sort of pioneer experimental unit, to prove it can be done by a unit from one of the princely states. There's another little complication, though. Since the Bhurtpores aren't regular Indian Army but belong to the Rajah, he can pick the officers. The junior officers are mostly ICOs. But the senior Indian officer, Major Naidu, is one of his men rather than a graduate of Dehra Dun. So's the adjutant, Captain Prithvi Singh. Anyway, there are only two British officers now, the CO and the 2 I/C."

"2 I/C?" I said, uncomprehendingly.

"Sorry. Second-in-command. Major Leslie. He's been with the Bhurtpores for donkeys' years. Started as a second-lieutenant in the regiment and worked his way up. The CO, Lieutenant-Colonel Holmes, isn't a Bhurtpore. He was posted in from a regular Indian Army unit and it shows."

"What do you mean?"

"I mean that he thinks it's a professional humiliation to be posted out of his unit to command a field service unit of the State Forces. He takes it out on the men. But you'll see. It seems to me that they're set up to fail."

This overdose of military minutiae made my head spin. The only clear thing I grasped was that Newman was right; it didn't sound like the Bhurtpores were a happy outfit.

"Anyway," continued Thornton, "the Club will admit the ICOs but not the VCOs as full members from the start. Mr Newman was very persuasive. He convinced the Wingco and the CO that it would be good for morale of the troops if there isn't discrimination against the Indian officers."

"The Wing-what?" I asked pathetically.

Thornton appeared a little put out. "The Wingco – Wing-Commander Jackson, our esteemed leader and Station Commander. You really must focus, old boy."

"Sorry," I mumbled. "But are you quite sure it'll work? I can't see European officers accepting Indians as their social equals."

Thornton made a face. "Mr Newman says that's the only way we'll be able to keep an eye on them – and he's right. If they mess separately, we're not going to be able to get anything on them. In any case, the deed is done. But you're right too. Not everyone in the squadron is overjoyed. There's a three-line whip for Friday night's do, so everyone will be there; but after that, it's anyone's guess who, if anybody, will turn up at the Club when the Indians are there."

"I suppose it'll be all right," I said doubtfully.

Thornton shook his head. "I think it'll be a ghastly shambles."

THERE WAS a lot to be done to get the Club in shape for the baptismal bash. I avoided contact with everyone, only venturing out to the station when I needed to draw something from the quartermaster's store. Since I was supposed to be mute, requests had to made in writing, scrawled in a childish hand on pieces of paper torn from a jotter book, countersigned by Thornton. As I did take some pride in my penmanship, I had to force myself to make my handwriting resemble that of a grubby 10-year-old.

I soon discovered that the quartermaster had christened me Dopey, after Snow White's dwarf, I presumed.

"'Ere yer go then, Dopey," he said, handing me the things I had requisitioned. The other clerks laughed. I smiled toothily at them, but my eyes shot daggers. The name stuck and spread. Soon, everyone on the station was calling me Dopey.

The Club was an object of curiousity for the camp-followers of the Bhurtpores. There were dozens of them, water-carriers, toilet-cleaners, barbers even. They formed a fringe to every Indian unit. Strictly speaking, no one from the Army side was supposed to cross the Boundary Brook to the RAF side without permission. The official prohibition didn't deter them. They crept up and peered through the windows when their duties gave them a free moment. I had to chase them away repeatedly. Thornton realised that we couldn't have them hanging around if we wanted to discuss things privately. He had a gate erected on the small bridge crossing the brook, with dire warnings in English, Punjabi and Hindustani proclaiming that the whole place was out-of-bounds except to officers. This had no effect since practically all the camp followers were illiterate in at least three languages. They just waded across regardless. More effective was the appearance of the formidable Subedar-Major, Rajindar Singh, an imposing six-footer with a fearsome moustache. He lashed them with his tongue and they slunk away.

Thornton also procured from the village an off-white mongrel of indeterminate parentage. I decided to call him Doc, since I was Dopey. Doc the dog was the sort of watchdog that would have caused a burglar to die of laughter. He did his job, though, because he would bark joyously at every stranger who came near the Club and rush out to lick him. This gave Thornton and me time to stop talking and take up a more innocuous position.

THE CLUB was officially inaugurated slightly over a week after my arrival by Lieutenant-Colonel Holmes and Wing-Commander Jackson. Extra waiters were drafted in from the officers' mess to cope. Thornton had procured a gramophone, which belted out a crackly selection of Glenn Miller and Vera Lynn tunes. There was a total lack of female company. Even if there had been any white women in the vicinity, they would have been put off by the presence of the Indian Commissioned Officers of the Bhurtpores.

There was a distinct lack of enthusiasm about the proceedings. The RAF crowd stood in one corner while the officers of the Bhurtpores stood in another. Wing-Commander Jackson opened the proceedings with a tedious speech of welcome, underlining RAF-Army cooperation. Lieutenant-Colonel Holmes followed, waffling on about being "brothers-in-arms against a common foe". The brothers-in-arms remained resolutely in their separate groups. Thornton made an effort to cross the floor and attempted to strike up a conversation with some of the Indians, but I could see it was a forlorn hope. There wasn't much that he had in common with any of them. The conversation degenerated into a discussion of the weather. Since this was the same all year round, day after day, there soon were uncomfortable gaps between sentences. I noticed one or two of the RAF fellows hovering at the fringe of their group as if undecided whether to join him; but as he seemed to be making no progress at all, they hung back.

The only other white officer among the Indians was Major Leslie, a mousy little man with a sparse moustache who looked more like an accountant. He stood apart from the rest of the group, deep in conversation with two officers, a Sikh captain and a major. I assumed the latter to be Major Naidu, the senior Indian officer. Naidu was a large man, running to corpulence. In mufti, I would have pegged him as a moneylender or tradesman. I heard them address the captain as Prithvi. So this was the adjutant. Like all Sikhs, he had a martial air andsported a full beard. Among the three, he was the only one who looked anything like a soldier.

The soirée soon wound down to its dismal end. Lieutenant-Colonel Holmes proposed a toast, "Gentlemen, the King-Emperor."

"The King-Emperor," chorused the company. I noticed that several of the Indian officers didn't do more than just raise their glasses slightly. There was a lighter-skinned officer with a thin pencil moustache who made a grimace at the mention of the King-Emperor. I thought he might be a Pathan, or at least a member of one of the tribes of the North-West Frontier. A couple of others looked at their feet. Of the two dozen or so Indian officers, maybe eight didn't drink the loyal toast. I mentally filed their faces away for future reference.

Thornton put on a record of "God Save the King". The company snapped to attention. That was the end of the party. The officers filed out silently, the RAF to their barracks and the Bhurtpores to their tents. Thornton dismissed the mess orderlies.

"Well," he said to me when everyone had gone, "that's that. Ghastly."

"Not entirely wasted," I responded. "It's pretty clear that some of the Bhurtpores aren't particularly taken by the King-Emperor. Not enough to drink to his health, at any rate. I suppose I'd better keep an eye ..."

We were interrupted by Doc's barking. Thornton hushed me and went to the window. There was nothing to be seen. He took a torch from behind the bar counter and went out for a look. After ten minutes, I became concerned. Arming myself with a stout broomstick, I went off in search of him.

He was lying face-down at the rear of the building. I went up to him. There was blood on the back of his head.

14

THE MEDICAL officer, Dr Hammond, was not pleased to be dragged from his bed at that time of the night. "What the devil do you want?" he growled at me, scowling ferociously. Hammond had the bedside manner of Sweeney Todd. Anyone who wasn't really sick when they went to see him would certainly be when he was through with them.

I tried to make him understand that he was needed at the Club urgently. He glared at me. "Can't you speak?"

I shook my head emphatically and pulled at his sleeve, feeling much like a dog trying to make a human understand what is required. Reluctantly, Hammond put on his dressing-gown and fetched his medical bag, muttering all the time under his breath.

We found Thornton sitting on the ground, rubbing his skull. Hammond called to me, "Get him inside in the light where I can see. Quickly, now!"

Together, we propped Thornton up on a bar stool. Hammond examined him and pronounced his diagnosis, "Trauma to the head, but no fracture. You might have mild concussion. Looks like a nasty wound, that. Needs a couple of stitches. Better get you to the infirmary. Can you walk?"

Thornton tried to nod, but evidently the effort caused him much pain. "I'll make it," he gasped out, holding his head.

"What happened?"

"I'm not sure," replied Thornton. "I heard a noise outside and went to investigate. I was standing at the back looking towards the fence when something hit me on the head."

"Could it have been this?" asked Hammond, holding up a piece of roofing tile. "I found bits of it near you."

"Don't know," said Thornton. "Might have been."

Thornton limped off, supported by Hammond. It was only then that I noticed. Doc hadn't barked when he arrived. I made a search, but there was no sign of him.

I DIDN'T see Thornton for a couple of days after that. He was confined to bed under observation. Doc had vanished. I assumed that he'd taken the opportunity to make a break for freedom. The perimeter fence didn't present much of an obstacle to a free-spirited mongrel determined to join his feral cousins. An examination of the area around the clubhouse in the morning revealed nothing out of the ordinary. As Hammond had noted, there were bits of roofing tile where Thornton had been found. I looked at the roof. It was in pretty bad shape. It could have been an accident. Somehow, I wasn't entirely persuaded. I went to the almeirah and checked my pistol. The feel of the cold steel was reassuring.

TO MY surprise, that evening about a dozen of the Bhurtpores turned up at the Club at opening time on the dot. They ordered drinks and took command of the cane chairs around the card table. A couple of them occupied the settees in the other part of the room. The Pathan I had noticed the previous night was there too. He seemed to be the leader of the group despite his relatively junior rank.

As I served the drinks, I realised the flaw in our brilliant plan. The Indians spoke in a mix of languages, mainly English laced with various Indian tongues. Fortunately, they had to use English since they came from a variety of races and tribes. If the Bhurtpore Regiment had had officers recruited entirely from the Rajah's domains, I would have been deaf as well as mute. To my consternation, I couldn't understand a word at first, even when they were speaking what purported to be English. It took me a good while to decipher their accents.

It soon became clear what was up. With the Indians scattered around the room, any other officer who turned up would have had to join one or another of the groups. A couple of the RAF chaps came in the door, had a look around and decided to go away after one drink at the bar. The Bhurtpores were left in sole occupation of the field.

This set the pattern for the following days. The Bhurtpores would turn up precisely when the door was unbolted and scatter themselves around the place. The white officers soon stopped bothering even to look in. The theoretically mixed club quickly became Indians-only in practice.

The only British officers who bothered to come regularly were Major Leslie, Thornton and a certain Captain Michael Ormonde. Ormonde was Thornton's army equivalent. He held the post of Deputy Air Intelligence Liaison Officer, which I gathered from Thornton meant that he and his superior officer, Major Franklin, were responsible for the defence of all the aerodromes in northern Malaya. Ormonde had Byronic good looks and a pronounced public school accent. He was from the regular Indian Army and took an interest in the officers of the Bhurtpores when he was around. His job took him away from Batu Sembilan often, so we would go days without seeing him in the Club. That was the reason for his absence from the inaugural party. When he was in camp, he made it a point to turn up at the Club and mix with the different groups. Judging from their comments after he left, the Bhurtpores seemed to tolerate rather than welcome his company, but they attempted to be nice to him since he was one of the few British officers who demonstrated any friendliness towards them.

Major Leslie usually appeared with Major Naidu and Captain Prithvi Singh. He at least made some effort to be sociable with his brother-officers. Lieutenant-Colonel Holmes did not deign to grace the Club after the opening fête. Naidu and Prithvi generally kept to themselves. I had the impression that the others looked down on them because they weren't from Dehra Dun. There was a certain snobbery among the Indian Military Academy graduates, since they were the cream of the officer corps of the Indian Army and destined for great things.

Gradually, I began to discern patterns of relationships. Lieutenant Habibullah Khan, the Pathan, had his group, a mixed bag of different races – Rajputs, Sikhs, Jats, Punjabis, Hazarawalas and even one Eurasian officer. As a Muslim, Habibullah didn't touch alcohol. He normally drank Green Spot, the local orange-flavoured concoction. He gave the impression of asceticism; I thought I detected a touch of fanaticism. That group was always in earnest conversation. No one paid the least attention to the dumb waiter. It was quite clear from their discussions that they were disenchanted with the Rajah and the Raj. I became convinced that if there was any subversion going on, Habibullah Khan was involved up to his neck in it.

BEING THE resident fool did have its advantages. I was allowed to wander around the aerodrome with little hinderance. The guards sometimes challenged me, but when they saw who it was, they would lower their weapons. "It's only Dopey," they would say and relax. At the beginning, some of the more loutish groundcrewmen tried to make sport by calling me names and throwing things at me. Although my blood boiled, I made an effort to control myself and smile blandly at them. The more decent ones soon got the louts to stop. In any case it was no fun, since I never responded.

My favourite spot was a bench outside the window of the Sergeants' Mess. I wasn't actually supposed to sit there, it being reserved for sergeants. But when they tried to evict me, I feigned incomprehension and they soon gave up. It became my regular perch. I would sit there beaming at all and sundry, feeding crusts of bread to the pigeons. That seat allowed me to hear a lot of what was going on inside. Generally, the conversation was about home, women, the war, women, the blithering idiots they had for officers, women ... It was informative, and not a little entertaining.

The RAF was by nature a more egalitarian organisation than the Indian Army, or for that matter, the British Army. The NCOs came from all over and all stations of life. What united them was a desire to get stuck in with the enemy. They universally bemoaned their fate, to be exiled in the Far East when the big show was in the Western Desert where the 8th Army was battling it out with the Afrika Korps (for some reason, nobody appeared to remember that the Italians were involved in any way). There was a general expectation that there would be war with Japan at some time, but they were unmoved by the prospect. The slant-eyed yellow men with buck-teeth couldn't shoot straight because they were all short-sighted. They couldn't even beat the Chinks, even though they had been at it since 1937. In any case, we had the most modern fighter in the Far East right here in Batu Sembilan – the Brewster Buffalo, which could fly rings round whatever the Japs might choose to put up against it. Let the sons of Nippon come, if they dared.

The Sergeants' Mess was also the source of interesting information about the officers. Wing-Commander Jackson was held in high regard as a veteran of the Battle of Britain. He had been shot down in his Defiant, an obsolescent beast eventually relegated to the night-fighter role. This didn't deter him from putting in for Hurricanes. He ended up having to ditch in the Channel after an epic dogfight with a gaggle of Messerschmitts. After that, his fighting days were over and he was packed off to Malaya with a gong for gallantry. The other pilots were young and wet behind the ears. The sergeants didn't have quite the same regard for these chinless wonders. Still, an officer was an officer, even if he was a twit.

Major Franklin and Captain Ormonde were regarded with some reserve. Part of this had to do with the natural tribalism of the British NCO as a class. They were army, which put them beyond the pale. Franklin was considered to be all right, as far as an officer could be, even if he was army. He was a Territorial who had been absorbed into the regular army for the duration of the war; in other words, not a toff. Ormonde, on the other hand, provoked stronger feelings, mostly negative. His accent put people's backs up. So did his aristocratic airs. There was a rumour that he was the illegitimate son of a belted earl. Whatever the truth may have been, Captain Ormonde was not a popular man in the Sergeants' Mess. Nor, for similar reasons, was Flight-Lieutenant Thornton. Any public-school boy was a public enemy. I hadn't realised before quite how much resentment there was against the ruling class in England.

Thornton's job as Ground Liaison Officer took him away from Batu Sembilan often. He kept company with Ormonde, who was his counterpart from the army. They went off together to examine the defences of the other aerodromes in the area and to check the preparedness of the infantry units assigned to guard them. But it was more than mere professional interests that they shared. Increasingly, during his free time, he was with Ormonde. This was unsurprising, since they both came from the same stratum of society. Thornton was not by nature gregarious. I thought him rather too sensitive and retiring to be a soldier. Ormonde was, by contrast, self-assured to the point of conceit. He had something of the air of an actor about him. I did not personally take to him, but the fact that he showed some interest in the Bhurtpores was a point in his favour. Ormonde had in fact gone out of his way to be friendly to Thornton when he first arrived. I believe that he was Thornton's only friend on the station. The two of them would often turn up before opening time for a private chat and tipple. I left them to themselves. As far as Ormonde was concerned, I was Dopey the invisible man.

ABOUT A month after the opening of the Club, there was a massive thunderstorm after midnight. I was shocked from my sleep by a tremendous clap of thunder and a blinding flash of lightning. The heavens opened and deluged us. The wind blew tiles off the roof and leaks sprang up in half-a-dozen places. I ran from room to room with a collection of buckets and rags to catch the water.

I soon became aware of pandemonium in the Bhurtpores' camp. Through the windows, I could see them milling around, illuminated by the flashes of lightning. It looked like the wind had taken down most of their tents. There was a crowd at the fence and on the RAF side of the Boundary Brook doing something which I could not see clearly. I was too busy and tired to pay attention. When the floor was mopped and the furniture dried off, I dragged myself back to bed.

There was no lie-in for me the following morning. I was roused at the crack of dawn by a hubbub from the Bhurtpores' camp. I wandered out onto the sodden lawn to see what was up. The damage was clear in the light. The storm had flattened most of the tents. Worse, the Boundary Brook had burst its banks. The clubhouse was all right, situated as it was on a small rise. But the Bhurtpores had built their cantonment in a lower-lying area, which now resembled a marsh. Tent poles stuck up forlornly from the water, looking like the trunks of a drowned forest.

Holmes had turned his men out and was harangueing them in a loud voice. It was his dulcet tones that had gotten me out of bed. His face was violet with emotion. He flung every pejorative epithet in his vocabulary at them – "bone-idle", "useless", "incompetent", "inept", "bungling", "blundering" and "shiftless" featured prominently. When he called them "dogs" and "pigs", I heard a murmur of dismay ripple through the ranks. There is no graver insult to Muslim troops. I don't know if his intention was to wound them, but wound them he did. Then, to my utter astonishment, he started laying about him with his riding crop, cursing wildly. I left without waiting to see the rest.

THORNTON turned up to survey the damage later that morning. "Everything under control?"

"Well, half the roof's gone and the ceiling in the dining-room is sodden, but otherwise we're all right," I answered.

"Could be worse," he commented. "Our next-door neighbours came a cropper. Have you seen their place?"

I nodded. "Their CO tore a strip off them this morning. He was practically raving."

"So I heard," said Thornton. "As I said, he takes out his frustrations on the men."

"What's the story?" I asked curiously.

"Well, the way I heard it, he was on an upward trajectory when there was a slip-up. Something to do with over-zealous punishment of defaulters. Had them locked up in his own personal Black Hole of Calcutta and one of them had the bad grace to die. Anyway, the upshot was that he was shuffled off laterally into the Bhurtpores. I gather being seconded to command a State Forces unit is the Indian Army equivalent of being cast into outer darkness. And being sent to a quiet sector like Malaya instead of the Western Desert just caps it all. His ambition, I am told, is to make the Bhurtpores the most efficient unit in the Indian Army or perish in the attempt. Or more likely, have them perish in the attempt."

"Poor blighters."

"Poor blighters, indeed. He's cancelled all leave and got them digging irrigation ditches all over the shop to drain off the water. They won't hear the last of this for a long time. He thinks that he's personally been made a laughing stock by the disaster. Everyone is confined to barracks for a week."

"I suppose this means that business will be slow tonight?"

"Yes, I'm counting on it. We'll be having someone new join us. An accounts clerk by the name of de Silva. You wouldn't happen to know him, by any chance?" he asked with a wicked smile.

AS I HAD anticipated, business was slow that evening. None of the regulars turned up. The RAF chaps didn't bother to come either. I closed shop at eight o'clock instead of the usual nine. D'Almeida came at quarter past nine together with Thornton. I was pleased to see him. He wasn't his usual dapper self. The normal coat and tie were absent. Instead, he wore a stiffly-starched white shirt buttoned to the collar and faded khaki trousers, with leather sandals. I shook his hand warmly and offered him a drink. He asked for kopi-o, black coffee without milk. When I brought it to him, to my surprise, he poured the coffee into the saucer, blew on it and sipped. I had never seen him so relaxed.

"Well, Mr d'Almeida," said Thornton, "what have you got for us?"

D'Almeida took off his glasses and began polishing them. "Very little, I fear, gentlemen. At least, nothing concrete."

We waited for him to continue. "As Mr Newman told us, there is a morale problem in the battalion. The officers are demoralised. The troops are discontented. This morning's incident has left a large scar. The men do not think that they should be blamed for an act of God. Two of the four companies are composed of Mussulmans. They do not take kindly to being called dogs and pigs. The other two companies, although Hindu, feel deeply the insult to their comrades and the stain upon the honour of the battalion. Altogether, it is not a very encouraging situation."

"But the subversives? Have you anything on them?"

D'Almeida paused a while before answering. "There is certainly talk of Indian independence. I myself have received a pamphlet published by the Indian Independence League. It appeared under my door one morning, anonymously. I have reason to believe that the source is one Mr Narayanan, who has a shop in the kampong. In the regiment, the talk is amorphous, theoretical. I do not sense that it is an issue among the rank-and-file. Their concerns are more practical. They are concerned about the sparseness of their rations and the poor quality of their bedding and tents."

"What about Lieutenant Habibullah Khan?" I interjected. "He has a group here. They come practically every night. I've heard them grumbling."

"Habibullah? Now, there is a young man to watch. A man with drive and a mission. He will go far if given rein. He is discontented, it is true. Disenchanted with the pace of reform in India and the Indian Army, certainly. But disloyal? I do not know."

"So we're barking up the wrong tree," said Thornton. "There's nothing out of the ordinary going on."

"I did not say that," said d'Almeida cautiously. "There is something going on. I do not yet know what. But there is most certainly something…" He stopped abruptly. We were sitting together in the dining-room. He was staring out the window towards the servants' quarters and kitchen at the back of the clubhouse.

"What is it?" asked Thornton.

"I thought I saw a glimmer of light. Out there, at the back."

Thornton looked at me. "I'd better take a dekko."

"I'm coming this time," I responded.

Arming ourselves with torches and broomsticks, we cautiously crept out the back door and looked around. There was nothing to be seen. The night was impenetrably dark. We kept our torches off so as not to betray our position.

Then, I heard a scuffling noise from the servants' quarters. "There," I whispered to Thornton. "There's something over there."

We approached the ruins with our sticks at the ready. "Now!" yelled Thornton, switching on his torch and rushing forward. I did the same. We plunged through the doorway into the room. Nothing. We charged into the adjoining kitchen. It too was empty. In the centre of the back wall was a brick fireplace with two earthenware charcoal stoves still on it. Weeds were growing in the corners. The ceiling had fallen in. There was an all-pervasive smell of rotting wood. I went to the back window and peered out. Ten yards away was the fence and beyond it the jungle. Only the metallic toc-toc call of the nightjars punctuated the silence. Thornton flashed his torch around the room. He held the beam on a pile of gunny sacks.

"You'd better have a look at this," he said.

I came over. In the beam of the torch lay a pile of bones. It was the skeleton of a dog. I recognised the collar immediately. It was Doc.

15

"THEY'RE ON to us, whoever they are," said Thornton when we had rejoined d'Almeida in the dining-room. "They killed the dog and bashed me on the head. We'd better be on our guard at all times now."

D'Almeida shook his head. "If they had wanted to kill you, why not finish the job properly that night when you were knocked unconscious?"

He had us there. "You think it was an accident, then?" I asked.

He shook his head again. "No, I did not say that. But many things puzzle me. If the aim was to kill or incapacitate Mr Thornton, they had the opportunity and did not take it. And why kill the dog? I must think further." He lapsed into silence. I knew it was no use trying to coax anything out of him prematurely. He would let us know when he was good and ready.

"Meanwhile," said Thornton, "I'd better drive you back to your place. You've got something in the kampong, I take it?"

"No," said d'Almeida, still apparently deep in thought, "It would be strange to have you, an officer, drive me, a clerk, home. I shall walk, as I always do. The night is dry and clement. It will be no exertion."

"Are you sure, Mr d'Almeida?" I asked, with concern. "I mean, they might do something."

"To me?" he replied, raising his eyebrows. "I am only a clerk, hired to assist with the accounts. We have had no prior contact. Why should they wish me harm?"

The scepticism must have registered on my face, for he continued, "It is good of you to be concerned, but I do not think I am in any danger. Whoever 'they' are, they do not seem to be intent on homicide. I shall be all right." He smiled slightly and took his leave, carrying his umbrella under his arm and looking every inch the innocuous retired civil servant he was supposed to be.

"Well," said Thornton when he had gone, "I'm not so sure they're not bent on getting us. You'd better watch out."

"We'd both better watch out," I replied.

I spent a restless night, waking at the slightest sound. I slept with my pistol under the pillow, fully loaded. Thinking back, I'm surprised I didn't blow my brains out by accident. It was comforting at the time, though.

THE FOLLOWING day, I walked into the kampong to get wood to fix the roof and ceiling. I was by then quite well-known to the villagers. During the first week, I had made the rounds of the shops purchasing various items for the clubhouse. They were inclined to be suspicious at first, but as I smiled beatifically at all and sundry, they eventually accepted me as harmless. I contrived to make myself understood by pantomime, which provoked a certain degree of mirth at my expense. No doubt I was known in the kampong by the local equivalent of Dopey. I went to the market every couple of days to stock up on essential things like soya sauce, ikan bilis and chillis. The RAF did not supply these necessities. They preferred to stick to their tinned bully beef and greasy sausages.

Emerging from the lumber yard, I was surprised to see Major Naidu deep in conversation with a couple of Chinese men in one of the coffeeshops. Naidu had his face pressed up close to the others, as if to exclude the world. He was in mufti, but I recognised his paunch immediately. I debated whether or not to stay, but decided in the end that it would be suspicious to evince too much interest in what he chose to do on his day off. I set off back down the dusty road to the aerodrome, pushing the plywood in a wheelbarrow I had contrived to borrow. The sun was already hot, although it was only ten in the morning.

When I got back, the Bhurtpores were still hard at work draining their swamp. The tents had been re-erected some distance away from the original site, on higher ground. The new irrigation ditches criss-crossed the cantonment in a neat pattern, dividing it checkerboard fashion into squares. I didn't envy them the work, especially as the CO had them at it all through the day, even when the sun was blazing. Noël Coward had remarked that only mad dogs and Englishmen go out in the midday sun. In this case, the mad dog was an Englishman.

D'ALMEIDA provided us with a constant stream of information about the goings-on among the Bhurtpores. He had a knack for connecting with people of all classes and races. He made friends with the bhistis and the syces. He mixed with the sepoys and the NCOs. No one who had known him in his previous incarnation would have recognised him. In court, d'Almeida was ferocious. He was feared up and down the Peninsula for his erudition, oratory and single-minded pursuit of the truth. Out of court and chambers, he doffed the persona with the wig and gown when it suited him. He could appear as the kindly old uncle – which was the part he played as Albert de Silva, retired civil servant and part-time book-keeper, confidante and friend to all.

There were two factions amongst the Indian officers. One was a group of Rajah's men, centred on Major Naidu and Captain Prithvi Singh, respectively the senior Indian officer and battalion adjutant. They owed their positions to their connections in the Rajah's circle of courtiers rather than to any outstanding professional merit. Most of the VCOs were with them, long-service professional soldiers who had worked their way up from the ranks but who found that the system did not allow promotion beyond Subedar-Major. They were conservative, hide-bound by tradition and suspicious of innovation. The other group was led by Lieutenant Habibullah Khan. It consisted mainly of the ICOs, who had graduated from Dehra Dun expecting to be treated with more professional respect. They were young and untried, eager to prove themselves and impatient with the glacial pace of reform in the Army. Poised uncomfortably between the two factions was the Subedar-Major, Rajindar Singh, a grizzled veteran who had seen action in Palestine during the Great War and in Afghanistan after that. He maintained a studied neutrality between the groups. His only loyalty was to the Regiment. Hovering ineffectually on the fringes was the 2 I/C, Major Leslie, who was ignored by his superior and unrespected by his subordinates. The only thing that united the Indian officers was hatred of the CO.

After the incident of the Great Flood, Lieutenant-Colonel Holmes had redoubled his efforts to whip the battalion into shape. Nothing they did was ever good enough. His disdain for officers and men alike was patently obvious. They were sent off, a company at a time, on long route-marches in full kit. They were engaged constantly in digging field fortifications, filling them in and digging them again – all for practice. The officers were lectured, criticised and chided for the smallest shortcomings of their men. Never was there a word of praise or appreciation. The men grumbled. The officers muttered. Open mutiny simmered below the surface.

I watched Habibullah Khan and his group in the Club carefully. More officers joined them. The talk was of renewal, of casting off the foreign yoke. This was sedition, pure and simple. They grumbled about Holmes and his unreasonable cavilling. They gave vent to their frustration at being considered second-class, despite the fact that in their view the battalion was in tip-top shape. They spoke in hushed angry tones of slights and insults endured by officers and men. When the CO himself despised the battalion, it was no wonder that other units looked down on them. Running through it all was the constant refrain that India should be free, free of alien domination, free to determine her own destiny. I had to admit that I found those arguments seductive.

All this was dutifully reported to Thornton. He had a hidden wireless transmitter installed behind a bookcase in the small administrative office that had been set up in the second bedroom. With this, he would transmit details of all we had learnt to Newman in Singapore. Pamphlets issued by the Indian Independence League circulated widely. It was also clear that Japanese propaganda touting an Asia for the Asians was being spread amongst the rank and file. But we were unable to pinpoint the source. D'Almeida, in his tight-lipped way, refused to share with us his suspicions. I suppose it was the habit of a lifetime spent in the law that caused him to wait until he had a proper case before making accusations.

I had my own suspicions, of course. I noticed Major Naidu several times in the village, sitting in the coffeeshop talking to several Chinese men. It wasn't always the same people. They had a conspiratorial air about them. I didn't like the looks of them. It struck me that the first time I had seen him there, the battalion was supposed to have been confined to quarters. Had he been absent without leave? It might all have been completely innocent, but I kept my eye on him nonetheless.

THE BEST thing about my new position was that I could get mail. Newman arranged for letters from my family to be forwarded to d'Almeida in Kampong Batu Sembilan. They were ostensibly letters to "Mr Albert de Silva", but the contents were re-copied by some functionary at Special Branch from the letters that the girls wrote to me.

I discovered that during the time I had been incommunicado, I had become the uncle of a baby girl. Ralph and May had had their first child before Christmas the previous year. Naturally, the whole household was in raptures. It gave me a pang to read about the domestic arrangements, but the pain of homesickness was better than the agony of isolation. I was not allowed to write back, for obvious reasons. D'Almeida however did his best to assure Mak that all was well with me, within the limitations imposed by our position.

Once a week, I was allowed a day off. After the first month, Thornton had decided that the Club should be closed on Fridays. I spent the time hanging about d'Almeida's place. The villagers thought nothing of it, since they knew we were associated through the Icarus Club. Rather than living in the cantonment, d'Almeida had rented a small brick house on the outskirts of the kampong, at the edge of the jungle. The house was by no means luxurious. There was no refrigerator. Instead, he kept his food in a wire-fronted wooden cupboard. The latrine was a simple hole in the concrete floor with a night-soil bucket underneath, cleared every morning by the toti-man. The kitchen was an old-fashioned one, with a concrete platform on which to place cooking stoves. Charcoal was stacked in the corner for use in the stove. The kualis and pans were neatly hung on hooks along the wall. A small sink completed the equipment. The bedroom was spartan, a simple camp-bed with a mosquito net and a plain almeirah. It was quite a change from his big house in Singapore. I couldn't help noticing that he had a

Webley service revolver in the room. He also showed me the jungle path that led to the back of his house. "One never knows when it might be necessary to come or go without being noticed," he said. D'Almeida was not one to leave things to chance.

D'Almeida had contrived to make friends with all the kampong kids. As he was an accomplished conjurer, they flocked to see him make coins appear out of people's ears or cigarettes disappear into his palm. The kids treated me as one of them, a large, silent, harmless presence. I was content to let them do so. I enjoyed watching them. There was something homey about having children about the place. I soon discovered that the kids were his eyes and ears in the village. He referred to them fondly as his band of Irregulars. There was not a coming or going within a radius of five miles from Kampong Batu Sembilan that was not reported to him.

The man on whom suspicion fell on was one Mr Narayanan, a shopkeeper in the kampong. He ran a provision shop full of sweets, books and stationery. The kampong kids were forever pressing their noses against the glass, leaving little greasy marks. D'Almeida paid them to go into the shop on the pretext of buying something, just to look around and see what they could find out. There wasn't a more light-fingered gang of artful dodgers in all Malaya. They brought back copies of seditious pamphlets published by the Indian Independence League. He had a whole cache of them in his back room. But possession of seditious literature was a far cry from subversion. And we had no idea who his contact may have been in the Bhurtpores or whether he was part of a wider network. At least, I had no idea. If d'Almeida knew, he wasn't saying anything.

LATER ON, as I gained confidence and familiarity with the place, I took the bus to Kota Bahru just for the change of scenery. D'Almeida suggested it. He supplied me a false moustache from his magic trunk full of such wonderful paraphenalia. I changed in the public toilet at the bus station, a disgusting, foul-smelling, sopping-wet cesspit that one would resort to only in extremis. With my moustache firmly in place and a suit rather than my usual tutup jacket, I felt a different man. I was a different man. It was good to shed the pretence and act normally for a while. Wandering anonymously in town, having lunch at a restaurant, spending an afternoon at the cinema, being able to speak – it was liberation. At the end of the day, batteries recharged, I would put on my costume and character again and return to the clubhouse.

I soon discovered that d'Almeida had a reason for suggesting my excursions to town. One day, he said to me, "I believe that Captain Prithvi Singh may be in Kota Bahru today. Perhaps you would so good as to keep an eye on this address and let me know if he comes?" He handed me a slip of paper with the name and address of a shop. I looked it up when I got to town. Stationing myself in a coffeeshop opposite, I bought a newspaper and ordered coffee and kaya toast. I sat there all afternoon. Prithvi Singh did not show up.

D'Almeida was not put out when I reported the news to him. He merely nodded and looked thoughtful. The next week, he gave me another address. Again, there was nothing to report. The third time, I got lucky. Prithvi appeared shortly after lunch in mufti. He could not disguise his military bearing, however. He disappeared into the bowels of the shop, where he remained for about half an hour. He emerged with a small envelope and headed off. I tailed him for a while, but I lost him in the tangle of unfamiliar streets. When I reported this to d'Almeida, he smiled slightly but again said nothing.

After that, d'Almeida sent me to watch the shop every time I had a day off. I saw Prithvi twice more, at roughly monthly intervals. The routine was always the same. All this I reported to d'Almeida. I was dying to know what was going on but knew

better than to ask. After nearly four years working with him, I was
used to his penchant for the dramatic denouement.

ON ONE of my days off after my birthday, I left early for
d'Almeida's place in anticipation of receiving a special letter from
home. The girls had previously written to say that they would be
sending up something special. I was not disappointed. The letter
came together with a parcel, delivered from Robinson's at a princely
price. It was full of little treats like Chivers jam, Cadbury chocolate,
Ovaltine and Marmite, all of which I sorely missed. I was in a fever
of anticipation to open them. Clutching my parcel and letter, I
excused myself and hurried back to the clubhouse.

I let myself in and went directly to my bedroom. To my surprise,
the door was closed. There were faint noises coming from within.
My neck hairs prickled. No one should have been there. After that
second nocturnal visitation, I was paranoid about possible assassins
lurking in dark corners. I took to checking and double-checking
the doors and windows every night. When I left the clubhouse, I
made it a point of locking up everything securely. I cursed myself
for having left my pistol in the almeirah. I debated whether or not
to sneak out and get reinforcements. In the end, I decided that it
would be foolish as well as inglorious to go running off for help
without even having a look. Arming myself with a broomstick, I
flung open the door.

I froze in astonishment at the sight that greeted me. It was
Thornton. And Ormonde.

In my bed.

16

"YOU BUGGER!" I exclaimed before I could help myself.

Such things went on in Fenton Abbey, that I knew. It was an open secret who was involved. Even the masters knew but turned a Nelsonian blind eye. But I hadn't known about Thornton. It was a tremendous shock. That, and catching them cavorting naked on my bed …! I turned to leave, white with anger. Both Thornton and Ormonde seem to have been startled into immobility by my sudden irruption. Ormonde recovered first.

"So," he said with his irritating upper-class drawl, "a miracle – the dumb speak. Should we expect the lame to walk next?"

Thornton tumbled out of bed. "The cat's well and truly out of the bag now," he said in a pained tone.

I rounded on him. "The cat's not the only thing out of the bag," I commented sharply. He snatched the blanket off the bed and covered himself.

"Listen, Dennis, I'm sorry. I know we shouldn't have … I mean, using your room and things without telling you. I really am sorry."

"Dennis, is it indeed?" said Ormonde, arching his eyebrows. "I trust I haven't intruded myself into anything …?" He pointed his finger at each one of us in turn.

"Good God, man!" I exclaimed, scandalised. "Don't be disgusting!"

"Michael, please," pleaded Thornton in an anguished voice. "There isn't anything between Dennis and me. I'll explain everything. Later."

He took my arm and ushered me out of the room. "Look, old chap, I really don't know what to say," he said when we were outside. "I … I didn't think you'd mind. But it was unforgivable of me not to ask. Believe me when I say that I am most awfully sorry."

I was a little mollified by his obvious contrition. "How long has this been going on?"

"Well, since you started taking days off, actually," he said, shamefacedly.

I was shocked. The thought of burning the bedclothes flashed across my mind. "Does he know about our mission?" I asked severely.

"I haven't told him anything. But I'm not sure how much he suspects," replied Thornton.

"I suppose you're going to tell him?"

Thornton looked uncomfortable. "After this, I'll have to."

"I suppose you do. But keep d'Almeida out of it," I said. "Don't say more than you have to. Can you trust him?"

Thornton nodded. "I'll have to tell him what we're doing here at any rate."

"What are you doing here?" asked Ormonde, who had gotten dressed and joined us.

I picked up my parcel and pushed past them into my room. I stripped the bed with disgust and bundled the bedclothes into the corner. Still simmering, I unpacked my parcel and put the things away in the almeirah. I had been looking forward to reading my letter and having a special feast to celebrate my birthday. The moment was spoilt. My eye lighted on my pistol. I decided to take it out into the lounge, looking for a convenient hiding place where it would be accessible whenever I entered the building.

Thornton had finished his hurried explanation when I reappeared in the lounge. They raised their eyebrows at the sight of the gun. "A Luger. What an interesting trinket," commented Ormonde.

"Where did you get it?" asked Thornton. "Surely Newman didn't give it to you?"

"No, it was a gift from a friend," I replied, emphasising the last word. "I prefer it to the Webley. It's handier and has eight shots rather than six."

"There's certainly much more to you," said Ormonde, "than meets the eye."

I ignored him. "Have you told him everything?" I asked Thornton.

"Yes, everything," said Thornton shortly.

"And what are we going to do about Captain Ormonde here?" I asked.

"Captain Ormonde is on your side, old boy," said Ormonde. "I can be of great help. The Bhurtpores trust me. I'm in the game. I have a feeling something's going to happen soon. There's tension building up."

I looked at Thornton. He nodded. "All right," I said, "I don't think we have any alternative, but I can't say I like it. I suppose you're going to tell Newman? He has a right to know if Ormonde's part of the game now."

A look of alarm flashed on Thornton's face. "No, I'd just as well not tell Newman. Not about this. Please." He looked at me pleadingly.

I could guess what was going through his mind. What he and Ormonde had done was grounds for prosecution under the Penal Code throughout all the British territories in the Far East. The legal penalty was imprisonment for a period of years. The social penalty was humiliation and ostracism for life. Men faced with public exposure had committed suicide before. I knew I didn't have a choice. He was my friend. I nodded unenthusiastically. Thornton seized my hand and shook it heartily without saying anything.

When he left us to get dressed, Ormonde took out a cigarette, put it in a cigarette-holder and lit it. "I suppose that you and James go back a long way together?"

"We're both Old Fentonians. But I didn't know him well in school." I replied shortly.

"It's not as if I didn't have some inkling something was up, the way you and James were always huddled together here," said Ormonde. "We're not all as stupid as we look. I certainly didn't think you were quite as simple as you affected to be. You know, even Davenport thinks you might be a spy."

That shocked me. He had shown no sign. "Davenport? Is he on to us?"

"Don't be alarmed, old boy," said Ormonde. "It was just a passing comment. He thinks you're a 'rum cove'. Said he wouldn't be surprised if you turned out to be a spy. But I don't think he was really serious."

I wasn't reassured. The odd nocturnal events of the past weeks came back to mind. Was it Davenport who had hit Thornton that first night and killed Doc? It didn't strike me as likely but one couldn't be certain.

Ormonde put the cigarette-holder down. "Look, I know it must have been a shock to you, finding me and James like that. But I really do want to help. If there's something rotten in the state of Bhurtpore, we're going to root it out." He put out his hand. "Friends?"

I hesitated for a moment, then took it. "Friends," I said, not entirely without unease.

ORMONDE'S comment that something was going to happen soon proved prescient. Within a few weeks, there was a major ruckus among the Bhurtpores. The two camps within the regiment had all along maintained a studied correctness in their mutual dealings. It transpired however that there had been a flare-up between Habibullah Khan and Major Naidu. They had almost come to blows. The affair was kept from the British officers. I managed to piece together what had happened from the conversations in the Club, supplemented by information that d'Almeida gleaned in the cantonment.

Apparently, Lieutenant-Colonel Holmes had occasion to criticise Major Naidu severely about the performance of some of the troops. Major Naidu had in turn berated Habibullah Khan. Some said it was justified, others thought it an overreaction on the part of Naidu, who was not particularly fond of Habibullah. Whatever the truth of the matter may have been, Habibullah had lost his temper and accused Naidu of being a thief and swindler. Insults flew and there would have been blood had they observed the old Frontier custom of carrying a knife at all times. Fortunately, both were unarmed. The two men had to be forcibly kept apart by other officers. Naidu could of course have had Habibullah court-martialled, but declined to do so ostensibly for the sake of the regiment's good name. Several of the officers thought it rather sporting of him. Others muttered darkly that he was merely biding his time. The atmosphere among the Indian officers became palpably strained. The two groups were not even on speaking terms in the Club. Major Leslie may have had an inkling of what was going on, but the CO continued in ignorance of the tensions in his unit.

Meanwhile, I continued to wander around the camp and listen in on the sergeants' conversations. Tension had been building up since the Japanese proclaimed a protectorate over all of Indochina and advanced into Cochin-China in July. With that move, northern

Malaya fell within range of their bombers based in southern Indochina. The Americans reacted by announcing an economic embargo. Rumours flew about regarding impending action. The Bhurtpores started digging field fortifications around the perimeter of the station. But the consensus was that nothing would come our way any time soon. When news came at the end of October that negotiations between the Americans and Japanese had broken down, there was an increased tenseness in the atmosphere, a feeling of anticipation. The dark clouds gathering on the horizon seemed to presage more than just the advent of the monsoon.

I was much more keyed-up too. After Ormonde's warning, I kept a wary eye on Davenport. He seldom came my way, but when he did, I fancied that he gave me a funny look each time. Thornton also was careful not to arouse his suspicions any further. According to him, relations between them remained the same – but then again, he had no reason to suspect that his brother officer had anything beyond the usual connection with a mere servant. There were no more untoward incidents. Nevertheless, I found myself more paranoid than ever. The nights were the worst. My room was between the office and the main lounge, so I did not directly face the servants' quarters and jungle at the rear. Despite this, I often fancied that I heard movement and scuffling in that direction in the quiet of the night. The least little sound jerked me awake. I knew that I was being foolish, but found it hard nonetheless to sleep soundly.

THEN, one day, d'Almeida said to me out of the blue, "I believe it is time to bring matters to a head. I have a theory that must be tested."

"What theory?" I asked.

D'Almeida shook his head. "It is premature to speculate," he said. "But I am going to spread a rumour among the Bhurtpores that they intend to pull down the clubhouse and rebuild it, starting next week."

"What will that do?" I persisted. "What do you hope to achieve?"

"Let us say that I am throwing a rock into the pond to see what surfaces." He refused to be drawn further. "It is imperative that no one else should know what I have done. Do not inform either Thornton or Ormonde yet." I had told d'Almeida all about them. He thought it ill-advised to have taken Ormonde into our confidence in such a way, but accepted the fait accompli. He avoided Ormonde and didn't come to the clubhouse after closing time any more. I used the jungle path whenever I visited his house in the kampong. As far as we knew, his cover at least was still intact. We wanted to keep it that way.

As he was leaving, he put his hand on my arm. "My boy, what I am about to do may put you in some danger. Keep your wits about you and take care. When things start to happen, events may move very fast. I would not want you to be hurt."

I was touched by his unaccustomed solicitude. He had always maintained a rather aloof formality with me when I was his pupil and later his employee. The other staff were terrified of him, except for George. Yet I knew that he had a gentler side, as he showed when he was with Mak or his kampong kids. Despite all the time I had spent working with him, I wasn't sure which persona represented the real d'Almeida – the stern and distant advocate or the kindly old uncle. He was such a chameleon. That day, I think I was moved a notch inwards in his magic circle. The thought pleased me immensely.

17

D'ALMEIDA was right about events moving very fast. Shortly after our meeting, I returned to the station late one Sunday afternoon from my usual shopping expedition in the kampong to find the place in a state of uproar. RAF personnel in steel helmets and full kit were moving in the direction of the Bhurtpores' cantonment. The guards at the gate challenged me with an unexpected firmness. They only let me through after examining my pass, which was something they had stopped doing months before. I swung by the sergeants' mess to see what I could pick up. Amid the excited babble of the clerks and cooks, I heard the word "mutiny" repeatedly. There was talk that reinforcements from 8th Indian Brigade in Kota Bahru had been requested to back up the RAF.

I got back to the clubhouse to find Thornton already there.

"What on earth is going on?" I asked. "What's happening over there?"

"I don't know for certain," replied Thornton. "I'm here because I got a note from Mr d'Almeida. Here." He handed a crumpled slip of paper to me. 'Imperative that you be at the clubhouse before dark', it read, 'go armed and ready for action'.

"It looks like he didn't have time to write more," I said, hoping that nothing had happened to him.

"Do you think I should get Michael?" asked Thornton.

"First, tell me what in heaven's name is happening."

Thornton rubbed his chin. "It's all a bit confusing. As far as we can make out, there's been a mutiny among the Bhurtpores. Something to do with one of their subalterns being put under arrest. The station has been ordered to stand-to. Brigade is sending a British company to assist."

At that moment, Ormonde appeared. "Do you know what's going on over there?" I asked him the moment he got through the door. He nodded. "I've just come from the Bhurtpores' cantonment. The trouble started just after lunch. Apparently, Major Naidu raided Lieutenant Habibullah Khan's tent and found a bundle of subversive leaflets. He put Habibullah under immediate arrest. They're going to ship him out to Singapore for court-martial. He was frog-marched under guard to the guardhouse.

"When his company heard about it, they refused to go on digging fortifications. Just downed tools and went on strike. The other Mussulman company joined them. The two Rajput companies started wavering. The CO had another fit and went out to tear another strip off them. Someone took a pot-shot at him. Missed. They don't know who did it. He beat a rather undignified retreat."

"So what's the position?" asked Thornton.

"The position's very delicate," replied Ormonde. "So far, there's been no violence or damage – apart from Holmes' injured ego. He's foaming at the mouth, but has the good sense not to aggravate matters by showing himself again. The sepoys and NCOs aren't going to do anything more until they're assured that Habibullah will be released. Our chaps have secured the Bhurtpores' armoury and the HQ block. But they've got rifles and a couple of Bren guns, so no one's resting comfortably. The situation's a tinderbox. One spark and the whole thing could go up in flames."

"When do the reinforcements get here?"

"Dashed if I know. 8th Indian Brigade has three Indian

battalions and no British. It's impossible to send sepoys to put down a sepoy mutiny. Major Franklin is over there trying to put together a scratch force of British troops – cooks, clerks, Line of Communications troops and whoever else he can get his hands on. Heaven only knows how long they'll be."

"That's damned serious," responded Thornton in a grim tone. Ormonde assented wordlessly. I knew what they were thinking. Ever since the Indian Mutiny in the middle of the 19th century, the great nightmare of the Raj was an uprising among the Indian troops. That was why there was no field artillery in the Indian Army. That was also why they usually brigaded a British battalion with two Indian ones. The exigencies of war had put an end to that practice. There were no British troops within fifty miles. Also at the back of everyone's mind was the memory of the mutiny of the 5th Light Infantry in Singapore during the Great War. The sepoys had run amok, killing Europeans. It was no wonder they were worried.

"Shall we get over to the Operations Block?" asked Ormonde.

"No," replied Thornton, "we're staying put. We've information that something might happen at this end tonight."

Ormonde raised his eyebrows. "Information, by Jove! A reliable source?"

"Eminently," responded Thornton.

"In that case, old boy, I think I'll stay with you. You might need a hand."

Thornton smiled gratefully. I was also thankful. If there was to be trouble, an extra gun would not be unwelcome.

WE DINED on bread and water. At Thornton's insistence, the lights were kept off. We sat and waited as the minutes ticked interminably away. In the distance, from the direction of the Bhurtpores' cantonment, came a muffled hubbub. Shadowy figures flitted back and forth in the distance. All the action seemed to be happening over there. It was only because of my faith in d'Almeida that I stayed on in the clubhouse rather than headed off towards the main cluster of buildings.

Around 10 o'clock, we heard a scuffling sound from the back. Thornton and I peered through the dining-room window. The night was dark despite the moon, which was shrouded by rain clouds. We could discern nothing in the gloom. Then came a more distinct sound – a kind of scraping. It was certainly emanating from the ruined kitchen.

"Right, this is it, chaps," said Thornton. "Michael and I will get up as close as we can. Dennis, you cover us from here. Keep the lights off." With that, they slipped silently out the back door. With a dry mouth and trembling hands, I looked out the window into the dark. The wait was unbearable.

Suddenly, Thornton called out, "You there! Come out with your hands up! We have you covered."

A fusillade of pistol shots rang out from the kitchen in reply. Thornton and Ormonde dived for cover and returned fire. I opened up with my Luger from the window, firing blindly at the dark mass while keeping my head well down. As far as I could see, there were two of them, judging from the muzzle flashes.

The exchange of fire brought a detachment trotting at the double from the Operations Block on the other side of the aerodrome. I heard their boots scrunching on the gravel outside the clubhouse. I ran to the side window to have a look. There were four RAF groundcrewmen led by a fresh-faced Pilot-Officer. A sudden panic seized me. If they found me there with a German pistol... Hurriedly slipping the gun under the dining table and keeping well out of sight, I called out in my best public-school voice, "You men there! Get into the clubhouse and out the back. Flight-Lieutenant Thornton needs suppport." The detachment came through the front door, stumbling over the furniture in the dark. "Sir?" called out the Pilot-Officer uncertainly. I lit a match to illuminate my face and cringed beside the table. The Pilot-Officer swung his revolver in my direction. I held my hands up and whined pathetically. He yelled at me, "Where are they? Out there?" I nodded vigorously, pointing to the back door and uttering a series of grunts. He led his men to the back. Just as he got to the door, some idiot flicked on the light switch, the better to see by. A volley of shots rang out from the outbuildings. The Pilot-Officer pitched forward with a low moan. I flung myself at the light switch and flipped it off. Leaderless, the RAF men milled about in the dark. I was aching to tell them to get out there and help. They didn't seem to have any initiative at all.

There was the sound of boots in the main lounge. The RAF men swiveled their rifles towards the sound. "Who's there?" one of them called out.

"Captain Ormonde," came the reply. "Who's that? Which bloody fool turned the light on? Who's in charge?"

"Flight-Sergeant Richards here, sir," said the voice. "Pilot-Officer Simmonds was in command, but I think he's copped it."

Ormonde found his way into the dining-room. Outside, Thornton was still trading intermittent shots with whoever was in the kitchen.

"Right, you men, listen to me," said Ormonde in an authoritative voice. "You two, over there at the door. Flight-Sergeant, at the small window. You, to the other window." He fumbled in the sideboard and found two torches. Tossing them to me, he said, "You, boy, you're coming along too. Hold on to these."

After inspecting his dispositions, he said, "At my command, give them four rounds of rapid fire. Aim there; there where the muzzle flashes are. Then when I say 'charge', the four of us go straight for them. The two of you at the windows give us covering fire but for

God's sake, stop when we're out the door. I don't want to be shot in the back by one of you clots. Understood?" There was a chorus of acknowledgement. He gave the order and the men loosed off four rounds in quick succession. Then Ormonde shouted, "At them, men!" and we poured out the back door with him in the lead. We got to the kitchen without return fire. I flung myself down next to the doorway and shone the two torches into the interior. Ormonde emptied his revolver into the room. There was no reaction.

Cautiously, I peeked around the door frame. The room was empty, except for a body sprawled on its back in the centre. Ormonde approached it gingerly. I followed in his wake, shining the torches on its face. It was Major Naidu, with an enormous red patch in the centre of his chest. It was obvious he was dead.

I swept the torches round the room. The cooking platform had been moved aside to reveal a flight of stairs leading downwards into the unknown dark. Thornton had joined us, along with the other two RAF men.

"There were two of them at least, I'm sure of it," said Thornton. Ormonde nodded in agreement. He looked around and saw the RAF men bunched together at the doorway.

"Flight-Sergeant," he bawled, "post two of your men out there as guards in case there are more of them! And keep your eyes peeled!" In an exasperated undertone, he added, "God preserve us from bloody amateurs playing at soldiers."

Thornton said, "There's nothing for it. Someone will have to go down there and check." There was no rush of volunteers.

"My kingdom for a Mills-bomb," Ormonde muttered. "The first one down will get it right between the eyes if someone's waiting there." He looked around for something that might serve as a shield. His eyes lighted on Naidu. He called out to me, "You, help me get him over there. Yes, you! Get a move on man, we haven't all bloody night!"

Reluctantly, I helped him manhandle Naidu's inert form over to the top of the stairs. It was the first dead body I had actually touched in my life. Naidu's head lolled loosely as we dragged him over. The sickly smell of blood and sweat nauseated me. I felt a warm, sticky rivulet trickle down my bare arm and drip onto the floor, leaving a trail that could be seen even in the faint moonlight shining through the empty windows and broken roof.

"Right," said Ormonde in his voice of command, "when I say go, we go." He gave Naidu's body a shove and it clattered down the stairs. "Now!" yelled Ormonde, "Go! Go! Go!"

He went first after the body, followed by Thornton. Caught up in the excitement of the moment, I followed them brandishing the torches. It was only later that it occurred to me that I would have been the prime target if anyone had been lurking there. Fortunately for me, there was no one. We jumped over Naidu's crumpled form and spread out in the small cellar. In the light of the torches, I could see that the room was stacked with boxes and blankets, emblazoned with the "WD" stamp. A dark passage led off in the direction of the jungle. I shone the torches down the passage but could see no end.

"Turn the torches off," commanded Thornton, "I'm going in." He disappeared into the darkness before anyone could stop him.

After what seemed to be an eternity, he returned. "It leads under the perimeter fence and into the jungle," he reported. "Whoever the others may have been, they're gone. No sign of any of them."

"No point hanging around then," responded Ormonde. "We'd best be getting back to the clubhouse."

The remaining RAF men carried away the corpses of Naidu and the luckless Pilot-Officer Simmonds. Ormonde and Thornton went with them to report. I was left alone in the clubhouse. It was about half an hour later that I was startled by a sound outside the back door. I immediately switched off the lights and retrieved my pistol from under the table. There was a scratching sound at the door. I held my breath. Then came a voice: "Chiang? Are you there?"

"Mr d'Almeida? Is that you?"

"Yes," he replied, "let me in, if you please."

I hurriedly unbolted the door and got him inside.

"How did you get by the guards?" was my first question.

"Through the tunnel," he replied.

"The tunnel? You knew all this time about the tunnel?"

"No, not until tonight. But I will explain …"

We were interrupted by the sound of boots on gravel. I hurriedly hid my gun again and motioned d'Almeida to get out of sight. It was Thornton and Ormonde returning. They came into the lounge and settled themselves in the most comfortable armchairs, calling for drinks. As I was serving them, d'Almeida appeared soundlessly like a phantom. Thornton almost choked with surprise. Ormonde leapt to his feet and reached for his revolver.

"No need for that," said d'Almeida imperturbably. "Captain Ormonde, I presume."

"Yes …," he replied confusedly, "but who the deuce are you?"

"My name is of no consequence," responded d'Almeida. "Let us just say that I have been supplying Mr Thornton with inside information about the 1st Bhurtpores. I understand that there has been trouble?"

"That, Mr … Mr de Silva is the understatement of the month," said Thornton. "Do you know what's been going on?"

D'Almeida smiled slightly at Thornton's valiant attempt to keep his identity secret. He sat down in a cane armchair, which he positioned so that his back was to a wall and facing the door and windows. I couldn't help noticing that there was a bulge in his coat pocket, looking suspiciously like a Webley.

"I think I can account for matters with some confidence now," resumed d'Almeida when he was comfortably seated. "Let us recount what we do know. Firstly, literature published by the Indian Independence League has been circulating among the Bhurtpores for some time now. Secondly, the morale of the troops is low. Thirdly, there are several officers – chief among them Lieutenant Habibullah Khan – who make no secret of their desire for a faster pace of reform in India and the Indian Army."

"So Habibullah is at the bottom of this," interjected Ormonde.

D'Almeida shook his head. "No, I am certain he is not. Habibullah is no fool. If he had been the one passing out the seditious literature and subverting the troops it would have been unwise to draw attention to himself openly. I became convinced after only a few days that the source was to be found somewhere else."

"Narayanan," I ventured. "You told me that he has a back room full of leaflets."

"Yes, my little troop of Irregulars determined that Narayanan is the ultimate supplier of the materials; but he could not have distributed them in the camp. That would have required someone inside. This has been the line of investigation I have been pursuing all these past months.

I discovered during my tenure as accounts clerk that something strange has been happening to the stores issued to the battalion. Unaccountably, the quality of things like blankets, tents and linen is inferior – far inferior to what one would expect, even taking into account the fact that the 1st Bhurtpores are a State Forces field service unit. This, more than anything else, has been the cause of the low morale among the rank and file. Furthermore, the battalion was paying an extraordinary price for necessary supplies of rice, meat and groceries. I came to the conclusion that embezzlement and theft on a grand scale were being carried on."

"Prithvi Singh!" I exclaimed. "So that was why you had me watch him in Kota Bahru."

"Precisely. Prithvi Singh. But he did not act alone. There is a ring of conspirators, led by Major Naidu."

"The late Major Naidu," said Thornton drily. "That bit of trouble you referred to – he was shooting at us. We shot back. There were others too."

D'Almeida looked solemn. "I had feared it would come to this. A pity that Naidu died. He could have confirmed everything. Did you capture anyone else?"

"No, unfortunately not," replied Thornton. "But how does this all add up? Did they know about Dennis and me?"

D'Almeida took off his spectacles and started polishing them. "It was the incident concerning you and the dog that started me thinking. The first incident occurred on the night that the Icarus Club was inaugurated. You were attacked – with a roofing tile, to make it look like an accident. I asked myself, why not kill you there and then? The answer was obviously that they did not need to do so. The next question was, why then kill the dog? Logic impels one to conclude that it was in their way but you were not. Therefore, there must have been something in the vicinity that they wanted to get access to without being noticed."

"The tunnel! It's full of War Department stuff," I said. "I suppose they must have been checking to see if we'd found anything that night."

"Precisely. That is the way they smuggled the goods out from the camp and replaced them with inferior goods bought outside. I suspected that there had to be something of the sort around the clubhouse. Perhaps Naidu had it dug when the station was constructed; or more likely, it is an old smugglers' hole. The border is porous and smuggling is endemic. The difficulty was to catch them in the act. That would have been proof positive."

"You might have told me at least," I said reproachfully.

"I might, but I decided against it for your safety," responded d'Almeida. "The conspirators had shown no inclination to kill either you or Mr Thornton. They had ample opportunity to do so. Had they the least suspicion that you knew, they might have decided to liquidate you. I thought it better that you should not know, lest by some unconscious act you raised their suspicions."

I subsided. He continued, "I deduced that they must have had a store of some sort from the quantity of goods that was missing. It would have been impossible to move such an amount without a substantial risk of being seen. The night of the flood, they returned to check their cache. You may recall that I noticed something at the back that night when I came here for the first time. That gave me the first real inkling of where their store might be located. Once I was quite certain of who was involved, I was determined to flush them out. This was why I spread the rumour that you were going to demolish the outbuildings and extend the Club, beginning next week. I presumed that this would induce them to act."

"No one told me anything about that rumour," said Thornton, looking accusingly at me.

"Again," said d'Almeida, "it was necessary not to alert them. It was crucial that you should not act in any way out of the ordinary. Otherwise, they might not have taken the bait."

"Well, they swallowed it hook, line and sinker," commented Thornton. "But how does this tie in with the subversion? Were they behind that too?"

"Indirectly. Their interest was to get the goods out and smuggle replacement goods in. They also wanted to inflate the cost of supplies, taking a commission from the supplier – this was what Prithvi Singh was doing in Kota Bahru once a month. For all this, they needed local knowledge and help. Narayanan provided that. He found the buyers and suppliers, and arranged removal of the goods. I have no proof of the exact nature of their arrangement, but I surmise that part of the price of his services was that they should distribute the IIL literature to the troops in camp."

"And Habibullah? How did he fit into all this?" I asked.

"It was an open secret that peculation on a grand scale was occurring, although nothing could be proven. That aggravated relations between the two factions. But there appears to have been a consensus that the British officers were not to be told. That consensus started to disintegrate after Naidu and Habibullah had their argument. Naidu became more and more concerned that Habibullah or one of his group would betray the secret. Then, when it became known that the outbuildings were to be torn down – with the consequent exposure of their cache – Naidu had to act. He needed a distraction. Placing Habibullah under arrest for subversion and threatening to court-martial him was bound to provoke a reaction from his men. Colonel Holmes' intervention aggravated the situation. With all attention focused on the Bhurtpores and all British troops concentrated at that end of the station, the conspirators were free to clear out their trove."

"So," said Thornton, "you've done it again, Mr ... de Silva. It's Naidu and Prithvi Singh who are the trouble-makers. With them gone, I suppose the battalion will settle down."

"Not quite," said d'Almeida gravely. "When I heard what was happening, I guessed that Narayanan would be at the other end of the tunnel to help remove the goods. I took the opportunity to search his house in his absence. I discovered a hidden wireless transmitter. I also found this."

He produced a jotter book from his pocket and opened it on the table. There was a list of words and letters incomprehensible to me. Thornton, however, immediately grasped their significance. "My God! It's the air recognition codes for the whole northern sector. Where the devil did Narayanan get this?"

"It appears, gentlemen," said d'Almeida with deliberation, "that there is a traitor in our midst."

18

WE WERE silent for an eternity after d'Almeida's bombshell. I broke the spell, "Could it have been passed to Narayanan by either Naidu or Prithvi Singh?"

Thornton shook his head emphatically. "Only a few people had access to the recognition codes – the Station Commander, the CO of the Bhurtpores ..."

"And don't forget, the Flight Operations Officer, Davenport," interjected Ormonde.

"And your boss Major Franklin, the Air Intelligence Liaison Officer," added Thornton. "I suppose that we can rule out the Wingco from the start. He's beyond suspicion."

"I would not rule anyone out at present," commented d'Almeida. "The least likely suspect is often the guilty party. Are you certain no one else can have obtained the document?"

"It's kept in a safe in the Wingco's office," said Thornton. "It isn't a question of just having had a look. Someone got hold of the codebook long enough to copy it out. The Chief Clerk has the key to the safe, so I suppose we could check with him who took out the codes in the last couple of weeks. That might narrow the field. Assuming that Chief isn't the traitor."

Our consideration of the problem was interrupted by the sound of distant booming. "Is that thunder?" asked Ormonde. "It doesn't sound quite right."

We listened intently. The booming was continuous. It seemed to be coming from somewhere to the northeast. Then, a breathless corporal ran up and saluted. "You'd better come right away, sir," he said to Thornton. "The balloon's gone up."

"What?!" exclaimed Thornton.

"The bleedin' little Nips 'ave landed up north. All officers are to report to their stations. The squadron 'as been scrambled."

As he spoke, we heard the sound of aeroplane engines being revved up. I ran to the window to look. The Blenheims were taxiing out of their dispersal bays onto the runway. I glanced at the clock on the wall. It was half-past midnight on Monday, December 8th.

I WAS AT a loss as to what to do with myself. Thornton and Ormonde had gone to their posts. The mission was over. War had come. I had no role.

"What are you going to do now?" I asked d'Almeida.

"There is little that can be done before daylight," he replied calmly. "I propose to return to my bed and sleep. I suggest that you do the same. Exhausting yourself will not affect the war in any way."

I marvelled at his sang-froid. "Shall I come in the morning?"

He did not seem to hear me. "I need to think about our next move," he said and started to leave, engrossed in thought. I followed him to the tunnel. As he started to descend, he turned to me and said, "I shall call together my Irregulars in the morning to see whether they can pick up Narayanan's trail. I fear that he may still be capable of causing mischief."

"Don't forget Prithvi Singh," I added. "He's armed and desperate."

"That may be so," he responded, "but I am certain that he will be more concerned with preserving his life than helping the enemy. Narayanan, on the other hand, may be part of a wider network. It is inconceivable that he was acting alone."

"Let me come with you," I pleaded.

"No," he said, "not at the moment. I am still not suspected. It may be to our advantage if the connection between us does not become apparent just yet. I will send for you. Wait in the clubhouse. Get some rest."

I wanted to escort him back to his house, but he declined firmly. He disappeared down the tunnel and into the blackness of the night. In the distance, the rumble of artillery continued. The horizon towards Kota Bahru was illuminated intermittently as if by lightning. I tried to take his advice, but sleep eluded me. The sound of aircraft landing and taking off punctuated the night.

AT THE BREAK of day, I was blasted out of a dreamless doze by the blaring of the station klaxon. At first, my befuddled brain didn't grasp the meaning of the sound. Then realisation dawned and I tumbled out of bed. Still in my sarong, I ran out the front door just in time to see a gaggle of enemy bombers appear over the aerodrome, flying so low that I could almost make out the faces of the bombardiers. Their wings were emblazoned with blood-red circles. I stood transfixed by the sight until the first bombs fell on the tarmac and dispersal bays. Some of the Blenheims were caught re-arming and re-fueling. They went up in a dazzling pyrotechnic display. I threw myself flat in the muddy grass.

The raid was over in a matter of moments. Black plumes of oily smoke snaked up from the burning wrecks. Some of the station buildings had been hit. The clang of fire-bells mingled with the sound of aero-engines. A quartet of Buffalos was scrambling belatedly in an attempt to catch the raiders. There had been no anti-aircraft fire, no fighter cover. We had been caught well and truly flat-footed.

I had barely gotten back to my feet and brushed the grass off my clothes when the sirens went off again. This time, a pair of fighters appeared to strafe the emergency vehicles milling around on the field. They were radial-engined like the Buffalo but sleeker, faster and much more deadly. I found out later that they were Nakajima Hayabusas, which the Allies called Oscars. The Oscars made one swooping pass, leaving destruction in their wake, pulled up and came around for another. The Buffalos bounced them from above. "Tally-ho!" yelled a young aircraftman near me. We stood there watching the dogfight along with practically everyone else on the station, oblivious for the moment to the chaos around us. The struggle didn't last long. The Oscars out-flew, out-turned and out-shot the hapless Buffalos. All four went down. I only saw one parachute. The Oscars, their ammunition expended, headed back northwards.

The station was in confusion. I knew I had no part to play there. I returned to my room to change and pick up my pistol. Then I headed off through the tunnel to d'Almeida's house. Keeping in the cover of the jungle, I skirted the road. The Bhurtpores had set up road-blocks and sand-bagged machine-gun emplacements commanding the approaches to the aerodrome. No one paid the least attention to the adjoining jungle though. I got past the pickets without being noticed.

AT D'ALMEIDA'S place, I caught him in the midst of packing. "You're leaving, Mr d'Almeida?" I asked incredulously.

"Yes," he replied. "Narayanan did not return to his house. I must find him before he does more damage. There is a network extending all over the Peninsula, I fear. Narayanan is only one cog in the machine, and not the most important one." He handed me a sheaf of papers. They were covered with Chinese characters.

"What are these?" I asked.

"From my very rough understanding of written Chinese," said d'Almeida, "I deduce that these are invoices for stationery and supplies delivered to Narayanan's shop. You will notice something peculiar about the quantities and prices."

I stared, but could make nothing out. D'Almeida prompted me by pointing to a column of numbers. "I don't see anything," I said, feeling acutely foolish.

"The columns do not add up," he said shortly.

"A code!" I exclaimed, finally understanding.

He nodded. "Indeed, a code. You will also note something else about the papers."

I looked blank again. He pointed to the letterheads. They were from a dozen different companies. Then I saw it. "They're all in Georgetown, Penang."

"Yes," he said. "And unless I miss my guess, that is where Narayanan will be heading."

"I'm coming with you," I said decidedly.

"No, my boy," he said in a mild voice, "I fear you would be an encumbrance. It would be hard for you to pass unnoticed and I must blend into the crowd."

I knew he was right, but that didn't make it any easier for me to accept. "But Mr d'Almeida," I protested, "you can't go alone. It's too dangerous."

"I am gratified by your concern," he replied, "but I shall not be alone. Two of my Irregulars will be coming with me." He called out and two young Malay boys appeared. They were barely in their teens. "These are Ramli and Ahmad."

The two boys smiled shyly at me, then retreated to wait outside the house. I knew it was useless to insist further, but I wanted to try. As usual, he read my mind. "You can be of greater service remaining with Mr Thornton. The traitor is almost certainly a British officer. He must be found and neutralised. You would be far more useful here than if you were to accompany me."

I assented with a heavy heart. D'Almeida was the best advocate in the whole of Malaya. It was impossible to refute his arguments. "Good luck," I wished him. "I'll see you back in Singapore." I seized his hand and shook it, with an awful feeling in my gut that I would probably never see him again.

"Good luck, we shall meet again, God willing," he said simply and left, a bundle under his arm and his two young companions at his side.

A wave of weariness swept over me. I climbed into his camp bed. I was asleep before my head hit the pillow.

I AWOKE with a start in the unfamiliar surroundings. The wall clock showed it to be well past midday. I was ravenously hungry. There wasn't much in the house, just a couple of stale crusts of bread and some kaya. I made a frugal meal of that and decided that I had better get back to the station.

Returning the way I came, I noted with some surprise that the ground defences were unmanned. Smoke was still hanging over the station, but the guards at the gate had gone. Of the Bhurtpores, there was no trace. I debated whether to try my luck getting in by the main entrance, but discretion got the better of me and I sneaked back under the fence through the tunnel. Only later did it strike me as strange that no one had bothered to even post a guard there.

The station and the Bhurtpores' cantonment were strangely quiet. There were no aircraft to be seen, save for the burnt-out carcasses of several Blenheims and Buffalos. None of the emergency vehicles was about; or any other vehicle, for that matter. I re-entered the clubhouse by climbing through the dining-room window, my gun at the ready. A sound came from the office. I cautiously opened the door.

Thornton whipped round, his revolver in hand.

"Don't shoot, it's me!" I called out urgently.

He sank back into his chair with a sigh. "You gave me quite a shock there," he said, "I almost plugged you." His face was haggard. A set of earphones dangled from his neck. Evidently, he had been hard at work with the wireless transmitter.

"What's going on?" I asked. "There aren't any sentries at the gate. I could have waltzed here and no one would have stopped me."

"I've been trying to raise Newman," he replied. "There's no reply."

"Surely they can't have bombed Singapore?" I responded anxiously.

"No, we don't have the range to contact Singapore directly. There's a series of relay stations. I can't get through. All I hear is static. I think they've hit the first relay station."

It was a few seconds before that sank in. Our communications were cut off. We had no way to report to Newman what had happened. "What's the situation?" I asked, with some concern.

"Desperate," he replied bitterly. "I was out this morning at Kota Bahru. 8th Brigade is holding on, but the Japs have a beachhead which they're steadily expanding. Our air strength in the sector was practically down to zero by midday. They kept catching our chaps on the ground refueling. They've got air superiority and our side's taking an awful pounding. Brigadier Key's got his men fighting back splendidly, but I don't know how much longer they can keep this up without air cover and naval support.

Meanwhile, our traitor's been hard at work. It's obvious that he's the one who's been telling them when our bombers return.

Then they hit us. Ormonde's over at Ops trying to get a lead on who it might be."

"But what about the station?" I persisted. "Where is everyone?"

"Gone," said Thornton shortly. "Around noon, as far as I can make out, a rumour got started that the Japs had broken through and were on their way. Someone panicked and gave the order to evacuate. All remaining airworthy aircraft have been flown off to Singapore. The groundcrewmen packed it in and did a bunk in anything with two or four wheels. When I got back, the last of them was scampering through the gate.

That set the Bhurtpores off. If the sahibs wouldn't stay, neither would they. They've all gone, as far as I can tell. Can't say I blame them. I've never been so ashamed of the RAF in my life, never!"

"Who gave the order to evacuate?" I asked.

"Damned if I know. It can't have been Wing Commander Jackson; he was with me at Group HQ in Kota Bahru. All the senior officers have left. There's only Ormonde and me still here."

I felt my spirits plummet like a ball of lead. Not only out of contact, but completely defenceless as well! I regretted bitterly my decision to come back. I should have stayed at d'Almeida's house and taken my chances. "So what do we do now?" I asked, as much to myself as to Thornton.

"I don't know," said Thornton in a tone of enormous resignation, "I just don't know. We've botched the job. The rot's gone right to the core. Both squadrons are gone – what's left of them. The Bhurtpores are gone. The Japs are ashore. There's no air cover. Heaven alone knows how long 8th Brigade can hold."

At that moment, Ormonde showed up. "You'd better come, James," he said in a serious tone, "I've found something that you should see."

"What is it?" asked Thornton.

"Only a wireless set hidden in a typewriter. In Davenport's room."

The news electrified us. Thornton leapt out of his chair, tossing aside his headphones. I followed. Ormonde looked doubtfully at me. "You'd better stay here," he said.

"Not on your life," I replied decidedly. I wanted to be in on the kill. He looked for a moment as though he would insist, but when he saw I was determined, he just shrugged his shoulders and led the way.

We crossed the deserted airfield and got to the Operations Block. Just as the two others disappeared into the building, there was a commotion from the Bhurtpores' cantonment. A crowd was approaching, maybe a hundred strong. They had no formation or cohesion. It was just an amorphous mass, out of uniform and apparently without discipline. They were chanting something. I stood at the door watching them. Ormonde and Thornton came to the window to have a look. "What are they saying?" asked Ormonde. "Can you make it out?"

I only caught one phrase. "Azad Hind," I said, "Free India. I don't understand the rest."

As the rabble neared us, I saw that they were dragging something with them. I stared at it. It was a body, the body of a white man. I didn't have to look much closer to know. It was Lieutenant-Colonel Holmes.

19

"GET DOWN!" I whispered urgently. "Out of sight! They're mutineers."

Ormonde and Thornton ducked just in time. The mutinous crowd was almost at the Operations Block. They had discarded their uniforms and were wearing a motley assortment of civilian clothes, some with webbing and pouches. All were armed. A couple detached themselves from the crowd and came towards me, their rifles levelled menacingly in my direction. I debated whether or not to run. In the end, I decided that it wouldn't make any difference. I stood my ground and smiled at them in my most vacant fashion. Fortunately, they recognised me. Evidently deciding that I was harmless, they returned to the group.

When they got to the gate, they hung Holmes' corpse on one of the posts. Someone got onto a box of some sort and started making a speech. It looked to me like Lieutenant Habibullah Khan. There was a lot of shouting and raising of guns. Small groups were straggling in from the direction of the cantonment. I bolted through the door lest anyone else decided to take an interest in me. My knees felt like jelly. I nearly collapsed.

"That was a bloody close call," said Ormonde feelingly. "I do believe you saved our bacon."

Thornton clapped me on the shoulder. "Thanks, Dennis. I

always knew you'd come through when the chips are down." I could only smile wanly at them. I had never been so scared in my life.

"So what shall we do?" asked Ormonde. "Davenport's room is in C Block, over there. With this lot all over the place, we can hardly saunter out and have a look."

I nodded dumbly. I hadn't recovered the use of my vocal chords.

The sound of boots interrupted us. Thornton and Ormonde whipped around, their revolvers at the ready. A young corporal appeared at the door. "Hang on! Don't shoot! I'm friendly!" he called out in a broad Australian accent.

The two officers relaxed. "Who are you?" asked Thornton.

"Me, mate?" he replied. "Corporal Dave Blake, RAAF."

"You had a close shave there, sneaking up on us like that. We might've shot you."

"Yeah, I reckon," he responded with a grin.

"Is that the way you address an officer?" asked Ormonde testily.

Blake stared at him. Ormonde stared back. "Yeah, I reckon, sir," said Blake with an almost insolent air.

Thornton interposed before things got out of hand. "What's been going on here, do you know? How did you end up here?"

"Yeah, well, me and me mates was sent up here from Kota Bahru to get stores. No one's around, no sentries, no groundcrew, nothin'. Soon as we get to the ammo dump, up comes this Pommie Lieutenant-Colonel and says we're to follow him. We didn't fancy that, but he pulls a gun on us and says come, so we go. He gave us each a rifle and says, 'follow me lads, I've got a mutiny to put down'. We didn't like the sound of that, but seein' as we'd no choice, we just went along. When we get to the Indians, they're all excited, jabberin' away. Seems that they let some bloke out of the chokey, some Lieutenant who was bunged in there by the CO."

"That must have been Habibullah Khan," said Ormonde.

"Yeah, that's right, some Khan. Anyway, the Pommie Colonel comes up and says, 'You're not going to get away with mutiny' and points his revolver at this Khan. Then one of the Indians shoots him through the chest, just like that. Me and me mates, we're not stupid, we put up our hands straightaway. They take us to the HQ block and post a guard at the door. There's all sorts of shouting outside. This Khan fellah is their leader or somethin' but he doesn't look real happy about what's happenin'. Then the guard goes off for a sec to see what's up and I take me chance to bugger off. I got out the window and here I am."

"And the others who were with you? What happened to them?" asked Thornton.

"Dunno, mate. I thought they was behind me, but when I looked back, they wasn't there. I wasn't hangin' around to find out though, I can tell you. Mebbe they made it out the back gate. Or mebbe not."

"Well," said Thornton, "it's pretty clear that we've got a full-scale mutiny on our hands. They've evidently killed Holmes. I don't know how many of them there are, and we can't count on any other white soldiers apart from us."

"Are they all gone?" I asked, "Surely somebody must have stayed behind. There's all these stores and things." When I left early in the morning, the place was abuzz. I couldn't yet accept the fact that everyone had gone without even seeing the enemy.

"The whole bloody lot just upped stakes and left," said Thornton bitterly. "There's been no attempt to destroy the ammunition stores or any of the spares. The Japs will have an early Christmas with all the stuff we've left behind."

"Yeah, mate," interjected Blake, "I heard that the Nips'll be along soon. We'd better get outta here."

"I don't see how, with all these sepoys around the place," said Thornton. "Maybe Dennis might slip by them, but the three of us would be stopped as soon as we show our faces."

"Or shot, just as likely," added Ormonde.

"Well, I'm not hangin' around waitin' for the Nips to pick me up," said Blake. "I'll take me chances with the Indians."

"No," said Thornton decidedly. "You'll stay here. We'll try to sneak out after dark. With this weather, the light should fade pretty soon. Dennis, take the watch. You're the only one who can safely be seen."

"Right," I agreed, without enthusiasm. I wasn't keen to test the ability of the Bhurtpores to tell a Chinese from a white man in the fading light. Blake didn't look too eager to stay either, but he must have concluded that his chances were better in a group than alone.

We settled down to wait for dark. I propped myself on a box and peered cautiously out the corner of the window. Blake kept the front door covered with Thornton's revolver. Thornton and Ormonde watched the back door to the room, sitting close together and talking in low voices. The crowd at the gate had thinned somewhat, but groups of sepoys kept drifting past the Operations Block constantly. Fortunately, they showed no inclination to investigate our refuge. I didn't see how we would get out the main gate, even in the dark; and the other gate was right in the middle of the Bhurtpores' cantonment. The thought of being captured by the Japanese or shot by the mutineers was depressing. It was hardly a glorious way to go.

BY 6.00 PM, it was almost pitch dark. The sky was completely clouded over. There had been no further air raids during the afternoon. Whether this was because of the weather or because the Japs knew that there was nothing else left worth shooting up, I did not know. The sepoys at the gate had gone. There was no one in sight.

"Time to get moving," said Thornton.

"What about Davenport?" reminded Ormonde. "We should at least put his radio out of commission."

"Yes, I suppose we should," agreed Thornton. "I'll have my gun back now," he said to Blake, who surrendered the weapon with reluctance. Evidently, he didn't relish being unarmed with the mutineers still loose in the aerodrome.

"Dennis, you and Corporal Blake stay here and keep an eye out for the Bhurtpores. Let us know if you see anyone. We'll be in C Block," said Ormonde. They were gone before I could protest.

I was left alone with Blake. He was young, maybe in his late teens or early twenties, still pimpled from adolescence. He regarded me curiously. Obviously, I didn't fit into any of his stereotypes of what the natives were like. "Where are you from?" I asked, uncomfortable at the examination.

"Me, mate? Coober Pedy, if you've ever heard of it." I shook my head. "Nah, didn't think so. And you?" he asked.

"Born and bred in Singapore," I replied, "educated in England."

He nodded his head knowingly. "Yeah, you sound just like a Pommie. Like your two mates there."

"They're not my mates. Well, I guess Thornton is, but the other's ..." I paused, not knowing quite how to put it.

Blake was surprisingly fast on the uptake. "Your mate's mate, eh?" He made a limp-wristed gesture and gave me a wink. I smiled but said nothing.

Suddenly, three shots rang out from the direction Thornton and Ormonde had gone. "Bloody 'ell!" exclaimed Blake, "the Indians 'ave got 'em."

I leapt to my feet and sprinted out the back door without checking whether anyone was about. C Block was just behind Operations. One long corridor ran lengthwise through the building from end to end. Smaller offices opened out from the corridor.

I found Ormonde at the door of one of the offices, his revolver smoking. He was staring into the room. Thornton lay crumpled on the floor, a vivid red stain spreading on his back.

20

"IT WAS Davenport," said Ormonde. "James was examining that..." He pointed at a typewriter, partially disassembled on the table to reveal a collection of cathode tubes. "We didn't see him at the window until it was too late. He got James in the back. I fired at him, but I don't know if I hit anything."

Blake came panting up to us. "Not here, man!" yelled Ormonde at him. "Outside! Look outside! He might still be there."

It was obvious that Blake wasn't eager to go out unarmed looking for Davenport. I tossed him my pistol. He signaled his gratitude and ran out. He was back in a minute. "Nothin' out there, mate," he said.

Ormonde went over to the window and stuck his head out. "Damnation!" he cursed. "The bounder's gotten clean away."

I was more concerned about Thornton. He was still breathing when I got to him. I rolled him over and tried to staunch the wound. He had been shot just below the right shoulder-blade, the bullet emerging on the left side, just missing the heart. "Get the first aid kit!" I called out urgently. Ormonde ran off. Thornton's eyes fluttered open. He grabbed my sleeve. "Tell ... tell Newman," he gasped in a weak voice. "Codebook ... Tell Newman ... shot right ... in back ..."

Ormonde returned with the first aid kit. "Steady, old man," he said in a soothing voice. "We'll patch you up."

Thornton brushed his hand away. "Newman … tell him … the traitor…," he said to me, pulling urgently at my sleeve. His voice trailed off and he slipped into unconsciousness.

We bound up his wounds quickly and pumped him full of morphine. "The first thing," said Ormonde, "is to get out of here before the Bhurtpores find us."

"We'd better head back to the Club," I suggested. "If anyone heard the shots, they'll be all over us in a minute."

Ormonde agreed readily. Blake and I carried Thornton, trying to stop the bleeding as we dragged him along. Ormonde kept a wary eye out for mutineers. Crossing the open ground to the clubhouse was hair-raising. We kept low, moving as fast as we could. The smoke from the fires on the airfield gave us a little cover. I saw from the corner of my eye little dark figures congregating at the main gate. Some were already moving towards the station buildings that we had just vacated.

We got to the clubhouse without being spotted. Thornton was still unconscious. "He's in a pretty bad way," I said. "We've got to get him to a doctor."

"Yeah," agreed Blake, "he ain't gonna last long."

Ormonde bit his lower lip. "What do you suggest we do? Walk up to the Bhurtpores and surrender? You saw what they did to Holmes."

It was a point. We couldn't be sure of the reception we'd get. Then a thought struck me. "We could get out through the tunnel. No one was guarding it when I came back."

"And then what?" said Ormonde bitterly. "The mutineers are probably all along the road. We'd never get by without being spotted."

"No, we can get by," I replied emphatically. "No one's watching the jungle. That's the way to go."

"Go? Go where? We can't carry him all the way to Kota Bahru or Kuala Krai."

My mind was racing like a sports car. The words came tumbling out without my having to think. "We don't have to. The sea's only a couple of miles from here. There's a path through the jungle to Telok Puyu. We could get a boat."

"What about the bloody Japs?" chipped in Blake. "Last I heard, they was ashore at Kota Bahru. We'd be bloody sitting ducks."

"No," I said, "we go south. To Kuantan. It's a day, maybe two days away by boat. I know someone there. It's the only chance we've got."

We glanced through the window towards the Operations Block. Groups of sepoys were methodically combing the buildings. It was only a matter of time before they decided to come our way.

Ormonde still hesitated. "Look, we've got to get away now, before they come here," I said urgently, "And my friend's got a short-wave radio. We could get in touch with Singapore. Newman's got to be told about the traitor."

That seemed to clinch it. "Very well, we'll head to the beach and then south," said Ormonde, resuming command. We cobbled together a stretcher with blankets and broomsticks, and fastened Thornton to it. I had done what I could to patch him up with our first aid kit, but his pulse was frighteningly weak.

As we were leaving, Ormonde pulled my arm. "What about the code-book? How did you keep in touch with this Major Newman?"

I shook my head. "Damned if I know. That was James' job. He's got the book hidden somewhere." For a moment, it seemed that Ormonde was going off in search of the code-book. "For God's sake, man, leave it! We've got to go now!"

He saw that I was right. A small party of sepoys was coming our way, their silhouettes black against the glow of the still-burning aircraft on the runways. We got to the kitchen and hurried down the stairs into the dark. Ormonde deftly replaced the false cover to camouflage the entrance. The tunnel was uneven and narrow, but we made it through and out into the welcome embrace of the jungle beyond the perimeter fence.

"Which way?" asked Ormonde when we were out. It took a while for me to get my bearings. Everything was different in the dark and we didn't dare show a light. "That way," I said, hoping for the best.

After a hundred yards, stumbling over tree roots and stones, I had to admit that I wasn't sure of the way. "It's no use guessing," said Ormonde. "We'd best wait until daylight."

"Your mate ain't gonna last till daylight if we don't get him a doctor soon," said Blake laconically.

There was silence. I couldn't see Ormonde's face. After a minute, he replied in a weary voice, "Do what you can for him. If we go on stumbling in the dark, the chances are we'll blunder into the mutineers or get ourselves hopelessly lost. I'll take first watch."

We settled down to a wretched night. The biting insects were out in force. The rain of the previous days had left the jungle sodden. The night was bitterly cold. In the distance, we heard the dull booming of artillery. Thornton groaned now and then. We injected him with morphine, which kept him quiet. Blake and I took turns looking after him.

Somehow, I drifted off to sleep. I was roused by Ormonde shaking my shoulder. "Time to go," he said shortly.

It was still dark in the jungle, but there was just enough light to see by. I felt more confident of the way. Ormonde and Blake took over as stretcher bearers while I led the party and kept a wary eye out for hostiles.

The going was rough. The path had been little used. I myself had only been down it a couple of times. Fortunately, it led in the general direction of the coast, so it wasn't hard to follow by dead reckoning. The main problem was Thornton. He had slipped into a coma in the night and his breathing was shallow and irregular. We had to pause frequently to readjust the makeshift stretcher.

After what seemed like hours, the jungle thinned out and gave way to a coconut plantation. Between the trunks, we glimpsed the sea.

"Thalassa!" I exclaimed to Ormonde triumphantly.

"What?" he said.

"Thalassa. The sea. That's what Xenophon's men cried out when they finally reached the coast. You remember?"

"Sorry, old boy," he replied, "my Latin's rusty. Never was any good at Roman history anyway."

I was puzzled by this remark. I didn't have much time to consider it though. From the shadows of the plantation emerged a group of armed men. They were Indians. I realised with dismay that their shoulder titles were the Bhurtpore Regiment's.

21

THE SEPOYS approached us cautiously, rifles at the ready. As my eyes adjusted, I saw others hidden in slit trenches among the trees. One had a Bren-gun pointed directly at us. Then I recognised someone.

"Subedar-Major Rajindar Singh!" I called out. "Don't shoot! We're on your side."

The Subedar-Major emerged from cover, eyeing me suspiciously. I could tell that he knew he had seen me somewhere before but couldn't quite place me. I decided we had nothing to lose by being frank. "Thornton-sahib has been badly wounded. We need help. Do you have a medical orderly?"

Rajindar Singh glanced at the wounded man, then turned and gave an order. A medical orderly came running up and began ministering to Thornton. "You'd better take over," I whispered to Ormonde. "They seem friendly."

Ormonde put down the stretcher and stepped forward towards the Subedar-Major. There was a moment's hesitation, then Rajindar Singh snapped to a brisk salute. "How many men have you here?" asked Ormonde.

"Two platoons, Captain-sahib," responded Rajindar.

"What are your orders?"

"We are to defend the beach and this path to the aerodrome, sahib."

Ormonde nodded with approval. "We need food and a boat. Can you provide them?"

"The food we can give, sahib," replied Rajindar, "but we have no boat." There was a pause. Then, breaking a lifetime's conditioning, the Subedar-Major asked, "The Captain-sahib has come from the aerodrome? What is the situation there?"

I tensed. It occurred to me that these men did not know of the mutiny of their compatriots. How would they react if they were told? Ormonde hesitated too, seemingly weighing whether or not to tell Rajindar what had happened. After a moment, he replied, "The aerodrome has been abandoned. The RAF has left. Your Colonel is dead. Did you know this?"

Rajindar Singh was silent for a while, then he nodded slowly. "Yes, Captain-sahib, we were told yesterday. And the Japanese?"

"Will your men fight the Japanese?" asked Ormonde cautiously.

"Yes, sahib, we will fight." He paused. "For the honour of our regiment, we will fight."

Ormonde relaxed at the words. "We must get Thornton-sahib to a hospital. We are going on down the coast. Have you a radio?"

"No, sahib," replied the Subedar-Major, "we only have a field-telephone. It works no more. The line is dead."

Ormonde frowned. "That must be because the switchboard isn't manned. Or maybe someone's cut the line. The Japanese are still fighting at Kota Bahru. 8th Brigade was holding them, the last I heard. They haven't reached Batu Sembilan yet. I will try to get reinforcements to you as soon as I can."

"Yes, sahib," said Rajindar Singh, his back ramrod straight, "we will hold our positions until we are relieved."

We got supplies and medicines from the Bhurtpores, whatever

they could spare. Thornton was still unconscious. Blake and I took up the stretcher and marched off down the path. The sepoys watched impassively as we passed them. What they thought of us leaving like that, I can only guess. When I glanced back, I saw the tall figure of Subedar-Major Rajindar Singh among his men. I never found out what became of them. I can only hope that somewhere, some time, their gallantry was properly acknowledged.

A MILE down the coast from the Bhurtpores' position, we finally came to a kampong of fishermen. The houses straggled along the white-sand beach, deceptively peaceful in the weak December sunshine. The monsoon had abated temporarily, but the sea was still rough. A strong easterly wind blew, rustling the fronds of the coconut palms and flapping our shirts.

The villagers came out to stare at us, not in an unfriendly fashion but rather warily. A grizzled old man whom I took to be the village headman approached Ormonde and began to speak. Ormonde shook his head, "Sorry, I don't understand a word." Despite the time he had spent in the country, he hadn't contrived to pick up any Malay. I lowered the stretcher and stepped forward.

The headman turned to me and reeled off a succession of long sentences that I struggled to follow. I found it impossible to understand his Kelantanese dialect, but fortunately he knew a few words of the Rhio Malay that we were accustomed to speak in the Straits Settlements. With fragments of phrases and many gesticulations, I managed to impart to him the fact that the Japanese were coming. He didn't seem unduly bothered by the prospect. I pointed repeatedly to Thornton, who by now was delirious with fever. After repeating to him the words "Kuantan" and "doktor" several times, the headman finally understood and motioned to us to follow him.

He led us up the beach, to where the fishing prahus were pulled up in a neat line. They were frail, canoe-like vessels which didn't appear capable of surviving even the smallest wave. In boats such as these, the men of the village drew their livelihood from the perilous sea. Moored to a stake a little beyond the line of prahus was a small sailboat, no doubt the pride of the kampong. It had an auxiliary engine besides the sail, the ultimate in modernity in this part of the world.

The headman indicated that we should get aboard. We waded waist-deep in the surf to the side of the boat, holding the stretcher as high as we could to keep the patient dry. A group of well-muscled young men helped us heave Thornton up and settled him amidships among the fishing tackle. The boat was open to the elements, with only a small wheelhouse aft to provide some shelter. We rigged a sort of tent out of blankets to cover the wounded man. One of the young men, named Yusof, remained aboard when the others went back over the side. He cast off and expertly raised the sail. We scudded away from the beach, where the whole village had congregated to watch us go. I waved my thanks to them. Some waved hesitantly back. The kampong kids kept pace with us along the beach for a while, but soon we left them behind. The land receded as the boat plunged through the waves, heading briskly south with the wind. Only the whistling of the wind, the flapping of the sails and the splash of the waves broke the silence. For the first time in an eternity, I felt relaxed. I closed my eyes, meaning to rest for a moment. Before I knew it, I was fast asleep.

WHEN I AWOKE, it was already dark. Blake was next to me, snoring gently. In the dark, I saw Ormonde curled up at the prow. Whether he was awake or not, I couldn't tell. I shifted myself carefully, so as not to disturb either of them. The wind had picked up somewhat and smelled of rain. In the wheelhouse, Yusof stood motionless like a pillar of rock, guiding us steadily on our course.

Around nine o'clock, the sea got much rougher and the first heavy drops of rain splattered on deck. Yusof decided that it would be foolish to risk ourselves in the storm. He made for shore and moored in a small sheltered bay fringed with coconut palms. We moved Thornton to the wheelhouse and rigged a shelter to keep the rain off him. The rest of us bunched up in the lee of the furled sail, which provided hardly any cover from the tempest. The night was riven by jagged bolts of lightning. Even in our little cove, the boat bucked up and down like a wild mustang with a stomach-churning regularity. Soon, everything we had was soaked through.

Respite came only with the dawn. The sun rose from the sea, driving the rainclouds away. We stood up, sodden, to bask in the welcome rays. Yusof offered us some cold rice for breakfast, which we devoured with gratitude. We washed it down with fresh rainwater. The only other supplies we had were army-issue biscuits, which we rationed stingily, not knowing where our next meal was coming from.

As we were about to hoist sail again, Thornton gave a gasp and tried to sit up. I rushed to his side. "James, it's me, Dennis," I called softly, holding him.

He grasped my arm and tried again to get up. "Dennis?" he croaked in a parched voice. I put a cup of water to his lips and he drank a little. He relaxed. "Wilberforce …" he whispered. Then he was gone. I laid him gently down again.

We stood silently around the body for a while. Ormonde said, "I suppose we'd better bury him at sea."

I indicated to Yusof, who only spoke Kelantanese, that we should wrap Thornton in the spare sail. He understood and helped me with the body. As I was going through the pockets, I found a small notebook. Opening it, I realised what it was.

"Here," I said, handing it to Ormonde, "it's the codebook. You'd better have it. You can call Newman and tell him when we get to Kuantan." He took it without a word.

When we were done wrapping up Thornton, Yusof took the boat out of the cove into the open sea. I thought that Ormonde as senior officer would say something – make a speech or funeral oration or improvise some ceremony. But he kept quiet, his face set in stone as he watched the preparations. In the end, I said a silent prayer in memory of my friend. Somewhere off the east coast of Malaya, beyond the sight of land, we commended James Thornton to the deep.

22

FORTUNATELY for us the day remained dry, though overcast. The sea was still rough, but by then we had found our sea-legs and no longer sported that distinct shade of apple green which had characterised our complexions on the first day aboard. No one felt much like talking. Blake had a dormouse-like ability to snooze in any position and at any time. He spent most of the day in a comatose state. Ormonde sat at the prow staring steadfastly ahead. I tried to sleep, but found myself maddeningly awake. Yusof continued to guide the boat, his face inscrutable and his thoughts hidden.

Just before noon, we were rudely jarred into consciousness by the drone of aircraft engines coming from the north. Ormonde climbed up onto the roof of the wheelhouse to have a look. He came down in double-quick time. "Hide!" he yelled, "they're Japs!"

Blake, who had been fast asleep, was yanked under a tarpaulin by the scruff of the neck before he was fully awake. I ducked under the spare fishing nets, which stank to heaven of the previous day's catch. The aircraft roared over us, flying low and fast towards the south. The boat rocked wildly in their wake. "What the bloody 'ell was that?" asked Blake, staring after the disappearing flight.

"Damned if I know," replied Ormonde in a serious tone. "But we'd better keep ourselves out of sight. There might be more of them. You might want to make yourself look a bit more Malay, Dennis."

I found an old sarong in a corner and knotted it around my waist, leaving my shirt hanging out. A handkerchief served as a sweatband around my forehead. I wouldn't have passed as Malay by any stretch of the imagination, but no Japanese pilot would have known the difference anyway. There was no way we could disguise Ormonde or Blake, despite their deep tan. Ormonde's blond hair would have given him away even to the blindest bombardier. All they could do was keep out of sight under the awning that we had rigged for Thornton. We scanned the sky anxiously for more signs of enemy activity.

"Are they heading for Singapore?" I asked.

"In broad daylight?" responded Ormonde. "Not unless our air defences have been totally destroyed." He was silent for a moment. "If what we saw up north is anything to go by, that might well be the case."

A disturbing thought suddenly struck me. "They might be heading to Kuantan. Isn't there an airfield there too?"

"Yes," said Ormonde, "the only one we have left on the east coast if the fields around Kota Bahru have fallen."

"Could Davenport have betrayed them too?"

"Very possibly. We don't know how extensive his network is. Narayanan must have been one of his key agents. He may have had others."

"This Davenport, he's a bloody Pommie bastard spying for the Nips?" interrupted Blake, who had been following our exchange.

Ormonde smiled sourly. "A spy yes, a bastard certainly, and unfortunately English to the very core."

"What on earth could have induced him to turn traitor?" I mused.

Ormonde shrugged. "Money. Sex. Politics. Could be anything. My guess is money. A man has a flutter at the racetrack now and then, and before he knows it, the debts are beyond control. It just takes a little push to get him down the slippery slope. The Germans are very adept at this, I'm told. He might have met someone when he was in the Dutch East Indies. He was there for a time, attached to their colonial army. Batavia's crawling with German agents."

"What about Malaya?"

"I would say, old boy," replied Ormonde, "that the Japs have enough people in Malaya so that they don't need any help from the Jerries. I wouldn't be surprised if the network goes as far as Singapore. We're going to be in a bad way if the Indian Army is as shot through with discontent as the Bhurtpores."

WE REACHED our destination that evening, after nearly two full days atsea. I had thought of sailing directly to Kuantan, but Ormonde rightly pointed out that with things the way they were, the garrison might well choose to fire first and apologise later. Fortunately, Courtois' plantation was situated near a distinctive promontory, which I recognised easily as we coasted along slowly following the shoreline. I collected all theStraits dollars we had and offered them to Yusof, but he waved the payment aside. In the end, I prevailed on him to accept my shirt, which he did with a broad smile.

We got off into the waist-deep surf and watched as the little boat tacked swiftly round and headed back north. The beach was deserted. There were no defenders in sight, which was a good thing for us. Evidently, this stretch of coast was not considered worth defending, since it was a good hour's drive away from Kuantan. I had been there many times before during my exile and the landmarks were like old friends to me. We walked along the beach barefoot, savouring the cool waves licking at our feet.

Rounding the promontory, we came into a small cove. To my surprise, there were four small flat-bottomed boats hauled up onto the sand. Some effort had been made to conceal them from the air as they were piled with coconut fronds. The promontory hid them from the sea.

Ormonde drew his revolver. My pistol was tucked into my waistband. I handed it over to Blake. I wasn't a soldier and didn't think I could actually bring myself to shoot someone if things got rough. We approached the boats cautiously. There was no one around. Some of the boats had bullet holes in them. We examined them carefully. Then Blake gave a low whistle. "Look 'ere," he said, pointing. I craned my neck to see over the side. There was a helmet under one of the benches. It wasn't British.

"IT SEEMS, gentlemen, that we've been overtaken by events," said Ormonde drily.

"What do we do now?" asked Blake. He looked around nervously.

Ormonde looked at me. "Is your friend far from here?"

"No, only about a mile. I don't think we've got much of a choice. The boat's gone and we can't jolly well hike all the way to Singapore."

Ormonde looked at the boats and made a quick calculation. "Thirty to a boat – unless there are more of them about, this looks more like a recce than an invasion. We'd better press on. Keep your eyes peeled."

We ran across the beach, carefully keeping within the tracks that the Japanese had left so as not to betray our presence. They didn't seem to have been concerned at all about covering their trail. Once we reached the cover of the undergrowth at the high-water mark, we paused and listened. There were only the sounds of the jungle.

Ormonde motioned me to take the lead. Reluctantly, I went forward, bent almost double.

"Stand up properly!" he whispered to me. "Act normally. They won't shoot civilians."

I wasn't entirely sure about that, but stood up anyway and tried to appear like a native out for an evening's stroll. Blake and Ormonde followed, keeping under cover as much as possible. It took us half an hour to cover the distance to Courtois' bungalow instead of the usual fifteen minutes.

THE bungalow was just as I had remembered it. There were lights on in the front room. On the evening breeze, I discerned the gravelly voice of Edith Piaf. I breathed a sigh of relief. "All clear," I said and sauntered up to the door. As always, it wasn't locked. Pausing only to knock once, I stepped into the living room.

Courtois was there, dishevelled, unshaven and twice as large as life. He was busy polishing one of his shotguns. Startled by my sudden appearance and no doubt disconcerted by my wild looks and strange dress, he snapped the shotgun shut and pointed it in my direction.

"Michel, non! C'est moi, Dennis!" I called out urgently.

"Dennis? C'est vraiment toi?" He blinked at me in amazement. Then a broad grin split his face, and he came up and gave me a gigantic hug. "Mon vieux! I did not think to see you again."

Ormonde and Blake entered. Courtois scowled and tightened his grip on his shotgun. I placed my hand on his arm. "They are friends."

"Anglais? Merde! I spit on the English." He actually spat, hitting the floor with a large moist gob.

"Charmed, I'm sure," said Ormonde, unperturbed.

"Hey, take it easy with me, mate," said Blake, "I'm Australian."

I explained to him briefly our predicament and begged for the use of his transmitter. He agreed reluctantly, and "only for friendship's sake" as he put it to me. He continued to glare hostilely at Ormonde. He led us to the room where his equipment was and indicated that we could use it.

I turned to Ormonde. "Do you know how to use this stuff? James did all that, so I haven't a clue where to start."

Ormonde nodded and took his place confidently in front of the transmitter. Referring to Thornton's codebook every now and then, he twiddled the knobs and fiddled the dials. The transmitter squawked into life. "Rainbow, this is Sunbeam. Rainbow, this is Sunbeam. Do you read me?" There was only the fizz of static in reply. He repeated himself over and over.

"The Japs must've hit the relay station near here too," I said despondently. Just at that moment, the static vanished. "Sunbeam, this is Rainbow. Identify yourself."

Ormonde flipped hurriedly through the codebook and said the password. "Rainbow, we must speak to Major Newman. Urgently."

There was a momentary hesitation at the other end. Then a familiar voice came on the air, "Who the devil's that? What d'you think you're playing at, transmitting in clear? Is that you, Thornton?"

I grabbed the microphone from Ormonde. "Major Newman, it's me, Chiang. Thornton's dead. I've got something important. There's a traitor passing our air recognition codes to the Japanese …" Ormonde interrputed. "You'll have to speak more slowly and clearly than that," he said.

Newman's voice crackled again on the transmitter. "Where the devil are you?"

"Kuantan, sir," I replied, "the house where we met."

"Stay there," he commanded. "Don't move. I'm coming to get you."

I felt a weight ascend from my shoulders. Blake was smiling broadly. Only Ormonde was serious. "This Major Newman, can he be trusted?"

"He's the chap who sent us out to Batu Sembilan," I replied. "As far as I can gather, he's in charge of anti-Japanese intelligence or something of the sort at Special Branch."

"Well," said Ormonde, "that's something." He turned to Courtois. "Have you seen the Japanese? Have they landed at Kuantan?"

Courtois scowled even more ferociously. I repeated the question more gently. He shook his head. Ormonde's brow creased. "There's at least a company of them out there. For all we know, they've got another invasion force off the coast."

"The Navy will stop them, surely?" I said. "They're in range of Singapore now. There are those two battleships."

"Yeah, mate," agreed Blake, "the Prince of Wales and Repulse. They'll show the bloody Nips a thing or two."

Courtois interrupted. "They will not stop the Japanese," he said shortly. We turned to him and stared. "You did not know? Today, the Japanese have sink both the *Prince of Wales* and *Repulse*. Near Kuantan. Poof! Gone. *Finis*."

23

IT TOOK some time for this to sink in. Ormonde left the room without a word. Blake sat down heavily in a chair, apparently stunned. The foundations of my world were rocking. I needed time to think. I went outside to clear my head. Instinctively, by force of habit, my feet took me along the path to the beach, where I had spent so many hours contemplating the ocean and eternity. The Japanese were completely forgotten. I stared out to sea knowing of course that there was nothing to be seen. The sound of the surf soothed me.

Events had moved so fast over the last three days, I hadn't had the opportunity to reflect on what was happening. My brain had been on autopilot while my body did what was necessary to survive. It was only now that I began to comprehend the significance of what had happened. I had always taken for granted that the British were superior to any Asiatic foe. The cocky confidence of the air- and ground-crewmen at Batu Sembilan was infectious and not a little comforting. The thought that the Japs could succeed in gaining a foothold in Malaya never crossed my mind for a moment.

But in just three days, the Japanese had not only successfully established a beachhead at Kota Bahru but also destroyed British air power in the north-east of the country. The despised Jap pilots had flown rings around the tubby Buffalos in their sleek Oscars and shot them out of the sky with scarcely any trouble. I had seen the invincible sahibs run at the rumour of the approach of enemy forces, like frightened rabbits with a fox on their tails. An entire Indian battalion had mutinied, shot its CO and evaporated, without a single shot being fired. There was a traitor – a British officer, no less – running loose, betraying our positions and secrets to the enemy. Now this – the pride of the Royal Navy, gone in the blink of an eye. This wasn't how it was supposed to be. It was too much to take in.

WHEN I returned, Blake and Ormonde had vanished. I found Courtois alone, still ministering to his guns. I sat down heavily.

"*Ça va?* It goes well with you?" he asked, looking up from his task.

I shook my head morosely. Courtois got up, went to his ice-box and thrust a bottle of beer into my hand. I leaned back in the chair and told him of what I had seen and experienced. He listened intently without comment.

"The bulletins are optimistic," Courtois said, at length. "They say the Japanese do not advance beyond the coast. They are being held by the valiant defenders and attacked by air."

I almost burst out in sarcastic laughter. "Attacked from the air by the valiant defenders? Thank God for 8th Indian Brigade. They're still holding on. Or were. Someone at least is salvaging the honour of the Empire."

"The little yellow men land here yesterday morning," Courtois said laconically.

I sat bolt upright. "Here? They landed here? Are they still around?"

He waved nonchalantly at the jungle. "They are out there."

"Didn't they bother you?"

"Me? Non, they come, they see, they go. I am not their enemy."

I was flabbergasted by his attitude. "They're allies of the Boches. They occupied French Indochina. And you say they are not your enemies?"

He shrugged his shoulders. "I am no friend of the English or the Vichy regime. I live here and do my business whoever may be in charge. Besides, I have a new patron."

I raised my eyebrows interrogatively. "A new boss? What do you mean, a new patron?"

"After you leave, the Japanese offer to buy my plantation. It is a good price. My brother is in accord. So we sell. I work for Mr Yamada now." His revelation rendered me speechless. "Stay with me, mon ami," he continued. "You do not belong with these English. They despise you and your people."

I shook my head. "No, Michel, I cannot. I have my family in Singapore. They need me more than ever now. I must return to them."

"I understand," he said shortly. He indicated that I should follow him to the radio room. He turned on the radio. We caught part of a bulletin. The announcer solemnly intoned that heavy fighting was taking place in northern Malaya and that our forces were counter-attacking the enemy vigorously. After a minute, I could stand it no longer. I turned away in disgust. He switched the radio off and put on a record. We listened to his whole collection twice through.

I TOLD Ormonde that the Japanese had visited the plantation and were still somewhere around. He received the news without comment, but insisted that we take turns keeping watch.

Nothing untoward happened. Wherever the Japanese may have been, they didn't seem to be interested in Courtois.

Shortly after daybreak, a car pulled up in front of the bungalow. A man got out, dressed in military uniform and bearing the pips and crown of a lieutenant-colonel on his shoulder straps. He was alone.

"Mr Newman," I said, advancing to greet him, "it's good to see you. Or should I say, Lieutenant-Colonel Newman?"

He took my outstretched hand with a firm grasp and pumped it up and down twice. "Mister will do fine. I have to wear this fancy dress so as not to get shot at while up here."

Ormonde joined us and gave a crisp salute, which Newman acknowledged. Blake managed a gesture which ended more as a half-hearted wave than a military courtesy. Courtois stood at the door and glowered at the newcomer. I made the introductions. Newman replied in fluent French, which mellowed Courtois a little.

He didn't waste much time on pleasantries. He had each of us report to him in turn. I was the last. He got to me after about an hour. As I sat down, he asked me, "Have you heard from Mr d'Almeida?"

That jolted me. I had assumed that d'Almeida was in contact. I shook my head. "No, we parted company … let's see, it must have been on Monday morning." Only three days ago. It seemed ages. "He said he was heading for Georgetown. I thought he had told you. I don't know where he is now."

Newman didn't comment. Instead, he asked me to recount my version of events. He asked the occasional probing question and jotted down details. I decided finally to do some probing of my own. "What's been happening down here? I know that the Japs have landed in the vicinity and sunk the *Prince of Wales* and *Repulse*. Have they taken Kuantan yet?

It was his turn to be jolted. "How did you know about the *Prince of Wales* and *Repulse*?"

I was confused for a moment. "So it isn't true? Courtois told us about it yesterday ..."

His brow darkened. "Yes, it's true, but the news wasn't public yesterday. How did your friend Courtois know?"

I felt a lump of apprehension rise in my throat. "He said that the Japanese came to see him – I don't know if that was before or after the sinking. The Japs own this plantation. His boss is a Mr Nada or Yamada or something like that."

Newman's eyebrows rose. "Yamada Takeyoshi?"

"I don't know for certain, he never told me the full name."

"I think," said Newman seriously, "we should have a talk with your Monsieur Courtois."

COURTOIS wasn't overjoyed to be bossed around in his own house. I was afraid he would blow up and reach for the guns. It took all my powers of persuasion to get him to agree to speak to Newman. He finally consented, albeit with bad grace. Ormonde and Blake were present too, as reinforcements. I'm not sure whether the four of us could have handled him though, if he had chosen to give trouble.

To ease the atmosphere, Newman spoke in French. I struggled to keep up. It was clear from Ormonde's expression that he was completely lost.

"Monsieur, it appears that you have sources of information that keep you well apprised of military matters, is that not so? I refer specifically to the matter of the sinking of the battleship HMS *Prince of Wales* and the battlecruiser HMS *Repulse* shortly after noon yesterday."

"What of it?" demanded Courtois truculently.

"The information about the sinkings was not public yesterday evening. May I know how you learned so quickly of these events?"

There was a silence. Courtois stared at Newman, who stared steadily back. It was a test of wills. After what seemed like an eternity, Courtois spoke.

"I see no reason to dissimulate. I was told by Yamada-san. He is the owner of this estate and my boss."

"Mr Yamada Takeyoshi, I assume?"

"Yes, that is so."

"Mr Yamada Takeyoshi is a known Japanese spy," said Newman. "We have been looking for him ever since the outbreak of war. Do you know where he is now?"

Courtois shook his head emphatically. "I do not know."

"You knew of his activities? He asked you to help him?"

"He said nothing to me of these. He only demanded of me on Tuesday evening that I should send a signal. Then yesterday afternoon, he let me know that the British ships were sunk near Kuantan. Beyond this, I have no knowledge."

"You have the signal that he asked you to send?"

"No, it is destroyed."

"Was it in English?"

"Yes. I was instructed to send it in Morse."

"You recall what it said?"

Courtois paused. He seemed uncertain whether to proceed. Newman waited. Finally, Courtois said, "The message concerned a Japanese invasion at Kuantan. It said that a Japanese force had landed and were fighting on the beach. It ended with a codeword, which I have forgotten."

Newman sighed deeply. "What did he say?" whispered Ormonde to me. "What on earth's going on?"

Newman answered, switching to English, "What's going on is that this gentleman has been the cause of the loss of Force Z and the death of a thousand British sailors. He sent a signal stating that the Japanese had landed at Kuantan. Admiral Philips was informed and decided to intercept the invasion force. His ships were caught without air cover, because of the loss of the fields around Kota Bahru and the evacuation of RAF Kuantan. The rest you know."

"You bloody bastard!" exclaimed Blake. "You should be shot!"

Courtois rounded on him. "Hold your tongue, *crapule*! I did not know the signification of the message I was asked to send. But now I know, and I am glad."

"Glad?" said Newman in a shocked tone. "At the death of a thousand of your allies?"

"*Oui*, I am glad," responded Courtois. "I owe no fidelity to the English. They kill my son François."

The English killed your son?" said Newman, confused.

"*Oui*! At Mers-el-Kébir. François was on the battleship *Bretagne*. The cursed English, they sink the *Bretagne*."

"That can't be!" I interjected. "You've got it wrong. It must have been the *Boches*."

"No," said Newman heavily, "he's right. The Royal Navy attacked the French fleet at Mers-el-Kébir shortly after the capitulation. Several ships were sunk. There was heavy loss of life."

I was thunderstruck. "Why in God's name …? They were our allies!"

"The exigencies of war. We couldn't risk letting the Jerries get their hands on the French ships. It's not something we're proud of," replied Newman wearily.

"I did not know when Yamada-san ask me to send the message that it would cause the sinking of the English ships," said Courtois fiercely. "But it is – how you say – poetic justice. My son is avenged. Do with me what you will."

24

THERE didn't seem much to say after that. I gazed forlornly at Courtois, who stared woodenly back. Newman gave instructions that he was to be placed under guard. Blake led him off to his bedroom. He didn't resist.

"Who is this Yamada fellow?" I asked when they had gone. "Is he part of the Shigeru Tate network?"

"No, not as far as we know," replied Newman. "We think it's a separate group altogether, based in Georgetown."

"Georgetown," mused Ormonde. "He must be Narayanan's controller. Or at least part of that network."

"Perhaps," said Newman in a serious tone, "but that's something we'll have to untangle later. Right now, we're going to have to get back to Singapore and take Courtois with us. It may be ticklish if there are Japs in the vicinity. How many did you say there were?"

Ormonde answered, "We counted four boats on the beach. At thirty men a boat, I make it a reinforced company at least. Of course, we don't know how many there may be elsewhere along the coast."

"What are they doing here?" I asked. "Have they attacked Kuantan?"

"No," replied Newman, "There was some firing the night

before. We haven't established the exact cause, but it appears that the Garhwals spotted something and opened up. That set off the artillery all along the beach. Some panicky blighter signalled that a major attack was in progress."

"We found bullet holes in some of the boats, and bloodstains," commented Ormonde.

"There's been no follow-up attack. I'd guess that they were probing our defences."

"Is that Yamada still out there with them?" asked Ormonde. "He might be leading the Jap force or at least guiding them to the airfield."

"It's a fair bet that he is, from what Courtois said. You got here when? Last night? Force Z went down some time after noon. Yamada told Courtois about it yesterday afternoon, according to him. That wouldn't give Yamada time to get far. He must still be somewhere in the vicinity."

"Who's defending the airfield?" asked Ormonde.

Newman laughed shortly, without mirth. "No one. It was the same story again as at Batu Sembilan and Kota Bahru. There was a raid on the 9th. The RAF and Australians got the wind up and left. There's something definitely wrong with our bloody troops. They've all bolted to Singapore. That was why Force Z had no air cover for its sortie. Yamada must have known this and baited the trap with the false news of an invasion."

"How will we get back to Singapore then?"

"My aircraft's still at Kuantan – or should be, assuming that our chaps haven't abandoned the beach defences and bolted too. Panic is an ugly thing and damned difficult to stop once it gets started. I saw it at Caporetto in '17. Once an army starts to run, there's no knowing where it will end up. The Japs hadn't cut the road when I drove here, but we can't count on that now. Is there another road from here to the town?" he asked, turning to me.

"Nothing metalled," I answered, "but there's miles of estate tracks and roads. There's no map, though."

"Monsieur Courtois would know, I'm sure," said Newman. "You'll have to persuade him to cooperate and not lead us into an ambush. We leave within the hour." He strode off with a quick salute.

"Right," said Ormonde briskly, "we'd better get ourselves organised. Dennis, you and Blake see to Courtois. I'll take care of the radio equipment."

I felt uneasy. Something was nagging at the back of my mind.

I CHECKED the safety catch of my pistol as I cautiously pushed open the door. He was sitting with his back to me as I entered. Despite my best attempt to move quietly, he caught the sound of my entrance and spun round in his chair.

"Dennis," said Ormonde, "you startled me, sneaking in like that. Are we ready to go?"

"You were supposed to have destroyed the radio. Who have you been calling?"

"No one, old boy," he replied. "Just having a last listen to the news before we go." At that precise moment, the radio squawked to life. The words were incomprehensible to me. But I knew that I had heard that language before – spoken by my barber Takeda to his wife.

"It's Japanese, isn't it?"

He saw the levelled pistol in my hand and smiled. "Do put that thing away, old boy," he said, "before you do yourself an injury." He calmly stood up. I raised the pistol threateningly. His smile widened. "It's empty, you know."

I hesitated. "Check it if you don't believe me," he said smoothly.

I didn't know whether to accept his word. He reached into his pocket. I squeezed the trigger more in reaction than as a conscious act. The hammer clicked harmlessly. Ormonde withdrew his hand. There were eight bullets in it. "I took them out last night."

"Why did you do it?" I asked, letting my hand drop to my side. I felt very weary.

"Do what?"

"Kill James."

"Did I?"

A sudden anger blazed in me. "Don't play games with me! I've had enough! You're the traitor, not Davenport!"

He smiled his infuriating smile. "All right, have it your way. I'm the traitor, not Davenport. Are you satisfied?"

"You gave yourself away just now," I said, struggling to keep my voice calm. "You said that Narayanan was part of Yamada's Georgetown group. D'Almeida only told me about the Georgetown connection with Narayanan when I saw him off. James wasn't there and neither were you. You couldn't have known – unless you knew already who Narayanan was in contact with."

His self-assurance slipped for a moment, but he regained his composure almost immediately. "Ah, a mistake on my part. Rather careless of me. So, your friend's name is d'Almeida. I must remember that." I cursed myself for having given that information away. With a fluid, snake-like movement, Ormonde drew his revolver from its holster. "Whatever shall I do with you now?"

"Are you going to shoot me too? I'll turn around now so you can do it in the back like you shot James." I was so angry I didn't know what I was saying.

He pretended to wince. "A low blow that, old boy. I didn't want to kill James."

"Then why?"

"Honestly, I really didn't want to kill James. But he realised when we were in Davenport's room that there was one other person who had access to the air recognition codes on a regular basis."

"You."

Ormonde nodded. "Yes, me."

"Why didn't you just kill me too and get it over with there and then?"

"I would have," he said cold-bloodedly, "but with all those mutineers around, it seemed that you might be useful – and you were. And then you had that brilliant idea of heading south to Kuantan to use your friend's radio. It would have been stupid of me to do it before then."

"And Davenport, your confederate? How did he get away?"

"Davenport?" laughed Ormonde. "Damned if I know. He might have buzzed off with the rest. I've really no idea, old boy. I doubt he had any inkling of what was going on."

I was confused. "But he suspected me."

He laughed again. "Poor Davenport wouldn't have recognised a spy if one came up and coshed him on the head. Davenport is the sort of chap who can't tell one native from another. I'd be surprised if he could even recognise you again. I told you that he suspected you, just as I told James that he had the transmitter hidden in the typewriter. It was, shall we say, a form of insurance for me in case the story of the traitor got out. You and James – had he lived – would have sworn that Davenport was the man. Even Blake has it in his head that Davenport is a spy."

"So it was you all along," I said bitterly. "Even when you and James were … were …"

"Yes," he said shortly, "Even when we were together. James wasn't cut out for this cloak-and-dagger business. I saw within the first week what he was up to. But I must admit that you took me by surprise. I really had no idea, until that day when you caught us together. My compliments."

"And what happens now?"

"What happens is that we wait. The Japanese are coming. I've made contact. They know that the head of the anti-Japanese section of Special Branch is here. It's quite a coup. All thanks to you."

I felt a sense of bitter failure. He was right, of course. Newman was there because of me. "Why?" I asked despairingly. "With all the privileges and advantages you've had, why betray your King and country to the Japanese?"

He laughed out loud this time. "With all me privileges and advantages, is it now?"

I recoiled in astonishment. The upper-crust accent was gone.

He smiled sardonically. "I see I've surprised you, me lad. Allow me to introduce meself. Sean Collins, at your service." He made a mocking bow. "Spawned and raised in the most ignorant, backward, benighted corner o' Connemara. It's Irish, I am. No subject of your King George, now."

I was dumbstruck. The transformation was so complete. "But I wasn't content to remain Sean Collins from Connemara all me life. I had some little talent, which brought me some little renown at the varieties. I reached the dizzy heights of the Abbey Theatre, Dublin. But it was the good life that I was after. So," he continued, resuming the aristocratic voice, "I became Michael Ormonde, gentleman and man-about-town."

"And spy and traitor."

"Ah, yes, well that came later. The good life was expensive. My creditors became a little too pressing. I thought it best to leave the country. I came out here, eventually. A White man can live very well in the East, on credit most of the time."

"How did you get involved with the Japs?"

"I see that I'm going to have to tell you my life's story," he said, with a sarcastic edge. "Let's just say that they took advantage of my little peccadillos. Careless of me. I was lured into a compromising position. Once I was caught, it was either cooperate or be exposed. But later, I came to appreciate the monetary advantages as well. Credit doesn't last forever, even for a gentleman."

"I should have known," I said bitterly. "You can't tell Greek from Latin. And you don't even speak a word of French. I should have realised right away that you weren't a public-school boy."

He smiled his most maddening, infuriating smile at me. "Yes, isn't it deliciously ironic? Here you are, an old Fentonian, a real Cambridge man. Your accent's genuine. And here I am, with my fake accent and background, pretending to be what you are. Yet, you're just a Chink, a native, while I'm a …"

He never got to finish the sentence. Blake, who had crept up behind him through the other door while he was speaking, whacked him hard over the head with a plank. "Bloody bastard Pommie poofter," he said with great feeling.

25

NEWMAN said, "So you were right about Ormonde."

"What do we do about him now?"

"I say we take the bastard outside and shoot him right away," answered Blake. Ormonde was sitting on the floor, nursing the back of his head. For once, he seemed not to have anything to say.

"Tempting as that might be," responded Newman, "he's more valuable to us alive. Shooting him won't solve our immediate problem either. The odds are now three to two rather than four to one. We can't watch him and Courtois, and fight the Japs."

I felt I had to speak up. "We could let Courtois go," I said slowly.

Blake stared at me as if I had just confessed to hereditary insanity. Newman said nothing.

"I don't think Michel is dangerous," I continued. "He's got this great anger against the world and he dislikes the British intensely, but I don't think he's actively helping the Japs. He didn't deliberately set out to sink those battleships. All he did was take instructions from his boss. If we let him go, he might help us get away. As you said, the odds are stacked against us otherwise."

Newman made up his mind. "Come," he said to me shortly.

Courtois was sitting on the edge of his bed, holding the framed picture of François and staring at it. He didn't look up when we unlocked the door and entered.

"Your friend Chiang has been pleading your case," said Newman. "He says that you aren't working with the Japanese. Are you?"

Courtois looked directly at Newman. At that moment, I realised that he was an old man, tired of the world and tired of being angry. "No," he replied shortly.

"We are going to leave now," continued Newman. "You may come or you may stay. If you choose to come, it will be as a free man. If you choose to stay, we will respect your choice. But I must tell you that the Japanese are returning to this house."

"I stay."

"Michel, come with us," I pleaded. "We have caught their traitor. It is the English officer Ormonde – or Collins, as I should call him. The Japs may hold you responsible."

"*Non, mon ami*," he replied wearily, "this is my home. I stay. The little yellow men will not hurt me."

I knew that I wouldn't change his mind. Time was short. I grasped his hand firmly and shook it.

"I will do what I can to detain the Japanese here as long as I am able. *Bonne chance, mon vieux*. How you say it in English – good fortune? Until we meet again."

"Take care of yourself. Until we meet again, my friend," I replied. Without looking back, I left to join Newman and Blake.

ORMONDE remained unflustered by the prospect of being taken out and possibly shot. He was a cool one, I'll grant him that. We left Courtois' house by the back door, having first disabled the car so it would not be of any use to the Japs. Newman had changed into mufti. Keeping a wary eye about us, we headed down a jungle path in the general direction of Kuantan. I had a vague idea where to go, but beyond the estate, the terrain was unfamiliar to me.

The sun was high when we started. It was stifling among the trees, with not a whisper of wind to cool us. I was in the lead, dressed in my sarong and singlet, followed by Ormonde and Newman with Blake bringing up the rear. It wasn't an arrangement I would have chosen myself, but it was hard to deny Newman's two-fold argument that I was the only one who knew any part of the way and that if we bumped into any Japs, they would be less likely to shoot a native than a white man. I wasn't so sure about the second bit myself, but he didn't seem to be in the mood to be argued with.

After about an hour, the trail petered out at the bank of a small stream.

"I don't know the way from here," I said to Newman.

"Follow the stream-bed," he replied. "It must lead to the sea. We'll keep to the coast."

I splashed into the stream, grateful for the cool lapping of the water around my ankles. The stream was shallow and pebbly, with the occasional deeper hole. Fortunately, the water was clear, so I could see the obstacles. The rocks were slippery and the going was slow. But after another hour, we heard the unmistakable sound of the surf. The jungle soon gave way to a more open terrain of coconut palms and sand. The sea lay beyond a thin white ribbon of sand. My legs were aching with the unaccustomed exercise of pushing through water. I was looking forward to throwing myself down on the beach and having a good rest. Then I saw them. I stopped suddenly and held up my hand to caution the others to be quiet.

Newman came up. "What is it?"

I pointed. A hundred yards away where the stream met the ocean stood four men. Three were short of stature, carrying rifles almost as tall as themselves. The fourth was a white man, dressed in khaki shorts and shirt, and wearing a solar topee. "What do we do now?"

Newman was silent for a while. Then he appeared to make up his mind. "Corporal," he said quietly, handing his Webley to Blake, "keep out of sight and keep this man covered. If he so much as squeaks, blow his head off." He beckoned to me. "Give me your Luger," he said. "I need you to come with me. Act as if it's perfectly natural for us to be out for a stroll in the jungle."

With my heart in my mouth, I walked ahead of him by the side of the stream. He had the Luger pointed right at my back. I wasn't sure what was in his mind, but I didn't like the possibilities.

The party spotted us. The Japs brought their rifles to the ready.

"*Nicht schießen! Wir sind Freunde!* Don't shoot! We're friends!" called out Newman, waving the Luger. I was taken totally aback. I hadn't known that Newman was fluent in German. He spoke it like a native.

The white man started at the sound and indicated to the others to lower their weapons. He was evidently confused at this sudden apparition emerging from the jungle speaking perfect German and claiming to be a friend.

"*Wer sind Sie?* Who are you?" he asked uncertainly, with a strong south German accent.

"*Oberstleutnant von Talheim,*" replied Newman, "*und Sie?* And you are …?"

The man's Japanese companions stared uncomprehendingly during the exchange. "*Ich?*" he responded, still not quite sure how to react, "*Ich bin Sergent-Chef Werner Pflug.*" We continued walking towards them. The hairs on the back of my neck prickled. The Japanese soldiers watched us warily.

"*Von der Fremdenlegion?*" continued Newman in a commanding Teutonic tone, moving ever closer.

"*Jawohl, herr Oberstleutnant. Ich war …*" He never finished. We had gotten within ten paces of the party now. With expert aim, Newman put two shots into each of the enemy soldiers. They hadn't time to react. They crumpled in a heap, with hardly a cry. I will never forget the expression of agonised astonishment on Sergent-Chef Werner Pflug's face as he slowly toppled over. I was frozen into immobility with shock.

"Corporal Blake!" yelled Newman. "Get the prisoner out here now! We'd better get going immediately." He prodded the corpses with his foot to make sure they were all well and truly dead.

I was still shaken. "Did you have to do that?"

"Yes," he replied shortly. "There was no other way. Get a move on. Others may be around. If they heard the shots, we'll have a hornets' nest on our tail soon. Have you any more ammunition?"

Dumbly, I passed him a fresh clip. He jammed it determinedly into the Luger, casting an eye over his shoulder.

"How did you know he was German?" I asked.

"We've had reports that the Japanese have been recruiting Germans from the French Foreign Legion garrison in Indochina. I guessed he was one of them — a calculated risk."

"And if you'd been wrong?"

"If I'd been wrong, we'd be dead."

We ran along in silence. Ormonde was very white. Evidently, he hadn't expected such ruthlessness. We put a couple of miles between us and the patrol before we stopped for breath. I was gasping for air and bathed in sweat.

"Five minutes, no more," said Newman. "Then we move again."

"Bloody slave driver," said Blake to me under his breath. "What did he say to that poor bugger there?"

"Save your sympathy," I replied, still trying to catch my breath. "That 'poor bugger' was a German working with the Japs. If Newman hadn't bluffed him into believing that he was German too, we'd be lying there instead of them."

That put paid to the conversation. We got back on our feet and headed south. I was so tired I could hardly think. I willed myself forward while every bone and muscle in my body protested.

I DON'T remember much about the rest of that terrible day. My body was burning and my mind was numb. All I have is a jumbled recollection of having to press on, constantly dogged by the fear that theenemy was on our heels. Once we stopped and hid in a copse of nipah palms while a Japanese patrol passed within touching distance. Newman stuffed a handkerchief into Ormonde's mouth to stop him crying out. I don't think it was necessary. He had a very strong sense of self-preservation. Having seen what Newman was capable of, he probably had no desire to test his resolve.

It was after nightfall when we were picked up by a patrol of Indian troops. They brought us to their officer, a young lieutenant who had the presence of mind to immediately send us back under escort to battalion headquarters. Once Newman had established his identity to their satisfaction, we were treated much better. There was hotfood and a soft bed. My head was breaking and I could hardly think. My body ached all over. The medical officer gave me a dose of something unspeakably bitter, which brought me welcome relief.

The following morning, just before daybreak, we were transported to the airfield at Kuantan. Newman's aircraft was still parked on the tarmac. It was a Hudson – an unlovely, rotund crate, but to me a vision of deliverance. Ormonde was seated between two hefty MPs. Newman and I had somewhat more comfortable seats forward. Blake had been allowed to rejoin the RAAF contingent – whatever remained of it in Kuantan after their precipitate flight three days before.

When we landed in Singapore, it was nearly noon. Fortunately, the Japanese didn't have any fighters in the air. Our lumbering Hudson would have been a sitting duck – or more precisely, a flying one. There was a staff car waiting. Newman got into it. "Do you need a lift?" he asked. I climbed in gratefully. My whole body was aching. My head was throbbing and my eyes felt as if they were going to drop out of their sockets. Newman gave instructions to his driver. The car pulled up on the gravel drive in front of the house. I stumbled wearily out of it. I couldn't focus. I saw dim shapes congregate on the steps. I felt their arms as they rushed forward to embrace me, heard the voices but could not make out the words. All this while, I had been holding on for the moment of return. Now I could hold on no longer. Everything went black.

26

IT TOOK me a week to get over my illness. Actually, it wasn't as serious as it sounds. After two continuous days of sleep, I felt much better. But Mak insisted that I stay in bed. She brought me a constant stream of kueh and fruits, plumped up my pillows regularly, supplied me with reading material and fed me all my favourite dishes. The entire household was mobilised to pander to my wants. I had no incentive whatsoever to oppose Mak. I had been away for two long years. I missed being pampered and fussed over. Upon Mak's insistence, I was kept isolated from visitors and world events. No newspapers were allowed at my sickbed. The radio was turned off. That suited me fine. I had had enough of the world outside.

From the girls, I pieced together an idea of what had been happening during my absence. They took turns to come into my room and nibble my delicacies. They told me that Mr d'Almeida had retired to the Cameron Highlands and left Cuthbert in charge of the firm. I tried hard to appear surprised by this news. Raja Aziz had left to join the army. George had been promoted to junior partner in his place and was making a name for himself at the bar. Ralph was still with the firm, but wasn't happy with the new arrangements. Cuthbert left the running of the firm very much to George, who apparently turned out to be a hard taskmaster.

Ralph wasn't the ambitious sort but I surmised that the fact that George had been promoted to partner while he remained merely an assistant rankled somewhat. Still, he couldn't afford to leave, and with the advent of the baby felt increasingly under pressure to be a good provider.

I discovered with astonishment that d'Almeida had continued to pay my full salary to Mak all the time I had been away. There was no need for him to have done so. Neither Mak nor the girls had any idea where I had been, since that would have defeated the purpose of my exile. They thought that I was working for the d'Almeidas up-country, not realising that I had actually left the firm. Of course, after I started with Special Branch, no one kept them informed either. All they had been told was that the firm would forward letters to me; which it did, by way of Newman and Special Branch.

I ached to tell them what I had been up to. But when I signed up, along with the cloak and the dagger, they issued an oath of secrecy which I was obliged to take. The oath wouldn't have stopped me, but for d'Almeida. With him still out in the field, I felt that it would be a betrayal of confidence for me to say anything. I contented myself with telling people that I had been in Kuantan, omitting to mention the events up north. As far as everyone was concerned, I had been sitting safely on the sidelines all this time.

There was little anxiety in the house about the progress of the war. The first air raid on 8th December had shocked everyone, naturally. The docks had been hit badly, as had Chinatown. But the official bulletins were optimistic and glossed over the damage. After the first week, the air raids ceased. The news from the front was censored. As far as the civilian population was concerned, the fighting was far away. Life jogged on almost normally. Of course, it was impossible to hide the loss of the *Prince of Wales* and *Repulse*. This jarred confidence a little. But Mak and the girls had a naïve

– one might almost say blind – faith in the ability of the British to defend Malaya. It was all I could do to hold my tongue, but I did so anyway. There was no need to upset them unnecessarily. After all, I told myself, the British would probably hold the enemy somewhere up north, far from the great fortress of Singapore. Setbacks were to be expected in wartime. In the end, the Empire would triumph, as it always had.

The only one who had any suspicion that not all was well was May. She had quit her job upon getting married, but when war broke out, she volunteered to return to the hospital. She had seen some of the casualties of war. Survivors of Force Z were brought to her ward – burnt, maimed, yet in remarkably good spirits. But from them, she learnt the awful truth that the great behemoths had sallied forth without air cover and had been sunk without even engaging the enemy. It was a sobering revelation for her. She alone among the girls talked about the war. Mostly, she spoke about her work and about Ralph being away nights. He had signed up as an air-raid warden with the local ARP. She didn't directly ask me about my experiences. She just skirted around them, as though afraid to broach the subject directly. Until one afternoon, a week after my return, she said to me uncertainly, "All is going well up-country?"

I hesitated. I wasn't keen on lying to May. I temporised. "What have you heard?"

"Nothing, nothing," she said, shaking her head. After a pause, she sighed deeply and went on, "All those young boys, so many killed, so many hurt. So sayang. They say it is impossible to win against the Japanese. They are not confident."

"It was a complete mess up north," I said. "There was confusion all over. The fighting was a lot worse than what you've been told here."

"You were up there, at the fighting?" she asked, surprised. "I thought you said you were all the time in Kuantan."

I bit my lip. "You mustn't tell anyone else. Both me and Mr d'Almeida were there, at Kota Bahru. Don't ask me why. Things didn't go well."

"So the Japanese are winning?" she asked with alarm.

I regretted having said so much. "No, not exactly," I replied, trying to assuage her obvious concern, "but the British haven't been doing too well – not as well as the newspapers and bulletins would like us to believe. But don't worry. The enemy's hundreds of miles away. They won't get here for months – if ever. They've got to cover the whole length of Malaya."

"The Japanese have captured Penang," said May shortly. "All the white people were rescued. All the Chinese and Indians and Malays were left behind."

I was stunned. "Penang? When?"

"The whites were taken off on December 13th, the day you came back. We do not know when the Japanese came exactly, but it must be soon after that."

My thoughts turned immediately to d'Almeida. "How do you know this?" I asked her, somewhat roughly in my agitation.

"The Government has just announced it," she replied, in a tone of reproach. "But we knew before that. We had some casualties in the wards. They told us of the bombing of Georgetown and the rush to get away. Only the white people were given the chance to escape by the Government. The rest had to stay behind and wait for the Japanese. People in the hospital talked of nothing else. The Asiatic staff were very upset. Matron had to give us one of her talks."

"None of the Asiatics got away?"

"Surely some did, but not with the Government's help. People are still angry."

I swung myself out of bed and started rummaging in the almeirah for my clothes.

"Where are you going?" asked May, shocked.

"To find out about Mr d'Almeida," I replied. "He was in Georgetown. I have to know if he got away."

I rushed out without even saying goodbye to Mak. The only thing I could think of was the possibility that d'Almeida might be trapped behind Japanese lines, pursuing a dangerous adversary to the death.

SINCE I HAD no way of contacting Newman, my only thought was to get back to the office and try to pick up the scent from there. Walking down through Government House Domain, I was disconcerted by the difference since I had been there last. Here and there were craters marring the perfection of the lawns. Soldiers in full kit were at the sentry posts. Just as I got down to Orchard Road, the sirens sounded.

For a moment, I stood transfixed. There had been a respite from the raids after the first week, so my convalescence had been untroubled by sirens and bombs. I saw people scurrying for the nearest cover. There weren't any air raid shelters. I later discovered that some genius in government had thought that it was impossible to dig shelters because of the high water-table. People cowered in doorways and under tables, wherever there might have been a modicum of cover. I had been in the middle of an air raid before. The prospect no longer petrified me. Gathering up my courage and trusting to luck, I ran down the deserted road towards the city. No one else was about. Orchard Road was empty, a ghost of its normal self. It was surreal.

Far off, I heard the crump of bombs and the coughing of the ack-ack guns. I saw in the distance that the bombers were over the harbour, their position marked by angry black puffs of anti-aircraft fire. When I reached the junction of Bras Basah Road, I had to jump for my life when a convoy of fire engines and ambulances sped along at full speed with bells clanging, heading towards the docks and Chinatown. Smoke was already rising from there. The all-clear sounded. There was no sign at all of any of our fighters.

I trudged past the familiar landmarks in their unfamiliar guise. Some were boarded up, most had windows reinforced with tape. There were sand-bagged emplacements at road junctions. After the all-clear, people were back on the streets again, intent on their business, as if the air raid had been a passing shower. Bicycles were all over the place. There didn't seem to be any petrol rationing, judging by the number of vehicles streaming back and forth. It was a strange sensation being back in the big city after so long away. I felt a vague sense of discomfort being surrounded by so many people. I crossed Cavanagh Bridge towards the GPO. Everything looked normal. Then I saw a collapsed building a couple of hundred yards along the quay, smoke streaming from the smouldering facade. There were little black shapes in front of it covered with cloths and newspapers. A small crowd milled around, morbidly curious about the sight of death. I had seen enough of death to last me a lifetime. I continued determinedly on my way without glancing back.

THE OFFICE gate was shut when I got there. I had long ago misplaced my pass-key, so I rattled the grille until someone appeared. It was Moraiss, the Chief Clerk. If he was surprised to see me, he didn't show it. "So you have come back," he said laconically.

"Yes, I'm back," I replied. I had an irrational urge to hug him, just to see how he would react. I contented myself with shaking his hand, however. "Nice to see you again, Moraiss. Is Mr d'Almeida here?"

"Mr d'Almeida has gone home."

For one moment, my spirits rose. Then I remembered.

240 | <small>THE DEVIL TO PAY</small>

"Mr Cuthbert, you mean?"

Moraiss looked at me strangely. "Yes, Mr Cuthbert."

I left it at that and went up to my old haunts.

George was in his room. He got up immediately when he saw me and came to shake my hand. "Look what the cat's dragged in," he exclaimed jovially. "We knew you were back, of course. May told us but your mother wouldn't let us see you. With good cause, I see. You're looking bloody awful."

I smiled ruefully at him. "I feel bloody awful. It's been a rotten two years. I don't suppose they've caught Lim Beow Sin?" He shook his head.

I was indifferent. Somehow, it didn't matter so much now. "You've been prospering at any rate," I commented.

"Not exactly prospering, but I can't complain. Pull up a pew and fill me in on what you've been up to." He offered me a cigarette and a chair. I took the latter and slumped down tiredly.

"I'm surprised you're still in business."

"Why shouldn't I be? Life goes on. The Blitz didn't stop London. A few Jap bombers now and then won't stop us."

"May tells me that Ralph has joined the ARP as a warden. And I heard that Aziz got a commission in the Malay Regiment. What about you? Have you signed up with the Volunteers?"

"Me? They wouldn't want me. They haven't reached the bottom of the barrel yet," said George in a mocking tone. "Anyway, they're not sure they want to arm the natives. The heaven-born mandarins of the Malayan Civil Service would have a collective fit. They can't bring themselves to think of us as allies rather than coolies. I have it on good authority that the non-European companies of the Volunteers aren't issued any ammunition. Besides, they're doing very well without me, if you believe the newspapers."

I decided to tell George everything. I needed to unburden myself. It took me the better part of an hour. He didn't interrupt.

When I got to the end, he stood up wordlessly and rummaged through a pile of papers on his desk. "Read that," he said, handing me a newspaper.

I looked at the column he indicated. It was the Order of the Day for Tuesday, December 9th, signed by no less exalted a personage than His Excellency Sir Shenton Thomas Whitelegge Thomas, Governor of the Straits Settlements and High Commissioner to the Malay States. I racked my brain to remember what I had been doing then. It was the day we had escaped from Batu Sembilan and met Subedar-Major Rajindar Singh and his men defending the beach. I read the Order. "We have had plenty of warning and our preparations are made and tested," it went. "We are confident. Our defences are strong and our weapons efficient ..."

"Bloody hell!" I exclaimed.

"Read that bit," said George, pointing to the end of the column. "Go on, out loud."

"Let us all remember that we here in the Far East form part of the great campaign for the preservation of truth and justice and freedom," I read. I stopped abruptly. My fists were clenched around the edges of the paper. I unclenched them slowly.

"Did they read this out in Penang, I wonder?" said George, gently taking the mangled sheet out of my hands.

"D'Almeida's in Georgetown. Or would have been, if he'd made it that far. Didn't anyone get out besides the Europeans?" I breathed in deeply, striving to master my emotions.

"Not that I know," said George. "I'll nose around and see what I can find out. It's really bad luck about d'Almeida. I wish there was something we could do. The only silver lining is that d'Almeida can take care of himself. All we can do is wait."

"Can't you think of anything?"

"No," replied George seriously. "We can't go haring off to Penang to look for him. It's behind enemy lines, and I don't suppose they'd let us through even if we ask politely."

"You don't seem surprised, despite the newspapers and the Orders of the Day," I commented. "Did you know how badly things were going?"

"I had my suspicions," said George slowly. "I've been following the personal announcements."

I didn't quite understand. "The personals?"

"Every time a new batch of refugees comes into town, there's a whole slew of announcements in the personals – so-and-so from wherever would like to contact Mr X, that sort of thing. And there are the announcements by the banks of branches that have been 'temporarily closed due to circumstances beyond our control'. I've been plotting the names of the towns on the map. It isn't a pretty picture."

It was too depressing. I changed the subject. "And how's Daphne?"

"Daphne?" said George with a short laugh. His brow darkened momentarily but the expression was gone in a flash. "Daphne's fine, I suppose. I haven't seen her for ages."

I perked up at that. "You broke it off then?"

"There wasn't anything to break off. It just … ended," he said insouciantly. "She met that magistrate friend of yours. What's his name… Higgins."

"Higgins …? You don't mean Bernie Higgins?"

"Yes, I was foolish enough to introduce them at the Bar dinner and dance. That was that. Like called to like and she was gone."

"Bernie Higgins? You're sure it's the same one?" I said with astonishment. Bernie was one of my oldest friends. We were in the same college in Cambridge. He was bookish, awkward and introverted, the complete opposite of George. Any decent bookmaker would have given very long odds on Bernie stealing a girl from George.

Anyway, I didn't hear clearly the rest of what George said. All I could think of was that Daphne was now available. For a brief moment, I wondered whether I should tell him of my own interest in Daphne. It seemed to me that there was an edge beneath the veneer of indifference. Perhaps he was still interested. I decided against it. He didn't own her.

I stayed a few minutes longer, then made my excuses and left. All through my exile, the companion I had missed most was Daphne. Having at last found someone to talk to, the deprivation was all the harder to bear. In Kuantan, I had been marooned in the middle of an intellectual desert. There was no one to have a decent conversation with. I tried with Chidambaram; his orchids provided me better companionship. I had nursed no hopes and no dreams about Daphne, knowing of George's interest and George's talents. Now that the way was free, I was determined not to let the opportunity slip.

It was only when I got to the bottom of the stairs leading to her flat that the cold grip of reason slowed me down. What if she had forgotten me? What if she was indifferent? I stood at the foot of the staircase, uncertain. Should I give up this fool's errand and just go home, dignity intact? What did I want? A romantic relationship? An intellectual partnership? A platonic friendship? I didn't know exactly what I had in mind. All I knew was that I had to try or regret it for the rest of my life.

I mounted the steps with trepidation. It was the same as I remembered it. I knocked on the door. Perhaps she was out. My courage failed me and I turned to go. The door opened. It was she. She recognised me. "You!" she exclaimed, and slammed the door in my face.

27

I WAS nonplussed. It certainly wasn't a reaction that I had expected. I went back downstairs, feeling utterly foolish. I hadn't gone ten steps when I heard the door open.

"Dennis," she called. "Come back. I'm sorry. It was unforgivably rude of me."

I hesitated momentarily, struggling with my wounded pride. Pride gave in without much of a fight. I went back up. "It's good to see you, Daphne," I said.

"I apologise," she said, taking my proffered hand and shaking it somewhat formally. "It was ... it was a shock seeing you there like that. It's been a long time."

She seemed agitated. I thought it a good sign. Indifference would have killed all hope. "Yes, it's been a long time. I'm sorry I haven't ..."

"Would you like some tea?" she interrupted.

"Yes, thanks," I answered mechanically.

She fetched the teapot and poured me a cup. "One sugar?"

"Thanks." I could hardly believe how banal our reunion was turning out. "You've been well, I hope?"

"Yes, well enough, thank you." Her answers were formal and oddly stilted. This wasn't the bubbly, vivacious girl I had known.

"As I was saying, I'm sorry I haven't contacted you for so long.

I was… well, it's a long story and I don't know where to begin."

"There's no need. You don't owe me any explanations …"

"Daphne," I said, rather more emotionally than I would have wished, "I really missed you all the time I was away. I didn't realise how much I cared for you before … and there was George …"

"Dennis Chiang," she said, in a funny choked tone, "you leave without a word of goodbye. You keep me in the dark about where you've gone. You vanish off the face of the earth for years and years and years. Not a word, not a letter, nothing to show whether you're alive or dead. And now out of nowhere and without warning, you come back and tell me that you missed me and care for me … and … and …" To my astonishment, she started to weep.

"Daphne, dear, don't …" I put my hand on hers. She attempted to brush it away weakly, but gave up the effort without much struggle.

"I hate you, Dennis," she said. I put my arm around her shoulder. She didn't resist.

"I'm sorry," I said, "I couldn't tell you. I had to disappear on account of a gangster. He would have hurt my family. I had to go up-country. I know I should have written or called or sent you a message of some sort. But there was you and George and I didn't want to get in the way …"

She smiled weakly through the tears. "Isn't that just like you, Dennis? The perfect English gentleman. So damnably correct …"

"But now George says that it's over between you," I continued, "so I thought … I thought that maybe we could … we could …"

"We could have a relationship?" she said. "We could become lovers?"

I shifted uncomfortably. She wasn't hostile and she didn't push me away. "We could start by being best friends," I said, "if that's what you want."

She started weeping again. "I'd want more," she said. "I missed you too. Terribly. More than I thought I would."

"Darling," I replied, my heart leaping. I wanted to embrace her.

"But it's too late, Dennis. I'm married. To Bernie."

I felt the floor disappear from under my feet.

I MOVED away a little on the settee. "When did this happen?" I asked, trying to keep my voice under control.

"Oh, Dennis, why couldn't you have said something?" She mustered herself and dabbed her eyes. "Stiff upper lip. Isn't that what you English always show? I'm afraid I haven't quite got the hang of it yet."

She took a sip of her tea, more as a means of buying time to compose herself than anything else. "It was nearly two weeks ago," she started, her voice still a little wobbly, "just when this horrible business started. Bernie…" She stopped abruptly, shook herself and said, "Look, I'm not telling this right. I'd better start at the beginning."

"Yes, I think you'd better," I said in a flat tone. I couldn't trust myself to say more.

"When you left, I felt … I felt, well, deserted. I know I didn't have a right to, and we were just friends and I told you that you were like a brother to me. But when you went without saying goodbye, I was mad at you. And I was mad at me for being mad at you 'cause I knew I had no right to be. I tried to find out where you'd gone, but all they'd tell me was that you'd gotten involved in some police business and that they'd sent you away for your protection. It wasn't satisfactory but no one would say anything more. And I thought, 'heck, if he cared for me, he'd have said something'. So I tried to put you out of my mind.

"I tried to make it work with George, I really did. But, as you know, he's not really into art or books or music or anything like that. I'm not as dumb as I look. I could tell he was putting up a front, that he was trying, but it wasn't the same. And soon I'd get irritated and I'd think of the times we had together and the long talks we had. Then he introduced me to Bernie at some Bar shindig. And you know, Bernie reminded me of you. He talked the same, and he seemed to know something – not just a fraud like George. We got to talking, and you know, I kept thinking of you all the time. And I realised there could never be anything between George and me. So we broke it off. Or I did, anyway. I tried to let him down gently. He seemed to take it okay."

"No," I said, "you misjudged George there. He's still upset."

She raised her eyebrows. "George? But he said he was okay. He's the sort that gets over a girl like people get over the 'flu. I mean, we parted friends and all that. But anyhow, it wasn't on account of Bernie. I just couldn't go on seeing George any more. I needed to get away from him. Bernie soon got to hear, and he came round a couple of times. He was sweet, and he was company. Elaine was … gone. You were gone. And the rest of my crowd had headed back to the States by then. You don't know what it's like to be lonely, to have no one to talk to."

"Believe me," I said with some feeling, "I know exactly how that feels."

"Anyway, Bernie soon became a regular fixture. He was company… and I needed company. My Daddy passed on last year, so I've no one left in this world, no one at all," she said quietly, evidently still trying to master herself.

"I'm sorry," I said, rather fatuously, to fill the gap.

She went on, her voice calmer now, "Bernie joined the Volunteers. When the Japs bombed Pearl Harbour and landed up north, he was called up. He came to me the Wednesday after that – December 10th, it was. Said that he'd been posted to some place up-country as a liaison officer with the regulars and that we might never see each other again. He asked me to marry him. And I said yes …"

"Do you love him?" I asked, my heart in my mouth.

"Don't," she said, tears welling up again. "Don't ask me that. I'm married. We got married that afternoon, just the two of us in the Registry office with his clerk as witness. Then he went. We didn't even spend the night together …" She broke off. I waited silently for her to carry on.

She took a deep breath. "They sent me something yesterday." She got up, went to the desk and handed me a thin slip of paper. "Read it," she said. It was a telegram couched in the inimitable dry prose of the military: "We regret to inform you that your husband Second-Lieutenant Bernard Higgins of the 1st Battalion, Straits Settlements Volunteer Force, has been reported missing in action …"

"Missing in action," she said in a voice drained of emotion. "Someplace up north – Jitra, I don't even know where that is. I came back here, 'cause I don't have anywhere else and no one to go to. And then … and then you come knocking on my door again …"

I got up to leave. "I'm sorry, Daphne," I said, fumbling for the words. "I shouldn't have come. I didn't mean to upset you. That was the last thing on my mind, believe me…"

"No, don't go, not yet," she said quietly, reaching out and touching my hand. "Hold me for a while. I need to be held."

I sat down again and drew her to me. I stroked her hair gently. We didn't speak.

28

I DON'T know how long we just sat there. All sensation of time disappeared. We were finally interrupted by the wail of the air raid sirens again. Daphne headed for the door.

"No, not outside!" I called out. "Isn't there an air raid shelter?" She shook her head. Taking her by the hand, I shoved her under the kitchen table. I pushed it up against the wall and the settee against it and put the mattress from the bed on top.

"Come on in," she said. There was only room for one. I told her so, but she insisted. I contorted myself so that my head was under the table while the rest of me sprawled out on the floor. I felt that my backside was uncomfortably exposed.

After an eternity, the all-clear sounded. Evidently, it had been a false alarm. I unwound myself from my awkward position and helped her out.

"You can't stay here," I said. "There's no protection and no one to look after you."

"I'll be okay," she said, without much conviction.

"No," I said decisively, "you're coming home with me." I continued hurriedly lest she got the wrong idea. "We've got a big house up at Cavanagh Road. There's plenty of room. I've got five girl cousins in residence, so you'll be properly chaperoned. If you stay here, you'll be exposed when the bombers come. We've got a garden. We'll dig a shelter at least – it's on a hill, so it won't fill up with water."

She seemed uncertain. "Daphne," I went on, "Bernie's one of my best friends. I owe it to him to take care of you." Even if I didn't have feelings for you myself, I refrained from adding.

"Okay," she said at last, "if you're sure it's okay."

"It'll be fine," I reassured her. "Mak won't mind in the least."

MAK didn't mind, though the household was in an uproar due to the alarms. I entrusted Daphne to Gek Neo, who in her businesslike manner took full charge. Then I went out to get the gardener, Dollah. We had a hurried discussion about the practicality of constructing an air raid shelter in the garden. It was decided that the best thing to do was to dig a couple of slit-trenches in the lee of the wall of the kitchen garden. At least that would provide us with some cover from flying shrapnel. Dollah went off to round up his sons and nephews, and was back with manpower and materials in a couple of hours. We spent the next two days hacking away at the tough clay with changkuls. By midnight, we had a fair-sized V-shaped scrape about waist-deep. We shored up the sides with planking and made a parapet of gunny sacks filled with soil along its length. I was worried about cover on the top. There wasn't anything to protect the occupants from debris falling directly from above. I couldn't think any more that night, though. I crawled back to my bed and slept like the dead.

The next morning, I ran into Daphne at breakfast. I had been too busy with the shelter to worry much about her. "Everything all right?" I asked.

"Yes, perfect," she replied, smiling at me. I felt my heart flutter a little.

"We haven't had much time to talk," I went on. "But the good news is that the trench is done and I can take a breather."

Julie and Augusta joined us, which put paid to any prospect of further progress. Their school had closed for the holidays so they were at a loose end. They spent their time interrogating Daphne on her life in the States, Jesselton and Singapore, marvelling at the fact that she had dared to live alone among strangers for so long. She took it in good spirit and answered all their questions frankly. I sat quietly by, unable to get a word in but content merely to be in her company.

My little reverie was interrupted by the appearance of a military despatch rider bearing an official missive.

"Trouble?" asked Daphne, in a concerned tone. "They're not drafting you, I hope?"

"No," I said, skimming the contents. "But I've got to be off tomorrow. I'm a prime witness at a court martial."

THE court martial was held in a nondescript room in Tanglin Barracks. Newman greeted me at the entrance and walked in with me. Blake was already there. He was wearing three stripes on his sleeve.

"Well, Sergeant Blake," I said, "I see that congratulations are in order."

"Yeah, well, thanks mate," he replied beaming. "Seein' as I was the only one of me unit to have stayed up north instead of buggerin' off with the rest, the brass-hats figured that I should get another stripe. Beaut, ain't it?"

"Are you still based at Kuantan?"

He lowered his voice. "We've been pulled back to Singapore. If yer ask me, it's a crock. The blokes are sayin' that we ain't never gonna stop the Nips if they keep pullin' the 'planes back all the bloody time 'cause they're scared we can't hold the fields. Gawd help our poor lads up there fightin' with no air cover."

Our reunion was interrupted by the summons to enter the courtroom. Under wartime conditions, the proceedings were simple and devoid of ceremony. The prisoner was arraigned before a bench of three officers, two majors and a colonel. As I was the first and primary witness, I got to view the proceedings from start to finish. The prosecutor was competent and marshalled the evidence clearly. I told my story in as much detail as I could recall. I glanced at Ormonde during the recital. He smiled at me. I looked away, not wanting to make eye-contact.

After Blake and Newman had given their evidence, the prosecution closed its case. The defence did not offer any witnesses. The verdict was inevitable.

"Does the prisoner wish to make a statement before sentence is passed?" asked the President of the Court in a solemn tone.

Ormonde looked around the courtroom with a sardonic smile on his lips. "I'm not going to beg for my life," he said in his aristocratic accent. If anything, he exaggerated it for the occasion. "I don't owe any loyalty to your King or Empire. I'm an Irishman, a citizen of the Free State. But I didn't come here to make any political speeches. I did what I did with my eyes open, at first, because I was blackmailed into it but later on, also for the money that it brought. I'm not one to shirk responsibility for my actions. I'll take the consequences."

There was only one possible sentence. The court martial rose and the prisoner was escorted from the room. As he passed me, he stopped for a moment. "Goodbye Dennis," he said, looking me right in the eyes, "try not to think too badly of me." I remained stonily silent, watching his back until he left the chamber.

As we filed out, Newman put his hand on my arm. "A word in your ear, if you please."

We repaired to a quiet corner of the room. "Any word from d'Almeida?" I asked.

"We've had some news," said Newman. "He got as far as Penang, that we know. He sent me a message from Butterworth. From our contacts, we learnt that he followed Narayanan to Georgetown. He then accused the man of stealing his umbrella and got the police to arrest him. Made quite a scene at the ferry terminal, I hear."

I couldn't suppress a smile. "That sounds like him. So that's over, thank goodness."

"'Fraid not," said Newman solemnly, "Georgetown was bombed shortly after, and the police were called out to maintain order. Someone got in and let Narayanan out before we could have him picked up. Then came the order to evacuate and there was confusion all over the place."

"Didn't d'Almeida get out of Penang?" I asked with alarm.

"I don't know," replied Newman. "We've lost contact again."

"I don't suppose any of your lot bothered to evacuate him when the whites left," I said accusingly.

"Bad business that, very bad show," said Newman seriously. "Some blithering idiots in high places thought it was the right thing to do. It's hit native morale all over Malaya. The Japs couldn't have done a better job if they tried."

"You're damned right about that," I replied.

"But there's no use going on about it now," he responded in his brisk manner. "I didn't call you over to talk about that anyway. I've a proposition for you."

"Not another one," I said suspiciously.

"Hear me out," he replied. "As you know, things aren't going well at the front. The Japs are through the Gurun line and have taken Penang. Everything I tell you is in strictest confidence, by the way," he added parenthetically. I listened in silence.

"Anyway," he continued, "we're gearing up for a long fight. The plan is to infiltrate parties of guerillas behind enemy lines. They'll be our eyes and ears, waiting for the time when we're ready to roll the Japs back. There's a special training school here in Singapore, very hush-hush. The Governor's given the green light for us to recruit among the local Chinese, including the Communists."

I arched my eyebrows. "You're arming the Communists? They're dead against your lot. They want to kick you out of Malaya."

"I know that," he went on, "but they're even more against the Japs. As far as they're concerned, the war here is part of the bigger war in China. They're willing to cooperate with us red-haired devils to fight the greater devil, at least for the time being. But we need more good men. I think you'd be ideal."

He waited for me to say something. I was torn. On one hand, I felt somehow that it was my duty to be doing something to defend my home and family. On the other, a little voice kept telling me that I'd done quite enough already and it wasn't my war any more. "Let me think about it," I temporised.

"Right, but don't take too long over it," said Newman. "Call me on this number when you decide. Don't spread it around. It's Fortress Command, so don't be surprised. You might have to try a couple of times before you get through. Ask for Skylark." With that, he left. I stared at the piece of paper, debating whether to chuck it into the wastepaper basket straightaway. In the end, I tucked it into my shirt pocket and wandered back home, irresolute.

THAT evening after dinner, May had news. Four of us had retired to the verandah to enjoy the night air. The stars were out. I had a steaming mug of Ovaltine. There had been no raids for some days. The war was far away.

"I gave my notice today," said May matter-of-factly.

"What for?" asked June. "You need more time with Baby?"

Baby Grace had been left in the care of Mak and Gek Neo while May was working at the hospital. There was no use letting Ralph take care of her. He could tell one end from the other to either feed or dry her as the case required, but that was as far as his talent as a parent went. In any case, Ralph wasn't around much. After office hours, he had his duties as an air raid warden. He popped in whenever duty allowed him. May had more or less moved back into her old room, which Daphne now shared with her.

"Yes, I need more time with Baby," said May with a sigh, "but I cannot take the time off now when I am needed so much."

"I thought you'd given your notice," said Daphne. "Surely this means you'll be home more often."

"No, I gave my notice not because I will stop nursing. I have been asked to join the Indian Army hospital up in Woodlands. They need so many nurses. There is no one to look after the poor soldiers. So, me and two other nurses have agreed to go. And they will pay me more also. $150 a month."

"Woodlands? That is far away. Nearly in Johore," said June.

"I know," said May. "But there is another reason also. We are not treated as equals in the hospital. Even though we have more experience, the European nurses are put in charge of us. Most of them are very nice, but some do not know how to behave. They do not like to treat the Asiatic patients. And Matron takes their side always, even when they are in the wrong. I think it is better to work in the Indian hospital."

"You'll still have European sisters," I cautioned.

"I know that. But they are different. Sister Agnes is the one who came to our hospital to look for help. She is a saint. Even though she is white, she does not see the patients as black men. Matron was very angry when we gave our notice. She said that we Chinese should not go and nurse the black men. She said that they are disloyal. She was not very pleasant. But I do not care.

I will go next week."

"Don't they need help? Auxiliaries or helpers or something of the sort?" asked Daphne.

"Yes, we are always short of staff. Anyone who wants to help is welcome."

"What about me then?" said Daphne.

I had been almost dozing, but now I sat bolt upright. "You're not serious. You haven't any training."

She looked at me with a pained expression. "I know I haven't. But I'm useless here. You've all been very kind and all that, but I can't take your hospitality forever. I want to do something, contribute something. Will they take me, May?"

"Yes, surely, you are welcome if you want to come," said May. "Sister Agnes will be very happy to have you."

I felt a pang. I had secretly nursed the hope that Daphne would stay with us indefinitely; or at least until Bernie came back – if ever. I hadn't counted on her leaving so soon. I knew though that I could say nothing against her decision without seeming selfish.

Gek Neo came to clear away the cups. "Daphne wants to come with me to the Indian hospital," said May.

"That is good," replied Gek Neo, wiping the table. "But you will come back here on your days off. You are welcome to stay here, as long as you want."

"That's so very kind of you, all of you. I don't know what to say. I don't know where I'd be if it wasn't for you – and Dennis, of course," she said, touching my hand briefly and smiling.

I hadn't expected her touch, and I felt my ears redden. "I might be going away too," I said, to cover my temporary confusion. "Mr Newman has asked me to sign up for some army work."

The girls rounded on me. "You cannot," said June vehemently. "You have just come back. You must stay here and look after Mak."

"No, but I've got to do my bit too …" I said defensively, taken aback by the strength of the adverse reaction.

"You go away for two years, not enough? You know when you were up-country, every week Mak made a Novena for you. Then she went to the temple to pray to Kuan Yin for you to come back safe. What for you want to go again? You want to kill Mak, is it?" said June, getting angrier.

"I have a duty …" I said weakly.

"Your duty is to your family," said Gek Neo in a quiet tone. "The war is not your pasal. The orang puteh can fight the Jepun. Mak needs you here. You cannot tell her that you want to go away and fight and die. She cannot take it."

I knew they were right. She wouldn't have stopped me if I insisted, but her heart would break, of that I was sure. But somehow, I felt that to refuse Newman's proposition would be a dereliction of duty. And deep down, I didn't want Daphne to think less of me for not serving. I spent a very restless night.

29

WITH daybreak came clarity. I knew what I had to do. Rising earlier than usual, I went down to breakfast hoping to catch May before she left for work. She was there, together with Gek Neo. My unaccustomed presence so early in the morning caused a certain amount of comment.

"May, I'd like to join up too. Would they have a place for me?"

"You?" said May in astonishment.

"Yes, me. I can't sit at home doing nothing. The shelter's finished. There's no work in the courts. It may be months before things get back to normal. I can't go on taking a salary from the d'Almeidas without doing any work. Surely they'll need dressers or stretcher-bearers or even peons."

"I do not know," she said doubtfully, "but I will ask."

"Besides," I went on, "this way I can keep an eye on you. Mak would want that."

She beamed at me. If she suspected that she wasn't the centre of my interest, she didn't show it. The matter was settled remarkably quickly. May called Sister Agnes, who was delighted at the suggestion. Not only would she get an experienced nurse but also a medical auxiliary and a general-purpose peon as well. They needed as many hands as they could get. Evidently, there was little coordination between the civil and military authorities, and the

Indian Army was left to fend for itself when it came to medical services. We were told to report the following morning.

Mak wasn't thrilled, but she didn't object. As I had anticipated, the prospect of May working way up north in Woodlands among all the Indian soldiers became more palatable since I was going along. The hospital would provide board and lodging, so we wouldn't have to make the long journey home every day. I sensed that Mak wasn't overjoyed that I would be away from home again, but the fact that I was still on Singapore Island within an hour's drive was some consolation. And, lurking at the back of her mind, was the realisation that Lim Beow Sin was still at large.

I WENT down after breakfast to square things at the office. Cuthbert wasn't there, so I spoke to George again. "I think you're barmy," he said, "but I won't stand in your way." I hadn't told him about Daphne.

"Tell Cuthbert that I'm eternally grateful that they kept on paying my salary to Mak. I'll never forget that. And when this rotten business is over, I'll be back, if you'll have me."

"Not to worry. We'll keep your seat warm," assured George. "Was there anything else?"

"You wouldn't happen to know where I could get hold of some tin hats? We've dug a shelter in the garden, but there's no overhead protection. I need a dozen."

"Tin hats?" said George. "Just sit tight, my son. I'll be right back."

He disappeared down the stairs. Half an hour later, he reappeared with our office boy in tow, carrying a large sack that clanked. With the air of a conjurer producing a rabbit, he announced, "One dozen tin hats, as ordered."

"George, you're a wonder," I said, marvelling. "Where on earth did you get these?"

"Friend of mine who works for the Auxiliary Fire Service has a whole crateful that no one wants. So, he was happy to let me have a few."

I retrieved one from the sack. I blinked. It wasn't the expected round British Army steel helmet. It had a distinctly Teutonic look. "They're German helmets," I said with dismay.

"Technically, they're Siamese. But yes, they're imported from Germany. That's why no one wants them. One poor AFS wallah was cycling along with this on his head when a mob nearly lynched him. They thought Jerry paratroopers had landed."

"I can't use German helmets," I said doubtfully.

"Listen," said George patiently, "shrapnel can't tell the difference between a German and a British helmet. You'll be jolly glad you've got something on your nut when the bombs are falling."

He was right as usual. I thanked him and made my way down, my sack on my back.

"By the way, Merry Christmas, Santa," he called to me.

I had completely forgotten. Tomorrow would be Christmas Eve.

"You might need this," he said, tossing me a set of car keys.

"I can't take your car," I remonstrated.

"Yes, you can," he replied. "Cuthbert has let me use d'Almeida's Rolls until he gets home. You'll need something to get you there and back."

I stuffed the keys gratefully into my pocket. "I don't know how I'm ever going to repay you for all this," I said.

"Don't you worry," George responded, "I'm bound to think of something."

THE 19th Indian General Hospital was located in Woodlands, near the fabled Naval Base and practically within sight of the Straits of

Johore. The Causeway linking Singapore to the rest of the Asian continent was just a short distance away. The three of us drove up on Christmas Eve, feeling little of the holiday spirit. It had been announced in the Government Gazette that the Christmas public holidays were cancelled, as was Hari Raya Puasa, which fell four days after Christmas. The news in the papers was depressing. True, Russia was pressing forward in the Crimea and our side was winning in the Western Desert; but in the East, the Japs had attacked Hong Kong. It would only be a matter of days before that port fell.

We reported to Sister Agnes, an efficient, energetic old soul who tried to give the impression of being a martinet but failed dismally. The laugh lines at the corners of her eyes gave her away. I negotiated a special deal for myself. Two days of duty followed by one day off so that I could get back to make sure everything was all right with Mak and the other girls. May and Daphne were accomodated in the same room in the nurses' quarters. This consisted of a series of wooden huts thatched with attap, scattered among the trees of a rubber estate. The wards and mess-halls were the same. There were ack-ack guns scattered around the perimeter and in-between the buildings. Evidently, the Japanese had a rather loose interpretation of the Geneva Convention's prohibition on attacking medical targets.

The scene which greeted us was one of indescribable chaos. The wards were full of groaning men, blood was all over the place and the stench was unbelievable. The incessant buzz of flies nearly drove me wild. They settled all over the place despite all our efforts to keep them away. Daphne was pale but carried gamely on. She was assigned to help with the surgical cases, which required a strong stomach. I had seen my share of casualties but I felt queasy all that first day. What struck me most was the stoic bearing of the troops, many of them barely out of their teens. Here they were in a strange land, fighting a stranger's war and dying for a cause that did not concern them, yet I heard no murmurs of complaint, no rumblings of discontent. The sight that affected me most was that of a British major practically in tears, holding the hand of a grizzled old jemadar gravely wounded in the belly. I found a portable screen, which I set up to give them some privacy. The major gave me a half-smile and a nod of appreciation. When I came by later in the day, both the major and the screen were gone. Another man lay in the bed.

DESPITE my arrangement with Sister Agnes, I didn't manage to get off as planned. May refused to leave her charges and Daphne insisted on staying too. This being so, I decided not to go myself. The casualties kept coming in, sometimes in ones and twos, sometimes by the truckload. News came that Kuching had been captured on Christmas Eve, Hong Kong on Christmas Day and Ipoh on the 27th. We remained indifferent, too overwhelmed to care. By the end of the month, we had been at it for almost a week without a break and were on the verge of collapse. Sister Agnes insisted that we should take two days off. I accepted with alacrity on behalf of May and Daphne. If I hadn't, May would have stayed on until she gave out physically.

We spent the whole of the first day and half of the second in a comatose state. Around tea-time, I finally got up, showered and went down, feeling ravenous. To my surprise, there was a message for me from George, asking that I call him.

"My dear Dennis," said George jovially when he heard my voice, "back in the land of the living at last!"

"Barely," I replied. "Is there something I can do for you?"

"As a matter of fact, yes," he said, "come and have dinner with me tonight. At the Raffles. It's New Year's Eve. Tomorrow, it will be 1942. Time to loosen up a bit."

"Thanks, George, that's really generous of you," I said, a little wearily, "but I don't think I'm up to merry-making tonight. It's been a hard week and …"

"You did say that you didn't know how to thank me for some trifling little things I did for you earlier," he replied. "Well, this is it. Come to dinner tonight. And bring Daphne."

"You know that Daphne's here?" I said, surprised.

"There are few things that escape me, my son," he said. "Ralph told me. Ask her to come. For auld lang syne."

I couldn't refuse, not after what he had done for me. "All right, I'll ask her," I said warily, "but I can't promise anything."

"Good. Excellent. I'll pop by with the Rolls say eight-ish. It's usually black-tie, but I'm sure under the circumstances, they'll understand if the dress-code slips a little tonight."

IT WASN'T with much enthusiasm that I broached the subject with Daphne. I didn't know what George was up to and that bothered me. Perhaps he still harboured hopes, now that Bernie was out of the picture. For a moment, I toyed with the idea of calling him back and reporting that Daphne had refused to go. But then I thought better of it. I told myself repeatedly that I wasn't afraid of competition from George. I almost believed it.

Daphne was surprised by the invitation. Initially, she seemed disinclined to go, which lifted my spirits somewhat. Unfortunately, Gek Neo heard us talking and persuaded her that it would be a good idea. She said that I needed a bit of a diversion, after all that I had been through. I don't know how much she suspected about my feelings for Daphne, but Gek Neo was pretty shrewd. I thought there was a little mischievous twinkle in her eye when she egged Daphne on.

Anyway, Daphne agreed that it might be nice to get away

from everything and just have some fun for one night. So we got dressed up and waited for George. She was gorgeous in all her finery. I said so and she beamed broadly. George turned up on the dot at eight, driving d'Almeida's Rolls. He looked very dapper in his tuxedo. I had on a rather less elegant version, a left-over from my college days.

"My dear," said George suavely, "how lovely you look. It's been too long since I've had the pleasure of your company."

"You're looking great yourself too, George," responded Daphne. "Everything okay?"

"Terrific," he answered, "especially now that I've seen you again." He gave her his arm and escorted her to the back seat. "Would you mind?" he asked me, handing me the keys. I sighed and took them. He got into the back with Daphne.

THE Raffles was a bit more sober than I remembered it, with black-out curtains covering the windows. The Sikh jaga was still there though. He took charge of the car competently when we went into the ballroom. It was crowded and a trifle hot, despite the multitude of fans whirling at full blast. An effort had been made to keep up appearances. There were balloons and streamers, and a large banner emblazoned with the words "Happy New Year 1942". The crowd was mostly white, with a few Chinese among them. We were the only mixed group as far as I could see, which attracted some attention. George, as usual, had contrived to get us a good table, with a bottle of real champagne. The band was playing a selection of popular tunes – Cole Porter, Irving Berlin, Gershwin, Jerome Kern. A few couples were on the dance floor.

Dinner was excellent despite the limitations imposed by the circumstances. It was almost impossible to believe that we were at war. George was at his best, witty, attentive, scintillating in conversation. Unlike previously, he didn't try to impress Daphne with his knowledge of art, music or literature. He kept to what he knew best – the courts, people and life in general. He had her in stitches with his anecdotes. She seemed to be enjoying herself immensely. I soon felt that I had made a bad mistake in agreeing to bring her along.

The atmosphere got merrier as midnight approached. We finished the first bottle of champagne and called for a second. I had never developed a taste for the stuff and nursed my champagne flute all night, barely sipping the contents. George was drinking a fair amount, as were the people at the table next to us. Daphne had quite a bit too, and soon began to giggle. Everyone except me seemed to be very merry. But beneath it all, I sensed a tenseness, a brittleness, as if the spell could be broken at any time.

The group at the next table grew louder. There were three couples, middle-aged, with the look of affluence about them, the ladies gilded and painted, the men exuding prosperity. From their clothes, I surmised that they weren't refugees from up-country. One seemed to be the tuan besar of a local trading company, judging from the scraps of conversation that I overheard. It wasn't difficult even with the band playing full blast, given the volume at which they were conversing.

"You'll see," said the tuan besar, "you'll see. We're leading them on. Stretching their lines of communication. Fight them on ground of our choosing, what? Like we did with the Huns back in '18. Elementary strategy, elementary. When the little yellow beggars are exhausted and hungry, that's when we'll hit them."

One of his companions, a bald man with glasses, begged to differ. Evidently, he had heard something of the dismal state of morale among the Empire forces. Only the Australians seemed to have any aggressive spirit. The tuan besar was scornful. What could one expect when the majority of the troops were Indian?

No fighting spirit, as usual. Leave it to the British to do the dirty work and stiffen their backbone. As for the Australians, they might be aggressive but they were just undisciplined colonials. There was a round of agreement. Common soldiers from the dominions were not held in high esteem. Certainly not fit for polite society. Not even the officers. There was another round of agreement. The bald man persisted in his more pessimistic assessment of the situation. He wouldn't be surprised if the Empire forces had to pull back into Fortress Singapore and wait for reinforcements before striking back. "Well, then," said the tuan besar, "we'll sit out the siege. Malta's been holding out for months against everything the Huns can throw at them. We've got the troops, even though they're mostly wogs and niggers. Still, with good British officers, they're more than a match for any slant-eyed Jappo. And we've got the British Army, thank God." He turned to our table. "Speakee English? Of course you do. A toast then. A toast to the British Army. They're the rock that'll stand when everyone else is running away."

George had been listening to the exchange with a strange glint in his eyes. I sensed that he was close to explosion. "No," he said politely, with a smile on his lips, "let me propose another toast — to the brave Indian soldiers, who are dying in a war that is not of their making, for a cause that is not theirs." He stood up. "To the Indian Army and the independence of India," he said in a loud voice, draining his glass. The band stopped playing. A scandalised murmur ran round the room.

"I shall take my leave now," he said. He bent over and kissed Daphne's hand. "It's been a real pleasure, Daphne." To me, he said quietly, "Please see that Daphne gets home."

He beckoned to a waiter, who trotted promptly over. Producing a wad of notes, he withdrew a couple of large ones and pressed them into his hand.

"Ngiam, see that my friends are well taken care of," he said. With that, he strode out, the waiters bowing as he passed.

"Well!" exclaimed the tuan besar, "I never heard such treasonous twaddle in all my life!"

That was too much for me. I rounded on him. "It's not treason to recognise what the Indians are doing up-country. They didn't join your Empire voluntarily because of your superior morals or civilisation. They don't have a say about how they're ruled. Yet, those men are fighting up there in your war to defend your way of life."

The group eyed me coldly. "Talking about fighting up there," said the tuan besar, "what are you doing here? You'd be at the front if you'd any backbone at all. I served in the Great War. In my day, they'd hand a white feather to fellahs like you."

I was dumb with rage, searching for a suitable retort. Daphne saved me the trouble. "Don't you start on him, now," she said fiercely. "I'll have you know that Dennis was at the front, at Kota Bahru when the Japs landed. We've been working in the Indian army hospital all this past week, tending to those poor boys who are spilling their guts for the likes of you. While you've been sitting here guzzling your champagne and brandy and gin and running them down. Don't you dare criticise my friends. They're worth ten of you any day!"

She grabbed her things off the table. "Come on," she said decidedly, "let's get outta here." She swept out briskly. All eyes followed her.

"Thanks for sticking up for me back there," I said when we got to the courtyard.

"No need. Guys like him just make me so mad! They're so snooty even about their own folks. You know, I was at tea with some of those society ladies a couple of months back, before the Japs landed. They were talking about the 'common soldiers' like they were slugs or worms or something you haul out of a garbage tip. I don't know how this place works, with people like that … I just don't know." She took a deep breath.

"How did you find out about me being at Kota Bahru?" I asked with curiosity.

"May told me. She said you were doing something hush-hush for the army. Something really brave and heroic. I think she was trying to make me sweet on you." She smiled.

There seemed to be a conspiracy to get me hitched to Daphne. It didn't displease me. "Nothing really heroic," I said, trying to appear modest while bursting with self-satisfaction. I didn't like to admit it to myself, but the fact that Bernie was a Volunteer and a war hero bothered me. It was good that Daphne knew that I hadn't just been a passive spectator.

"Look," she said, "let's go for a walk. I don't feel like going home yet." I acceded readily.

The night was warm and the stars were out. She hitched her arm through my elbow. We strolled to the sea-front and along the esplanade. At the Cenotaph, she leaned against the railing, letting the breeze blow her hair. She shimmered in the starlight, an ethereal vision in satin and silk. I couldn't help myself. I took her in my arms and kissed her. "Don't, Dennis," she said softly, "I'm married." It didn't carry much conviction. I kissed her again. She kissed back.

It may have been hours or minutes, I don't know. The sound of the air raid sirens brought me back to earth. There was nowhere to run to, so we crouched down in the shadow of the Cenotaph. I put my arms around her, as if that would have been any use against the bombs. She snuggled her head against my shoulder. Above the harbour, the searchlights traced a filigree of light in the night sky. The puffs of ack-ack fire punctuated the blackness like flowers of fire.

It would have been beautiful if it hadn't been so dreadful.

30

THE JAPANESE air force ushered in the New Year literally with a bang. The raid on New Year's Eve was the biggest since the start of the war. After that, the bombers came regularly twice or thrice a day, sometimes in gaggles of forty, fifty, sixty or more. Our tubby fighters were impotent, even on the rare occasions that they managed to catch the raiders. Towards the middle of January, some Hurricanes arrived on one of the reinforcement ships. We had great hopes, but they soon went the way of the Buffalos, swamped by the sheer number of nimble Oscars. Eventually, we heard that what remained of the RAF, RAAF and Dutch Air Force had been withdrawn to the safety of the East Indies. The storm was coming closer and our umbrella had been taken away.

In the second week of January came news that the Empire forces had been beaten at Slim River. KL fell on the 11th. The Japs kept coming relentlessly down the Peninsula. Morale went south in tandem. More reinforcements arrived. I knew this from the changing mix of patients that we received – Rajputana Rifles, Madras Sappers and Miners, more Punjabis and Jats from different regiments. I don't know why they bothered to send them. They were so pathetically young and almost completely untrained. It was a case of off the ship, into battle and to the hospital – for the lucky ones.

We worked like automatons at the hospital. The days just ran together in a formless blur. I saw Daphne when I could. We never again managed to get another day off at the same time. There was just too much to do. We snatched a little time here, a moment there, a fleeting instant elsewhere. Despite the carnage and the chaos, the pain and the privation, I felt something akin to happiness.

I went back to check on Mak and the other girls on my rare days off. The house was right next to Government House. Bombs fell regularly in the vicinity. The gardens of the Domain were now pitted with craters, but the Union Jack still flew from the flagstaff and the sentries remained stolidly at their posts. The bulletins remained unwaveringly optimistic. The Government had not ordered any large-scale evacuation of women and children – which we assumed they would have done if there had been any real danger of a siege. Mak remained convinced that it was impossible for an Asiatic power to beat the British. I wasn't so sure, but couldn't bring myself to disillusion her.

We laid in stocks of rice and cooking oil. Even if the Japs never got as far as Johore, the price of food was sure to go up. Shopkeepers stopped allowing Europeans to sign chits for their purchases, which took many by surprise. From time immemorial, a white man was given credit as a matter of course. No longer. It was strictly cash from then on. The white community tried to hold their collective chin up, clutching the tattered remains of their superiority around them like rags to cover up their nakedness. They seemed to have harboured the belief that if they gave up, the natives would utterly lose hope and curl up in a ball and die. All this stiff-upper-lippishness began to jar on my nerves. It was almost a relief to return to the hospital.

ON THE last day of January, I finally managed to arrange our schedules so that Daphne and I both had a break at the same time.

There was no question of being able to drive back into town. We decided to go for a picnic by the sea instead. I had scrounged enough petrol from my meagre allowance for just such an occasion. At daybreak, before everyone roused themselves, we packed some food from the canteen, borrowed a couple of bedsheets and headed off down the road. The great Naval Base, of which so much had been expected, lay forlorn and abandoned ahead of us. After the destruction of Force Z, there didn't seem to be much point holding it. The relief fleet from Europe would take months. The Royal Navy decided to pull out and wait elsewhere. We skirted the perimeter. The docks and cranes appeared intact. No one was about. There were a couple of guards at the gate but none patrolling the fence. It was as if everyone had gone off on holiday, leaving everything behind.

We found a small hillock by the sea, within sight of the Straits and the Causeway. On the other side, the Sultan's palace shone clearly in the early morning sun. We spread the bedsheets on the ground and laid out our repast. The birds were twittering in the trees. Butterflies flitted in and out of the shadows. It all seemed so very peaceful. There was only an intermittent, indistinct rumble from the north to remind us of what lay beyond. We spoke of beautiful things far away and munched our stale sandwiches. I wanted very much to hold her, but I feared that if I tried, I might spoil the moment. I found myself hoping that we would soon receive news of Bernie's death – then pushed away the thought, horrified at myself for letting my mind wander down that road. The idea kept re-intruding nevertheless, no matter what I did. I determined to enjoy the moment, whatever the future might bring.

Our attention was diverted by a curious wailing sound.

"What on earth's that?" asked Daphne.

"If I didn't know better, I'd say it was bagpipes," I answered.

The sound was coming from the direction of the Causeway. We moved a little further up the hillock for a better view. There was a lot of activity on the Singapore side. Lines of troops were filing down the road towards Woodlands. They still marched proudly, unbowed despite all the reverses and defeats. Amid all the bumbling and ineptitude, the Argylls were one of the few regiments which had stood out. At the tail end of the column were two bagpipers, heads held high and backs straight, playing as if they were on parade at Edinburgh Castle. The sounds of 'Hielan Laddie' came to us on the still air. For one brief moment, my spirits rose. With men like these, we can hold the Japs, I thought to myself. But there were so pitifully few of them. A single officer brought up the rear, walking at a measured pace as though all the Japanese in the world could not chase him from Malaya. When he stepped off the Causeway onto Singapore Island, he stopped and cast a defiant glance at the mainland.

Suddenly, without warning, there was a terrific explosion. We were thrown off our feet. Debris rained down into the Straits, making huge splashes. My first thought was that it was a Japanese raid. I scanned the sky anxiously. It was Daphne who first realised what had happened.

"My God!" she exclaimed, "They've blown up the Causeway!"

I glanced in that direction. There was a gap a hundred feet wide in the middle of the Causeway. The railway line, the water pipes, the roadway, all lay shattered. Water was coursing through the broken link. The officer turned and followed his men down the road. We were cut off from the mainland. That could only mean one thing. The siege had begun. At that moment, my one thought was that I had to get Daphne off the island as soon as possible.

IT TOOK me more than a dozen attempts before I got through to Newman on the number that he had given me. He sounded very tired.

"I've made up my mind about that proposition you put to me," I said.

"Good," he replied, "I'll have someone pick you up in the next couple of days."

"There's just one thing else before you hang up. I'd like a favour in return."

"Yes?" He wasn't hostile, just wary.

"I need a pass to get off the island. For a friend of mine. A young American lady."

He seemed surprised. "You don't need a pass for that. Any white woman who wants to go can and should. All she has to do is book passage. The Government will even pay for it if she hasn't got the money. P&O will take care of everything. They're at Agency House in Cluny Road."

I was astounded. I had thought that the process would be very much more complicated now that the Fortress was besieged. "You mean that's all there is to it? Just sign up and leave? Why hasn't this been announced publicly?"

He heaved a deep sigh. "It's another brainwave from the top. After that business in Penang, the Governor thinks that telling the European women and children to go will be bad for native morale. He thinks it'll reduce our prestige. If we had a military governor, he'd order all useless mouths out now, before the siege really takes hold. But we haven't, so no one's been ordered to leave. Heaven help us all if rations start getting short. It'll be a damn sight worse for our prestige if women and children start starving."

"What about the natives?" I asked, but I already knew the answer.

"Ah, that's a bit more difficult," he replied wearily. "Priority for the Europeans, but if you can get a berth, by all means. You'll have to pay for it yourself though. Except for essential personnel and those most at risk. We've given out passes for some of the members of the China Relief Fund Committee. If the Japs catch them, the end won't be easy or merciful."

I wasn't surprised. But I was beyond resentment by then. Actually, I thought it was rather a good idea to get the Europeans out. If it came to a long siege, there would be no question of share and share alike. Despite the Governor's fine words about all of us being in it together, I had no illusions about where the non-white population stood if it came to a choice about who would get priority for rations.

NEWMAN'S information put me in a much better frame of mind. I hadn't thought that it would be so easy to get Daphne out of danger. I didn't reckon with her obstinacy.

"Are you going?" she asked defiantly when I put the matter to her.

"You know I can't. There's Mak and the girls ..."

"Is May going?"

"No, she's staying as long as Ralph is here."

"So there!" she declared. "I'm not going either. Everyone I care for is here in Malaya."

I noticed that she had said "Malaya" rather than "Singapore". I didn't press the matter further.

NOW that the Japanese were firmly ensconced on the northern shore of the Johore Strait, a new menace was added to our daily visitations by their bombers. They established their headquarters and an artillery spotter in the Istana, which had an unrivalled view of Singapore Island. Soon their guns were lobbing shells all over the place. There was no warning, unlike in the case of an air raid. Just a whoosh like an express train, then an almighty bang. I wondered why the British didn't shell the Istana, but one of the officers said that they didn't want to offend the Sultan, who was reputed to be a good friend of the British. Others said that he had turned his coat and gone over to the Japanese. The Johore Military Force had been ordered to disarm without firing a shot. I can't say I blamed him. He was the sovereign of a British-protected state. The British had singularly failed to provide the promised protection. Life had to go on, whatever colour the emperor may have been.

Woodlands was getting too hot. Smoke rose from the burning oil tanks of the Naval Base. The smell pervaded the hospital. May and most of the nurses were ordered to report to the 12th Indian General Hospital in Tyersall Park, near the Botanical Gardens and not far from the Sultan of Johore's mansion. Daphne and I went along too. I still had hopes of persuading her to leave, but she remained adamant. I could understand her motivation, even though I didn't agree with her. It would have seemed too much like desertion in the face of the enemy to leave at that time. None of us really believed that the Fortress would fall, not with all the Empire troops entrenched here. The Orders of the Day were stirring in tone. Malta and Leningrad had suffered far worse. There were many who believed it all. The call of duty was very strong. In retrospect, it would have been a kindness if the Governor had just ordered all non-essential personnel to be evacuated. The misguided solicitude of the authorities was to be the death of many a faithful wife.

I received my marching orders the following day. A Morris 3-cwt truck turned up at the hospital driven by an RASC corporal. I was told to pack my gear and follow him. I went to find Daphne. She was busy with a surgical case. I waited until she was done and took her to a quiet corner.

"I've got to go now," I said, holding her hand.

She took it away. "Damn you, Dennis," she said, avoiding my gaze, "why do all you men have to play the hero?" I thought I saw a small tear flash momentarily at the corner of her eye.

"Look," I said tenderly, "the Japs are going to come whether I go or stay here. Newman's got a job for me. I'll be back, I promise."

We embraced briefly. There wasn't time for more. On my way out, I looked in on May.

"Take care," I said. "Don't tell Mak. I'll come back as soon as I can."

"You do what you must do," she said, giving me a big hug. "Thank you for looking after us. I will look after Daphne for you."

I smiled slightly at that. The corporal hooted impatiently on the horn. It was time to go.

THE driver handed me an envelope. It contained instructions which I read on our way, as well as a sealed letter of introduction to the Officer Commanding, a certain Captain Gavin. I was being inducted into 101 Special Training School, at some place called Tanjong Balai. Their job was to train guerillas for action behind enemy lines. After a long, bumpy, hot drive, I was unceremoniously deposited at the door of 101 STS.

The place was like an ants' nest. I entered the orderly room and presented myself to the private on duty. "You've come to the wrong place, mate," he said. "We're bein' evacuated to Rangoon."

"That can't be," I protested. "Lieutenant-Colonel Newman has just ordered me here."

"Can't help you, mate," shrugged the clerk. "Orders is orders."

I hung around the door irresolutely. My transport had left and there was no question of hailing a taxi back into town. All around, soldiers were packing things into lorries. I had just resolved to hitch a lift when a young captain came over. He spoke to me in Chinese. I stared blankly at him. Seeing my confusion, he switched to Malay. "What is it you want here?"

"I have come to join," I answered automatically in Malay.

"Who has sent you?"

I handed him my letter from Newman. He read it and turned to me, still speaking in Malay. "Do you know what is in this letter?"

"Well, yes, as a matter of fact. I read it on the way here. Except for the sealed one."

The captain started a little at my answer. "You might have told me you spoke English," he said reproachfully.

"Sorry, you never asked."

He held out his hand. "Swift's the name. I used to run a plantation up-country, near Jemaluang. Welcome aboard."

I shook his hand warmly. "Thanks. What do I do now?"

Swift scratched his neck. "You've caught us at a bad time. We've just been told that we're to leave for Burma. The whole unit's packing up. I'll have a word with the OC. Don't go away."

I sat myself down in the shade of a rain tree and waited. Swift returned after half an hour. "Sorry, but you've missed the boat. We've just sent off our last batch of graduates across the Straits."

"Well, in that case, I suppose I'd best be getting back to town," I said resignedly.

Swift sized me up. "Keen to get stuck in, eh?" he said. "Some of us aren't leaving. There's a unit of Chinese irregulars being formed by Colonel Dalley. 'Dalley's Desperadoes' we call them. You're welcome to join us for the show."

I made up my mind immediately. "Right, I'll just tag along if you don't mind. But I haven't any military experience."

"Not to worry," said Swift cheerily, "none of us have. We'll soon fix you up."

I SPENT the next few days with Swift and some of the remaining instructors of 101 STS. They gave me a crash course in weapons handling and explosives. Since I was the only one left, I had their undivided attention. I learned to strip and fire a Sten and a Thompson, to work a radio and picked up the rudiments of demolition. On February 5th, the last truck left for the docks. Swift, me and a couple of officers headed off to join Colonel Dalley's Desperadoes.

I was appalled at what greeted us. I had expected a military unit of some sort. But the Overseas Chinese Volunteer Army – or Dalforce in army-speak – had the appearance of a band of bandits. Instead of the usual British Army khaki, they were wearing a mix of blue uniforms and civilian clothes. None had steel helmets; they wore cloths round their heads, wound like turbans. A few lucky ones had haversacks. The rest carried their equipment in a blanket, slung around the body in the Russian fashion. It was their weapons that shocked me the most. They carried an assortment of shotguns and single-shot civilian sporting rifles, with not a single military weapon among them. But one only had to study their faces to know that this was no mere militia rabble. There was a look of grim determination about them. I had never seen hatred before. I saw it then.

I was luckier than most. Since I had the pick of the stores of 101 STS, I had a proper uniform, complete with steel helmet and a Sten gun with ample ammunition. Captain Swift decided that I should be his orderly, which suited me fine. I couldn't communicate with the rest of the men, who spoke only Chinese. In fact, communication was a problem as many of them could only speak their own dialects. The few educated ones were appointed NCOs and did their best to transmit orders to the others. Morale was high and they were eager to have a go at the Japanese.

Swift and I joined 'A' Company at a point codenamed 18-Keppel, in a rubber estate a few hundred yards off Jurong Road at the 18th milestone. We were next to a unit of Australians. Our front line was within sight of the Johore Straits. As we moved into our positions, I noticed that several of the men were eyeing me closely. It made me slightly uncomfortable. I thought they might be wondering why I was so differently equipped. There were other things to occupy me though, and I soon forgot the matter.

That night, we had our baptism by fire. A few of the men, eager to take the war to the enemy, swam across the Straits camouflaged with floating crates. They ambushed a Japanese patrol on the Johore side. All hell broke loose. Searchlights pierced the night and there was indiscriminate firing all over the place. The patrol returned safely, well pleased with their exploits. Their escapade was trumpeted all over the newspapers the next day.

The following night, the Japs got their own back. They opened up on our positions with mortar and artillery fire. We took several casualties. I watched the men under fire. None had been in action before. Though they were tense, no one broke. There was a certain fatalism among them, a fanaticism that I had never encountered before. It was as if they were determined to pay the Japanese in full for all the atrocities committed in China. After years of bitterness, at last they had the chance to hit back in some small measure.

I was in a forward trench with a British sergeant when a salvo of mortar bombs came over. They detonated among the branches of the rubber trees, splattering the area with sharp fragments of wood. Some of the Volunteers were caught in the open and went down. The sergeant rushed out to get them, heedless of enemy fire. "C'mon," he called to me, tossing over the medical satchel. "You 'ad some Red Cross training. They need 'elp." I followed him, ducking as more rounds exploded along the beach.

Two of the casualties were too far gone for us to do anything. The third was groaning in agony, a gaping wound in his side. I pumped him full of morphine and did my best to bind up the injury. He turned to face me, gasping out his thanks. With a shock,

I recognised him. He was one of Lim Beow Sin's teenaged goons. The look on his face confirmed that recognition was mutual.

A few Volunteers scrambled up with a stretcher. They coolly loaded the wounded man and carried him to the company aid post. I heard them jabbering among themselves. One cast a glance over his shoulder at me. I didn't have time to worry about it. The sergeant and I made a dash for the nearest trench as the next instalment from the other side came crashing down.

As we cowered in the trench, the sergeant introduced himself. "Sims," he said, "from the Norfolks. But I'm a Londoner meself."

I shook his proffered hand. "Chiang," I replied, "of no specific unit. Born right here in Singapore."

"You're the Chink wot speaks English ... I mean, the Chinaman ...," he floundered in confusion.

I couldn't help smiling a little. "Yes, I'm the one. Pleased to meet you."

"No offence, mate, but I ain't never met anyone of your kind wot spoke so genteel. Like a real toff. 'Ave a fag?" He offered me his packet of Players.

I took the cigarette with trembling hands. When I followed Sims out of the trench, I hadn't had time to be scared. Now the reaction set in. He lit the cigarette for me. His hand was steady as a rock.

We were squatting on our haunches, having a peaceful smoke, when there was a sudden sound from above. A dark shape flitted by. Something bounced off the parapet and rolled onto the floor. My mind didn't register what it was until Sims yelled out. "Bloody 'ell, it's a bleedin' grenade!"

Before I could react, he had flung himself down on it. The grenade exploded. I felt a searing pain in my elbow and was knocked off my feet. My head connected with the wall of the trench with a resounding whack.

I WAS transferred to the Field Hospital with concussion. My left elbow hurt like the blazes, but it was only a graze. Sims took the full blast with his body. It was with profound sadness that I learnt he hadn't made it. I felt guilty to be alive. That grenade had been meant for me.

Newman came to see me at the Field Hospital, much to my surprise. "How are you feeling?" he asked, not entirely sympathetically.

"As well as can be expected under the circumstances," I answered, rather testily.

"I sent you to be trained in guerilla warfare, not to go off and join Dalley's forlorn hope," he said.

"Too late. By the time I got there, they were off. Captain Swift invited me to come along and I thought it was a good idea."

He shook his head sadly. "For a young fellow, you seem to have a lot of enemies. Pity about the sergeant. We can't afford to lose good men like that."

"It was Lim Beow Sin's goons, I'm sure of it. I saw at least one of them."

"I don't doubt it. The question is, what do we do with you now? You can't go back to Dalforce. I'm going to give you a pass to get away. Considering the part you played in catching their man Ormonde, I'm not sure you'd want to be here if the Japs ever get a firm foothold on the island."

"Is it as bad as that?" I asked with astonishment.

Newman didn't answer. He drew a document from his pocket and signed it, offering it to me. I stared at it. There were literally thousands who would have killed for something like that. But somehow, I felt I couldn't take it. It seemed too much like a betrayal – of those who were staying and above all, my own family and Daphne. I shook my head. "I can't go."

"Don't be stupid," said Newman. "We need men like you for

our deep penetration groups. What use are you here? We've men enough for the front. We're pulling out all our valuable assets. Go to Rangoon. 101 STS will set up shop there."

I shook my head determinedly. "You can't order me to go. I'm a civilian."

Newman sighed deeply. "Very well, stay if you must. But take this anyway. I haven't filled in the name of the ship or the date. You might need it sometime." He held it out to me. I took it and put it in my pocket. He left without saying anything more.

I WAS discharged from the Field Hospital and went back to Tyersall Park. Ironically, that grenade saved my life. I learnt later that my unit of Chinese Volunteers was overrun when the Japs landed on the island. They fought until their ammunition gave out, then they fought on with their bayonets and their bare hands. The Japs took no Chinese prisoners. Only one officer and a handful of British ORs escaped. Swift wasn't among them.

THE first thing on my agenda was to get Mak and the girls away from Cavanagh Road. Government House had become a regular target for the Japs. There seemed to be something about the Union Jack flying on the roof that irritated them. They kept lobbing shells and bombs in that direction. The fact that the British had emplaced a battery of 25-pounders in the Domain didn't improve their mood. It was a miracle that our house hadn't already been hit. I sent word that they should pack up everything and bury the few items of value that we had in the garden. We had relatives enough to put them up for the time being.

When I got to the house, I was confronted with insurrection. Mak refused to budge. "This is my house," she said quietly, her lips pursed firmly. "My husband bought it for me. I will not go."

Gek Neo was practically hoarse pleading with her. "Mak, it is only for a little while. We will stay with Kim Poh Cho. They have a big house in Joo Chiat. They are happy to welcome us."

"What for stay with Kim Poh Cho?" responded Mak. "This is my house. It is your house. We should not trouble relatives."

A shell burst in Government House Domain. "See, Mak, it is not safe," I cajoled. "You *must* go."

"And the house?" she asked. "Strangers will come into the house."

It suddenly dawned on me what this was about. I hadn't realised till then how territorial the average Nonya was. The house was the focus of their lives. They ran the domestic affairs of the family. A Baba husband interfered at his peril. When it came to the household, the wife's word was law. To be evicted, to live with strangers – that was almost like giving up one's identity. To have strangers take over the house, disarrange the kitchen and trespass in the rooms didn't even bear thinking about.

"We will lock up the house, Mak. No one will get in. I promise," I said with as much conviction as I could muster. In my heart, I didn't believe it. Looters were already active, picking over the carcasses of empty mansions like vultures. The Japanese had no inhibitions about helping themselves either.

"If you promise..." she said, wavering. We pressed our advantage.

"Yes, Mak, Denny promises. We will lock up the place. All will be well." Gek Neo took her arm and firmly steered her off to the kitchen to pack.

There was no question of emptying everything out of the place. It would have taken a fleet of lorries, even if we had the time. I insisted that everyone be limited to a large bag each. All the crockery and cutlery were locked in the kitchen. I fashioned several large signs: "Danger! Unexploded Bombs," illustrated with suitably graphic skulls and crossbones. These were placed in conspicuous places. I hoped fervently that we would attract a better class of looters who could at least read.

Just as we were about to leave, June gave me a large parcel tied up in brown paper. "What's this?" I asked.

"Your barber friend – the Japanese one – he gave this to you before he left Singapore with his wife."

"When was this, for heaven's sake?" I responded, rather peeved.

"Don't be like that lah. He gave it when you were up-country. We forgot after so long."

There was a letter with it. "Dear honoured friend," I read, "I cannot thank you enough for what you have done for me and my wife. I have nothing to give except this. If one day, the Imperial Japanese Army should come, this will help you." He signed it in beautiful flowing calligraphy. I tore open the package. It was a portrait of the Japanese Emperor.

I had an immediate urge to slash it up. "Does anyone have a knife?" I called out.

Gek Neo came out of the kitchen with a large bread knife. "You want this? What for?"

"To chop that up," I said, "I'm going to hang it on a tree in the garden."

"No," said Gek Neo in her matter-of-fact way. "That is no good. If the Jepun come, they will be angry to find their Emperor's picture destroyed. I think it is better we hang it in the hall. Then if they come, they will leave us alone."

"You're not serious," I said.

"I am serious," she replied. "Mrs Chan's Jepun friend told her last year to get such a picture. Before they all went away in

October. We did not believe them at that time. Now some people are already making flags."

I was flabbergasted. "You mean people want the Japanese to win?"

"No," replied Gek Neo, "but the orang puteh are running away. We must be ready."

It made sense. The British could go, but we had to stay whether we liked it or not. Trying hard to suppress my revulsion, I hung the picture up in the hall so that anyone coming in would see it immediately. It was our insurance policy. I couldn't help myself though. I stabbed it right in the eye with a knitting needle. Then we bolted and barred all the doors and windows. It was with a heavy heart that I pulled out of the driveway, all our bundles and boxes tied to the roof of the car with string. It took three journeys to get everyone and everything away to Kim Poh Cho's place in Joo Chiat.

We passed forlorn groups of refugees at every street corner. At some points, I had to nose the car through a dense throng of rickshaws, hand-carts and wheelbarrows piled high with furniture, bedding and boxes. Perched on some piles, amidst the rest of the baggage, were frail, shriveled old women. We are the lucky ones, I kept telling myself. We have somewhere to go.

31

THAT Monday, we awoke to the sombre news that the Japanese had landed on Singapore Island itself. We had been expecting that. They made a feint landing on Pulau Ubin but the main thrust came in the west. As usual, the bulletins spoke of 'heavy fighting' and 'spirited defence'. I had become cynical by then. It was obvious by Monday evening that the Japs had established a firm foothold. No amount of official obfuscation could hide the fact that our troops hadn't managed to throw them back into the sea.

During my trips into the city with the ambulance crews, I was disconcerted to see groups of soldiers wandering aimlessly around town. Mostly they were white, with a scattering of Indians. They didn't seem to be injured, but all semblance of discipline had evaporated. Not a few were roaring drunk. I saw a grey-haired European man berate a group of rowdy soldiers for their behaviour. "Give it up gramps," they jeered at him, "it's all over. If the bloody natives won't fight for their own country, count us out." A hail of bottles followed. The man beat a hasty retreat, to the hoots of the soldiers. I just gritted my teeth and went on with my job.

The idea of getting Daphne out of Singapore preyed on my mind constantly. It wasn't a simple proposition. The docks were under constant bombardment now. Even as late as January, ships still left with places to spare. Now there was a rush for all available berths. The Japanese had no compunction about bombing and strafing civilian ships. Those who sought to get away had to run the gauntlet of their aircraft and submarines. The waters south of Singapore became known as "Bomb Alley". The difficulties proved to be academic anyway. When I even mentioned the notion of leaving, she brushed me off curtly. I gave up pestering, but that didn't stop me worrying.

THEN on Wednesday morning, something happened to change things. We were just coping with a new rush of patients when the air raid sirens went. We tumbled pell-mell into the nearest shelters. Usually, the raids passed us by. The hospital was marked with prominent red crosses on the roofs of the buildings. This time, to my horror, I heard detonations in the compound. Sticks of bombs came down, hitting the ground one after another like the drumming of gigantic fingers. The ground heaved. We were choked by clouds of dust thrown up by the explosions.

When the explosions stopped, I heard the staccato rattle of machine-guns. Fighters had followed the bombers and were strafing the hospital. The crew of a nearby Bofors struggled manfully to return fire, but the attempt was futile. I saw two of them go down under the fusillade. I wanted to rush out to help them, but my legs froze. Then, above the din, came a more ominous sound. It was like the rushing of a high wind in the trees. "Fire!" yelled someone. "The wards are on fire!"

I stared stupefied at the inferno that engulfed the wood and attap constructions. The monsoon had ended early that year and the attap was tinder-dry. Dante himself couldn't have imagined such a hell. The pitiful cries of the wounded mingled with the crackle and roar of the flames. The walking wounded were hobbling away, some burned terribly. The invalids were roasted where they lay.

We grabbed the water pails. Men formed a bucket chain, oblivious to the bullets and falling embers. The heat was intense. It singed the hair and blistered the skin. It was almost too much to bear. Our puny efforts were useless. I will never forget that smell until the day I die.

THE fires had burnt themselves out by afternoon. I wandered around the charred wasteland, dazed, soot-blackened and fire-scorched. Over two hundred had perished. I hunted desperately for Daphne, heart stopping every time I came across the body of a white woman. I found her sitting on a fallen tree-trunk, covered with grime but otherwise unharmed. She looked up when I called her name.

"Now will you go?" I asked roughly. I was angry – angry with the Japanese, angry at the senseless destruction, angry at her obduracy.

She looked at me with eyes that had no more tears to be shed. "I can't. I can't desert you all now ... all I care for, everyone I care for is here ..."

I softened. "It isn't desertion. The military sisters have already been evacuated. We've just received word that the Chinese nurses are to leave too. May has already gone to fetch Baby. They'll be off tomorrow. You have to go ..."

"But Bernie ... ," she said, "I can't leave without knowing ..."

My anger flared up again. "For God's sake, woman, face the facts. Bernie's dead! 'Missing in action' is just a euphemism. The Japs don't take prisoners. You've heard the stories. He's dead!"

She placed her face in her hands. I sat down beside her and put my arm around her shoulders. "I'm sorry ... I'm sorry ... But there's nothing more for you to do here. I love you, Daphne. I can't bear the thought that you might be killed here. If you feel anything for me, anything at all, please go now ... while there's still time."

She buried her head in my chest. "I love you too ..." she said, so softly that I nearly didn't hear.

After a while, she looked up. "Will you leave too?"

"Yes," I replied tenderly, "I'll leave too."

THE queue to the P&O manager's bungalow at Cluny snaked all the way down to Bukit Timah Road. They clutched their pathetic bundles and shuffled forward under the pitiless sun, a forlorn, bedraggled, uprooted legion of lost souls.

We took our place at the end of the queue. No one spoke. Palls of dirty black smoke rose from the burning oil tanks at Normanton, stark against the blue sky. The smoke looked like the angel of death hovering over the dying city. Beneath it all was the constant subliminal rumble of war.

By the time we got to the front of the queue, dusk had fallen. There were two desks: one marked "England" and the other "Colombo". I automatically steered Daphne to the England desk. The one-way fare was a flat £120 – almost $1,000 Straits dollars, half a year's salary for most people. Daphne baulked. Her hand wavered irresolutely over the booking form.

"Sign for it," I whispered in her ear, "we'll find the money."

"It's not the money," she whispered back, while the booking clerk tapped impatiently with his pen.

"Please," I pleaded.

She signed. We got a boarding pass and a cyclostyled sheet of instructions. Only one small piece of luggage was allowed. Bring a fork and knife, they instructed. Bedding would be provided, but no sheets. 'Do not miss your boat, there will be no substitutions' they cautioned in bold letters at the bottom.

IT WAS only when we met Ralph and May back at their flat that I realised with horror that we'd made a terrible mistake; or to be more precise, I had made a terrible mistake. All along I had merrily assumed that we would all be heading to the same destination. I was so fixated on getting Daphne out that I hadn't checked where May was going. Now I learnt that the Chinese nurses were being evacuated to India.

"It is all right," said May understandingly. "I will be with the other nurses. You must look after Daphne. She has no one else."

I was sorely tempted. My head pulled me one way and my heart the other.

"Go with May," said Daphne. "She needs help with Baby. I can fend for myself."

"I can't leave you alone ..." I said, trying to rationalise the decision my emotions told me to make.

"Look, Dennis, you've been at me all this time to be sensible," she said, "You be sensible yourself now. She's going to be alone with a young kid in a strange land. Ralph won't be there to take care of them. You're the only one they can depend on."

"But ..."

"But me no buts, buster," she said decidedly. "You're going with May or I'm staying put. And I mean it."

I knew I had no choice. I watched Ralph sitting quietly with May in his arms, both of them watching Baby as she played unconcerned on the floor. No one was making any arrangements for non-Europeans to get away. There would be no escape for him. Someone had to look after his family. I copied the details from May's boarding card onto my ticket with a heavy heart.

We ate in silence. The mood was sombre. Only Baby was happy, toddling around the room trying to lick everything that her chubby hands could pick up. The dark thoughts of the adults didn't affect her.

After dinner, we went to say our goodbyes to Mak and the girls. There were tears, but beneath the tears, I sensed a feeling of relief. Mak was glad that we were getting away, though parting with Baby Grace was almost unbearable. We comforted each other that it wasn't forever. I assured her we'd all be back soon, trying to make myself believe that it was all true. I don't think I was very convincing. My words rang hollow in my own ears.

THE following day, we made our way to the docks. George had generously agreed to drive Daphne and me while Ralph took care of May and Baby. He reclaimed his car, which had served me so well in the weeks past. It was the worse for wear, scorched, scratched and dented, but still running. The streets were crowded. People were streaming east, away from the fighting. There were troops all over the place, wandering around looking lost or just sitting in dispirited groups under the trees. We passed the Padang with the Supreme Court in the background. There were pylons on the green lawn, to prevent the landing of enemy paratroopers. The face of the city was lined and scarred. The smell of burning was everywhere.

At the harbour, we could get no closer than five hundred yards with the car. There was a queue ten people wide and two hundred deep trying to get in. The crowd funneled down to a single line at the gate. The harassed sentries let a trickle through. Those who got by scampered away gratefully, dragging their children with one hand and lugging their suitcases with the other.

Daphne turned and gave George a big hug and a peck on the cheek, for old times' sake, she said. "Thanks, old man," I said with feeling. "I'm sorry you're not coming with us."

"I'm not. What would I do in India except get in trouble for trying to overthrow the Raj? Take care of Daphne now." He got back into the car and drove off with a wave.

We beat our way through the throng. It took us more than an hour and a half. At the gate, we waved our tickets in the faces of the overwhelmed MPs. We were pushed by the crowd through the gates. I almost lost sight of Daphne in the crush. Fearing that we would be separated, I grabbed her by the arm. The quays stretched out to the distance interminably. I had no idea that the harbour was so big. The docks were in a state of total confusion. There were craters everywhere. A godown was still smouldering. To the south, the oil tanks of the Asiatic Petroleum Company on Pulau Bukom were burning like funeral pyres. There wasn't any sign of organisation.

Daphne was booked onto the *Duchess of Amalfi*, which had been a liner in an earlier life. We traversed the unending quays looking for the right berth, feeling like we had been walking forever. Suddenly, there was a commotion behind us. The crowd parted. A group of Australian soldiers, armed to the teeth and led by a captain, came striding purposefully towards one of the waiting ships. A naval officer came down the gang-plank to remonstrate with them. He was obviously trying to stop them getting aboard. The soldiers were in no mood to argue. The Australian captain drew his revolver and shot the man at point-blank range. Then the whole gang of them forced their way aboard the ship, elbowing women and children out of the way. "Cast off," yelled the leader, and the cables were thrown overboard. There was a howl of anguish from those left behind on the quayside as the vessel began to move away.

"Come on," I said to Daphne with grim determination, "we've got to get you aboard your boat before something else happens."

The Duchess was tied up alongside the quay two hundred yards away. With relief, I handed Daphne's boarding pass to the guard. He waved her through. When I tried to follow, he put his hand on my chest. "Not you, mate. This one's headed to Fremantle," he said gruffly, not even bothering to ask for my ticket. "Your lot get off on one of the other tubs over there." He jerked his thumb in the direction of another line of ships moored a couple of hundred yards away down the quay. I began to protest that all I wanted to do was to make sure that she was properly settled. I didn't have much of a chance. Others began pushing their way past me. Daphne was swept up the gang-plank. "Goodbye," she yelled. "Take care ..."

Her voice was drowned out by the cough of the ship's engines. The pressure of the boarding passengers forced her inexorably upwards until she was lost from view. I didn't even have the opportunity to kiss her goodbye. The crew made ready to cast the lines off. I couldn't bear to watch her leave. My eyes were misty as I made my way down the quayside to my own ship.

RALPH was there, holding Baby in one arm and May in the other. He was taking leave of the family that he might never see again. It was heartbreaking to watch them. I turned away to give them some privacy.

Someone tugged at my sleeve. To my astonishment, I saw the boy Ramli, who had left with d'Almeida all those weeks ago.

"Tuan," he said, "come quick. The Indian tuan want to speak to you."

"Indian tuan? What Indian tuan?" I asked, bewildered.

At that moment, George appeared from the crowd.

"There you are!" he exclaimed. "I thought we were too late."

"George? What the devil's going on? How did you get here?"

"There's an unofficial back door that a friend of mine was kind enough to open for me," he replied. "This clever lad Ramli brought me the news. D'Almeida's here. On Singapore Island."

"Here?" I said incredulously. "Where?"

"Somewhere out there," he said, waving his hand in the general direction of the fighting. "He's a prisoner."

"Of the Japs?" I asked, my heart sinking.

"No," said George, "of the Indians. Apparently, he and Ramli bought a boat and landed on the coast last night. They ran into a patrol of sepoys. He's being held for questioning as a suspected fifth columnist. We've got to get him out. I know you're supposed to be getting away, but I need your help. I can't do it alone. Are you with me?"

Ralph and May were staring open-mouthed. I knew what I had to do. Grabbing Ralph's hand, I thrust my ticket into it. "Take this," I said, "and get going."

Ralph protested. "I can't take this. It's your ticket out of this damned hell-hole."

"Go on!" I said to Ralph. "Your wife and your daughter need you. Get going before the ship leaves without you."

He hesitated still. I hugged May. "Go on, quickly!" I urged her. "And take your dimwit of a husband with you!"

"Thank you, Denny," she gasped, embracing me. "God bless. We will see each other again soon."

I pushed Ralph and he stumbled off in a dazed fashion after May and Baby.

"What now?" I asked George.

"Now," said George, "we stage a jailbreak."

32

"YOU'RE mad! Stark, raving bonkers!" I had just heard what George proposed.

"Not in the least," he said evenly, "it could work."

"You don't seriously think we can just commandeer a platoon of soldiers, march up to the guardhouse and demand d'Almeida's release," I continued. "This isn't fiction, you know. It's the real thing."

"Ah, but it worked for that Captain from somewhere-or-other that you told me about. You know, the one who dressed up as an officer and hijacked a troop of soldiers and stole the town safe. That wasn't fiction."

I subsided a little. "You mean the Captain from Köpenick. I know that was a real case. But they were pickelhaubed Prussians."

"Prussian pickles they may have been, but the principle is the same," George went on. "All you need is an army that is trained to obey rather than think. The Indian Army fits that description admirably. Besides, we need to get him out now. Tomorrow will be too late. Do you have any better ideas?"

"No," I admitted reluctantly. I knew time wasn't on our side. Even if the Indians didn't shoot him, the Japs probably would.

"Good," said George. "Then it's settled. Don't look so glum. What have we got to lose?"

"You mean besides our lives?" I answered sourly.

IT took a little while to organise things. Briefly, George's plan was that I should dress up as an officer, find a platoon of stray soldiers, pretend to be from HQ and demand that d'Almeida be released into our custody. When I protested that as the brains behind the scheme he should play the part of the officer, he said, "No, I thought about that, old son. Can't do it. I haven't any experience of the military. I won't make a convincing officer. They'd rumble me in no time. You, on the other hand, have the experience and the gumption to pull it off. That's why I came for you."

I saw the sense of that, though I still wasn't happy. "They shoot people who pretend to be officers, you know," I grumbled as I got into my uniform. George put the pips on the shoulder straps.

"Under the circumstances," he said, "I'd have thought they'd be jolly glad someone wanted to join up rather than run away." He stepped back to appraise his handiwork. "Marvellous. Perfect. You look exactly the part."

I looked at myself in the mirror. I must admit I did rather like being an officer. I suppressed my apprehension. "What are you going to do?" I asked George.

"Why, come with you, of course," he answered nonchalantly. "You didn't think I'd let you go alone, did you? Besides, as an officer, you need some privates. I can march around, you know. I learnt that much from the Boy Scouts. Now all we need are some troops."

George had managed to procure an Austin army truck from somewhere or other. Apparently they were just lying about for the taking, their drivers having abandoned them. He drove and I sat in the vehicle commander's seat. We cruised the streets looking for a suitable body of men. White troops were out of the question. They would never have followed a Chinese officer. Besides, most of the white soldiers we passed were dead drunk or heading for the harbour. We ignored them and they ignored us.

After about a mile, we came across a group of Indian soldiers sitting by the roadside. Unlike others that we had seen, they still carried their weapons.

"All right," I said, "let's try this lot. Wish me luck."

"Luck," said George and pulled the truck over.

I descended from the cab and approached them. The troops stirred and stared at me. My stomach was knotted with tension. I hadn't forgotten the fate of Colonel Holmes.

"You men there!" I called. "What regiment are you from?"

A havildar came up and said, "Coke's Rifles, Lieutenant sahib."

"Where is your officer?"

"Dead, Lieutenant sahib," answered the havildar. "We were surrounded by the Japanese and lost contact with our regiment."

"Come with me then," I commanded, in my most military tone. "Havildar, form up your men and get onto the truck."

He saluted and barked out a couple of orders in Urdu. The men got wearily to their feet and formed up. Another order and they began obediently filing onto the truck.

Back in the cab, I wiped the sweat from my forehead. "Well, that's done. I hope you know where we're going."

"Alexandra Barracks," replied George. "They took them both there. D'Almeida managed to distract the guards long enough for Ramli to get away. With any luck, he'll still be there."

ALEXANDRA Barracks was in the west of the island. The Japs were pressing all along the Jurong Line. If I had had my choice,

I wouldn't have headed in that direction. We passed several large bodies of troops on our way. What disturbed me most was that they all seemed to be going into town. No one was moving towards the front. I hoped fervently that the enemy hadn't broken through already. My spirits sank with every mile we drove west. At length, we drew up at the gate of the camp, which appeared to be deserted.

We got the troops off the truck and marched them to the guardhouse. There were only a couple of Malay sentries on duty. The guard commander came out. He was a young British corporal, evidently taken completely by surprise by our arrival.

"We've come for the prisoner," I said to him.

"Prisoner?" he repeated, bemused.

"The man who was brought in this morning. He's still here, isn't he?"

"I don't rightly know …" he replied, rubbing his neck.

"For heaven's sake, man," I blustered. "Who's in charge here?"

"That would be Lieutenant Parsons," he said.

I glared at him fiercely. "What was that again, corporal?"

"Ah, well … yes … I mean, that would be Lieutenant Parsons, sir." He saluted. I returned his salute.

"Lead the way," I commanded.

WE found Lieutenant Parsons in the Camp Commandant's office. The Malay Regiment had been billeted there until a few days previously. I gathered from the corporal that they had been moved into the line at Reformatory Road. The Japanese were pressing hard. There was only a skeleton guard present and Parsons was the last remaining officer.

"Chiang, Straits Settlements Volunteers," I said by way of introduction. "My orders are to take custody of the prisoner."

Parsons looked suspiciously at me. He wasn't used to English-speaking Chinese officers in command of Indian troops. He showed no inclination to cooperate. I began to sweat. "I've heard nothing about handing the prisoner over," he said. "My orders were to keep him here until further notice."

"Well, Lieutenant," I said, trying to keep my tone even, "you can take this as further notice. I'll have him, if you please."

"Let me see your orders," he replied.

For one moment, I had a powerful urge to bolt. I suppressed it. My only chance was to bluff it out. "Good God, man!" I stormed. "At a time like this, you want to play by the book? I haven't anything in writing with me. With the Japs beating at the door, you want me to go back and ask for a written order?"

Parsons stuck to his guns stubbornly. "I don't know who gave you your orders. I'm not releasing the spy to you if I don't have something. If I had my way, I'd just as well shoot him now and be done with it."

Checkmate, I thought. Then a last despairing inspiration struck me. I fumbled in my pocket, praying that I hadn't thrown it away. I found the piece of paper I was looking for. "Here," I said, "call this number. Ask for Skylark."

He took the paper and dialled the number, still keeping his eyes on me. Someone came on the line. "Hello, who's that?" said Parsons. "Fortress Command ... yes. Lieutenant Parsons, Alexandra Barracks here. I'd like to speak to Skylark. Yes, I'll hold on ..." My palms were getting very clammy indeed. "Yes, what ... you can't get him ... very well." He replaced the receiver. "They can't connect me to Skylark. But that was Fortress Command at Fort Canning, wasn't it?"

"Yes, of course it was," I replied, staring directly at him.

"Very well, then," he said slowly, "I'll release the prisoner to you."

D'ALMEIDA was brought to the Camp Commandant's office, escorted by two soldiers. I nearly didn't recognise him. His skin was as dark as an Indian's and he sported a full beard and moustache. To my horror, he seemed to be at the point of collapse. He staggered a little and had to be supported by his escorts. His eyes widened with surprise when he saw me. I frowned, hoping that he would take the hint and not betray the fact that we knew one another. He caught on immediately. Hanging his head down, he was the picture of a man resigned to his fate.

"All yours," said Parsons.

"Right, I'll be going then," I said. We exchanged salutes again. Parsons' men handed custody of d'Almeida over to my troops. We marched off to the gate and boarded the truck. I indicated that d'Almeida should get in the cab with us. He climbed in with an effort and slumped in the seat.

When we were safely on our way, I couldn't contain myself any longer. "Mr d'Almeida," I said, shaking his hand warmly, "I'm so glad to see you. I can't tell you how worried we've all been."

"I am eternally in your debt," he said in a weary voice, "both of you. I did not think I would live to see the dawn again." He patted me and George on the shoulders.

"Don't mention it, Uncle," said George, smiling. "Now to get you home."

"No, gentlemen, not just yet," said d'Almeida. He straightened up. "The game is still afoot. I followed Narayanan here. He can still do mischief. We must stop him. It is the endgame now."

33

D'ALMEIDA was in a bad way. His two-month odyssey down the length of the Malay Peninsula had taken its toll. In the past week, he had been hiding in rubber estates and avoiding Japanese patrols, waiting for a chance to get back to Singapore. The Japanese had forcibly evacuated practically the whole southern coast of Johore in preparation for their attack. He and Ramli had finally managed to buy a boat from a fisherman who thought them raving mad for wanting to get into Singapore rather than out of it. After his latest ordeal, during which he had been kept in an airless cell without food and water for nearly a day, he was at the end of his strength. Nevertheless, he still insisted that we should bring him to Special Branch Headquarters in Robinson Road.

George negotiated our truck through the lines of dispirited troops clogging the roads. The sounds of battle could clearly be heard, even from town. Fires burnt uncontrolled in Chinatown. The gallant members of the fire services fought the flames tenaciously while the city ground to a sickening halt around them. The civil defence volunteers stuck to their posts to the last, unlike some others. Ambulances still ferried the wounded and teams of auxiliaries dug through the rubble to reach the trapped. The Colonial Government ceased to function. They had lost all authority, moral as well as legal, and were shunted into irrelevance.

Singapore needed an inspiring leader in its hour of crisis. There was only Shenton.

We got to Robinson Road after an endless series of detours to get around shell-holes, collapsed buildings, rubble and corpses. After instructing the havildar to ensure that no one looted our truck, George and I practically carried d'Almeida into the building. There was only a single Chinese man in sight, burning files in the courtyard. I collared him. "We need to speak to Lieutenant-Colonel Newman urgently," I said.

The man looked blankly at me. "Newman? Who is Newman?"

"Head of the Japanese Section. Japanese Section," I repeated slowly, "you understand? Fighting Japanese spies?"

Light dawned. He disappeared into the building. We looked around the yard. Reams of paper had been put to the torch. The ash eddied in the wind.

The Chinese man returned with a European in tow. "What's this all about?" he demanded.

"This is Mr d'Almeida. He's been following Narayanan from Batu Sembilan all the way through Georgetown down here," I said, rather incoherently.

"Batu Sembilan?" said the man with a ferocious frown. "Georgetown? What the dickens are you blathering about?"

"Look," I said, trying to keep from showing my irritation, "it'll take too long to explain. We'd like to speak to the Head of the Japanese Section. His codename is ..." For one horrifying moment, my mind was blank. I racked my brain trying desperately to remember what was in James Thornton's codebook. Then it clicked. "Rainbow. That's right. He's Rainbow. We were Sunbeam."

"I'm Major Morgan., the Head of the Japanese Section," responded the man angrily. "I've never heard of Sunbeam or Rainbow. I don't know what you think you're playing at but I don't take kindly to idiots wasting my time!" With that, he turned on his heel and stalked off.

I was absolutely speechless with astonishment. D'Almeida pulled at my sleeve. He drew a piece of paper from his pocket. "Here," he said weakly, "try this number. Newman gave it to me for emergencies."

We found an unattended 'phone in the building. No one was about and I didn't think they would have minded anyway. I picked up the receiver, not really expecting that it would work. To my pleasant surprise, it did. It took me a couple of tries, but we got through. This time they knew who Newman was. I passed the 'phone to d'Almeida. He summoned up his last reserves of energy and told Newman the essentials of the case.

"He says to wait here for him," said d'Almeida exhaustedly at the end of the conversation. We found a sheltered corner and let him sit down. He closed his eyes. Within moments, he was snoring softly.

NEWMAN got to us after about an hour. He looked extremely harassed. He raised his eyebrows interrogatively when he saw me in a lieutenant's uniform. I was embarrassed. "Don't ask," I said, "it's a long story."

"I thought I told you to get out," he said.

"So you did. And I nearly took your advice." We left it at that.

D'Almeida stirred himself and outlined what he knew. The Indian National Army had been formed from Indian troops who had defected to the Japanese. It was led by a former captain in the 14th Punjabis who had been captured at Jitra, one Mohan Singh. The Bhurtpores had surrendered wholesale after the mutiny. A large number of them had joined the INA, swayed by Mohan Singh's oratory. Habibullah Khan had been promoted to major and put in command of them. They had crossed with the first wave of Japanese invaders. Narayanan went with them and was behind British lines. His role was to function as liaison with the INA, in particular with the Bhurtpores. He had a wireless transmitter with him and was undoubtedly busy relaying information on British positions to the other side. His main task was to identify which portions of the line were held by Indian or Malayan troops. The INA was then called in to try and subvert them. They had met with considerable success using these tactics during the long retreat.

"Damnation!" exclaimed Newman, "Our line's already leaking like a sieve. The last thing we need is more defections. And it doesn't help that the bloody Australians haven't any discipline. Half of them have deserted already. We're trying to plug the cracks with paper and spit."

"He must be stopped," said d'Almeida, his voice giving out.

"He will be stopped," replied Newman with determination. "Are those your men?"

I nodded. "For the time being, yes."

"Good. They'll come in handy later. Wait for me here. I'll be back as soon as I can." He left without further explanation.

"I'm going to get d'Almeida home," said George when Newman had gone. "He's all in. He needs a bed and something hot in him."

"Aren't you staying?" I asked with alarm. I had been counting on George's help.

"No, old son," he said, "it's your show. I'm a lover, not a fighter. And besides, I'm not sure I want to help capture this Narayanan fellow. His methods may be questionable, but his aims are laudable."

I was sorely disappointed. I tried not to let it show. "All right then, better get d'Almeida away while there's still time."

"Dennis," said George earnestly as he was leaving, "watch yourself. This Newman isn't all he seems to be."

305 | WALTER WOON

I looked at him with narrowed eyes. "What do you mean by that?"

"His real name is von Talheim. Friedrich von Talheim. And he's German."

"What are you talking about?" I asked, astonished. "How do you know that?"

"He gave some work to the firm, a spot of conveyancing. Some old biddy made a gift of land to one Friedrich von Talheim before the Great War. Near Admiralty House in Grange Road, right next to the Behn-Meyer bungalow. Quite a choice bit of property. Newman wanted to sell it. He retained us. Produced a deed poll showing the change of name – from von Talheim to Newman. All nice and legal, drawn up by a leading London firm of solicitors."

"When was this? The deed poll, I mean."

"Early-'twenties. Everything was perfectly in order. He sold the land...let's see, it must have been the end of '40. Got a good price for it too, over $50,000."

I was thunderstruck. "There must be a good explanation ..."

"There probably is," said George, "but I thought I should mention it. Take care of yourself. Don't be a hero. I'll see you soon."

I had an odd feeling in the pit of my stomach. I didn't know whom to trust any more.

NIGHT fell. It crossed my mind that I should leave, now that d'Almeida was safe. But my little section of riflemen looked to me for leadership. I couldn't abandon them. "Havildar," I called out. He came running. "We need supplies. I will take some men to forage. Have the rest pitch camp around the truck. We will stay here tonight."

"Yes, sahib," he answered. He detailed the naik and two men to follow me. We set off to look for food.

THE STREETS of Chinatown were deserted. Bodies lay where they fell. The stench was overwhelming. Now and again, a shell would whine overhead and explode some distance away in Tanjong Pagar or Telok Ayer Basin. The street lighting was off, whether because the power had failed or on account of the blackout I couldn't tell. We picked our way through the rubble by the light of the fires.

We headed towards the Jinrickshaw Station, a few hundred yards away. There had been several restaurants in the area. I had hopes that we might be able to scrounge something there. We passed groups of men, mostly Chinese, who scuttled away furtively when they saw us coming. They clutched bags and bundles. All order had broken down. It doesn't take much to liberate a man from the bonds of civilised behaviour. They saw nothing wrong with helping themselves to whatever they could get. I came to myself with a start. I was in no position to be judgemental; we were on the same errand, except that I justified it as military necessity.

The restaurants had been ransacked for the most part. However, in a store cupboard in a back room we discovered several tins of corned beef and spam. It looked like someone's hoard, carefully husbanded for the dark days to come. The restaurant was deserted, the doors and windows smashed. I had no idea whether the owner would be back; or indeed whether he was in fact still alive. Quelling my conscience, I instructed the men to take the tins, together with a small sack of rice that we found. To assuage my guilt, I left an IOU behind, with my name and address written clearly in bold letters.

We were halfway back when it struck me. "Naik, are your men Hindus?"

The naik made a face. "No, sahib. We are all Pathan."

We had half-a-dozen tins of spam and only two of corned beef. It looked like I was going to have a feast while my men had starvation rations. When we got back, I explained the situation to the havildar. The men took it in good spirits. They were glad to have food, little though it may have been. I felt guilty and contented myself with half a tin of spam though my stomach demanded more. We made a fire from wood that we pulled from the wreckage of a house. Theoretically, there was supposed to be a blackout. But with all the fires burning in town, one more made no difference. The men sat around conversing in low tones. The smell of the wood-smoke made me drowsy.

I GOT up with a start, not expecting that anyone would still be around. To my surprise, all the men were still there. No one had deserted in the night. The havildar had taken it upon himself to organise guards. He greeted me with a steaming hot mug of char. I took it gratefully. Evidently, I had been adopted as an honorary member of Coke's Rifles.

NEWMAN finally got back at mid-morning, riding in a truck with a strange array of antennae sticking out of it. I had almost given up on him and was on the point of instructing the section to disperse. "Get your men together," he called, "We're going hunting."

I hesitated. What was he up to? Should I follow him? He misinterpreted my hesitancy. "It's radio direction-finding equipment. I got these stout fellows to cobble something together," he said, indicating a pair of grimy Australian signallers in the back. "There's another truck over at Bukit Timah Road. Between the two of them we've managed to narrow down the area of Narayanan's transmissions. He's somewhere in the Pasir Panjang area. We can't be more exact than that."

"Where are you going then?" I asked.

"To pull the plug on him," he answered shortly.

My riflemen clambered back onto the truck. They had had a good rest. Their bellies were full too – relatively speaking, anyway. I had expected that there might be some reluctance to get back into the fray, but they obeyed orders without trouble. We followed Newman westwards, to the St James Power Station in Telok Blangah.

The staff were still at their posts, gamely keeping the power going. They were among the heros of that dark hour, like the unknown British PWD engineer and his wife who kept the pumps at the reservoir going while the battle raged around them. They remain unnamed and unsung to this day.

Newman found the chief engineer. "Shut the power down, sector by sector," he commanded. The engineer protested. It might not be possible to get the generators going again. "At this point," said Newman, "that's the least of our worries."

I wasn't clear what he was up to. He was peering intently at the Australian signaller, who was listening at his makeshift DF set. Suddenly, the signaller called out. "Gotcha, yer bastard!" He turned to Newman triumphantly. "The bugger's just gone off the air."

"Right," said Newman, "quickly now, which sector was that last one?" The engineer showed us on the wall map in his office. We sprinted back to the truck and roared off.

Our destination was a cluster of bungalows off Ayer Rajah Road. These had been occupied by civil servants before the war. Now, they stood deserted. They were uncomfortably close to the front line. We could clearly hear small arms fire and the cough of mortars.

"I hope he hasn't flown the coop," I said. Personally, I wouldn't have hung around so near the fighting if I had a choice.

Newman nodded. "He hasn't any reason to suspect that we had anything to do with the power-cut. With any luck, he'll be lying low until his Jap friends come and get him. From the sound of things, that could be anytime now. Deploy your men. Search every house. Arrest anyone you find. You're the only one who can recognise him. I'm counting on you."

I gave the orders and the riflemen spread out. They began combing the houses systematically. Looters had already visited. Everything worth taking was gone. In an orgy of pure vandalism, they had broken every door and window, even the bannisters were shattered. I found a teddy-bear in one of the bedrooms. Some poor child must have lost his friend in the rush to escape. I picked him up and dusted him off. The fur was rubbed off in places, evidence of his little owner's rough affection. I placed him gently in a nook in the wall, hoping that someday he and his young friend would be reunited.

We made steady progress through the row of houses. The sepoys were seasoned veterans of the Frontier Force. They were used to the task of clearing out hostile villages. Two men would keep watch outside while the others went through each building. They dashed from cover to cover, methodically isolating each bungalow.

Suddenly, a man dashed out of one of the houses ahead of us.

"Is that him?" called out Newman to me.

I wasn't sure. It was a long time ago and so much had happened. As I hesitated, the man put matters beyond doubt by firing at us. The sepoys returned fire. The man dropped.

We rushed to his side. When I saw him, I had no doubt that it was Narayanan. A bullet had hit him in the throat. He was evidently in a very bad way. Every breath he took caused the blood to gurgle in the wound. Newman rummaged roughly through his pockets. He found a small notebook, which he thumbed through. "It looks like we've got something. These must be the Japanese codes," he said with satisfaction.

"Shall I get an ambulance?" I asked, foolishly forgetting our situation.

"No," said Newman grimly. He drew his revolver and right before my horrified eyes, shot the man once in the head.

"What did you do that for?" I cried. "He might have had some information we need."

"He had no chance. It was for the best," said Newman shortly.

After we had destroyed the wireless set, we piled back into the truck. I held one hand with the other to stop it trembling. Newman sat silently by my side, looking through the codebook, completely unperturbed by what had happened.

As we passed Alexandra Barracks, a staff-sergeant flagged us down. Newman ordered the driver to stop.

"I gotta couple of POWs here, mate," the staff-sergeant said in a thick Australian accent. "I can't be responsible for them. Will yer take 'em off me' ands?"

"Japanese?" asked Newman.

"Nah," replied the Australian, "black blokes. Indians. We caught 'em tryin' to sneak past. We killed three and these ones 'ere gave it up."

Newman got out of the truck, indicating that I should follow. "Lead the way," he said.

"Good on yer, mate. I gotta get back to me unit. Most of the division's buggered off. I can't leave me lads all alone out there."

"Which unit is that?"

"2/4 MG Battalion, 'B' Company, 3rd platoon. We attached ourselves to the Malays on Reformatory Road. They've been takin' a pastin', I can tell yer that. We've been pushed back. The Malays are diggin' in up there." He waved at the ridge above us. "The Japs'll be along anytime now. Any troops you can spare will be mighty welcome."

He led us through the deserted camp to the lock-up. Parsons and his men had gone. "Right, leave them to me," said Newman. The Australian signalled his thanks and trotted off back down the road.

Newman drew his revolver and indicated that I should unlock the door. I felt a knot in my stomach. He was going to shoot them too, of that I was sure. I opened the door gingerly, heart beating. I wasn't sure I could shoot anyone in cold blood if that was what he wanted of me.

The two of them were sitting in one corner of the cell. I had my revolver out too, just in case they took it into their heads to jump us. With a start, I realised that I had seen these men before. "You're Bhurtpores!" I blurted out.

"The sahib knows our regiment?" said a lance-naik with surprise.

"These are Habibullah's men," I said to Newman. "I suppose we should have expected that since Narayanan was in the vicinity."

"You have eaten the salt of the King-Emperor and yet betrayed your Rajah and regiment. You have lost your honour," said Newman sternly. "Who has led you down this path?"

The men hung their heads. "We were taken by the Japanese, Colonel-sahib," replied the lance-naik with apparent contrition. "An Indian officer came to us and said we would be free if we joined the Azad Hind Fauj. They told us that the British Raj is over."

"There is only one penalty for such betrayal," said Newman in a solemn tone. I braced myself. "But I will let you go. On one condition. You must give me your word, on your honour, that you will no longer bear arms against the British." The two Indians quickly nodded their assent, the relief plain to see on their faces.

I was completely astounded. All my doubts suddenly crystallised. "No!" I said. "Drop your gun. We're not letting these men go."

"Have you taken leave of your senses, man?" asked Newman, looking at me with wide eyes.

"Not at all, Herr Oberstleutnant von Talheim," I said grimly. "You're German – a German agent. I don't know what your game is, but I'm not letting these fellows loose."

"Not German," said Newman calmly, "Austrian. My family comes from South Tyrol."

I wavered a little. "You said you were at Caporetto in 1917. That was a lie."

"No," said Newman. "I was there. On the Austrian side. I was a Rittmeister of hussars."

"But ... you changed your name ..."

"Yes. After the war, we left South Tyrol. The Italians took it in the peace settlement. My family were from Sankt Ulrich. We've been there for generations. Now, it's called Ortisei. We didn't want to be Italian so we went to my mother's people in England. I changed my name because it didn't do to have a Germanic name at that time. Lots of people did it during the War and after. Like the Mountbattens."

I wasn't sure of myself at all now. "You're not the head of the Japanese section of Special Branch. Major Morgan is. Don't deny it."

"I never said I was," replied Newman. "You're right about Morgan."

That took me completely aback. "But you've been doing all these things ..."

"Behind Morgan's back. The man is a complete idiot, blind and blinkered. He couldn't see what was happening in front of his nose and wouldn't let anyone tell him. I'm in charge of keeping tabs on the Communists, but I couldn't just let things go on like that. So I went off and set up my own network, with my own money, I might add."

I was completely confused. The man had an answer to everything. "How do I know all this is true?"

"You don't. You'll just have to trust me," he said. He laid his revolver slowly on the window sill and spread his hands. The Indians moved. I jerked my gun in their direction and they cringed backwards.

I didn't know what to do. It seemed that time had stopped and we were frozen in that tableau. The answers were plausible; yet that was what would be expected of a German spy. Then abruptly, I made up my mind. "All right," I said, hoping that my instincts were right.

Newman picked up his revolver again. "Go now," he said to the Indians. They scampered off quickly.

"Don't ever do that again," he said, wiping his brow. "I suppose it's my fault for not letting you know. I forgot you have a knack for finding things out."

"Why did you let them go?" I asked.

"What good would it do to keep them now? No doubt they've had their heads filled with all sorts of rubbish about what would happen if they fall into our hands. This way, at least they can spread some doubt among their fellows. I don't think that everyone who joined the INA did so out of conviction. If they know they won't be shot, some of them might just come back."

It made sense in a perverse way. I felt very foolish. "I've made a complete ass of myself, haven't I?"

"Not a complete ass," said Newman, with the ghost of a smile on his lips. "Come, we'd better be off. Unless you want your commission to be permanent, I think you'd better get changed. There's still time for you to get away from here. By the way, I hope your lady friend left in good time."

"Yes, thanks," I said, "I saw her off myself yesterday morning. On the *Duchess of Amalfi*."

Newman's face darkened. I had an awful sense of foreboding.

"What? What is it?" I asked anxiously.

"I'm sorry," he said sadly. "The *Duchess* was bombed as she left the harbour. She went down like a stone. I don't think many got out."

34

IT took a full minute for me to absorb the import of what Newman had said. Then I felt as if someone had reached in and wrenched out all my guts. "It isn't true!"

"I'm afraid it is," said Newman. "I'm really sorry to have to be the one to tell you."

"Weren't there any survivors?"

"A few," he said, "most of them badly injured. Some were picked up by other passing vessels. It wasn't easy. The Japs were strafing people in the water."

There were survivors. There were survivors. I clung to that thought like a shipwrecked sailor to a life-belt. But deep in my heart, I feared the worst. I was racked with guilt. She hadn't wanted to go. I made her. I chose the destination for her. I forced her to sign the booking form when she hesitated. I might as well have signed her death warrant.

"We'd better get going," said Newman. "The Japs might be here anytime."

At that moment, I hated him for being so cold-blooded. I hated the Japanese even more. No one had asked them to come. The British may have been arrogant and overbearing, but we would have worked something out, given time ... but we hadn't been given time. War had been forced on us, against our will. This was no war of liberation. This was naked aggression, pure and simple. At that instant, I understood what the Chinese Volunteers had felt. I wanted so desperately to hit back.

"I'm not going," I said firmly.

"Don't be mad," replied Newman, "there's nothing you can do. You can't fight the whole Jap army alone."

"I won't be alone. You heard what the Aussie said. The Malay Regiment is up there. One of my friends signed up. Maybe he's there. I'm going to join them."

Newman shrugged his shoulders. "You are without doubt the most pig-headed idiot I have ever met in my life," he said. "Good luck."

I shook his hand firmly. He looked me straight in the eye and said, "If you need me, I'll be at Fort Canning."

IT was a stiff climb up the Gap. There had been some fighting there earlier in the day but that had died down. I proceeded cautiously, rifle at the ready, keeping to the edge of the road as it wound its way sinuously along the side of the ridge. The sun was setting. I had a marvellous view. I paused to watch and breathe the air. It was peaceful for a moment. Then the burning oil tanks on Pulau Bukom reminded me of where I was.

The pickets of the Malays picked me up and brought me to their officer. 'C' company of the 1st Malays was entrenched at Point 226, not far from the old opium factory. The locals called the place Bukit Chandu, opium hill. The officer commanding was a trim British captain with a neat moustache, on attachment from the Federated Malay States Volunteers. After the exchange of salutes, he sized me up. "Heading back to your unit?"

"No, sir," I replied. "I'll stay here if it's all the same with you."

"You're welcome to stay. Every man is a bonus. We're desperately short. We were pushed back yesterday from Pasir Panjang Village. Lost a lot of good chaps." He called to a sergeant. "Take the lieutenant to Lieutenant Adnan's platoon."

I was introduced to Adnan, a young man with a determined jut to his jaw. His platoon was entrenched in the front line with a Bren-carrier in support. He had left his wife and young child up in Malaya. The Regiment was his family now. He went from man to man, encouraging them, keeping their spirits up. Most were very young. They had been bloodied in battle, but they hadn't broken and they hadn't run. They waited fatalistically for the inevitable onslaught.

I shared a trench with Sergeant Rahim and a couple of privates. Rahim was in his thirties and had been one of the original members of the Regiment. He was from Port Dickson, a place I knew from holidays long ago. He was glad to have someone to talk to about home and even more pleased to be able to converse in Malay. The night was long and punctuated by the boom of artillery. Above, the stars shone in the moonless sky. They seemed to be reflected on the earth. From where we were, I could see the town, speckled with red where the fires burned unchecked.

THE Japs didn't make a push in the dark. No doubt they were consolidating after the battles of the last few days. Surely they must be at the end of their tether, I said to myself. They had been going non-stop for two months down the length of Malaya. No human being can keep this up, I thought. They have to run out of steam soon. I knew it was wishful thinking. After the first sharp anguish had subsided to a dull ache, I began to have second and third thoughts about my foolhardiness. What am I doing up here, waiting to be killed? I could have gone off with Newman and gotten away with honour intact. I cursed my quixotic impulsiveness. The thought of sneaking away crossed my mind. Looking around, I put the thought aside. Even if I could get out without being seen, I knew I wouldn't be able to live with the thought of having abandoned these men to their fate.

Dawn brought no relief. The sounds of fighting drew ever nearer. Around 10 o'clock, we were buzzed by enemy aircraft. We braced ourselves for bombs. Instead, we were treated to a shower of leaflets. I picked one up. It was written in bad English, trumpeting an Asia for Asians. There was a crude picture of a Japanese soldier booting a Briton out of Asia. Some of the men glanced dispassionately at the leaflets, then tossed them casually away. I could never understand the urge to scatter bits of paper written in English among soldiery who couldn't read the language. From our point of view, it was at least a much better use of their air superiority than the usual deluge of munitions.

Around lunchtime, there was a commotion at the front. A body of men was approaching. We were ordered to stand-to. There had been no preparatory bombardment and the group was advancing in close order with rifles slung, so we were unsure whether they were hostile. They appeared to be Indian troops. Word went round that we were being reinforced. A wave of relief swept through the ranks.

When they got within two hundred yards, I could discern their faces. They looked like Punjabis. There were about fifty of them, led by an officer – a major, from the shape of the rank badges on his shoulder straps. I suddenly grew uneasy. Indian majors were rare. They were only to be found in Indianised regiments. There was only one such regiment that I knew of in the whole of Malaya …

On impulse, I called out, "Habibullah Khan!"

The major halted and stared in my direction. I looked him full in the face.

"It's a trick!" I yelled, "They're with the Japs."

Galvanised by my cry, the Indians surged forward yelling and firing. They almost reached our foremost trench. The Malays returned fire and after a short, sharp exchange, the remnants of the Indians withdrew down the slope. They left twenty of their number in front of our lines. I didn't see what became of their officer.

WE ONLY had a temporary respite. Within minutes, the enemy opened up with mortars and artillery. The din was indescribable. I felt my eardrums would burst. The earth heaved and it was difficult to breathe. When the barrage lifted, the Japs charged at us, blowing bugles and screaming like banshees. I thought that most of the company would be too stunned to fight. But they were up and firing. My brain ceased to function. I fired and reloaded mechanically, not bothering to aim, oblivious to what was going on around me. The Lee-Enfield had a kick like a mule, quite different from the Sten I was used to. I really didn't care if I was hitting anything or not, it was just a matter of loosing rounds in the general direction of the oncoming horde.

The Japanese were crazed by our resistance. They attacked with medieval ferocity. They overran the company headquarters and swarmed over the trenches. Sergeant Rahim, who had a cooler head than me, realised what was happening. "Tuan, we must pull back," he said, urgently pulling at my sleeve. "The Japanese are surrounding us. We will be cut off." There were only three of us left alive in the trench. I nodded dumbly. We scrambled out and dashed to the nearest cover. Our Bren-carrier was burning fiercely, unused ammunition cooking off with a crackle and a shower of sparks. The smoke shrouded us from the enemy. We tumbled into another trench, but saw quickly that it had been overrun before. The occupants were dead. Some had been savagely bayonetted. The Japs were taking no prisoners.

I heard the sound of shouting and firing down the hill to the left of us. The battle had swept past, heading towards the beach. It was futile to run that way. I indicated to Rahim and the other man – just a boy really – that we should strike out northwards, to Ayer Rajah Road. We threaded our way through the belukar bent double, ears straining for the sounds of pursuit. From the hill-top, we heard isolated shots. They were shooting the wounded.

The oil tanks at Normanton were still ablaze. The air was thick with choking black smoke. It was a blessing. The smokescreen hid us from the enemy. We reached a concrete drain at the foot of the ridge. It was filled with burning oil, a river of fire two yards wide. The heat was intense. We recoiled from the licking flames.

"We must jump," said Rahim.

"I cannot," cried the boy. "I cannot cross." Fear was written all over his face.

Rahim seized him roughly and spoke in his ear. The boy swallowed hard and calmed himself. Gathering his courage, he dashed forward and made a prodigious leap. He landed on the other side, stumbled, then recovered and gave us the thumbs up. Rahim turned to me. "No, you first," I said. He nodded, undid his webbing and ran. His jump was short; he reached the lip of the drain and tottered. For one brief, horrifying moment, I thought he was finished. But he regained his balance and staggered forward, scorched but still alive.

Now it was my turn. My courage failed. I looked around to see if there was any other way across. The sounds of pursuit came to my ears. Rahim and the boy looked expectantly at me, waving their hands in encouragement. I took a deep breath, ran like all the demons of the pit were on my tail and leapt. The flames licked at my feet as I soared over the drain. I landed hard on the other side, the breath knocked out of me. I felt strong arms pulling me away from the inferno.

MY ONE thought was that I had had enough. I dismissed Rahim and the boy, telling them to make their way to safety as best they could. I was tired and burnt and deafened. My heart was dead in me. I staggered towards town. No one tried to stop me. There were no MPs about to round up stragglers. Everyone had just disappeared. Smoke from the many fires obscured the sun. It was a funeral shroud for the dying city.

I gave no thought to where I was going. My feet took me past Tyersall Park, where the ruins of the Indian hospital still smouldered. I was totally shattered. When I reached the Cold Storage building, the prospect of the climb back to Cavanagh Road was just too much. The house might not even still be standing. I decided to head to May and Ralph's flat. I didn't have a key, but under the circumstances, I don't think they would have minded if I had just forced the door.

It was already dark when I reached the end of Orchard Road. I was near her flat. I couldn't even bear to think her name. Impulsively, I decided I wanted to see it one more time. I knew that it would pain me, to see her things, to touch them, but I just had to. I turned aside and dragged my weary legs up the staircase. It had been nearly three years ago that I had first walked up those stairs – a lifetime.

The door was closed but not locked. Someone had forced it. Looters, I thought. Couldn't they have had the decency to leave my memories alone? I braced myself to confront the mess.

The door appeared to be stuck. I pushed it harder. As it opened, a chair scraped out of the way. Someone had placed it against the door to keep it closed. I walked in without a thought as to what I might find there. The room was in perfect order. The light of the fires outside cast a yellow glow. In the shadows, I saw a figure – a woman. I thought I was hallucinating. "Daphne …" I said, holding out my hands to the mirage.

"Dennis? Is that you?" came a voice. Her voice.

For a moment, I stood immobile. Then we were all over each other. It was no mirage.

"How ... how did you ...? They told me that the *Duchess* had been sunk," I gasped when we finally stopped kissing.

"I couldn't go ... I just couldn't. I didn't even have a chance to say goodbye properly, there were too many people. When I saw you go, it broke my heart." The words tumbled out in a breathless rush.

"Then I knew I didn't belong there. I was afraid to be alone among strangers, with nothing and no one. All I care for was here ... is here... I got off the boat and gave my ticket to some nanny who had come to say goodbye to her children. It felt so good, seeing the look on their faces. But you'd gone. My life was empty. I didn't know what to do. I came back here."

I held her close. "We'll never be apart again. I'll never send you off again."

In the half-light, we found some candles and bread. It was a banquet such as I had never had before or since. We set up her old wind-up gramophone. Only one record had survived – Rachmaninov's *Rhapsody on a Theme of Paganini*. Embracing, we danced in the dark, to the accompaniment of Rachmaninov and the bombs.

35

THAT Sunday, February 15th, was Chinese New Year's day. It was the year of the horse. We had waited practically all day in Daphne's flat. The popping we heard in the distance wasn't crackers though. It was small arms fire. I had no idea how close the Japanese were. All I knew was that they were too close.

"We've got to get you out of here," I said to Daphne.

She frowned. "I'm not leaving you again."

"No, darling, never again," I replied. "But this isn't the place to be. The line's cracked. Any minute now, the Japs may be here. We've got to get away."

I had discarded my uniform and donned some clothes that we had raided from Elaine Gilbert's former flat across the landing. Dr Tate hadn't given it up even though he left the island before the outbreak of war. I just broke open the lock. Knowing it was leased by the head of the Japanese spy ring in Singapore made the task that much more pleasurable. I found the wardrobes still full of his elegant shirts and tailored trousers. He was shorter and stouter than me, so the fit left much to be desired. Still, sartorial splendour was the last thing on my mind.

We emerged cautiously onto the road. There was an eerie calm. For one brief moment, the shelling and the firing had stopped. It was as if the war had paused to take a breath. It was our chance to get away. I knew that there were still people in the blocks of flats along our way. Curtains surreptitiously parted as we walked by, but the inhabitants remained hidden.

"Where are we going?" asked Daphne.

I hadn't the faintest clue. The main thing on my mind was to get Daphne set up with some family where she could spend the duration of the war. I racked my brains to think of someone. Then, I had a sudden inspiration. "Fort Canning," I answered. "There's someone there who might be able to help."

It wasn't far to Fort Canning. We skirted the YMCA building and headed to the top of the hill. In the time of the ancient kings, this had been Bukit Larangan, the forbidden hill. I had thought that it would still be forbidden now that it housed Fortress Command. To my surprise, nobody stopped us. Signs of disorder were everywhere. Clerks were running in and out of the HQ building bearing piles of files. Great bonfires were burning all over the place. All the minutiae of government, the records of over a century of bureaucracy, were going up in smoke.

I halted one of the harassed clerks. "I'm looking for Colonel Newman. Do you know where he is?"

"Search me," the man replied and shook himself loose. Four other inquiries turned up similar answers. My spirits began to sag. The fifth man we stopped was different though. "Newman? You mean the cloak-and-dagger bloke?"

"Yes, that's the one," I said, optimism revived.

"His outfit's in that building over there. You'd better get a move on, chop-chop. Last I heard, they were ready to get out."

I flung a hurried thanks to the man and grabbed Daphne by the wrist. We sprinted the last couple of hundred yards. A group of lorries was parked in front of the building. Their motors were already growling. I made a quick scan of the crowd. Newman was there. I panted up to him, out of breath.

"Your guardian angel's been working overtime," he said drily. "The Malay Regiment was overrun yesterday. I never thought I'd be seeing you again."

"Allow me to introduce you," I puffed, trying to regain my breath. "Daphne, this is Lieutenant-Colonel Newman. Daphne Ford."

He gave her a salute. "Charmed, I'm sure."

"She's the young lady I told you about."

Newman's eyebrows rose. "The one who was supposed to have been on the *Duchess of Amalfi*?" He glanced at me. "You're a very lucky girl."

"I need a favour," I said, still breathless. "Can you find a family who'll take Daphne in for the duration?"

"Just you hold on there one darned minute," interrupted Daphne hotly. "You can't go around setting me up without so much as a by-your-leave. Don't I get a say in this?"

I was abashed. "I'm sorry. I've been so concerned about getting you somewhere safe I forgot to ask. It's just that I don't want to lose you again. I couldn't bear it."

She softened a little and smiled. "Can't I stay with your family?" she asked me plaintively.

"Mak and the girls are staying with relatives. There's barely room for all of them. The house is boarded up; I don't even know if it's still standing." It never crossed my mind that we could stay together in May's apartment. I wouldn't have dreamed of suggesting it and she would probably have been scandalised if I did. With civilisation as we knew it crashing down around our ears, we were still bound by our social codes.

Newman cleared his throat to remind us of his presence. "General Percival has surrendered the island to the Japs. Ceasefire is at 2030 hours. It's only a matter of time before they're swarming all over the city. There isn't anywhere safe now. But I'll do what

I can. If the young lady wants it."

I looked at her. To my intense relief, she nodded. Newman gave instructions to one of the drivers to take care of her. We had one last hug before she mounted the truck. "Write me," she called out. I waved with a tinge of deep sadness as the truck pulled away.

"Thanks," I said to Newman with feeling. "Is there anything I can do?"

Newman answered, "There is just one last thing, if you want to. It's only right, since you were in on it from the beginning."

"Ormonde?" I asked.

"Yes, Ormonde. I'm damned if I'll let him cheat the noose, surrender or no surrender. He's in the lock-up at Tanglin Camp. Get him and bring him to the docks. There'll be a firing party waiting for him there."

I hesitated. I was done with killing, I thought. Then I looked around me. I saw the city lying in ruins, my family's life in tatters, my friends dead. Ormonde was responsible for all this in great measure. James Thornton's face flashed before my eyes. "All right," I said coldly, "I'll do it."

"Good man. You won't be alone." He called to someone.

"Sergeant Blake!" I exclaimed.

"Yeah, mate, it's me. You're still in one piece I see," he said, coming up to pump my hand.

"The two MPs will go with you," said Newman. "I'll see you later."

WE got to Tanglin Camp without incident, though the Japanese were still shelling the city. The ceasefire wouldn't take effect for some time yet and they evidently intended to keep up the pressure until the last minute. I heard that they had captured the reservoirs. I saw with a pang water running to waste from the broken mains.

Even if we had wanted to, we couldn't go on fighting. The curtain was coming down fast.

There was very little formality at the lock-up. Our two redcaps produced the order and the guard released Ormonde into our custody. He was unshaven and there were rings around his eyes, but the sardonic smile still curled his lips.

"Well, Dennis, me boyo" he said in his Irish voice, "Come to bid me farewell, is it?"

"Let's get on with it," I answered coldly.

Blake and one MP sat up front in the cab. I was in the back with Ormonde and the other MP. I was afraid that he'd try to make conversation. To my relief, he didn't.

We drove slowly because of all the obstacles in the road. Ormonde sat with his head cupped in his hands. To my astonishment, he started to sob. He ended by retching violently. The sight of this man, who had been so cool under fire, breaking down like that disturbed me profoundly.

The MP reached over and said, "Stop it! We'll 'ave none o' that now."

Without warning, Ormonde smashed both fists upward into the unsuspecting MP's chin. As the man went down, he kicked him viciously in the groin. The MP recoiled and crashed his head against the hard bench. He slid down onto the floor of the truck. With the fluidity of a striking cobra, Ormonde grabbed the man's revolver from his holster before I even realised what was happening.

"Ah," he said, resuming his aristocratic accent, "the tables are turned, my friend. Fate has intervened."

Fate intervened indeed. At that precise moment, there was a blinding flash and thunderous explosion. The truck was lifted bodily off the ground. It ended up on its side in a monsoon drain. I was flung violently against the roof, which fortunately was of canvas. Ormonde went flying out the back.

I recovered myself before he did and lunged for the revolver. He shook his head, calculated the odds of getting to me before I could fire and decided to run. Blake was scrambling out of the cab, blood streaming from a gash in his forehead.

"He's getting away!" I yelled.

"Oh no, he's bloody well not," said Blake grimly and set off after him.

ORMONDE stumbled through the rubble-choked streets, trying to shake us off. We hung doggedly on his tail. After the incessant din of the previous days, the city was unnervingly silent. My arm hurt like the blazes.

It seemed that we had been running forever. He was beginning to flag. We gained on him steadily. A scant fifty yards ahead of us, Ormonde came to a halt. "We've got the bastard," growled Blake at my side through gritted teeth.

Ormonde turned his head and gave a small, wan smile. Deliberately, he raised his arms in a gesture of surrender. Turning his back on us, he walked straight towards the crossroads ahead. Blake and I traded puzzled glances. A peculiar way to surrender, I thought, walking away like nobody's business.

"Oy, you bastard," yelled Blake, "you bloody well better come back here!" Then I saw them. At the corner of the road was a patrol of Japanese. The slanting rays of the sun flashed on their bayonets. Ormonde was giving himself up to them.

Blake saw them too. We flung ourselves behind an abandoned rickshaw. "He's gonna get away," he muttered grimly. "The murderous bugger's goin' over to his Nip pals."

The Japs didn't seem to have noticed either him or us. Evidently, they had been celebrating the imminent fall of Singapore a little too heartily, with captured Tiger beer from the looks of it. I knew what I had to do. I raised my revolver and aimed at his broad back. The range was less than a hundred paces. I could hardly miss. Ormonde walked on steadily.

My hand trembled as I willed myself to squeeze the trigger. The barrel of the Webley shook a little. "Go on, mate!" Blake hissed at me. "What're you bloody waitin' for?"

A shot rang out. I didn't feel the recoil. Ormonde stopped, swayed a little and then crumpled to the ground. Stupefied, I looked at my revolver. No smoke coiled from the barrel.

Blake, who was as stunned as me, recovered first. "Christ! The Nips 'ave shot 'im!"

I looked up. One of the Japanese had his rifle levelled in our direction. A thin wisp of smoke wound lazily from the muzzle. The others, jolted out of their alcoholic stupor, were rising to their feet.

"Time we made ourselves scarce, mate," said Blake, dragging me along.

BY the time we got back to the dockside, it was almost dark. Here and there we passed groups of drunken Aussies, huddling in doorways amid piles of empty bottles or staggering uncertainly in random directions. Blake's jaw was set grimly like a rock. He said nothing to them or to me. No one bothered to stop us at the gate. The endless lines of quays were deserted, except for a few small boats.

Newman saw us as we came up. "Good God, man, where have you been? Where's Ormonde?"

"Dead," answered Blake laconically, ambling off to find his kit. Newman turned to me. I explained the whole tale briefly. He shook his head. "Shambles," he muttered, "absolute bloody shambles."

"Bloody poetic justice I call it, mate," said Blake, who had rejoined us. "His pals saved us the job of shootin' the bastard."

Newman shrugged. "Well, sergeant, you're welcome to join us. Last boat off the island," he said, indicating a small tongkang tied to a bollard nearby. There seemed to be a lot of pips, crowns and red gorget tabs in evidence among the passengers.

"If you think for a sec that I'm goin' to get in that cockleshell with a bunch of bloody Pommie brass-hats ... thanks, mate, I'll take me chances findin' a native who'll get me over."

"Not British. They're Australian," replied Newman coolly. "It's your General Bennett and some of his officers. He was quite insistent that he should get away. Apparently, he's indispensable to the Australian war effort," he continued, scarcely able to conceal the disgust in his voice. Following news of the capitulation, Bennett had just that very afternoon ordered his men to stand fast within their unit areas and wait for the victors.

Blake grinned his crooked grin. "Yeah, so he's buggerin' off. Well, lots of luck to all of you. I'm off." With that, he slung his knapsack over his shoulder and started off. "You comin'?" he shot to me.

"No, thanks, not this time," I answered. "I've got to stay."

He grinned again. "Good on yer, mate." Off he went into the dusk without a backward look.

Newman turned to me. "There's a place for you if you want."

I shook my head ruefully. "It's kind of you to offer, but you know I can't leave. Not at this time."

He nodded. "Well, good luck." He began to stride off. Then abruptly he stopped, turned and came back. Seizing my hand, he pumped it decisively a couple of times. "You're a good man," he said with feeling, "you, d'Almeida and all the rest of your people. We've made a bloody hash of things. There'll be the devil to pay for all this, the very devil to pay. When word of this shambles gets out …"

"Take care, Colonel," I replied tiredly. "Till we meet again."

With a last squeeze of the hand, he left to join the others in the tongkang. As they chugged off into the gloom, the last rays of sunlight died.

I knew that I had just watched the sun set on the British Empire. Tomorrow the rising sun, blood-red, would bring another day.

GLOSSARY

25-pounder	British field gun
3-cwt	three-hundredweight military truck
achar	pickled vegetables
Afrika Korps	the major German army formation in North Africa
AFS	Auxiliary Fire Service
almeirah	cupboard
Argylls	2nd Battalion, Argyll & Sutherland Highlanders
ARP	Air Raid Precautions
attap	thatch made of the dried fronds of the Nipah palm
Azad Hind	Free India
Azad Hind Fauj	Indian National Army
babi pong teh	pork in black sauce
bakwan kepiting	crab and pork soup
BEF	British Expeditionary Force
belukar	secondary jungle
bhisti	water-carrier
Blitz, the	the German bombing campaign against Britain in summer 1940
Blitzkrieg	literally, "lightning war"
Boche	derogatory French term for a German
Bofors	British anti-aircraft gun
Bren	British light machinegun
Bren-carrier	light fully-tracked reconnaissance & utility vehicle
changkul	gardening tool, like a mattock
Chap Goh Mei	the fifteenth and last day of the Chinese New Year season
char	tea
chop-chop	quickly
CO	Commanding Officer
Coke's Rifles	1/13 Frontier Force Rifles

dekko	Anglo-Indian slang for "a look"
Force Z	Royal Navy task-force built around HMS *Prince of Wales* and HMS *Repulse*
Fremdenlegion	German translation of *la Légion Étrangère*, the French Foreign Legion
Garhwals	2/18 Royal Garhwal Rifles
GHQ	General Headquarters
GOC	General Officer Commanding
godown	warehouse
GPO	General Post Office, at that time in Fullerton Building
gunny sack	sack made of jute fibre
Hari Raya Puasa	festival marking the end of the Muslim fasting month of Ramadan
havildar	Indian Army NCO equivalent to sergeant
Huns, the	derogatory British term for the Germans
ICO	Indian Commissioned Officer, viz, graduate of the Indian Military Academy
IIL	Indian Independance League, an organisation agitating for the independence of India
ikan bilis	anchovies
INA	Indian National Army, formed by the Japanese from Indian prisoners-of-war
Inggeris	the English
Istana	palace
jaga	doorman or guard, often a Sikh
jemadar	lowest Indian Army VCO rank
Jepun	Japanese
Jerries	Germans
kampong	Malay or Chinese village
kaya	paste made from eggs and sugar, eaten spread on bread
Kim Poh Cho	grand-aunt by marriage
KL	Kuala Lumpur, the capital of the Federated Malay States
KNIL	Koninglijke Nederlands-Indische Leger – the Royal Dutch East Indies Army
kow-tow	to bow
kuali	Chinese cooking utensil, a wok
Kuan Yin	the Goddess of Mercy
lallang	razor-grass
lance-naik	Indian Army NCO equivalent to lance-corporal
Lee-Enfield	standard British rifle
Luger	German Parabellum 08 pistol

matelot	French sailor
memsahib	white woman, usually British
Mills bomb	standard British hand-grenade
MP	military policeman
mufti	civilian clothes
naik	Indian Army NCO equivalent to corporal
nasi kunyit	yellow rice
NCO	non-commissioned officer
Nips	derogatory British term for the Japanese
Norfolks	Royal Norfolk Regiment
Oberstleutnant	lieutenant-colonel
OC	Officer Commanding
ORs	Other Ranks, viz, privates and non-commissioned officers
orang puteh	white man
P&O	British steamship company
pasal	business, affair
peon	general-purpose worker
petas padi	small firecrackers
Pickelhaube	German spiked helmet, in general use until 1915
POW	prisoner of war
prahu	small unpowered fishing canoe
PWD	Public Works Department
RAAF	Royal Australian Air Force
RAF	Royal Air Force
Raj	British rule, especially in India
redcap	military policeman
Rittmeister	captain of cavalry in the German and Austrian armies
Sahib	Sir; used as an honorific by Indians. Used in the third person to designate white men.
samfoo	Blouse and trouser ensemble worn by Chinese women
sarong	cloth used as a nether garment instead of trousers by Malays and others in Malaya
sayang	in this context, "such a pity"
sayur lodeh	vegetables in coconut gravy
sepoy	Indian soldier
shilling	local slang for "coin"
Sinkhek	"newcomers" – non-Baba Chinese, whether born in British Malaya or not
Si-Peranchis	the Frenchman
Sitzkrieg	literally, "sitting war"
Sten	British sub-machinegun
stengah	an alcoholic cocktail
subedar	Indian subaltern, VCO

subedar-major	senior Indian officer, VCO
syce	groom; by the 'thirties, a driver
Thompson	American sub-machinegun
three-tonner	military truck
tiffin	lunch
tiffin carrier	container for food, consisting of tin pots stacked one above another
tongkang	motorised lighter, usually wooden, for transporting goods to and from ships moored in the harbour
toti-man	nightsoil carrier, the man who clears the latrines
towkay	Chinese businessman, a boss
Tuan	Sir; used as an honorific in Malay. Used in the third person to designate white men.
Tuan besar	big boss, i.e, managing director or chairman
tutup jacket	high-collared jacket fastened with brass buttons
ulu	literally, the headwaters of a river; figuratively, the back of the beyond
up-country	in the Malay Peninsula
VCO	Viceroy's Commissioned Officer, viz, Indian officer not holding a British-equivalent rank
Webley	standard British army revolver
Wehrmacht	the German army

ABOUT THE AUTHOR

Walter Woon was educated at the National University of Singapore and St John's College. Cambridge. He has been at various times the Sub-Dean and Vice-Dean of the NUS Law Faculty, a nominated Member of Parliament, a director of two listed companies, legal adviser to the President, ambassador to several European countries, Solicitor-General and Attorney-General. He is presently a Senior Counsel, David Marshall Professor of Law at the NUS Law Faculty and Dean of the Singapore Institute of Legal Education.

He is married with two sons.

The Devil to Pay is the second installment of *The Advocate's Devil* Trilogy.